BOOKSHOP

For Dave, my Owl: I hope I always find you the perfect book.—J.F.

For the Cameron Kids' team and all their wonderful books.—G.A.

Text copyright © 2021 Julie Falatko
Illustrations copyright © 2021 Gabriel Alborozo

Book design by Melissa Nelson Greenberg

Published in 2021 by Cameron + Company, a division of ABRAMS.
All rights reserved. No portion of this book may be reproduced,
stored in a retrieval system or transmitted in any form or by any means,
mechanical, electronic, photocopying, recording, or otherwise,
without written permission from the publisher.

Library of Congress Cataloging-in-Publication Data available.
ISBN: 978-1-951836-20-7
Printed in China

10 9 8 7 6 5 4 3 2 1

Cameron Kids is an imprint of Cameron + Company

Cameron + Company
Petaluma, California
www.cameronbooks.com

YOURS IN BOOKS

Julie Falatko & Gabriel Alborozo

cameron kids

Pine: A Bookshop
Knobby Pine Northeast of the Big Fir

Dear Sirs:

I received your marvelous catalog in the mail and
spent many long hours reading the descriptions of
all the books. Enclosed is my order form for *How to
Soundproof Your Forest Dwelling*, so that I might read
in peace, alone.

Sincerely yours,

Owl T. Fencepost

Top of Oak
Near the Clearing
and the Noisy Small Animals

Dear Owl T. Fencepost,

I regret to inform you that the book you requested is currently out of stock. Let me know if there is a different title you'd like instead, and I'll send it right away.

Yours in books,

B. Squirrel

Pine: A Bookshop

Dear Sir:

I would like to place an order for a particularly intriguing title,
The Can-Do Guide to Moving to a Remote Tropical Island.

Regards,

Owl T. Fencepost

Oaktop
Near the Noise

Dear Owl Fencepost,

Unfortunately, I no longer carry the book you requested. I sell many books to tourists interested in moving here from the city. I am sending one such title I think you'll enjoy: *Yes You Do Want to Live in the Woods: Why Life in the Trees Is the Bee's Knees.*

Yours in books,

B. Squirrel

Pine: A Bookshop

Dear B. Squirrel,

I am well aware of the influx of new families. In fact, I was reading aloud earlier today, and suddenly all of the new noisy neighborhood children were knocking on my door, wanting me to read to them. Which I did. But shall not do again. (Even though I do have a lovely speaking voice.)

I have enclosed payment for another book, *How to Build a Very Tall Fence*. Please send it quickly.

Sincerely yours,

Owl T. Fencepost

Atop the Majestic Oak
So Far Above the Chattering

Dear Owl T,

The fence-building book is only available through special order, which I would be happy to do. In the meantime, I have a feeling you'll like the enclosed book, *The Big Woods Book of Cooking and Baking.* I use its recipe for milk toast most mornings for breakfast.

Yours in books,

B. Squirrel

Dear Squirrel,

Thank you for the cookbook. I will admit that most of my meals are beans from a can. I tried the milk toast recipe, and it was quite fine. However, the aromas of warm food heating on my stove brought all the noisy neighborhood children to my doorstep. Please send *The Busy Owl's Guide to Food That Will Not Entice Neighbor Children to Stop By Uninvited.*

Sincerely yours truly,

Owl

Dear Owl,

The book you requested does not seem to exist. Is it possible you were making a joke? If so, I am delighted. It sounds like you and the children might enjoy *50 Fanciful Biscuits and Cakes*, which I have enclosed, of course.

Yours,

Bessie

P.S. You should visit the shop. There are so many books to discover by browsing the shelves!

Dear Bessie,

Yesterday afternoon, several young creatures knocked upon my door, wanting to "hang out," as they say. They brought me a book to read to them, and we made cookies from the cookbook you sent me. Did you know there is a recipe for a cake shaped like an acorn? We started it but it was very complicated, and apparently now the children are coming back today to finish it. How is an owl supposed to get some peace and quiet? You see why I cannot leave my house to come visit the bookshop? I would be mobbed by children!

Please send *Disguises to Make Owls Look Boring, Invisible, or Somewhat Menacing.*

Yours,

Owl

P.S. Okay, yes. I am joking. Just send me the next book you think I should read.

Dear Owl,

You, my friend, are a surprise. Two jokes! I am sending you a new title that might come in handy, *Crafts Children Can Do While You Nap on the Couch*. And I do hope you stop in sometime.

Yours,

Bessie

Bessie,

The squirrel children are fighting with the dormice about whether to make woven pot holders or decorated pencil cups. I thought it was loud before, but this is too much. Oh heavens, now they are dancing and want me to join. I am not a dancer. I would love to leave the house, but I'm certain they'd destroy it the minute I stepped out the door. All I want is a peaceful cup of tea.

Owl

Owl,

Tell them to make pom-poms. They can string the pom-poms into garlands. I loved to do that when I was a little squirrel! I am enclosing another book, *The Art of the Tea Party*. Good luck.

Bessie

Bessie,

You were right. The pom-poms were a hit. The children love the tea party book and are now making lists and folding napkins. From my perch on the couch, they appear to be scheming. I do not understand children.

Owl

O,

A little bird told me to send you glue, stickers, glitter, and paper,
so I have enclosed them, as instructed. What are you planning?

B

B,

I am not planning anything, except for that quiet cup of tea that I still have not had.

O,

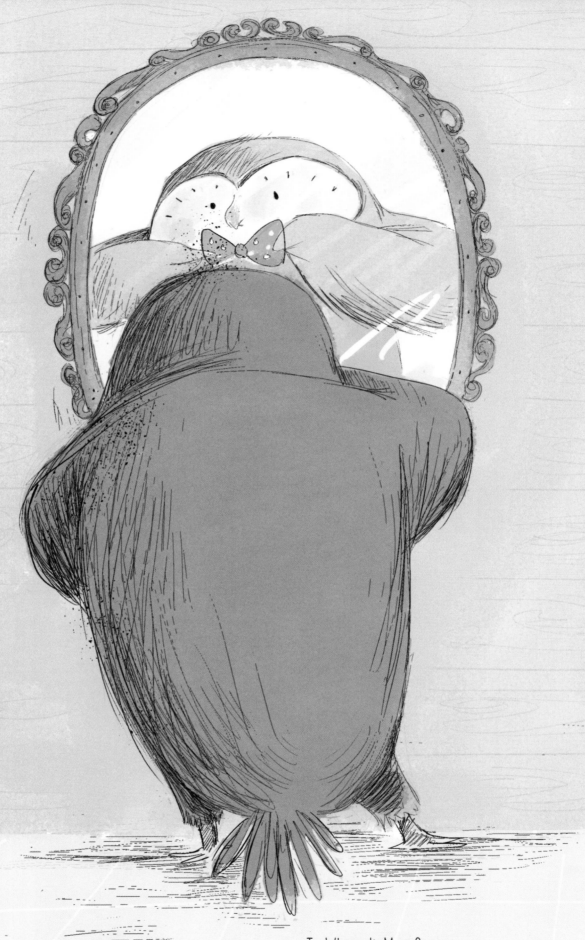

I would be delighted to
attend your tea party!
See you tomorrow!
Bessie

To Whom It May Concern:
All right, yes, fine. I'll come to your party.
Owl

Dearest Owl,

Thank you so much for such a lovely, lovely party. Are you sure you had no idea? Those children are quite crafty. I can see why you're so charmed by them. They do know how to put together a festive spread. And you said you weren't a dancer!

I have been thinking on it, and I can't decide which book to send next. What do you want to read now?

Bessie

B,

Don't send anything, please.
I am on my way.

O

TOWN AND
BOOKSHOP

THE HIGH SIERRA

BY KIM STANLEY ROBINSON

THE HIGH SIERRA

A Love Story

KIM STANLEY ROBINSON

Little, Brown and Company

New York Boston London

Little, Brown and Company
Hachette Book Group
1290 Avenue of the Americas, New York, NY 10104
littlebrown.com

First Edition: May 2022

Little, Brown and Company is a division of Hachette Book Group, Inc. The Little, Brown name and logo are trademarks of Hachette Book Group, Inc.

The publisher is not responsible for websites (or their content) that are not owned by the publisher.

The Hachette Speakers Bureau provides a wide range of authors for speaking events. To find out more, go to hachettespeakersbureau.com or call (866) 376-6591.

All photographs taken from author's private collection, unless otherwise cited
All illustrations by the author, except for illustrations on pages 14, 17, 269, and 361
    by Elizabeth Whalley, used with permission
Woodblock prints on pages 86, 179, 359, and 432 by Tom Killion, used with permission
Map on pages xviii–xix by Jeffrey L. Ward
Endpaper map and satellite images on pages 18, 323, 399, and 401 used courtesy of Planet
    Labs PBC.
The poetry of Gary Snyder on pages 417–18 and 422 reprinted with permission from
    New Directions Press

ISBN 978-0-316-59301-4
LCCN 2021943100

10 9 8 7 6 5 4 3 2 1

WOR

Printed in the United States of America

To the memory of
Terry Baier

Or I can say to myself as if I were
A wanderer being asked where he had been
Among the hills: "There was a range of mountains
Once I loved until I could not breathe."

—"Morning Star"
by Thomas Hornsby Ferril

CONTENTS

ACKNOWLEDGMENTS

For the illustrations on pages 14, 17, 269, and 361, thanks to Elizabeth Whalley.

For the satellite photos on pages 18, 323, 399, and 401, and in the endpapers, thanks to Will Marshall, Sarah Bates, Rob Simmons, and everyone at Planet Labs PBC.

Thanks to Declan Spring and New Directions Press for permission to quote from the poems of Gary Snyder.

Thanks to Tom Killion for the use of his woodblock prints on pages 86, 179, 359, and 432.

Thanks to Jeffrey L. Ward for the map on pages xviii–xix.

The photographs in this book are by Joe Holtz, Darryl DeVinney, Carter Scholz, and me, except for the one on page 214, by Tobias Menely, and the one on page 425, by Christopher Woodcock—my thanks to them.

For all our Sierra days, thanks to Joe Holtz and Darryl DeVinney.

Thanks also to Victor Salerno and Dick Ill, and Carter Scholz and Daryl Bonin. Also Casey and Mark Cady, and Neil Koehler and Cindy Toy, and all our Village Homes gang. Also David and Tim Robinson. And Chris Robinson. Also Brian Bothner and Brad Ill, Shelby Smith, Robert Crais, Paul and Lucius and Miranda Park, Pamela Ronald and Raoul Adamchak, and Mario Biagioli and Joshua Rothman. Also Tobias Menely, Yutan Getzler, and Jake Furnald. And Michael Blumlein, in memoriam.

For help with this book, thanks to many of those listed above, and also to

Casey Handmer, Laurie Glover, Tom Marshall, Donald Wesling, Gary Snyder, Hilary Gordon, Terry Bisson, John Kessel, Karen Fowler, Dan Gluesencamp, Dan Kois, Tim Kreider, Julie Dunn, Tim Holman, Michael Pietsch, Elizabeth Gassman, Evan Hansen-Bundy, Ben Allen, William Tweed, Armando Quintero, David Robertson, Colin Milburn, Djina Ariel, Curt Meine, Roberta Milstein, Margret Grebowicz, and Leonie Sherman.

Thanks for everything to Lisa Nowell.

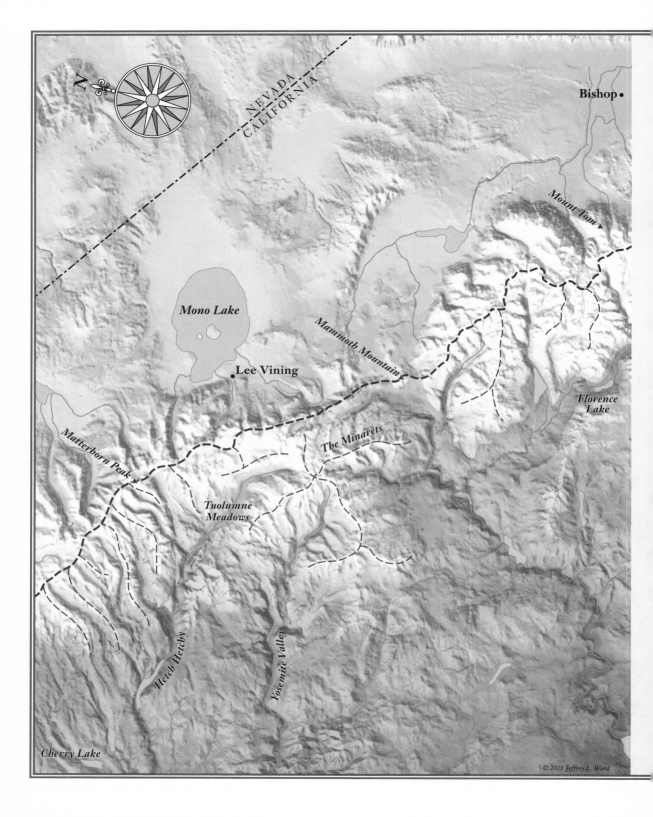

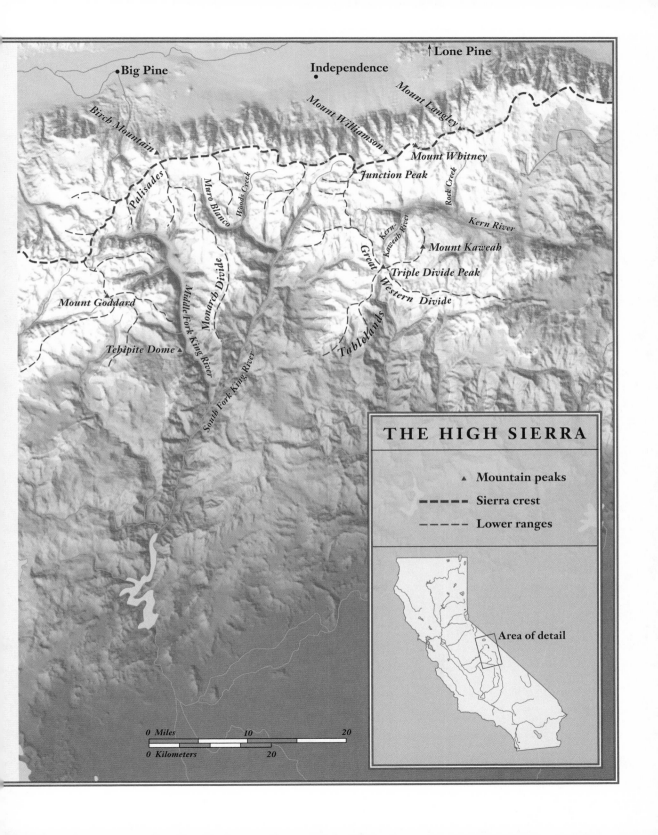

Big Pine

Independence

↑ Lone Pine

Mount Langley

Mount Williamson

Birch Mountain ▲

Palisades

Mount Whitney

Junction Peak

Rock Creek

Muro Blanco

Woods Creek

Kern River

Kern-Kaweah River

▲ Mount Kaweah

Great Western Divide

Triple Divide Peak

Mount Goddard

Monarch Divide

Middle Fork King River

Tehipite Dome ▲

South Fork King River

Tablelands

THE HIGH SIERRA

▲ Mountain peaks

– – – – Sierra crest

– – – – Lower ranges

Area of detail

0 Miles   10   20

0 Kilometers   20

THE HIGH SIERRA

MY SIERRA LIFE (1)
Not to Touch the Earth

I woke in my sleeping bag and saw Terry sitting up in his. I had gotten some sleep and now it was time. It was still dark but the sky was blue in the east, beyond the great gulf of Owens Valley. I had slept poorly, a little high on Diamox and altitude and the knowledge I was back in the Sierra. Around us stood tents and picnic tables and grills: the car campground at Horseshoe Meadows. A girl in a nearby tent had put us to sleep the night before by reading aloud to her friends, her musical voice like a lullaby. Now tall pines soared over us, black in the dawn. All the people around us were still asleep. Where else do you find so many people sleeping outdoors together? It's a thing from an earlier time. We packed as quietly as we could and took our stuff to the nearby parking lot. Sitting on the asphalt by my old station wagon, we brewed up some coffee and finished packing our packs. It was cold but not too cold. With a final check we were off. Destination Mount Langley, the tallest peak at the south end of the Sierra.

The sky was lighter now. Sunrise would catch us in a forest on the eastern slope. We had done it again: another Sierra trip. Well over 50 of them at this point, Terry and I, almost half of those just the two of us. Rambling the Sierra with my moody friend: at various times he would be gloomy, exuberant, calm, remote. It didn't matter. Both of us were there for the Sierra. In that sense we were a good match. For sure we were used to each other.

Now we flowed up the trail, hiking fast through shadows. A long gentle uphill walk through narrow meadows, threading an open forest. Everything was cool and still, the shadows horizontal, the light yellow. I felt the energy of the trip's first hour, and yet things were still a little dreamy too. Sometimes hiking involves a lot of looking down to be sure of your footing, but other times it's like strolling up a sidewalk. Minute follows minute, they unspool with nothing in particular to mark their passing. You're just walking, and you're only going to be walking for the rest of that day. And so you begin to shift into hiking's different time, its altered state of consciousness. Sierra time. In that morning light, at the start of a trip, I sometimes laugh out loud.

That feeling is one of the things I want to write about here. Crazy love. Some kind of joy. There are people who go up to California's Sierra Nevada, fall in love with the place, and then live the rest of their lives in ways that will get them back up there as often as possible. I'm one of those, and in this book I want to explore various aspects of that feeling, thinking about how it happens, and why. Analyzing love: Is this wise? Possibly not, but I notice we do it all the time. So I'll give it a try.

On that particular day in 2008, we came over a rise to a sudden huge view. Cottonwood Lake One stretched before us, a narrow blue expanse banked by reeds. Over the pine trees on the far shore loomed the Sierra crest, here a stretch of broken gray cliff blocking our way, 2,000 feet high and topped at its north end by the summit prow of Mount Langley, the southernmost of the Sierra's 14,000-foot peaks.

We followed the trail along the grassy south shore of Cottonwood One, and stopped at the far end of Cottonwood Two for second breakfast. It was very satisfying to look up at the giant rocky wall facing us and see that the rest of our day was going to be above tree line, and here it was only 9:30. When I remarked on this, Terry told me that the Pacific Crest Trail's thru-hikers always start early. "Ten by ten," they call it, meaning ten miles by 10:00 a.m. To me that sounded awful, but in the actual performance it had been quite nice.

Two fishermen wandered by and stopped to chat. I asked them if they had visited Cottonwood Lake Four, which would have given them a view up to Old

Looking north over Cottonwood Lake One to Mount Langley

Army Pass. The evening before we had asked a horse packer about that long-abandoned route, and he had growled, "You'd need crampons to get over that one."

The two fishermen replied that they had indeed seen such hikers. There was no snow on the pass, and the hikers headed up that way had not returned.

Horse packers! I said.

They don't like backpackers, Terry noted.

I suggested we try this Old Army Pass, and with a little frown Terry agreed. He had a long day ahead of him, and New Army would have been the sure thing. But we wandered toward Old Army, and found that Cottonwood Four filled the floor of a glacial embayment in the crest wall. Above the far end of the lake reared the pass, not a deep U or V, just a little cleft at the top of the great wall. The trail over this break hasn't been maintained or marked on maps since New Army Pass was built in the 1930s, but some guidebooks describe it as the best route to Mount Langley, a popular peak, being one of California's fourteen 14,000 footers. For me the interesting thing was this long-abandoned trail, which turned out, as we started up it, to be just as distinct as any other trail in the Sierra. It ran to the west end of Cottonwood Four, right under the steep headwall, then circled the lake and traversed up the slope on the lake's south side, going away from the headwall. Finally it made a hairpin turn and headed back toward the pass.

Here the problem with the old trail came into view: the final rise to the pass ran on top of a long ledge, like a broken rising sidewalk. Great when dry, but because it was on a north-facing slope, snow would cover this ledge long into every summer, and cliffs above and below it meant that when the ledge was under snow, the pass would be blocked. Probably the trail was passable only in August and September, with a few weeks to either side of those months, depending on snowfall. Thus the blasting of New Army Pass in the '30s, around a big turn in the crest that gave it a south-facing slope.

The trail is still there over Old Army Pass. Part of the Miter Basin is in the upper left corner of this USGS topo.

Now there was no snow at all. I was really pleased to be hiking this old trail, which had been built in the 1890s by a squadron of Black US cavalry soldiers under the command of Charles A. Young, the only Black commissioned officer in the army at that time. He had been the third African American to graduate from West Point, and later became the US military attaché to Hispaniola and Liberia, among other achievements; when he died, the funeral parade in New York drew 50,000 people, the interment in Arlington National Cemetery 60,000. A forgotten hero. His squadron's defense of Sequoia National Park from illegal sheepherders and loggers had set a standard that the army units up in Yosemite seldom matched. Another of his assignments had been to improve access to the new park; thus this trail, which had created a new way into Sequoia from the east. The north-facing wall ledge was admittedly an unfortunate route placement, but probably they had had no better alternative. New Army Pass had taken a lot of dynamite.

From the slope between New and Old Army Passes, looking north to Langley after a summer storm

These days, climate change may keep Old Army Pass open more than ever before. And obviously the 14er peak baggers are keeping it well-trodden. But it will never take much snow to shut it down.

Up in the pass we found ourselves in the low point of a broad ramp in the sky, rising in an undulating wave to Langley, which looked much like Mount Whitney from the same angle. The ramp was covered with sandy decomposed granite, and here and there some ground-hugging tundra plants. A sky island, this ramp, always sticking out of the ice caps during the ice ages. Now it formed a high road to the peak, which looked nearby, though the map told us it was a few miles away.

It was still early and we decided to go for the peak. We hustled up an intermittent faint trail, passing a big group that was losing steam. Terry put on the jets as he passed them, shaking his head in silent disapproval of a group that big and slow. Not that we were the fastest people up there: a clutch of runners ran down past us, quadriceps bouncing foursquare over their knees.

We flowed up in our usual silence. Langley's summit is a block about 200 feet higher than the ramp, its tilted flat top covering several acres. We found shallow cracks in the side of this block, even used our hands a bit. Up on the summit plateau it was back to easy walking. The eastern end of the block was the high point, overlooking immense drops to east and north. I had to lie on my stomach to look down these sheer cliffs.

A nearby circle of granite plates made rough benches, and in the middle of these lay the peak's aluminum summit register box, holding a notebook and a few pens. We signed it, then stood looking around. Peaks and ridges, ridges and peaks, scores of miles in every direction. This year there was no snow to be seen, and the bare granite of the range looked lifeless and forbidding. Ten thousand feet below us, the weird expanse of the semirehydrated Owens Lake was cut by dikes into quadrants of poisonous green or yellow, surrounded by an even bigger area of arsenic white, the exposed playa left behind after LA's water grab. It was like the view out an airplane window, but without the airplane. We were standing in the sky.

Clarence King, in 1864, trying to describe this same scene from the top of

Mount Tyndall, 12 miles to the north and visible to us now: "The serene sky is grave with nocturnal darkness. The earth blinds you with its light. That fair contrast we love in lower lands, between bright heavens and dark, cool earth, here reverses itself with terrible energy."

This catches something essential. The range of light: up here the rocks seem to glow from within, to pulse with an internal light, under a sky as dark and solid as enamel.

When we left the peak, Terry led the way off the summit block by a different route from the one we had ascended, steeper but more direct. He was always one for the direttissima. If he could see a route that went for him, he didn't like to fool around. We had to turn in and use our hands a little. Our ascent route would have been easier. But impatience would sometimes come on him like a fit.

When we got down to the big ramp in the sky, we dropped fast back to Old Army Pass, then turned right and came to the intersection with the trail from New Army. A little farther down we came to a cleft where water emerged without warning from a patch of sand. This startling spring soon became a narrow stream running between grassy banks. We sat on a boulder and stuck our faces in the cold flow. We had neglected to take any water with us from the Cottonwood Lakes, and thus had gone dry from second breakfast to 4:00 p.m. Our usual foolishness. Terry felt it was criminal to carry water while backpacking. Two pounds per quart on your back, for a species that evolved to go for days without drinking? Ridiculous!

So it felt good to drink a lot and then lie there on the grass, absorbing it like a sponge. A couple of miles downstream, our paths would diverge. I would join an artists' and writers' camp already there, spending a week with strangers, taking day hikes and talking around the campfire at night. This struck us both as a somewhat bizarre way to spend a week in the Sierra, but I was going to give it a try. Terry would meanwhile hike north on the Muir Trail, long miles every day, meeting me at the Pine Creek trailhead nine days later, where we would join our backpacking friends and make a tour of the Bear Lakes region in our usual hard-driving style. This plan was nothing unusual; Terry often tacked our group trips onto his longer treks up and down the Muir Trail, and we made arrangements accordingly. So it's strange to think this pause by a stream was the last peaceful hour we ever spent together in the Sierra.

The Baier on Langley, Whitney in the distance over his head, the Great Western Divide on the far left skyline, Mount Williamson on the right skyline, August 2008

GEOLOGY (1)
Batholith and Pluton

To think about the Sierra's allure I'm going to consider all kinds of things, but will start with the obvious main fact: it's a mountain range. So geology has to be part of the story.

I'm not competent to go too deeply into this, but some basics of geology will help me to explain its effects on the mind (or at least my mind), a topic which naturally should be called *psychogeology*. So in this book there will be some chapters devoted to geology, and many more, in one way or another, to psychogeology.

The geological terms I'll discuss include the following, briefly defined here:

THE BATHOLITH: the whole mass of Sierra granite

PLUTONS: individual blobs of granite that make up the batholith

THE CREST: the long and continuous highest ridge of the range, from which its watersheds flow west or east

DIVIDES: high ridges that tend to run west from the crest, or stand alone

BASINS: high headwater regions held in a curve of ridges

CANYONS: in the Sierra these are mostly U-shaped, being glacier-carved

MASSIFS: high areas isolated by deep bordering canyons

ROOF PENDANTS: older metamorphic rock stranded atop the batholith

GLACIERS: ice rivers and ice fields, mostly gone now

These terms (many already well known) will help me make my claim that the Sierra Nevada is the best mountain range on Earth, if backpacking is the game you want to play. This book will be making that case more or less continually.

There are some good books by geologists about the Sierra, and one great one, by James G. Moore; if you want more detail on this topic, they have it. For my part, I'll be keeping it simple. I'll split this strand of the book into short chapters, and insert them in an order that helps me make myself clear.

First up, then, very naturally, are batholith and pluton, because these terms describe the basic substance of the Sierra. How did this big raft of granite get where it is, floating near the eastern border of California, high above the rest of the state?

Mountain ranges are usually the result of one tectonic plate ramming into another one.

It's interesting to note that before the theory of plate tectonics was developed in the 1960s, no one could understand why mountains even existed. Earlier theories of *orogeny*, the term of that time for mountain formation, were completely lacking the basic mechanism involved, so their ideas were badly off. As Wolfgang Pauli once remarked about an incoherent theory in physics, these concepts were "not even wrong."

One theory of orogeny had it that the Earth had been shrinking as it cooled since its birth, and thus the surface of the planet was bunching up in places like the face of a shar-pei dog. Another had it exactly the opposite, that the Earth was still swelling from the action of interior radioactive heat, and as it swelled its surface cracked, releasing lava that poured up and hardened into mountains.

Oh well. In the early twentieth century Alfred Wegener pointed out what anyone could see on a globe, that Brazil and West Africa seemed to fit together. He suggested this could not be a coincidence, that some kind of continental drift must have occurred; but no one could see how that would happen. Then sonar and magnetic studies of the ocean floor in World War II found a mid-Atlantic rift from which the ocean floor seemed to be spreading in both directions. In a rush the theory of plate tectonics came together. John A. Stewart's

Drifting Continents and Colliding Paradigms is an excellent study of this paradigm shift.

By 1975 geologists mostly accepted this new theory of Earth's history. Big plates of the lithosphere were sliding around under the pressure of convective currents in the mantle below. Intense work since then has refined the picture, and the history of the Earth's surface going back millions of years has been established. Pangaea, Gondwana, Laurentia—these are previous configurations of the big continental islands, which geologists have been able to work out by computer models and fieldwork. Now we know there are nine large tectonic plates, and about twenty minor ones. Sometimes they're sliding past each other, sometimes they're colliding head-on and one is getting shoved under the other, and sometimes they're pulling away from each other. Much gets explained by this model, including mountain ranges. The Andes resulted from a Pacific plate's subduction under South America; the Alps show where Italy is shoving under Europe. The Himalayas mark the place where India is shoving under Asia, in the biggest collision of our time.

California's Sierra Nevada is the result of the Farallon Plate subducting under the main mass of North America. It got shoved under and began to melt about 120 million years ago. Just the rounding error here is several million years—think of that! It's one of the stunning facts of psychogeology. The span of so many years creates a kind of temporal foreshortening in our minds; but at the time these things happened, the present was passing at the same speed as our present. It's a long time. Mountains grow at about the same speed as your fingernails.

Mountain ranges far older than the Himalayas, Sierras, and Alps are still around, much worn down from their original size. They have sometimes broken up and drifted far from their original location. The Appalachians and the Scottish Highlands, for instance, are fragments of the same ancient mountain range. In another example, a mountain in Gondwana got split in two; now half of it is Table Mountain, overlooking Cape Town, South Africa, while the other half, Mount Wellington, overlooks Hobart, Tasmania. It's hard to imagine such lengths of time, such anchorless wandering of the landscape. Possibly it's completely beyond us. It's one of the wonders of geology for sure. It's also something that being in the mountains can give you a feeling for—intimations, like mental shivers, as you look at the bare bones of the Earth, newly exposed to the world—meaning around 20 million years ago.

So the Farallon Plate shoved under the North American Plate and dove into the mantle, where the leading edge melted, five to ten miles down. If that melted rock had risen to the surface while still melted, volcanoes would have resulted, and the emergent lava would have quickly cooled to become various kinds of volcanic rock. The Cascades are a volcanic range like that. It happens quite often.

In the Sierras, the Alps, and the Himalayas, the melted rock never made it to the surface. It pushed up against the rock over it, but that roof held, so the melted rock slowly cooled down there. That deep slow cooling of melted crustal rock creates granite; and a big mass of granite is called a *batholith*.

The Sierra Nevada batholith emerged into the light of day only after the vertical miles of Earth over it eroded away. Now it extends from a bit north of

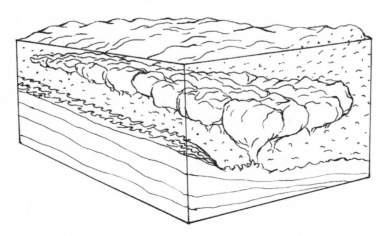

Around 100 million years ago, the Sierra was a mass of cooling rock five to ten miles below the surface—a buried ground pad, rising to support its friends. Drawing by Elizabeth Whalley.

Lake Tahoe to Tehachapi Pass in the south. If you could see the whole batholith free and clear in the air, it would be shaped something like a backpacker's air mattress: 450 miles long, 60 miles wide, and, because it still extends about six miles deep into the earth, while standing two to three miles above the land surrounding it, about eight or nine miles thick.

None of this was a uniform process. The batholith never looked exactly like an air mattress down there; it was maybe more like a band of cumulus clouds, with individual blobs of melted rock mashed together at their edges. Those individual blobs are called plutons. They're lumped together like party balloons, or the bumpy top of a parasail. That's the range as we see it: the slightly rounded tops of about 20 oval blobs, all pressed together. They're often oval rather than circular, averaging around 10 miles by 20 in size.

The rock is a bit different chemically from blob to blob. Granite is a mix of minerals, with silica composing 60 to 80 percent of the mass. Silica is the whitish part of granite, and the black flecks are mostly feldspar and hornblende; there's also often a reddish dash of iron oxide, and crystals of quartz. The slower the rock cooled, the more time there was for quartz crystals to grow. Taken all together, this mineral mixture makes a white or gray (or pinkish or orangish) speckled rock, its components present in differing proportions, such that many geologists don't even use the word *granite*, except to refer to a family of rocks, or to make a concession to the common language of non-geologists.

I call it granite.

The pluton called the Whitney Intrusive Suite is one of the biggest and youngest in the Sierra. Being large, it took longer to cool, which allowed bigger-than-usual crystals of potassium feldspar to grow. These crystals are called phenocrysts: you can see them as the large cube shapes that stud many boulders in the area. "It is as if the rock itself is hobnailed," as Kenneth Rexroth once said.

The Whitney granite is between 69 and 73 percent silica; there are whiter granites farther north, as in the Cartridge pluton. The Cartridge pluton, as seen from Pinchot Pass, is one of the most visible examples of an individual pluton that I know.

The Cartridge pluton's top is easily visible from Pinchot Pass.

Since the plutons were emplaced, the miles of rock over them got slowly worn away by glaciers, rain, stream action, freeze-thaw cycles, wind, and sunlight. Slowly the batholith got closer to the Earth's surface, and as the weight of the overburden on it grew less, the rock in the plutons expanded a little, thus causing them to crack in something like onion layers.

Eventually the batholith was exposed to the surface. There must have come a day when granite first peeked out of some broken metamorphic rock and looked up at the sky. The metamorphic roof continued to erode; a lot of it ran west into the Pacific, or filled California's Central Valley, which is a big V-fold in the subducting plate, a bathtub trench eight miles deep, now filled with the rock that used to overlay the batholith.

So the granite mass rose, the east side of it more than the west, helping to give the Sierra its characteristic lifted-trapdoor appearance: long gentle rise on the west side (200 feet per mile, for 80 miles), sharp drop on the east side

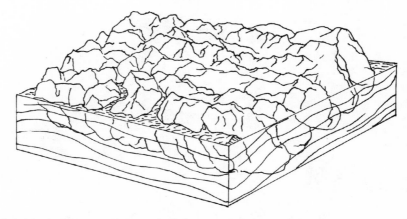

As the batholith broke through to the surface of the Earth it was also tilting upward on its east side.
Drawing by Elizabeth Whalley.

(1,000 feet per mile, for ten miles). Finally it burst into the open air, and kept lifting. It's been rising from Cretaceous times until now, and the speed of its rise seems to be accelerating. The overall rise has been something between four and nine miles. It's rising about one foot every thousand years.

Not the eternal hills, then. But eternal enough for us.

This view from space shows part of the Whitney Intrusive Suite, the biggest pluton in the Sierra batholith; Mount Whitney and Tulainyo Lake (still frozen) are near the center, on the crest; under them you see the 10,000-foot drop to the Owens Valley floor, including the road up to Whitney Portal. Photograph by Planet Labs PBC.

MY SIERRA LIFE (2)
Break On Through

About a hundred yards up the trail from the parking lot at Emerald Bay on Lake Tahoe, Terry stopped Joe and me, hand out like a traffic cop, blue eyes sparkling with pleasure. A fine morning. "Boys it's time to drop."

Happily we agreed and he handed us little squares of blue construction paper soaked in LSD. We ate the little scraps and continued up the trail. Thus began my first day in the Sierra Nevada.

Naturally this brings up some questions. Did taking LSD affect my first day in the Sierra Nevada? No doubt about it. Sometimes I've joked that I got high in the mountains that day and never came down, not from then till now. And it's true! But not exactly.

It definitely made for a cosmic day, as we used to say. Hilarity often overcame us, as it did quite a lot in those days, whether we were on drugs or not; we liked to laugh, and the world struck us as funny. But what struck me most that day, and has lingered since in me, was a stupendous sensation of *significance*. This was not just me encountering the real world at last, which as a child of the suburbs was certainly part of it—it was more than that. It seemed to me that this mountain range I found myself in was *more than real*. I didn't know what I meant by that, and I still don't. *Surreal* is suggestive, given its etymology, but not right. Neither is *spiritual*, or *mystical*, or *metaphysical*, or *existential*, though all these words reach for the feeling. Naturally *the ineffable* and *the inexpressible* are also appropriate, given the elusiveness of the feeling, or its inexpressibility. I keep coming back to my original formulation: what I was seeing was more than real. That's the feeling that stuck with me, and has never gone away. More real than real—the real reality—something like that.

We were hippie college students, yes. It must be obvious. It was the summer of 1973, and in a month we would begin our senior year at UC San Diego, and after that be cast loose in the world without the slightest idea what to do. Joe and Terry and I had been friends since junior high school in Orange County, and we called ourselves the Florida Trio because we had driven to Florida and back, right after graduating from high school in the summer of 1970. On that trip we had been clean-cut, clean-living Orange County kids, already very silly; the Florida trip had been a laughfest every day, no matter how slight the pretexts. We were high on nothing more than getting out of high school. Not that that kept us from drinking a bottle of bourbon with three Florida girls on the beach one night and getting even sillier. Aside from that, it was just happiness.

A few weeks after that trip, we drove from 1955 to 1970 in a single hour. Fifteen years in 90 miles: that's how I describe our drive from Orange County to UCSD. A time machine, taking us to the future! Even in Florida we had already felt that escape to freedom.

Three years then passed in a flash, and yes, in that time we became long-haired stoner hippie college students, steadfastly opposed to the Vietnam War (our draft numbers were all under 100) and living the now-mythical life of the '60s, like everyone else we knew: sex drugs and rock and roll, sure, but also bodysurfing and playing sports of all kinds, very precious to us. We were hippie jocks, not at all a contradiction in terms, for those who may be wondering. We had been bodysurfers in Orange County, and had tried to keep our hand in that game at UCSD, but the long rolling waves of San Diego were not as suitable for bodysurfing as the steep violent walls of OC, and besides, in the summers, when the ocean was warmest, we were back in OC working odd jobs and going to the beach there.

That was my life up to that point, and I was happy with it: books, the beach, sports, my friends, my girlfriends. Many of the women going to UCSD in those years were also stoner hippies, and way more adventurous and wild than my high school women friends had been, and I loved them all. Life was good.

But Terry was looking for more. He had always been a seeker, and in that junior year at UCSD we had been joined in our on-campus apartment by a new friend from a nearby OC high school, Daryl Bonin. Bonin was an adventurer, passing through on his way to bigger things than college, and he left UCSD even before that year was up, headed for Costa Rica. But by then he had changed Terry, and therefore me and Joe, by giving us adventurous ideas. For Terry, it was mountains. He ventured into the Sierra a few times on his own, and after that was completely focused on that range. Talking Joe and me into going up there with him was easy; we were happy to try it. We too were on the hunt.

I had had a bad Boy Scouts career, marred by an ex-Marine troop leader, and the dusty chaparral of the local campgrounds. We had practiced marching, shooting rifles, and surveying plots of land. I burst out laughing one morning while playing "Reveille" on my bugle, amused at the idea that I was waking up 300 people at once; I got fired from bugle duty, and soon afterward quit the Boy Scouts, thinking I did not care for the outdoor life.

And even the ocean, our refuge and salvation in high school, had begun to pall. This was my fault, as the third of my three near-drowning experiences had been entirely the result of my own stupidity: I had swum out at La Jolla Shores that spring into cold water and big surf, stoned and out of shape, and gotten thrashed to within an inch of my life. I came crawling up onto shore spitting seawater and feeling thoroughly chastened. Mother Ocean didn't seem to love me anymore. It was all too much like the rejection I had suffered from a girl I had adored that spring. Things were changing, everything was upended, I was ready for something different. Bonin had given us the key, and now Terry was bashing through the door and dragging Joe and me along. Up to a new world!

For this first trip I had bought ridiculously heavy hiking boots, and a beige North Face backpack with an internal fiberglass frame, not bad for its era, also a cheap sleeping bag and a tube tent. I got some days off from work at Sears, where I was a bike assembler and repairman. Off we went in my rattly old Cortina, the Florida Machine. We drove from San Diego to the foothills west of Lake Tahoe, stopping late in the day because all the gas stations were closed (it was during the gas crisis). We slept on the tilted surface of a side road off Highway 50, behind the Cortina so we wouldn't get run over in the night. Bridal Veil Falls State Park; I remember that night every time I drive by. The next morning we rolled back down to Pollock Pines and gassed up before continuing on.

In driving all the way to the Tahoe region, we were passing all the glories of the southern Sierra. But Terry had become convinced that the best part of the Sierra Nevada was the Desolation Wilderness, a rectangle of the Eldorado National Forest just southwest of Tahoe. It's true that Desolation is great, but to drive past the southern Sierra to get there, which we did many times in the following years, was an act of great ignorance. We did it mainly because Terry liked the name, and none of us bothered to check his expertise. He was already our mountain expert. And surely with a name like Desolation, it had to be the best part of the range! We sang it like the Moody Blues: DES-O-LAYYYYY-*SHUN*! It is a great name, but what a romantic thing, what a crazy misapprehension. That was us. We learned by doing. Terry never trusted guidebooks, and Joe and I always trusted Terry. At least back then.

So there we were, midmorning on an August day in 1973, hiking uphill from Emerald Bay to the first lakes in the Desolation Wilderness on that trail, the Velma Lakes. Coming on to acid in a powerful way. Within the first couple of miles I had developed big blisters on both heels, and on the front of one ankle. My giant Raichle boots, which I have still in the garage, weigh 2.7 pounds each (I just weighed them, it's appalling). And they were new, and as stiff as ski boots.

The LSD made the blisters seem trivial, even funny. I named one Jacob and the other Crouch, and the one developing on the front of my ankle I named Achilles, which I thought was very funny. Yes, I was stoned.

Then the bare rock of the mountains began to emerge out of the forest. All kinds of rocky majesty, though I didn't know it at the time: dark metamorphic rock to the left, which I later learned was Dicks Peak; white granite to the right, later known to be Phipps Peak. These were my own personal Pillars of Hercules, and between them, floating above the Velma Lakes far to the west, lofted my own personal Atlantis: the Crystal Range. Now that's a good name! At that very moment of first sighting they became my Isles of the Blessed. They looked higher than Everest and a thousand miles away. Terry said we would be there by evening. I couldn't believe it. Terry said there was lots of time, and he stopped at the first Velma to dive in and cool off. Turned out the lake's water had been snow the day before, and in my very jumpy vision I saw him dive in headfirst and then immediately shoot back out of the water, also headfirst. A miracle! I got in to my ankles and soothed my blisters. The cold water chilled my whole body by cooling the blood in my feet. This I found marvelous.

Sitting on the perfect meadow verge of that lake, I had an inspiration. I was carrying my soft Sears work shoes to wear around camp in the evenings, and it occurred to me I could cut squares in the leather heels of these shoes, leaving holes a bit bigger than my blisters; then I would hike in these shoes, and feel better. I did that, using a massive Swiss Army knife I was carrying, and the plan worked. With my horrid boots on my back, and the minor distraction of Jacob and Crouch removed from my consciousness, I could focus better on the astonishing Crystal Range.

Hiking down the slope from the Velmas we came to a broad creek or shallow river, running left to right and blocking our way. Terry said it was called the Rubicon. This made me very happy. I was most certainly crossing my own Rubicon. We waded across the creek, continued up a trail. We had not brought a map, and now Terry was so high he couldn't remember exactly where he had been on his previous hike in this region, made the year before. He wasn't sure if we were where he had gone that time or not, but it didn't matter, he explained earnestly; we were somewhere. Joe and I without looking at each other solemnly agreed that we were somewhere. When we came to a trail sign, Joe took out his camera and shot photos of Terry and me standing by it, twirling our hats on our fingers and grinning like idiots. We were definitely somewhere. *Eight miles high . . .*

We hiked on. The sun was now behind the Crystal Range, it was hard to believe it was already late afternoon. When we came to Lake Schmidell, Terry said it was too early to stop. Little did Joe and I know that this was going to be our afternoon mantra for the rest of our lives. Terry never wanted to stop; darkness made him stop. Hopefully. But we didn't know that then, and on this first day we hiked on, over a low ridge to Lake Lois. By now it was maybe a little past sunset, who could tell.

Lake Lois looked great; its back wall was the Crystal Range itself, and it had a picturesque little island out in the middle of it. But then Terry pointed across the lake.

There's people over there! he declared. We can't camp here!

Joe and I could barely see these people, they were the size of ants. Okay, we said. Lead on. And Terry led on, down Lois's outlet stream.

A few hundred yards down this stream there was a flat spot beside the burbling water. By now it was twilight, but our pupils being the same size as our irises, we could see like night creatures. Terry declared this was camp. I took my backpack off and flexed my shoulders and had to grab a tree to keep from floating away. Orgasmic waves of relief poured through my shoulders.

We laid out our cotton sleeping bags on beige Ensolite ground pads, useless things that tortured my sleep for years. We ate Kraft mac 'n' cheese dinners, cooked in pots balanced on Bleuet stoves that burned with blue flames.

After dinner I got in my sleeping bag and lay there listening to the little creek beside us chuckle its way downstream. Same clucks, over and over, but not quite: a beautiful music, low and beguiling, like Debussy noodling around. The moon came up, and the granite landscape on the other side of the creek glowed as if lit from within. The million shades of gray and black were etched on my retinas, and the scene as a whole—little plants, piles of rocks—was so articulated and balanced that it looked as if Zen gardeners had worked for thousands of years to make such a beautiful composition. I wasn't the slightest bit sleepy, on the contrary I was still seriously electrified, and didn't want to sleep. I lay on my side watching the scene and listening to the creek for the whole of that night. It was a night both long and short. Eventually I saw the sky go gray and the stars pop out of existence as the sky to the east got lighter and lighter. I didn't know that my life had changed for good, I couldn't know that, it was too new. But I did know I had just lived one of the greatest days of my life. And I knew that this granite world, holding me in its cupped hands as I lay on it, glowing luminously in the moonlight, was a magic place. I loved it. I loved it.

That feeling has never gone away. I trust now that it never will.

The rest of that first trip was just as fine. The second day we crossed over the Crystal Range, crawling up a knife-edge ridge to the top of Red Peak, then dropping down its western slope to Lake Five or Nine, I've never been sure which. The morning after that, we ate acid again and made toy boats out of twigs and aluminum foil. In the process of digging a mast hole in a flat piece of wood, using the tip of my big Swiss Army knife, I snapped the knife blade down onto the middle finger of my left hand and cut it right to the bone. For a moment I could see how deep the blade had gone, see that it was the bone itself that had stopped me from cutting my finger off. Big deal! I used a twig as a splint and wrapped the cut with Band-Aids. The scar is still quite visible. After setting our boats onto their voyages (mine came in last because it worked too well, which caused it to capsize), we hiked a long way up the ridge holding in the lake, and finally, from the far side of this ridge, we looked out over the glacial canyon running west from the big deep U of Rockbound Pass. Across this giant trough stood the curving wall we later called Neapolitan Mountain, because of its big boles of orange, white, and black rock. This view seemed truly huge—rocky—windy—sun in the west, blasting everything side-ways—again, more than real. This was the third great event of the trip, along with that first glimpse of the Crystal Range, and the night by the Lois outlet stream. This view in particular had a wild, scary vastness to it; we were on the edge of a cliff, overlooking an infinite gap of air, facing a granite wall of Hima-layan majesty.

Later that day we scrambled down to Lake Doris, a sweet little figure 8 of a double lake, nestled just under the east side of Rockbound Pass. It struck us as the perfect lake, and it still can seem so any time I get there.

By now I was completely won over. This was the most gorgeous and gigantic

The Crystal Range, looking south along it toward Mount Price

wilderness imaginable. The dusty chaparral hills of Southern California had left me entirely unprepared for what high glaciated granite peaks were like.

That night I burned my fingertips when taking my pot out of a campfire we made, and my chopped finger was kind of sore too, as were my blisters, and my shoulders. In fact, by the time we got back to the car the next afternoon I was somewhat of a wreck, in physical terms. But my heart was soaring. I was smitten, in love in somewhat the same way I had been with that girl back in the spring. A four-day conversion experience, a road-to-Damascus event. Now I was a Sierra person.

That's stayed true from then till now. I'm a husband, father, and friend; I'm a writer; and I'm a Sierra person. That's me.

So, but why? It wasn't just the LSD. In the years between 1973 and 1980 I took quite a few LSD trips, and did all kinds of things while tripping. I went to rock concerts, I don't care about them now. I went to the beach, it was nice but also rather alarming; the ocean can kill you with the back of its little finger. I wandered in the desert once, and felt oppressed; I drove the length of California once, not advisable, and was mostly appalled by what I saw and thought. Driving down one pass on the interstate I felt my trusty Cortina detach from the road and begin to float down the hill, and only by the most delicate of nudges on the steering wheel could I guide it back down to the flatlands of OC. Etc. Very much not recommended, most of what I did on LSD, and indeed taking drugs you don't know the provenance of, or the amount of, is undeniably stupid. Yes, I was a hippie youth, enjoying the careless life of a young man in the 1970s, a state of mind not easy to remember or explain. That these acid trips were the stupidest things I did back then is maybe a testament to how sensible I was compared to many of my generation.

Not that I want to renounce them now. It was stupid to take unknown quantities of unknown substances, yes; no doubt about it. But it seems, by the results of what happened to me and my friends, that some kind of weird honor system existed back then among the drug dealers, because mostly the trips were consistent with each other, and enjoyable. Sometimes not: once I foolishly dropped before taking out a woman I didn't know well, thinking I would wander Blacks Cliffs for the day and then be mellow by the time I was to pick her up that evening at her parents' house in Pacific Beach; didn't work out that way, and I spent a couple of hours at a car wash that afternoon, frantically trying to make the Cortina a little more presentable. That was a bad idea, an infinite regress of fractal hypercleanliness, which led me to think that my soul was likewise not clean, as I had no idea what to do with my life, and no prospects, and the world and history and time were big and scary—the closest I ever came to a bad trip, in short, although I have to say it was redeemed that evening by my lovely date, as we went to San Diego's Old Globe theater hoping to see Shakespeare and having to settle instead for the musical *I Do! I Do!* and then laughing ourselves sick.

That summer of 1973 was wild, those years were wild. Life itself was big. I always felt it as being stuffed with a huge significance, and myself embarked on a great adventure. That was true no matter what drugs I took or didn't take, and had to do more with literature, and the beach, and my friends both men and women. It was a literary feeling most of all, and a youthful feeling. It began when I read *Huckleberry Finn* in second grade, and has never stopped. Literature itself is the real psychedelic, the actual cosmic trip.

Now, in the last few years, LSD is being rehabilitated to some extent, as an unexpected and unexplainable help for some otherwise intractable human problems. Addiction, depression, pain, end-of-life anxiety; all these have been helped when the sufferers take LSD under the guidance of a counselor. Even a single trip is reported to be helpful, and seldom are more than three required to create effects of reconciliation to reality that endure, and greatly help people. Michael Pollan is good on this in his book *How to Change Your Mind*, as is the documentary movie *Fantastic Fungi*. Possibly this form of treatment will become a regular part of certain therapies; in the meantime, it's very strange that something interesting is going on during this small and temporary change in brain chemistry.

For me, as a young hippie and literary person, Ram Dass and Aldous Huxley and the various Buddhist writers were all very helpful in giving me a context. Psychedelics were an eye-opener, figuratively as well as literally, but they didn't do anything in themselves; or, they did what they did, a rather strange temporary alteration in consciousness, and then you had to learn from that, if you could, and move on. Which I did. With the end of the '70s lots of things went away for me, including some I regretted, like waterbeds, or youth itself; but an end to psychedelic experiences I didn't regret. The time for that was over. It was the Sierras that mattered, and the Sierras that stayed.

SIERRA PEOPLE (1)
The First People

Sometime in the late '90s we were hiking up the Muir Trail toward Mather Pass, in the highest part of Upper Basin. There was sure to be a nice campsite in the great stretch of high fellfield and ponds under the south wall of the pass. Late afternoon on a sunny day, hiking along feeling tired but not wasted. I suggested to Terry we needed a rest, so he veered off trail up onto a rise on our left, going up there mostly for the view, but also because it got us away from other hikers who would be passing by on the Muir Trail.

We followed him up onto a broad-topped sandy old moraine, threw off our packs, and sat down. Time for a sip of water, if we had any, and a late snack. We could see all the way back down the long stretch of Upper Basin, one of those perfect curving granite half-pipes that appear all over the range, this one especially big and fine: Split Mountain to our left, Vennacher Needle (not a needle) to our right, the Pinchot Pass ridge of red rock in the far distance, ten miles to the south. Then, just looking around—and I have the impression that we all saw this at once—looking westward into the sun, the rise we were sitting on was sparkling as if seeded with diamonds. Scores of sparks of reflected sunlight jumping out of the ground, which was the usual glacial till found in any moraine anywhere. What the hell?

We stood up, walked west to the nearest sparkle. Ah: a black glass shard. Then another. Then another. Then another. Only the ones angled correctly were sparkling at us; tilted at different angles were many more. We were standing in the midst of a field of obsidian shards. Thousands and thousands of obsidian shards.

We knew just enough to realize this was a Native American knapping site. We had recently learned that there is no endemic obsidian in the high Sierra, so that whenever you find it up there, you are seeing something that humans brought and left behind. So this was a place where Native Americans, Paleo-Indians as they are sometimes called, or the first people, had sat around, smacking blocks of obsidian maybe the size of bread loaves, using stone tools to knock off shards that they then knapped further, until they had arrowheads, spearheads, hand tools with cutting edges, and so on. There were so many shards under our feet that it had to have gone on like that for—who knows? Hundreds of years, it looked like. This place had been a human place for hundreds of years, you could see that just looking around.

Why here? Well, it was as clear as could be: for the view!

They were just like us, Terry mused, looking around. I had seldom heard him sound so content. Our sudden realization of this place's human past had impressed him, pleased him in some deep way. It validated his way of life; his love for these mountains was revealed to be a thing from deep time, a primal love. A first peoples' love. Just to be up here looking around.

We wandered from shard to shard, picking them up to inspect them. The view to the west continued to spark in an amazing way. Big rock candy mountain—a thousand broken mirrors—it was uncanny, spectacular. We were walking on sacred ground. We peered at the black glass shards' concentric spall marks, their concave and convex curves. Terry warned us to keep only one piece each, a warning not all of us heeded. One day we'll throw some chips back onto that moraine. It will be yet another Terry ritual.

When I was clearing out my dad's desk after his death, I found three egg-shaped pink granite stones, smooth as could be. I knew just where he had gotten them: Hunters Beach, Mount Desert Island. It's a pebble beach, and waves have tumbled the glacial till there until many of the pebbles, chunks of Mount Cadillac's beautiful pink granite, are egg-shaped or spherical. It's against the law to take these rocks away, as I told my dad that day. But my dad liked rocks, as do I. He must have slipped these three into his pocket when I wasn't looking. I took them from his desk to my home, and later that summer, back at Hunters Beach, I gave one each to my two boys, and took the third myself, and counted to three and we threw them back into the surf to tumble some more. My dad had forbidden any memorial service to be held for him, so I laughed as we did this. Memorials can take funny forms. That one felt like a good one.

People came into the Americas around 20,000 years ago, or maybe more—possibly 25,000 or even 30,000 years ago. Throughout my life this first arrival date has gotten pushed back further and further, as the archaeologists find evidence dating it to an older time; that seems likely to keep happening. Anomalous finds in both North and South America keep being discovered, their initial estimated dates a surprise to all. At first these dates get bracketed as being so outside the paradigm that they're probably wrong. It's that way still for sites in Brazil and South Carolina, both yielding dates well over 20,000 years old. But the famous anomaly found on the coast of Chile, called Monte Verde, a camp or small village dated to somewhere between 14,000 and 18,000 years ago, has held firm after extensive investigation. That find changed our understanding not only of when humans came into the Americas, but how. Before Monte Verde, it was assumed that people came south from Alaska through a gap in the ice sheet covering Canada that opened up around 13,500 years ago. The resulting continent-wide culture that poured through that gap, called the Clovis culture, is dated as starting about 13,000 years ago, and was considered to be the first human culture in the Americas. Now, even if the Clovis overland migration happened, as it almost certainly did (linguistic evidence can supplement physical traces to date separate surges of arrival), that wave of incoming people has been joined in our understanding by one that looks like it happened quite a bit earlier, made by sea travelers moving down the west coast of the Americas, south from the Aleutians all the way to Tierra del Fuego. Since sea level was around 200 feet lower during the last ice age, any coastal settlements these people might have made are now under water. Monte Verde was 30 miles up a river, and by a stroke of luck got well preserved in a peat bog. Now footprints well-dated to 21,000 years ago have been identified in New Mexico.

So, we still don't know exactly when humans first occupied the Americas, but for sure by 12,000 years ago, they were living in many places on both continents. Extinctions of megafauna from around that same time might have been caused or accelerated by human hunting; the Clovis style of stonework, mostly found in spear points, was widespread.

California's Sierra Nevada was still blanketed by its own little ice sheet in the time of these earliest Native Americans, but it was much less iced over by about 10,000 years ago, and by 5,000 years ago its ice cover was reduced to something quite like the remnant glaciers we see up there now. And there are well-dated sites up and down the California coast that go back as far as 7,000 years, and others even older in the basin-and-range country east of the Sierras. So, were they up in the high Sierra too during those years?

Yes, they were. We know this with certainty because these first peoples used obsidian that they obtained in the Owens Valley, often at Obsidian Dome, these days located right next to Highway 395. Scientists can identify by chemical composition where obsidian flakes originated, and they can even determine when chips or tools were flaked, by measuring how far water has penetrated any newly exposed glass surfaces; this happens at a regular and measurable rate (which I find amazing). These methods have allowed the archaeologists to trace a long history of obsidian gathering and distribution all up and down the Owens Valley, a system of distribution that shows expansions and contractions that appear to be tied to drought cycles. Also, obsidian from the Owens Valley is often found west of the Sierras, all the way out to the coast. In symmetrical fashion, seashells from the coast have been found in the Owens Valley.

Then also, as I said before, the high Sierra itself has no in situ sources of obsidian. Any obsidian found up there was brought there by people.

And bits of obsidian are found all over the Sierra. Several meadows in the high Sierra, where summer camps could easily have been set up, feature extensive fields of obsidian chips, like the one we stumbled on that day, clearly indicating knapping sites that were used over and over.

It's not surprising people would go up into the Sierras in the summers. Both the Owens Valley and California's Central Valley become baking hot in summer, so it makes sense that people would migrate up to the high meadows to get out of the heat. We still do that now. Back then, people from the two sides could meet up there, share camps, and mingle as they enjoyed their summers, exchanging goods that weren't available on the other side. Summer festivals, you might say; but it has to be remembered that for nomadic people, all their various seasonal settlements are their homes. In this case, the fact that the Paiute language on the east side and the Western Mono and Monache languages on the west side are mutually comprehensible dialects of the same language is very suggestive. There was surely a regular intermingling, perhaps including marriages. I would say, almost certainly. These neighbors were in-laws, cousins, family.

The obsidian chips scattered over the high Sierra are almost all that remains to support these speculations, but they're enough. Sites like the one we stumbled on are proof that they were occupied for a very long time. We once ran into a California state archaeologist near Bishop Pass, and asked him how long he thought people had been going up into the Sierra; he said they had good dates going back 5,000 years, but he thought people had been there for more like 10,000. He told me the lake we were standing next to was a knapping site, and while we spoke one of his assistants wandered off and came back with a black glass flake, reminding me of the great Thoreau story, of Henry telling his brother there were arrowheads wherever you looked, and reaching down randomly and picking one up from under his feet.

We told the archaeologist about our find in Upper Basin, and he thanked us for telling him. He said it was interesting because most knapping sites they knew of were near the east-west passes across the Sierra known to have been used by Native Americans for crossing the range. There were big knapping sites near Bench Lake, for instance, downcanyon from our Upper Basin find, and also in Taboose Pass itself, on the crest to the east of Bench Lake. Taboose was one of the major Native American passes, he told us, and the little meadow just west of Taboose Pass still had oval rings of stones, like tipi rings, used for the foundations of summer shelters, which no doubt had been newly constructed every year. These ovals are among the most substantial remains of Native Americans in all the high Sierra, enough to suggest that this area west of Taboose Pass had been a regular summer village. So the site we had found, about five miles away, might have been a place where young people would go to get away for the day, with the knapping something to do while they were there. Excuse for a party—sacred ceremonial site—both at once—who could say?

Later the archaeologist emailed me his paper on the Taboose Pass site, which had a map showing some of the places where objects had been found. There were about 20 marks in a space half a mile across, all over the small high meadow west of the pass. He mentioned they had decided not to include the map in the published paper, so that people wouldn't use it to find relics and take them away.

Ten thousand years of Sierra summer camping.

The road from Three Rivers up to Sequoia passes Hospital Rock, where an active Native American village existed until well into the nineteenth century, when its inhabitants were driven off by Europeans. Now there's nothing left but mortar-and-pestle holes in the rock by the river, and one wall of overhanging rock, a big boulder face that is somewhat protected from rain by its overhang, so that on it are almost all the pictographs that remain in the Sierra. Paints of various colors, but mostly red, were used to make patterns and what could be interpreted to be bird-human hybrids, or perhaps people with birds flying out of their heads—very suggestive for those of us with a psychedelic introduction to the range. Shamanic traditions are worldwide, as old as humanity itself; spirit voyages are a very ancient thing. This wall makes it look like such voyages took place here.

There could have been such painted rock surfaces all over the Sierra, but if they were directly exposed to rain, they would have gotten slowly washed away, until the rock was left clean again. It's beautiful to imagine the high Sierra with painted rock walls everywhere—and perhaps much of the world the same. Now the paintings left to us are in caves, or in very dry regions, or sheltered by overhangs, as at Hospital Rock.

The grinding holes down by the river are also very suggestive. The idea that people wore these holes into the rock with stone pestles as they ground acorns, year after year, testifies to how long they lived and worked here. The

Hospital Rock, Sequoia National Park

rock is hard, the holes pretty deep. In them people ground oak acorns to be able to leach the tannins out of them, and thus turn them into flour for food.

There are also bigger shallow basins in flat-rock areas, in the southernmost reaches of the range, at about the elevation of Hospital Rock and other village sites. Mixing bowls? Stew pots? Their purpose isn't clear, nor is their method of excavation. Sierra geologist James Moore took an interest in these and co-authored a paper that described a scientific experiment trying to determine whether people could have dug the basins by hand: 42,000 strikes over five hours yielded a hole 11 centimeters in diameter and 2 centimeters deep; so at this rate, calculated to be 17.5 milliliters per hour (bone-jarring work, it is reported), a basin of the size seen in the field could be created by five years of continuous work. Very funny, scientists. They judged their experiment to be inconclusive. But the basins are there, and their shape and location suggest that humans dug them, one way or another. Maybe five years isn't that long.

*   *   *

Petroglyphs are more durable than pictographs, being etched rather than painted. There are many petroglyph sites all over the Owens Valley, where the dark red stone takes a lighter hue when etched. Fish Slough, north of Bishop, is an area of rounded rock hills with great views of the Sierra to the west and the White Mountains to the east. The steep walls of these red hills are crowded with petroglyphs, like Newspaper Rock in Utah; many mural faces are etched until all the space on them is occupied. These drawings are mostly abstract patterns, resembling basketry weaves, or spirals. (Some archaeologists interested in shamanism have noted that these patterns, seen on rock walls all over the world, are the first hallucinations of people coming on to a psychedelic plant: see *The Mind in the Cave*, by David Lewis-Williams.) Laurie Glover took a group of us to visit Fish Slough in 2009, a group that included Gary Snyder and Tom Killion, two of the greatest Sierra artists of our time. To see them together viewing the ancient artists was a special thrill, a touch of deep-time aesthetics.

The second most famous pictograph in the Sierra, being almost the only other one that exists, is located under Tehipite Dome, in the riverbed of the Middle Fork of the Kings River.

Tehipite Dome

Tehipite Dome is a spire on the west wall of the canyon of the Middle Fork, almost twice as tall as Half Dome. That the ancient ones thought it was a special place is not surprising, although the little valley in the river floor below, really no more than a wide spot in the canyon, is hard to get to now, and probably then too. You have to bushwhack a long stretch of the canyon to get to it, or drop over the lip of the west wall just south of the dome and make a steep descent of about 5,000 feet. This wall now has a trail on it, which may be based on an ancient Indigenous trail, and is the easiest way to get there.

In any case we know they went there, because a village midden was found in the little valley, and some obsidian chips, and best of all, a boulder called Painted Rock, very near the foot of the dome, near the river. This boulder also has an overhanging rock face, and the simple black painting on the pro-tected surface is an abstract of some sort, what some have called paramecium shapes.

I've seen photos of this painting, but not the thing itself. Terry and I hiked to Tehipite in 2007, from the Wishon Reservoir up a forest trail to the rim, then down the long descent of the wall, the tall dome to our left the whole way down. When we got to the flat oval valley next to the river, we hunted for "Painted Rock" for most of two hours, but couldn't find it. I had read there would be a side trail leading to it, with an old wooden sign, but we saw neither. And we had no GPS, nor did we have a map location for the rock fine enough to help us. The topo map I had with me actually named it, but the printed name PAINTED ROCK covered an area of perhaps 50 acres. And the riverbed of the Middle Fork turned out to be dotted with many boulders of about the right size, from house size to storage-locker size. These had either fallen off the steep walls of the canyon, or been carried downstream by the glacier that had once filled the canyon, or both. So we wandered around from rock to rock, inspecting their sides and looking for any overhanging faces. No luck.

Eventually we gave up and hiked upstream on the old canyon trail to Simp-son Meadow. That was one of the most beautiful days of canyon hiking in my life, but I was disappointed not to have found Painted Rock, and decided I would return someday. So far I haven't, but I still hope to; the longitude and latitude for the rock are published down to a point of precision that seems to delineate about one square foot, and with this entered into a GPS device, we will presumably be led right to it. We'll see.

It's a strange thing that Tehipite Dome is almost completely forgotten now, and the trails leading to it disappearing from lack of use. I say forgotten, because in the nineteenth-century Sierra literature it's often referred to as "the famous Tehipite Dome." A round-topped plinth, quite a bit taller than El Capitan: it's really something to see. And in the nineteenth century, when every part of the Sierra was difficult to get to, access as such was not the decisive issue. But now, the road system and the trail system have combined to make some places in the Sierra very easy to get to, while others have remained almost as inaccessible as they were in 1890. You can drive to the foot of El Capitan, and walk in 15 minutes to the foot of Half Dome, and they're visible from all over that famous valley. So they're icons. But Tehipite Dome takes a real commitment to see. If just glimpsing it were your only goal, that would take a couple of days. To see it from below could take six days. Quite a trip! But if you don't make that commitment, you won't see it; and if you don't see it, you won't really get it. Photos are not good at conveying scale, and thus they don't convey reality very well.

Now, when flying from Sacramento to Los Angeles or San Diego, I sit on the left side of the plane, and looking down to the left I spot Kings Canyon, and then as the plane passes it, I look back and see the Middle Fork extending northeast from its confluence with the South Fork; it's all quite huge and obvious. Thus oriented, on clear days I can spot the top of Tehipite Dome, sticking above the west wall of the Middle Fork. As the plane continues south and west, more and more of the dome is revealed, and it's really tall, but very distant, and very small. Then it's gone from view.

When we reached Simpson Meadow that day of our failed search, we twice disturbed rattlesnakes. The next day we continued up the Middle Fork all day long, a glorious walk in glacier-carved granite depths, the scrapings of the glacier visible as horizontal lines on the side walls of the tight sinuous canyon. We never saw a soul. Hundreds were on the Muir Trail that day, just one massif over.

A Middle Fork moment near the Devils Washbowl. When ice filled this canyon, water pouring down its bottom under enormous pressure carved this granite cleft.

In 2016, my friends Darryl and Carter and I started and ended our trip by going over Taboose Pass, and we gave ourselves some hours on the way in and out to explore the high meadow the archaeologist had told us about. Carter transferred the marks on the archaeologist's map to his topo map, and on the last afternoon of our trip, we put down our packs and slowly wandered the meadow, trying to find the places marked on the map.

Sometimes it was easy. Right on the trail we crossed a low mound covered with obsidian chips. Other times the map marked knobs we thought we could recognize, and on these knobs were more clusters of black glass. That was very satisfying, like a treasure hunt. But it became clear yet again: the map is not the territory. Despite the seeming precision of the contour intervals, translating that information to the landscape is never obvious or easy.

In this case, whether we were in the right places or not, we were finding obsidian. I hoped also to find a shelter's foundation stones. These were said to be oval rings of low stone, about 20 feet long and almost as wide. Having been to the Orkney Islands and seen the incredible stonework in the archaeological sites there, I had an image of these rings that was no doubt overly elaborate. Tipi rings in the Rockies are a better analogy; these are unobtrusive for the most part, and there are said to be millions of them. I saw one recently in Wyoming, and this gave support to my notion that I may have found a couple in the Taboose Pass meadow; they looked much the same. As in the Rockies, the stones involved were used to stop flexible framing branches from sliding outward. These stone rings were always casual, and later, modern campers have also sometimes camped inside them. So it was a bit elusive that day, but I found two rises that seemed to have cleared tops, and one had a rough oval of stones bordering the cleared area; just the usual glacial stones, but there they were.

Obsidian, however, was everywhere: clusters of it every hundred yards or so, and individual chips scattered everywhere we looked. Clearly people had lived here. People just like us, not in some general way, but in the sense of having exactly the same DNA. They might not have had the lactose tolerance gene, which evolved in some populations starting around 17,000 years ago; but on the other hand maybe they did.

I tried to see it as it had been: a little village, with big oval huts standing here and there in knots of trees. People sitting around talking, prepping food, working on tools and clothing, eating meals together. Columns of smoke rising from campfires. Village life. It had been like that. They had not been on summer vacation; they were nomads, living in the right place for that time of year, perfectly at home. Songs and laughter, in different dialects that leaped the gap from person to person and culture to culture, the language variations no doubt an endless source of curiosity and amusement. Talking story, sharing cooking tips. In the fall when the days got shorter and the light slanted from the south, they must have held some final party and promised to meet again here the following year. Some new couples would have had to decide whether to stay together or not, and if staying together, which way to go down. That certainly must have happened.

That afternoon was a very different experience from our first discovery on the moraine mound. That first time, my feeling was one of joy: they were here! This time, seeing the meadow that had held a high village for thousands of years, my feeling was more complex, and suffused with sorrow. They were here, yes; but now they aren't.

Thus some traces left by the original inhabitants of the Sierra, which I have seen. They summered in the high country, and wintered at around the 4,000-foot level all around the range, including in all the great canyons. Of course what I've written here, and what anyone can still see, is inadequate to convey the thousands of years they spent in these mountains.

Between 1850 and 1870 they were driven out of the Sierra by newly arrived white people. Before that, following the arrival of the Spanish in the 1760s, they died in great numbers from European diseases new to them. Indigenous Californians were especially hard-hit by these. By 1880, the surviving Native Californians had mostly been forced onto reservations, often located far from home. They lived on as best they could.

This sorry tale of expulsion and genocide is one part of a larger American crime. The current reality is also disturbing. I spent part of the summer of 1966 on the Navajo reservation north of Flagstaff, staying with my great-aunt who was a missionary there, and I saw that even though Navajo culture has remained strong to this day, the destructive impacts of settler colonial rule have been huge, and are ongoing. It was one of the great shocks of my life.

In this chapter I've focused on what I've seen in the high Sierra of that early way of life. From those few traces it's hard to imagine the people and cultures that lived here for so long. But one can try. Those people went to the high Sierra and made it their summer home for the same reasons we do now: to get out of the heat and bustle, and spend some time in a beautiful place. That's very clear.

Now, given the past and ongoing crimes against Native Americans, we need to support the living as they pursue their lives; and it's not a bad thing to spend some time in the Sierra to walk around as they did for so long, and remember. In my novel *Shaman* I tried to imagine what life was like for Paleolithic people on this planet. No modern person can do this very well, but I tried. And for sure my Sierra wandering helped me write that book. If you want to know what I think it might have been like for the first peoples to live in the Sierra, that novel will tell you. Not that all Paleolithic cultures were the same, but they were far more like each other than any of them was like any culture since the Agricultural Revolution, not to mention the Industrial Revolution. Many of them seem to have included some kind of shamanism in their habits; and they all seem to have had a deep and active regard for their fellow animals.

Here in this book, I'll just say that to see those black chips of glass on the land is to feel something deep. We all are descended from people who evolved in Africa, some of whom walked out of Africa around 120,000 years ago, and kept on walking. It's important to remember that. Sometimes I think when you're walking all day, it's easier to remember that, and to imagine what it must have been like. Possibly that's one of the greatest values of walking up there. It's a chance to imagine the deep time of human history, and feel it in one's body, in the act of walking all day.

Last year we camped near White Pass, a remote spur high on the north side of the Monarch Divide, next to a small stream. Over a low granite rise lay a couple of ponds we had been thinking of as campsites, but the meadow flanking the little stream was better for that purpose. After Joe finished setting camp, he went over to check out the ponds. He came back after a while, face lit with a big smile. Look! he said, and held out his hand; half a dozen obsidian chips. Over by one of the ponds, he explained.

They would have had a view down the steep drop of the south fork of Cartridge Creek, and across the giant gap of air to the Ionian Basin and the Goddard Divide. They would have had names for some of these features. It was an awesome place, as we saw very clearly during that sunset. But very far from any possible village. Simpson Meadow was maybe the closest place they could have lived, even as a summer camp, and that was ten hard miles away, and thousands of feet below us. No: we were tucked up in a little cirque, a world of its own, a private miracle. It must have been shaman business that had brought them up here, or so it seemed. For an initiation of some sort, maybe. Or just a party, sure. In any case, a night out under the stars.

Joe went back and returned the chips to their places. We stayed in camp while he did that, letting the exact place be his secret. We knew we were someplace special. That would have been true even without the obsidian, but with it, that sunset turned mystical. We felt again the touch of deep time, of the humans who came before. These mountains are haunted, they were emptied by a genocide. We walk on sacred ground. And listen: that is true wherever you are as you read this, if you are anywhere in the United States, or anywhere in the Americas. Don't think otherwise. Remember.

Ten thousand years.

MY SIERRA LIFE (3)

Artists in the Back Country

That Artists in the Back Country camp that I joined in 2008 turned out to be a lot of fun. During the days we were free to do what we wanted; at night we talked by the fire. So after breakfast on the second day I took off on my own, up into the Miter Basin.

The west side of the Miter Basin, from Elizabeth's Pond

It had been many years since I had wandered in the Sierra by myself. It felt good. All those trips trying to get friends into the same campsite at night—but forget about that, here I was. And this basin was looking fabulous.

Up the slot to Elizabeth's Pond (I had named it the day before, on a hike with photographer Elizabeth Carmel; it's on the cover of her book of Sierra photos), then onto the big green floor of the lower basin, walled by white pillars to each side. Goal for the day, Crabtree Pass. One of two cross-country passes over the circling ridge that holds the basin.

Quick across the grass to the upper end of a long meadow, past its meandering creek. Wind pushed from the west, bringing scattered clouds. A foxtail grove hugged the wall under Sky Blue Lake. Foxtails don't dwarfify like other Sierra trees such as lodgepole and juniper, which miniaturize at higher altitude and form krummholz, German for "crooked wood" or "elfin wood." For foxtails it's all or nothing. These big trees I passed were more like ents than dwarves, and obviously ancient. Cousins to the bristlecone pines over in the White Mountains, almost as long-lived, and much bigger. I stopped by one and fingered the blond spiral grain in the exposed parts of the trunk, also its flaky cinnamon bark. Sudden shade from scudding clouds deepened the tree's rich colors.

A stream fell down some steps and slides in the lower basin's headwall. Clouds flowed over it, height and distance shifted with the moving light and shadow. Looking back I saw the lower basin's big curve, like that of so many Sierra canyons. This curve of Rock Creek ran up the Miter Basin like a spiraling fern, its highest curl tucking right into a glacier on the north side of Mount Pickering.

Up a grassy slope west of the stream, which was here a staircase waterfall. Above the waterfall a granite knob gave me an excellent view of Sky Blue Lake. Cloud Gray Lake today, a big round sheet of water, steely, wind-ruffled, forbidding. The west shore cliffed in a way that said no one ever went there. The east shore was a grassy verge. Circled on that side and climbed next to the lake's inlet stream, which rose in short leaps through a steep meadow. The clouds began to spit a little rain, but there were still big shafts of sunlight striking granite here and there, making a patchwork of light and shade, constantly changing.

Higher still, I came into a gorgeous region of chiseled orange rock shot with veins of white quartz. The creek dropped from pool to pool, each set between rough walls, so that I seemed to move from room to room, each only a few steps higher than the previous. Looking back I saw Mount Langley framed by rock walls, lit by sun when I was in shadow, then vice versa.

A pond high in the Miter Basin, on the way to Crabtree Pass. Sierra crest on the skyline, just north of Mount Langley.

A world of rock, and yet under my feet grass and flowers grew in the cracks. Higher still the grass was replaced by lichen, with moss pads clustering on flat places bordering the creek. The Persian carpet look, my favorite: exposed stone and sand, liberally dotted with small cushion plants and various lichens, all harmoniously spaced and fitted tightly to the land. The filigree of living color is crucial to the beauty of the stone. Sensuous advantage of a cloudy day:

colors leaped into my eye. I sauntered upstream, stopping often to look around. I didn't want to get past this place or this moment. I was here.

A moraine at the bottom of the high little glacier blocked my way, its rock unstable in the usual way of terminal moraines. About 50 feet high, tilted to the angle of repose and then a bit more. Nothing grew on it.

Its right edge had piled onto exposed bedrock. Scramble up the intersection of these two faces. Up to a tiny pond and lawn. From the lawn I had a good view of the little glacier above the moraine, a steep slope of ice almost entirely covered by rubble, but with a bergschrund at its top that revealed its nature. My map showed six glaciers in the Miter Basin, this one the largest. Maybe a quarter of a mile long, on a sharp tilt, in the shade of a north-facing cleft. Soon to be gone from this world.

Two upper lakes, one at my level, the other in a deep hole. A rock rib between them, leading toward the pass. Now I could finally see that the scree slope at the top of the pass was actually well beyond it. Crabtree Pass was a thousand feet lower than I had thought! I was already as high as the pass, and almost there. Just around a small shoulder, clean hard rock all the way. It was going to be easy—and had been all along!

Going around a final shoulder it got rumply. Little trail ducks marked the way, exceptionally small and shapely stacks of three little rocks, the top ones sometimes rounded. I usually hate trail ducks and destroy them on sight, but these struck me as helpful, and witty.

The pass was a narrow spine of hard handsome rock, smooth as aplite and intensely chiseled by the ice that had filled this pass at some point. Now I could see northwest, down a narrow slot with a lake filling its floor. In the V gap beyond the lake I spotted a wedge of the distant Kaweahs, dark and spiky as usual. Scree slopes impounded the lake, a view constricted and lunar. Much less beautiful than the Miter Basin. Nothing on the map could reveal this.

Clouds raced overhead, throwing a constantly varied quilt of shadow and light on the ridges. A pass for a scrambler is like a peak for a climber: the goal, the destination. An expansion in space. A rise to a new reality.

*   *   *

On the way back I took it easy. There were rain showers but also sun showers, and camp would be luxurious compared to what I was used to. Rain today was just a Turner effect.

I sat in the grove of foxtail pines below Cloud Gray Lake and brewed up a little pot of Greek coffee to fuel my stroll home. Stopped to take pictures of flowers, moss pads, grass, sedge. Saxifrage, asters, buckwheats, sedrum, polemonium, more I didn't have names for. Scattered in the granite cracks, under the darkening clouds, these glossy living beings filled their spaces almost to bursting.

A breath, a step, a heartbeat. The shadow of a cloud, racing over the land. Cloud and granite; moment and eon. Same laws of physics for both, but—different affect. Or the composite affect of the two interpenetrated: very much a Sierra feeling. The eon in every moment.

Walking takes thought. Rain matters. Hunger matters, and breathing. Being warm or cold matters. And always choosing where the next step goes. Hiking cross-country is the true mountain walking. Trails are thin roads; only when hiking cross-country do you choose your own adventure, in every step you take. The freedom forces a certain attention to process. This is possibly true in other contexts. There are no trails at all in the Miter Basin. Where every way will go, trails become unnecessary. Every hiker takes a personal route here, never repeated by anyone else. That individual route makes it your place. Your life can begin to look like that. When is it ever different?

I came back into camp at happy hour, and joined a lively party of men and women standing around, drinking white wine and eating Brie on crackers—olives, hummus, roasted red peppers. Extreme cognitive dissonance: I was stunned, it felt surreal.

But also, pretty easy to get used to. Our cook Ariana made the kitchen a cheerful place, and Mando Quintero and Bill Tweed did a good job of hosting what seemed a kind of continuous party. That night around the fire we read aloud from Snyder, Jeffers, and Rexroth. When I read, I used my headlamp to help me see the page — this would have been very useful in some of the dim little bars in San Francisco where I've done readings.

Better still was just chatting round the fire. The conversation kept returning to the Sierra, because we were in it, and everyone there had a relationship to it, even if it was only that of a first-timer, which in itself was interesting. There were a lot of Sierra years around that fire. My angle on it was so narrow: I backpacked, and I backpacked, and I backpacked. That's all I knew. So I had a lot to learn. I always like that feeling. Especially around a big campfire.

And my bed, packed in by horses, was really comfortable too.

A cirque is by definition arcuate in shape. Looking at the map, I noticed that the Miter Basin's boundary ridge is as arcuate as can be: it forms an almost perfect circle.

If you stick the point of a compass near the outlet of Sky Blue Lake, and put the other point of the compass on the Major General, you can run it all the way round to the spur between Primrose and Erin Lakes. Rock Creek then exits a narrow gap in this circle. The diameter of the circle is roughly three miles, the circumference ridge is therefore around ten miles long. The gap where Rock Creek exits the basin is about a mile wide, so, something like one-tenth of the big circle is broken by this gap.

Then also, from the circumference ridge, five or six spur ridges run in toward the center, somewhat like broken spokes headed for an absent hub. Up between these spurs extend little cirques, higher than the lower basin floor, each holding lakes.

The main basin and the cirques look somewhat like a right hand, palm up: the thumb is Iridescent Lake, the forefinger goes up to Arc Pass, middle finger up to Crabtree Pass, ring finger to Primrose Lake, little finger to Erin Lake. Rock Creek is the wrist.

Do other Sierra basins have this circular shape? The tops of the plutons must have formed underground as blobs with almost flat lobate tops; then, after they emerged into the air, ice lay for a long time on these broad dome tops, and that ice would always flow down the path of least resistance. Like when hot wax melts a break in the top of a fat candle: afterward that break is

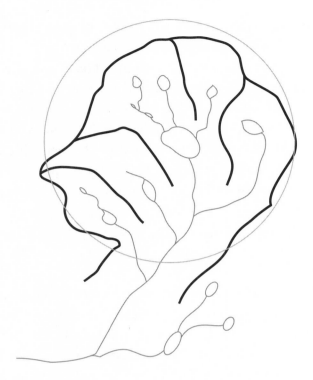

where the wax will always leave the top, and so the exit stream quickly deepens. Glaciers also eat back into the rocks banking them, like hot wax eating into the solid wax of a rim. So eventually the stone top of a pluton will become a hollow with a rim around its edge and a gap somewhere in that rim, leading out and down. Everywhere true, but seldom so obvious as in the Miter Basin.

The next day I went out again, and immediately noticed something: I knew this place. Third time in the same area; another thing I'd never done. Always we moved on and on and on. We were nomads in the Sierra, that was how we lived up there, it was what we wanted. Now I was settling into a place.

    Up the slot from Lower Soldier Lake to Elizabeth's Pond, eager to see the view up to the Miter. Big green trough flanked by white pillars: the basin, opening to the south, and at the southern end of the range, has a Mediterranean look.

I headed up the thumb slot toward Iridescent Lake. Another day of solo wandering: I felt blessed. Long lengthwise cracks in the granite made sidewalks. At the bottom of every avalanche gully to my right, alluvial meadows poured out over the blocky talus. Small grabens like sunken rooms. A chunk of white quartz like a vase inlaid in sand, holding a red buckwheat.

A bunch of tall pink flowers standing in a broad expanse of grass. Up into a shallow mini canyon between the Miter and the crest. The Miter revealed itself to be a spur coming off the crest. Iridescent Lake was held between the Miter and the Sierra crest, meaning 800-foot cliffs backed most of the lake.

When I came up to it, I saw that Iridescent Lake was iridescing. Here was a good name! Startled, I searched for the cause of this opal shimmer. It wasn't hard to find: the cliff backing the lake was made of the usual white granite, here strongly banded horizontally by three or four reddish stripes. All that was reflected in the lake, which being deep in the middle, but with sandy shallows, was yellow near the shore, then green, then blue in the depths. And it was a cloudy windy day, so the surface of the lake was alive with cat's-paws, reflecting all the various colors as they swirled. The lake *iridesced*.

I oohed and ahhed and tried to take pictures. Got a few frames that looked like Monet at Giverny, but the total scene could not be captured, of course. Very little of the high Sierra makes it into its images. If you see a pretty photo from the Sierras, you always have to remember, it was a zillion times more beautiful than that!

Off again. It was still early, I knew I had time to drop into the main channel of the basin, cross Rock Creek, and hike up into the cirque holding Primrose Lake, only about a mile away. Dropping into the basin I felt like a skateboarder in a half-pipe; down one side, up the other. Finding the cleanest line, the most stylish way. Sometimes you can walk as if on a sidewalk or staircase inlaid into the landscape, discovering it as you go. And it's easier to see it when alone, free from the magnetic effect of fellow hikers.

The western side of the basin, below Primrose Lake, was studded with isolated dead foxtail pines, all their bark gone, the spiraling grain of their trunks revealed like flesh, or bone. Primrose Lake lay in a tight steep horseshoe of a cirque, with Mount Pickering looming above the middle of the headwall. Edward Charles Pickering, nineteenth-century Harvard astronomer, founder of the American Astronomical Society. Joe Devel Peak, the next peak down the ridge, named after a packer in the Wheeler expedition of 1875. Not good names. Indeed the peaks on this ridge all have names that are candidates for replacement, like Pioneer Basin to the north. More on that later.

The cliffs hemming Primrose's exit gap stood like matched towers, each a thousand feet tall. The lake looked big against this backdrop of steep granite, its steel-gray water blinking with afternoon sun.

Coming down from Primrose Lake I followed its outlet stream, which dropped stepwise in a shallow gorge. I saw I could get around and up into Erin Lake on a traverse that never got much lower than Erin's altitude. Three cirques in one afternoon! I was definitely skateboarding.

Around the corner of the big tower between Primrose and Erin, a sudden steep traverse. The granite tilted so hard I could reach out a little with my right hand to hold on to creases in the rock, creases deep enough to be filled with grass, and always providing flat surfaces for walking, even if they were only as wide as my shoe. It felt steep, but the walking was as easy as ever. I followed rising horizontal cracks up to the gateway of the Erin cirque. It was funny how easy this basin was.

Black lichen marked Erin Lake's exit stream. The lake tucked a bit farther back in its cirque than Primrose had. It too looked big in its cliffy setting. The glacieret bulking above its south shore was covered by a cladding of gray rock. Grassy shore under the wall by the outlet, nice spot for an afternoon coffee. Little stove, titanium pot, throw a couple spoonfuls of Turkish grind into boiling water, soon a really fine coffee. Freshies from Ariana: mandarin orange, apple, chocolate. The wind shattered the sunlight on the lake into a bright glittering. It rustled through me and I was both cool and warm at once. A granite outcropping held up a knob of pure black rock, not obsidian. Hornblende? Olivine? Let's sit here forever and figure it out.

Reluctant goodbye to this cirque, which I saw on the map has higher ponds above the big lake; I wanted to scramble up and see them. Instead, back out the exit stream. The drop onto the big basin's wall was a steep boulder pile. I had to turn into the slope and use my hands. Fun to have a little challenge: suddenly I thought, This basin is *too* easy. But the tower over me loomed so ominously that I hiked in silence, forgoing my usual narrative monologue so that I wouldn't dislodge any rocks above with the sound of my voice. In the midst of this cautious silence a navy jet from China Lake zoomed by with a huge sonic boom. No rocks fell. I went back to babbling.

From below, I saw that Rock Creek's main glacier had swept its side walls clean, but later a little residual Erin glacier had dumped its terminal moraine out onto that clean sweep: thus the pile of boulders. It's as Muir said: once you know glaciers shaped this landscape, you can read it like a book, the sentences are everywhere. A pleasant walk through forest brought me to Lower Soldier Lake, and soon afterward to camp, and abruptly back in society.

What a beautiful day. More than ever I realized how much I liked wandering alone. I described my day to Bill Tweed, but as I did so, I realized that I couldn't do it justice. A day like that can't be shared; that must not be what they are for. There was no reason for anyone else to be interested. Maybe they are like dreams in that sense. It was a walk only, not an adventure. Writing about it might resemble writing about gardening more than writing about climbing. Contemplative writing, landscape writing, the experience of peace . . . I need here to take on this problem, which possibly can't be solved, although really every human experience should be legible.

In writing, maybe; but not in casual conversation. That hike was for me. It could not be shared, and did not need to be shared. Tweed seemed to know this. He had spent many years in these mountains. I had done so little solo hiking that I had not realized how private it was. If I hiked like a maniac or lazed around a pond all day, no one would know or care; I would be doing it for myself alone.

All of a sudden I saw the trust in me extended by Bill and Mando. My National Science Foundation hosts in Antarctica would never have allowed me to go off alone. Of course the land there is more dangerous, but many group leaders in the back country would have required me to go with companions.

To let me go alone was a sign of their confidence in me, and in the "gentle wilderness" that is the Sierra in summer. They knew I would be okay.

The end of that week taught me more things. A subset of the larger group hiked up to the lake under Arc Pass, to support Elizabeth in her expedition to get shots of Mount Whitney at dawn. We spent the night at the highest lake under the pass, which Mando and Tom Killion had named the Riviera, and down by the lakeshore after dark I played with Mando's green laser pointer, a device so powerful it could create a bright green dot on rocks far away. I aimed it downward into the lake and saw green dots appear on the lake surface, on the lake bottom, and on rocks high on the opposite shore. The lased light must be splitting, I exclaimed, as in those experiments used to explore quantum mechanics. We were seeing a quantum effect in the real world! The others just laughed. And in fact the real explanation turns out to be more mundane; a half mirror is just a half mirror.

Long before dawn we hiked up to Arc Pass by headlamps, helping Elizabeth lug her gear: massive Hasselblad camera, massive tripod, massive tripod head, laptop. Hasselblad had loaned her the camera for a year and it was a monster. Up a barren sandy chute between two jagged ridges, stars overhead. Hiking in the predawn night was another thing I had never done before. As we neared the pass the sky turned indigo, the ridges a blue-tinted ivory, subtle and rich. Dimensionality seeped into the world. Then we were in Arc Pass, seeing its sudden big view. Whitney was prominent to the north, showing yet another facet from this unusual angle. Directly below us lay a glacier, mostly cladded by rock, but with a fair bit of exposed ice too, and a melt stream down its middle that was pure white in the dawn. At the foot of the glacier lay Consultation Lake, a flat black circle. The dark slope of its far shore was dotted by little points of light in a line: headlamps of people making their predawn ascent up the trail to Whitney. Looked like photos of the pilgrimage on Fuji, or the final scene in *Fantasia*. On the ridge to our left loomed a tower that looked like the Chrysler Building. The ivory rock was everywhere chiseled and solid, luminous in the predawn.

Elizabeth got her Hasselblad set up. Sunrise hit and everything lightened at once. The flush on Whitney was a pale yellow. As the light grew the yellow turned a deeper yellow—never pink, cleaner than that, very brilliant and horizontal, with black shadows still covering a lot of land below.

Mount Whitney at dawn from Arc Pass. That high point to the far left is Mount Muir.

Ariana lay wrapped in her sleeping bag sketching the view, adding a golden eagle after it flew overhead. Mando filmed Elizabeth at work. I checked out the north side of Arc Pass, listed as class 3 in the Secor guide, but looking easier than that to me, if you were to take a certain cleft on its east side. The sunrise unfolded in a leisurely way. Time to look around, watch the shadows change, drink coffee and chat. When Elizabeth was done, we packed up. The pass was still in shadow, and would be for much of the morning, standing as it does under Mounts Mallory and Irvine. And I had to be back in Davis that evening, a strange thought.

Long solo hike back to Foxtail Camp, pack up and say goodbye. Two crows stood on the trail in Old Army Pass, putting a farewell curse on me. Cottonwood Lake Four's surface was shredded by violent cat's-paws, I got shoved hard in the back by gusts of wind. After that it was a march down through forest to the car, and by 3:00 I was on the road home.

Every basin deserves a week like that.

GEOLOGY (2)
Basins

Thus the Miter Basin; but what is a basin? We need to be clear on this, because basins are the crucial feature that makes the Sierra the great walking range that it is. And not all mountain ranges have basins the way the Sierra does.

Mountain ranges have ridges, standing over lower areas tucked between them, typically canyons. At their upper ends these canyons are walled on three sides, with the open side leading out and down. In California's Sierra Nevada, these high horseshoe-shaped enclosures are called basins.

A basin in your washroom is shaped like a bowl, and there are geological features shaped like that too, such as the Tarim Basin in China. But a Sierra basin is shaped like half a bowl. That the same word should refer to both shapes—well, that's language. "Basin, 1. a bowl. 2. a half bowl." Really? Yes.

The *Dictionary of Geological Terms* lists both these definitions, and for the *half bowl* definition it notes that the usage is specific to the California Sierra, with a few places also named that way in the Rockies. It adds some synonyms to this definition: "an amphitheater, cirque, or corrie."

An amphitheater is a good image for our kind of basin. A cirque, we learn in this same dictionary, refers to "a deep, steep-walled recess in a mountain, caused by glacial erosion." A Sierra basin is indeed a cirque.

This is one of those times when a picture is worth a thousand words.

In Sierra history, the word *basin* came into use pretty early. Theodore Solomons, the early Sierra explorer, was using the name Granite Basin in 1896. In 1902, Joe LeConte wrote about "the lake basin," now called Lakes Basin.

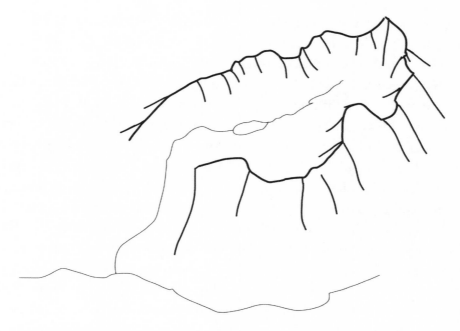

Schematic of a typical Sierra basin

(Granite Basin, Lakes Basin: these are not good names.) Both these particular basins can appear to be walled all the way around, so maybe that's how the use of the word began.

So, basins are made by glaciers. They're the empty rock containers of the upper ends of glaciers that are now gone. Their floors were therefore under ice for thousands of years. The ice scraped the floor as it flowed down and away. The ridges walling the basin, often in a horseshoe shape, were plucked at by the freeze-thaw cycle of water and ice; chunks of rock broke off after water seeped into cracks, then froze and expanded. When newly broken-off rocks fell on the ice, or got caught in its texture lower down, they were carried downhill and away. The ice mass resting against the curve of the headwall thus slowly ate back into it.

Now that the ice is gone, or confined to little residual strips in the shade, the basin floors left behind are typically bare rock, dotted with boulders dropped wherever they were when the ice melted. They're also dotted with ponds, filling hollows behind ribs of rock. Because granite has both onion-layer cracks and vertical cracks, basin floors can end up looking pretty chaotic, like disarranged rock mazes. Other times the glacier slid over the top of a hard onion layer of rock, polishing it to a finish as smooth as a marble floor. These patches are called glacial polish, and in the late afternoon they reflect sunlight like a mirror. Rocks carried by ice over these smooth floors sometimes got jammed down so hard they left lines call striations, or crescent-shaped inden-tations in the rock called chatter marks—a good name—you have to imagine the deep slow clunk of rock against rock, like teeth chattering with cold.

Ice filled these basins so completely that often it overtopped their border ridges, meeting ice from the next basin over. High enough accumulations of ice can create a broad plateau called a *mer de glace*, but in the Sierra there was usually an extensive system of ridges poking out of the ice. Year after year, century after century, these exposed ridges got eaten away from both sides.

Always the glaciers moved downhill under the force of gravity, flowing into lower canyons that also were carved by ice, a carving that created U-shaped valleys, typically much deeper than the high basins feeding them. Because the biggest canyons got cut so deeply, many littler upstream basins now form hanging valleys, their exit streams plummeting down the steep sides of much deeper canyons, sometimes as waterfalls, as in Yosemite Valley, but more often as rushing downhill cataracts.

The Sierra Nevada's basins are its crucial aspect, its distinguishing feature. This is to shift from geology to psychogeology, because what I mean here is that basins are where you want to be as a walker and camper. They are the golden zone.

But when you look around at other mountain ranges of the world, you find that basins like these, seen all over the Sierra, are actually quite unusual else-where in the world. This is because basins require glaciation, which is of course common in mountains, but if a mountain range gets more glaciation than the Sierras have had, which is also common, its basins get ground away by the very action that created them in the first place.

The Swiss Alps are a good example of this. The two ranges are similar in age and geological origin, and I'll be comparing them throughout this book, in part because of their different glacial histories. The Alps are about ten degrees of latitude farther north than the high Sierra, and they're on the receiving end of the Gulf Stream's immense load of precipitation, so they have lain under a much heavier lifetime load of ice than the Sierra—roughly ten times as much. That's made major differences. Canyons in the Alps are often twice as deep as those in the Sierra, and at the upper ends of these deeper canyons, ice has also carved the headwater basins deeper—often fully as deep as the canyons they debouch into. And in that harsher scouring, the canyon floors were almost completely smoothed, so that the high ponds that dot Sierra basins just aren't there in the Alps. What remains in the Alps are clean downhill runs, from the tops of the highest peaks all the way down to the giant lakes that pool at the foot of the range.

Then also, the ridges separating these deep Swiss canyons have been eaten back until they are classically alpine: knife edges with tall steep side walls. Where they meet other ridges, you see spiky horns, *horn* in German referring to a peak that glaciers have gnawed back into from all sides, until nothing remains but a single isolated spire. Matterhorn, Finsteraarhorn, Weisshorn— *horn* is a technical term there.

So the Swiss Alps are steep and dramatic, no doubt about it. My attempts to hike in them as if I were in the Sierra led me into more than one fiasco, as I will relate. But the point here is that the Alps have very few basins, and very few high ponds and lakes, because they've all been ground away.

That the Sierras are less steep than the Alps is not that obvious when you're hiking in the Sierra. There it's up and down, up and down. But compare it to the Swiss Alps, and you can see that the Sierras are actually a kind of high plateau, lightly etched by ice. In fact, although a few peaks in the Alps stand a bit higher than Mount Whitney, the Sierras have much more land over 10,000 feet than the Alps do—4,700 square kilometers in the Sierra compared to 1,900 square kilometers in the Alps. When you're walking, this difference between the two ranges is hugely important. There's a reason for all those cable cars and chairlifts you see in the Alps, beyond the Swiss desire to be accommodating to tourists; those aids make walking the Alps practical. Without them it would be an extreme schlep just getting from one valley to the next. People did that in earlier times, and still do it occasionally, but now most walkers take the chairlifts and cable cars and funiculars when offered.

The other mountain ranges I've seen around the world have reinforced my impression that the Sierra's basins are rare. I've walked in the Alps, the Scottish Highlands, the Himalayas, and the Transantarctics, and none of them has basins like the Sierra's. So the formula seems to be this: to get a basin, you need glaciation, *but not too much glaciation*. It's a Goldilocks phenomenon. Not too little, but not too much.

A famous drawing by William Morris Davis illustrates this situation pretty well. Davis made his studies in the Alps and in Norway, in the 1890s. In his now-classic drawing, the upper right corner of the middle panel contains by accident a sketch of what glaciers did in the Sierra.

William Morris Davis's illustration, from Geographical Essays, *1909: the peak on the far right in the middle drawing models Sierra glaciation very well.*

When glaciation has done some of its etching, but not as much as in the Alps, some remnants of the original rounded hills will appear as narrow long plateaus—as seen in the Sierras often, such as on that high crest road running up to Mount Langley. In the Alps you seldom if ever see these high ramps.

Another range that helps us understand the effects of glaciation lies just to the east of the Sierra, in the White Mountains that straddle the California-Nevada border. In a rough way this range can serve to show what the Sierras might have looked like before the glaciers did their work. Existing in the Sierra's rain shadow, the White Mountains never had many glaciers, and so are still basically a line of gigantic rounded hills. The Alps then illustrate the other end of the process, having lived under so much ice that the basins got ground away. These are the "too little" and "too much" examples, and the three ranges are thus somewhat like the three panels in Davis's graphic.

Glaciation, but not too much of it: and this particular ice history is somewhat rare in the world. Which makes sense, given that the Sierra Nevada is unusual in its combination of a Mediterranean climate and great height. There aren't that many Mediterranean climates on Earth, found as they are behind west-facing mid-latitude coasts, with their brief cool damp winters and their long hot dry summers. There are five, in fact: the Mediterranean itself, southwest Africa, west Australia, Chile, and California. Tall mountain ranges in these regions occur only in California and Chile, with lower (and thus less glaciated) examples around the western end of the Mediterranean itself, in Spain's Sierra Nevada and Morocco's Atlas Mountains.

So the rare combination of height and climate needed to create high basins means there are only a few mountain ranges on Earth that have them. And basins are the golden zone for walkers. This is psychogeological, yes, but I'm convinced it's quite real as an explanation for the Sierra's particular joy, and over the course of this book I want to unpack a little of why that should be so.

Looking at the maps, I count 15 named basins in the southern Sierra, and I'll list them with the compass orientation of their open ends, which matters a lot when it comes to how they feel when you're in them: Kaweah Basin northeast, Nine Lakes Basin south, Center Basin northwest, Humphreys Basin west,

Palisades Basin south, Dusy Basin west, Ionian Basin south, Gardiner Basin north, Lakes Basin west, Upper Basin south, Sixty Lakes Basin north, Evolution Basin north, Blackcap Basin northwest, Crown Basin south, and Pioneer Basin southwest.

The maps also show many more basins not named as such. Indeed if basins are defined as what melted glaciers leave behind at their top ends, then there are a few hundred of them in the Sierra. No one can visit them all, unless this was made a goal early in one's life. That would be a good project!

Dusy Basin under summer snow

MY SIERRA LIFE (4)

How We Met

I met Dick Ill in Cub Scouts, where we discovered we lived on the same street. After that we got together to zoom around on our bikes and play in construction sites as our suburb got built out. Then Dick went to a private Catholic school for a while. When he came back to our junior high he became the quarterback of our flag football team, and threw to me as his wide receiver. This was great fun, but socially he hung out with a different crowd from ours—the cool crowd, including girls, and guys from older classes. That lasted through high school. Later he rejoined us at UCSD, and became again one of my closest friends. As an adult he became a cellular and molecular biologist.

Victor Salerno I met in fifth grade, when we were in the same class and began to do stuff after class at our homes. That never stopped, right through our undergraduate years, when we were often roommates, until he got married and I headed to graduate school in Boston. We've stayed close all our lives. He is a criminal defense attorney, living in Los Angeles.

Victor and I met Terry in sixth grade, though we didn't know him well; he was in another class, and we played with him at recess, where he was a sports star. He was the playground's tetherball champion, and in dodgeball a dangerous foe, as he threw really hard. I caught his throws a few times, but his response to that was to throw at me even harder. So I dodged his shots if I could. Most of our interaction that year came that way, as a kind of duel, but in a team sport context, so it wasn't like fencing or tennis. He was just a star on a rival team.

Then in seventh grade Victor and I did more with him after school, and also met Joe Holtz, on the track team. Joe and I jumped the high jump together, though neither of us got very high. This was pre–Fosbury Flop. Joe ran at the bar full-speed and leaped from many yards away, achieving height as a function of huge horizontal distance. He was also a budding wrestling star. In one PE class a coach matched us against each other, and Joe pinned me in seconds; it was the first time I realized that some people are much stronger than others, even when they're the same size. The coaches also raced us against each other, as we were among the fastest boys in our class. We tied in the 50-yard dash with a time of 5.2 seconds, not bad for tennis shoes on grass. The coaches urged us to run track in high school, but I chose tennis, and Joe wrestling. As an adult Joe became a tax accountant, living in Honolulu.

In ninth grade we all moved together to El Modena High School, in its first year of operation. We were a little gang by then, Victor, Joe, Terry, and me, also our friend Robin, and a few other guys—Sheldon, Paul, Dave, Mike—also an equivalent gang of girls whom we knew in a group-to-group way. Steve Lamb, my best friend from second grade on, died of leukemia in tenth grade. That was something I couldn't think about for many years; 21 years, in fact, when Dan Jansen's sister died of leukemia on the day he had to race in the 1988 Olympics, and he slipped on the final turn. At that moment Steve's death fell on me like a wall.

Anyway, for me high school consisted mostly of these guys. I liked a number of our corresponding group of girls, and even had girlfriends the last two years. But mainly we were a little gang of jocks, hanging out in the usual high school way. That we eventually ended up going to the Sierras together as adults was maybe the unusual thing. To a certain extent it was like adding a new sport to our repertoire.

Through high school we played touch football and volleyball many afternoons after school. When there were just four of us, we often played volleyball. We butchered volleyball on purpose, palming and hooking the ball, even pulling down the net; for some reason we liked to make a mockery of that game. Later when we tried to play it straight, we were bad. Football we always played straight, and we ran so many plays, some quite elaborate (one was called

McDonald's Golden Arches), that when we joined together as a single intramural flag football team at UCSD, we were good. Joe and I finally got to play with each other rather than against each other, and being the two defensive backs in a 3-3-2 zone, we stymied every offense we ever met. Truly fun. In college we tried all the intramural sports offered, including oddities like innertube water polo, and basketball for people shorter than five foot ten, at which we were terrible. Hippie jocks, playing for the fun of it.

High school passed. Suburban boredom. But I've left out our salvation: the beach. It was ten miles away, and we drove there every chance we got. Before we got driver's licenses, my mom drove us; she was happy to do so, being a jock herself—baton twirler, golfer, bicyclist, walker, and workout devotee. She liked to see us having fun, and helped make it happen when she could.

Living where and when we did, if it hadn't been for the beach and bodysurfing, we very likely would have gone mad. Because bodysurfing wasn't just a sport; it was the natural world. Ten yards offshore and you were in wilderness and swimming for your life. That gave us a taste for what came later in the high country.

So in high school we were very straight, and very silly. At UCSD we became hippies on the move, as I've said. Victor and I roomed in a dorm on campus, Terry was in the room next door. I joined the fencing team, and one of my teammates, Darryl DeVinney, joined us in our sophomore year's on-campus apartment, quickly becoming an integral member of our group. In later years he became a computer systems specialist in Northern California.

I met Carter Scholz after both of us had our first stories published in *Orbit 18*, an anthology edited by Damon Knight. I wrote him a fan letter, and we became first pen pals, then hiking buddies and semi-neighbors, as he lives in Berkeley and we get together often. He's a writer and jazz pianist.

In our junior year at UCSD, Joe and Dick rejoined us from OC, and we also welcomed another high school friend, Dave, who brought along Daryl Bonin from the town next door to ours. That meant eight of us in two adjacent on-campus apartments, which meant too much fun; we were flying high.

Terry majored in chemistry, and as a group we were majoring big-time in recreational chemistry; but he was on the hunt for something more. He was good at chemistry but he didn't have a passion for it. So in that context, when he found the Sierra, it satisfied a hunger in him. He was definitely one of those people who fell so hard for the Sierra that everything else in his life had to be adjusted to that. He was not unique in that regard; a lot of Sierra lovers have that story. But he's the one I knew the best.

Left to right: Dick, Terry, Victor, Joe, Darryl, me, and my brother Chris's son Lantz, the morning after Lisa and I got married

SIERRA PEOPLE (2)

John Muir

Speaking of Sierra lovers!

Of course there were many other European Americans in the Sierra before John Muir got there in 1868, but he's the one that the modern history of the Sierra turns on, so I'm going straight to him. For the gold rush and other semi-Sierran events, I refer you to Kevin Starr's *Americans and the California Dream 1850–1915*.

He was born in 1838, in Dunbar, Scotland, a coastal town south of Edinburgh. His father was a strict evangelical who often beat his children—Muir only wrote about this after his father died. Muir's grammar school was similarly free with corporal punishment, and this was how he learned English (his mother tongue was Scots), Latin, and French, and how he memorized all the New Testament and much of the Old Testament. "We were simply driven pointblank against our books like soldiers against the enemy.... If we failed in any part, however slight, we were whipped."

As a child he climbed in the ruins of Dunbar Castle, and escaped his bedroom at night by climbing out the window onto the roof. He also climbed on the local crags. In Scots this was called *scootching*. "I was so proud of my skill as a climber that when I first heard of hell from a servant girl...I always insisted that I could climb out of it."

When Muir was 11, his father moved the family to Wisconsin and bought 40 acres of forested land. He set John to clearing it, while he read his Bible on the porch. John worked from dawn till dusk, six days a week, for ten years. As he put it, "We were all made slaves through the vice of over-industry.... I was put to the plough at the age of twelve, when my head reached but little above the handles, and for many years I had to do the greater part of the ploughing.... For the first few years this was particularly hard on account of the tree-stumps that had to be dodged. Later the stumps were all dug and chopped out.... I had nearly all of that to myself...on my knees all day, chopping out those tough oak and hickory stumps."

A youth of continuous hard labor; and the beatings continued. "The old Scotch fashion of whipping for every act of disobedience or of simple, playful forgetfulness was still kept up in the wilderness, and of course many of those whippings fell upon me. Most of them were outrageously severe."

When Muir was 17, his father bought a half section, meaning 320 acres, and the whole process of clearing the land began again, with Muir again doing all the work. He wrote, "I remember as a great and sudden discovery that the poetry of the Bible, Shakespeare, and Milton was a source of inspiring, exhilarating, uplifting pleasure; and I became anxious to know all the poets." His father wouldn't allow him to read after dinner, but he was allowed to read before breakfast, so he began getting up at 1:00 a.m. to read history, poetry, and mathematics. In these predawn hours he also began to make mechanical toys and inventions: saw tables, clocks, thermometers, barometers, timed stove starters. When one of their neighbors saw these contraptions, he suggested Muir take them to the Wisconsin State Fair and enter them in the fair's competitions. At age 22 Muir bundled several of these devices together and caught a train to Madison. It was his first train trip, and he sat out on the cowcatcher at the front. "I seemed to be flying."

Except for brief visits to see his mother and siblings, he never went home again. His harsh upbringing left its mark on him, and it's his own testimony that accuses his father of brutality, laziness, and absorption in a version of religion without love. The first photo we have of Muir was taken soon after his arrival at college; he looks like the proverbial deer in the headlights, like some kind of stunned feral child hauled out of the woods. It wasn't far from true.

John Muir's freshman photo at the University of Wisconsin, 1860, age 22

His four years at the University of Wisconsin gave him a good education and changed his trajectory completely. He took all kinds of classes while working odd jobs to pay for school. He read Emerson, Agassiz, and Humboldt. His main interests were scientific, especially botany. He was taken in hand by a science professor, Ezra Carr, and even more importantly, by Carr's wife Jeanne; they served as his advisors and surrogate parents.

He kept making mechanical devices, including some that have survived: an alarm clock that wakes you by tilting your bed and rolling you onto the floor, a desk that rotates every 20 minutes to change the book lying under your eyes. Jokes, in other words, like Rube Goldberg machines; comic images of people caught in mechanical systems.

The end of Muir's college career came in 1864, when Lincoln called for the drafting of half a million more men into the Union army. Muir decided to make botanical studies in Canada. They called such northward youths skedaddlers. He walked around the Great Lakes to the north shore of Lake Ontario, and ended up working in a rake handle factory, improving the machines until they could make 20,000 rake handles a day, probably more rake handles than Canada needed. He stayed until the Civil War was over.

He then moved to Indianapolis, where again he took a job in a factory and started improving its machinery. One day at work a shard of metal shot off a lathe into his eye; the punctured eye lost fluid and then sight, and in a sympathetic nervous reaction, the other eye also lost sight. He was totally blind for three weeks. Kindly acquaintances took care of him as he recovered. In that interval there was no certainty that he would regain his sight; it was possible he had been blinded for life.

But his sight came back. And then John Muir walked out of his life—literally, in that he took off on foot for Florida, intending to board a ship for South America. With this walk he gave up on being an ordinary person, and started the process of becoming what he later called a "self-styled poetico-trampo-geologist-bot. and ornith-natural, etc.!-!-!" A hippie poet, in other words; a psychogeologist.

In Florida he caught malaria. Again he was cared for by strangers, in this case one Sarah Hodgson, who dosed him with quinine and took care of him in her home for three months. During his recovery he decided that the Amazon, being notorious for malaria, was not the place for him. He saw a magazine article about Yosemite in the Hodgsons' house, and when he was well enough to travel, he sailed to San Francisco by way of New York and Panama. From San Francisco he took stagecoaches to San Jose, then walked across the Central Valley and up into the Sierra.

By then he was 30 years old. All his childhood and youth had combined in a powerful way to make him spectacularly ready for the Sierra—he was *primed*. Humboldt was his model for how to study a landscape, but the high Sierra was more than just an object of study to him—it was an ecstatic encounter. The next photo we have of him, after he had spent five years living in the Sierra and exploring it, shows us a man completely unlike the stunned college freshman—a person alert, bold, happy beyond any expectation—transfigured. He had fallen in love.

What he found in the Sierra was a landscape that in some ways must have reminded him of Scotland. But it was bigger—not just more expansive, but

John Muir after five years in the Sierra, age 35

higher, which changed the quality of air and light. He had never been higher than the Appalachians, never been above tree line, and never been on open expanses of granite. The Sierra's granite looked alive to him—new, scrubbed to a polish. He climbed peaks on the crest of the range and saw mountains stretching north and south for a hundred miles, and tucked among them, meadows green with new life. All his balked religious feelings, so intense in him and yet so twisted and beaten down by his father, burst out and found expression here. The Sierra Nevada became Muir's religion.

Then they became his profession. He lived in Yosemite Valley, working for the owner of a sawmill, and from that base camp he ranged up all the local canyons to the higher back country. Typically he took off for a few days wearing a long wool coat with some loaves of bread and tea bags in his pockets, and matches: he got through the nights with the help of campfires. If it rained he tucked under low trees on beds of pine needles, and kept the fire going.

During this wandering he came on a living glacier, high in a northeast-facing cirque, and realized that glaciers must have carved all the Sierra's canyons, including Yosemite Valley. After that he systematically explored to find supporting evidence for this theory, so these ecstatic years of mountain wandering were also a scientific field study. His science was a form of devotion.

In this endeavor he became a glaciologist before there was glaciology. Louis Agassiz had proposed his theory of ice ages around the time of Muir's birth, and now, in the early 1870s, it was mostly accepted by other scientists, but only as an explanation for features much farther north. Ice was thought to have covered the Arctic, where it still remained, and also Scandinavia, Britain, other parts of northern Europe, Canada, and New England. But there was little awareness of the altitude-latitude equivalence, which says that areas of high altitude can resemble lower landscapes much closer to the pole. The Sierra's southerly location and its Mediterranean climate kept anyone from imagining it could have been covered by ice during the ice age.

So Muir had his opportunity. His first published words were in the *New-York Tribune*, in 1871, when he was 33 years old:

> Two years ago...I found a book. It was blotted and storm-beaten...but many of the inner pages were well preserved, and...whole chapters were easily readable. In just this condition is the great open book of Yosemite glaciers....[I] am now searching the upper rocks and moraines for readable glacier manuscript.

His transformation into a writer came about because of Jeanne Carr. She and her husband had moved from Wisconsin to California, when Ezra took a position at the new university in Berkeley. Muir and Jeanne had stayed in touch by way of letters: they were close friends. Now she became something like his social secretary and literary agent. She arranged for him to meet Emerson when Emerson visited California, and also sent Joseph LeConte, another new professor of science at Berkeley, to Yosemite to visit Muir, where

Muir showed LeConte around and explained his ideas about the glacial formation of the valley.

After that encounter, Muir worried to Carr that LeConte seemed to be promulgating Muir's theories, without giving Muir credit for them. She told Muir that publishing was the only way to claim priority for an idea.

So the pure years of ecstatic wandering shifted into a new pattern, in which Muir summered in the Sierra and wintered in San Francisco or Oakland, locked in hotel rooms writing articles. He always complained about writing, but that first article for the *New-York Tribune* earned him $200 (approximately $7,000 in current value); this for a mere 4,000 words, cobbled together from letters already written. It seemed he could fund his Sierra life by writing about it; and thus he became a professional writer.

His first dozen articles mixed the ecstatic language of the transcendentalists with mechanical descriptions of the work of glaciers on rock. They laid out the case for the glacial origin of Yosemite Valley, and thus initiated a public scientific controversy, no doubt part of their appeal: an ordinary citizen was going up against the head of the California Geological Survey, Josiah Whitney, who continued to claim that Yosemite was the result of a great earthquake.

Muir pointed out that there were other valleys like Yosemite in the range, so a single catastrophe could not explain them all. To emphasize his point he began to call all such canyons yosemites, turning the name into a common noun. His articles assembled the glacial explanation from a thorough knowledge of the range, expressed on every page he wrote.

Whitney replied by writing that Muir was "a mere sheepherder and ignoramus." This ad hominem attack did nothing to forward his case, and scientists and the general public were mostly convinced by Muir.

These articles and the resulting public controversy formed the foundation of all Muir's later fame. He was *the* expert on glaciers. And he had a larger vision too. He often tried to describe the Sierras in ways that reached toward conceptual systems that didn't yet exist, like watershed ecology, or conservation, or even fractals: in one article he wrote, "Were we to cross-cut the Sierra Nevada into blocks a dozen miles or so in thickness, each section would contain a Yosemite Valley and a river." Then his vision floats up into the sky, giving readers something like the satellite views now so familiar to us:

> The whole state of California, from Siskiyou to San Diego, is one block of beauty, one matchless valley; and our great plain, with its mountain-walls, is the true Yosemite—exactly corresponding in its physical character and proportions to that of the Merced.... The only important difference between the great central Yosemite...and the Merced Yosemite...is, that the former is double—two Yosemites in one...meeting opposite Suisun Bay.

This image of California's Central Valley as a double yosemite is not geologically correct. But here Muir is thinking fractally. It's a shift to a larger scale; then in other articles he went small, calling Twenty Hills Hollow, a glen less than a mile long, a "miniature Yosemite."

This fractal thinking was structural and also aesthetic, an early example of psychogeology. It was also the start of an ethic: Muir was saying there should be no exceptionalism in our values, just as there was none in geology; if one valley is worthy of our reverence and protection, then they all are.

It's a shame Muir's use of *yosemite* as a common noun wasn't taken up. There are scores of yosemites in the Sierra; but more than one is now under water.

These early articles made Muir famous, and he became one of the first national figures to represent an attitude toward the American landscape that we now call preservationist. He spoke for the Sierras as an expert and advocate, a scientist clearly in love with his object of study. And there was a hunger in the country for what Muir represented. His readership often had close relationships to land and animals, and they were post-traumatic in the wake of the Civil War. The hope that the war might somehow have made America a better place was disintegrating in the experience of a rapidly growing robber-baron capitalism, a Gilded Age filled with inequality and greed. In this time of turmoil and disillusionment, Muir represented a potential way of fulfilling the American dream, despite all: through love of land, love of nature.

Important in this was Muir's often-expressed love of animals. His reader-ship was much more connected with animals, both domestic and wild, than we are now; and Muir's writing is particularly good on animals, both descrip-tively and in his sympathies. During his childhood, farm animals had stood in for the human friends he never had; he regarded them as intelligent and wor-thy of our care, even our reverence. He often used the phrase "our horizontal brothers and sisters," which even now speaks to us in ways we have not taken on.

At the end of this first rise to fame as a writer, Muir married Louie Strentzel. It was Jeanne Carr who introduced them, thinking they might hit it off, and that Muir would enjoy marriage. He did, and settled down as manager of his father-in-law's orchards in Martinez, California. He threw himself into the project of orchardist and family man, and for more than a decade wrote very little. With Louie he ran the orchard and raised two daughters, Helen and Wanda. Things might have remained like that, and Muir might even have receded from that moment of national attention and be forgotten now. But a few more things happened.

First, Louie saw that he was growing frustrated with life as an orchardist, and encouraged him to travel again—in particular, to visit Alaska. Second, there were people in San Francisco who were ambitious for California, and aware that the Sierras were being devastated by rampant logging and sheep-herding. City officials, prominent citizens, the leaderships of both Stanford University and the University of California—all wanted to protect what was already understood to be the top of their watershed, and a world-class attrac-tion among natural wonders. A group of them began discussing how to do this, and around 1890 Muir was invited to join them. He became a linchpin figure in a big network gathering to protect the Sierra from exploitation. The Sierra Club was founded in 1892, with Muir as its president and figurehead, also its organizing principle.

The third thing that happened was that Muir was now being published in *Century* magazine, which had a circulation of 1 million, in a nation of about 62 million people. *Century*'s editor, Robert Underwood Johnson, had an inter-est in land protection by way of expanding the national parks, which at this time included only Yellowstone and Yosemite. Johnson enlisted Muir in a campaign to write a series of articles advocating for more such land protection.

These three factors created the Muir we know now. His widely read essays from this period are, ironically, among his least scientific and least soulful pieces. Magazine writing can be like that. But now Muir was writing in service of a larger national project. The Sierra Club joined National Geographic and other organizations to advocate for land protection, and later they were joined by allies like Secretary of the Interior Stephen Mather, also Ned Harriman, one of the richest of the railroad magnates. Together all these people formed a powerful actor network, and as actor-network theory helps make clear, the Sierra Nevada itself was an important actor here too, in that it inspired many people to act in its interest.

A high point for this emerging actor network came in 1903, when President Theodore Roosevelt came to Yosemite and camped out with Muir. Roosevelt had requested the meeting, and for three nights he and Muir slept out at Glacier Point and elsewhere in Yosemite, keeping only a cook on hand to attend them. TR went back to Washington and pushed hard for conservation and preservation of wild lands, encouraging Congress's passage of the American Antiquities Act, which gave the president power to designate national monuments, something Roosevelt did with enthusiasm, sometimes, as with the Grand Canyon and Petrified Forest, following Muir's suggestions.

So in this period, roughly 1890 to 1910, sometimes called the Progressive Era, Muir was one of the most famous people in America, a prominent public intellectual. He spoke for the protection of animals, forests, and land.

There was pushback to this new movement, a pushback that continues to this day. Unsustainable extraction continued on a huge scale. And when the Hetch Hetchy yosemite was proposed as a reservoir to hold water for San Francisco, Muir found himself right in the thick of the fight. He understood that drowning Hetch Hetchy, which was within the new boundaries of Yosemite National Park, was a deliberate attack on the idea of wilderness protection, made by people involved in all kinds of extraction industries. It was well understood even at that time that lower foothill valleys could be used to store the same amount of water as Hetch Hetchy: going after it was a strike in a war, a stab at the heart, just like today's attempts to drill for oil in the Arctic National Wilderness Area.

But in the political fight over Hetch Hetchy, the Sierra's newly formed actor network splintered. Warren Olney, mayor of Oakland, and a founding member of the Sierra Club, wanted Hetch Hetchy dammed. He had seen the Bay Area's need for water; the local supply was paltry, and in private hands. He wanted a big public supply, and after the 1906 earthquake destroyed San Francisco, he was only one of many Bay Area luminaries, including many active in the Sierra Club, who wanted a better water supply. A bitter schism thus split the new club.

Muir was then forced to make a sort of experiment: Could he succeed on his own, without the Sierra Club, using nothing more than his writing? He could only try it and see; and so he threw himself into it. His scores of essays from this time all used variants of his slogan message: "Drown Hetch Hetchy? You might as well use your cathedrals for water tanks!"

This was his signature rhetorical move, insisting that the natural features being destroyed by civilization were more precious than anything humans made by their own art and craft. His analogies were as satiric as Jonathan Swift, as angry as Jeremiah. Cutting down trees was like smashing pianos. Killing muskrats for their fur was like killing children for their clothing. A dismembered sequoia was like Christ on the cross.

But writing alone is never enough; you need an actor network to make real change in the world. Muir was abandoned by crucial allies, and newspaper cartoons portrayed him as an old woman in skirts. The Hetch Hetchy dam project was approved, and logging across the American West proceeded apace.

Muir wrote, "Any fool can destroy trees. They cannot defend themselves or run away.... Through all the eventful centuries since Christ's time, and long before that, God has cared for these trees, saved them from drought, disease, avalanches, and a thousand storms; but he cannot save them from sawmills and fools; this is left to the American people."

Muir died thinking his political project had failed. But in fact the fight for the biosphere had just begun, and he is remembered as a founding inspiration for it. Some quality in him, not just his gift for writing, but some kind of cha-risma, kept him in the culture's memory, as an ideal for those who followed. Now his childhood home in Scotland is a museum devoted to him. The site of his family's Wisconsin farm is a national historic landmark. His adult home in Martinez is a national monument. In Indianapolis, on the street where his factory was located, there is a sign commemorating his eye injury. There's even a sign at the ruins of his rake handle factory, put up by the Canadian Friends of John Muir. He remains the most famous environmentalist in world history.

Charisma is mysterious. Perhaps it's created by a passion for some cause outside the person expressing it. Muir was a passionate scientist, which in our time sounds somewhat oxymoronic, but that's wrong, as he serves to show; one can work passionately and scientifically on a project at the same time, and sci-entists very often do this. For Muir, the project was the Sierra. Athlete philos-opher—psychogeologist—wilderness advocate—passionate scientist—these were all manifestations of his Sierra love.

I'll end this quick ramble through Muir's life with a photo of one of the trail-head signs that the US Forest Service places at every trailhead on the high Sierra's east flank, an area now administered by the Inyo National Forest, and called the John Muir Wilderness. Copies of this sign are posted at every trail-head, and they all include the well-known quotation from Muir that you see. The US Forest Service is not a notably philosophical agency, I think it's safe to say, and I'm pretty sure most USFS workers would agree. But someone in the agency caught the Muir spirit, it seems, when it came to designing these signs. Now every hike on the Sierra's east side begins with this little existen-tialist blessing from our government, a reminder to pay attention and be thankful. And this is what Muir's story can do more generally.

They even chose the right photo of him, which people seldom do, tending to go for the old-man-with-a-beard profiles. This one captures him best. I always touch it with my finger at the start of every backpacking trip, for good luck. And I've been lucky!

Touch the photo and take off!

MY SIERRA LIFE (5)
The Pinball Years

Those first Sierra years of ours were pretty ramshackle. Our trips were mostly planned at the last second, and for almost all of them we went to Desolation, despite the fact that we were living in San Diego, so the southern Sierra was both nearer and grander. Our gear was mediocre at best. Cotton clothing was probably the worst of it, or the heavy boots. Or the miserable ground pads.

More striking than our poor gear was our ignorance. Our sense of the Sierra was still limited to what we had already seen. We tended to do what we had done before, because it was what we knew.

But we kept trying. That first trip with Terry and Joe was in August of 1973. Our senior year of college occupied that fall and winter, and the following spring I was wandering the Hawaiian islands. That was a great event in my life, a real coup, because at the same time I was in Hawaii I was also enrolled at UCSD, completing two independent studies which earned me the final credits I needed to graduate. This cool plan wouldn't even have occurred to me if it hadn't been for Bonin, who had taken off for Costa Rica some time before. Going to Hawaii was my version of that kind of wander, and it felt great, because I could still finish my degree while having an adventure. The two professors who allowed me to write stories and poems for them were very supportive of my plan. Later, when I became a teacher myself, I discovered a student proposing to disappear made for the best kind of independent study. Gone all quarter, mail in your work? Good idea! Still, it was generous of those two to approve my plan.

So I wandered the islands that spring, sleeping on beaches or up on the volcanoes in my mountain tent, using my three-pound down sleeping bag—not much chance of getting cold! But a great adventure, and a big step in my thinking about what I wanted. I read Ram Dass, and saw him give a talk in Honolulu. I also read D. T. Suzuki and Alan Watts, and most important, Gary Snyder. Snyder's translations of Han Shan introduced me to Chinese poetry, and one of my UCSD professors, Wai-lim Yip, turned out to be the best translator into English of Wang Wei. After I took a class from Yip, Chinese landscape poetry became my model and lodestar. I thought of myself as a new manifestation of Han Shan—Han Stan—and wrote many poems designed to be read as if translated from Chinese. This was a useful ploy in excusing their simplicity, but it was also a style, or more importantly, a mindset—not just an aesthetic, but a lifeway. I ate magic mushrooms on Maui and had a transcendent day dropping through steep volcanic jungle to a black sand beach; I bodysurfed on Oahu and Kauai; I hitchhiked and met travelers and mystics; I wrote a poem a day as a discipline; and over those luminous weeks became more and more a hippie poet and wanderer.

Seven Sacred Pools, Maui

1. Fresh water meeting salt:
Foam pushed about by waves.
I sit under a hala tree
Hanging over the ocean:
Nothing to do,
Nowhere to go,
Watching pools become pools.

7. Or the sea so calm
That clouds sailing above
Like a fleet of galleons
Gleam perfectly reflected
In the ocean's mirror surface,
Clouds in the sea upside down.

*   *   *

So it was June of 1974 before I got back to the Sierras, with Darryl DeVinney and my girlfriend Julie. Terry joined us at the start of this trip, but only to begin his first long-distance hike, from Desolation to Yosemite. He was anxious to get started on that, and on our second morning disappeared ahead of us without a goodbye, the first of many such departures. The three of us continued to move around Desolation, lake by lake. Not a happy trip for Julie and me, as we were in the process of breaking up, not for the first time or the last, but it was upsetting to have it happen in the Sierra. I read Hayden Carruth's wonderful anthology *The Voice That Is Great Within Us*, and brooded on the fate of the foolish poet in love. A trip to forget, but I'm not good at forgetting.

At the end of that summer I went to Desolation again, with Terry and Bonin and Robin. It was a quick circuit of our usual places, plus the Hobbitland Loop, as we called it, the small ponds north of Lake Schmidell. Not a whole lot was added to my Sierra knowledge on that one either. When we came out, I drove across the country to my first year of graduate school, at Boston University. On that drive I called my parents from Rawlins, Wyoming, and found out I had sold a short story to Damon Knight, editor of the anthology series *Orbit*, which launched me in a different way. Sierra person, hippie Buddhist poet, and now, science fiction writer. An unusual mix, I'll admit.

But not a winter person. In Boston I was shocked at the cold. It was the first winter of my life. I hiked the snowy streets to my classes wearing my Sierra down jacket and boots, and sat in my apartment with my bare feet right on the radiator. This made me like many another young person who had come to Boston to go to college and been stunned by its arctic winter. I enjoyed my studies, my fellow students, my apartment roommates, and my professors, but I felt like a poet exiled to some colder planet. I wanted out, and by the turn of the year made arrangements to return to UCSD the following fall.

Then spring arrived in Boston and I began to realize that arranging to go back to San Diego had been a big mistake. Just as I had never seen a winter, I had never seen a spring. And now I had friends I loved. To my immense surprise, I was growing fond of Boston. But I had committed myself to returning, so in May of 1975 I loaded my car with my worldly possessions, mostly books, and drove back across the country. The subsequent feeling of living out a giant mistake persisted in me for many years, but there was nothing I could do about it but forge on.

As soon as I got back I returned to the Sierra. First I went to Desolation with Terry and Victor, in the snow-clad June trip that I wrote up in my first mountain story, "Ridge Running." That trip was a little masterpiece of comedy and beauty, and when we came out at Echo Lake, Robin picked us up, and he and Terry and I said goodbye to Victor and drove down to Bishop, and hiked from South Lake over Bishop Pass into Dusy Basin, then down into LeConte Canyon and up to Muir Pass. In other words, the southern Sierra at its finest.

This was the best trip yet. How did we decide to go in over Bishop Pass? It must have been Terry's idea, and it was a great one. From the South Lake trailhead to Bishop Pass is six miles of ever-increasing beauty, ending with a dramatic set of switchbacks stitching their way up a black buttress from the last lake to the pass. Not that we saw those switchbacks on this first trip, as they were still snowed under. We had to kick-step up a snow gully east of the trail to get over the pass. This I did in my white leather Stan Smith tennis shoes, so my feet were always soaked and cold, but I was so much happier in those slippery shoes than I had been in my monster boots that I felt I had solved my footwear problem. This was very far from true, but a nice feeling at the time.

Camped in Dusy Basin that first night, I had another overwhelming sensation of vastness, beauty, and significance. This was not psychedelic but rather the high Sierra itself, so much bigger than Desolation, so much more magnificent. Everything that I had been loving in Desolation was here magnified by a factor of six. I say six because the average distances and heights are all around six times greater in the high Sierra than in Desolation. In any case, all numbers aside, it blew my mind. Tom Killion's print *Isosceles Peak from Dusy Basin* captures very well the look and feel of my first evening in the high Sierra.

Isosceles Peak from Dusy Basin, *Tom Killion, 2012*

The hike to Muir Pass on our second day was several miles long, and in places very steep, a major endeavor with the trail buried in snow. We didn't notice it as a problem, except for one scary leap Robin and I had to make to get across a nearly vertical gully. Late that afternoon, up in Muir Pass, the immense stretch of Lake Wanda to the north was mostly iced over. The only source of water was a pond about halfway down to Wanda, which we hiked to with Robin's five-gallon collapsible plastic jug. Then we took turns lugging it back up, getting an early lesson in the weight of water; maybe this was the origin of Terry's religious aversion to carrying water in the Sierra. That night we slept in the pass itself, next to the round stone hut the Sierra Club built there in the 1930s. From my sleeping bag I looked at the stars, the blackest sky and the fullest array of stars I had ever seen, and I knew more than ever that this was the life for me.

So, a great trip, and a great introduction to the southern Sierra—nothing clueless or ramshackle about it, which made it kind of a first for me.

Soon after that I drove out to the Clarion science fiction writing workshop at Michigan State, so I didn't have any more chances to go to the Sierra that summer. After the workshop I drove to Boston to see my friends there, then drove back to San Diego. The pinball years: I bounced back and forth across the continent several times, the old Cortina barely managing each crossing.

In the fall of 1975 I was back in San Diego, starting graduate school. You can't go home again; but I had. And yes, it was completely changed, and not as good. Most of my friends were gone, scattered to the winds. The feeling of having made a huge mistake haunted me, to the point where I introduced myself to my new acquaintances at UCSD as Kim. It was Kim who went to grad school; I wasn't really there. This lame ploy only confused people. Kim or Stan, I had in fact gone back to my old school, something Steely Dan warns us never to do, and with good reason. But the deed was done.

And bad move or not, at least I was closer to the Sierras. By this time I was fully obsessed with them. Before grad school got started I went to Whitney with Terry, Bonin, and Bonin's friend Jeff, to hike the Muir Trail. They were going all the way to Yosemite, and my plan was to get as far north as I could before bailing out and returning to San Diego for the start of the fall quarter.

Again I hiked in my heavy boots, hated them, and put on my tennis shoes, carrying the Raichles on my back. I'm amazed I didn't throw them in a lake at some point. I carried them more miles than I wore them. But hiking the Muir Trail in tennis shoes was a mistake. With no snow to cushion the blows, I soon was afflicted with plantar fasciitis, which had bothered me on the tennis team in high school, and the fencing team in college. My painful arches hit me hard, which was too bad, because we needed to go long every day. I kept up, but it hurt, so my enjoyment of that hike was much reduced.

One day I took LSD in an attempt to transcend my feet, and led the way over Muir Pass, going so hard I didn't see the others all day. In the pass I sat down to rest, and watched a single woman hiker come up from the other side. She stopped, took her pack off, took a drink of water, put her pack back on, then she was gone. In those five minutes I had a complete lifetime's relationship. She was the one. I saw her as if by X-ray. Dirty-blond hair in a thick braid, swimmer's arms in a tank top, strong legs. She met no one's eyes, least of all mine, which were no doubt spinning in my head like pinwheels. She was calm and self-contained. She was trustworthy, loyal, helpful, friendly, courteous, kind, obedient, cheerful, thrifty, brave, clean, and reverent. Actually I doubted she was obedient. She wasn't even friendly. But she was the one. A hippie mountain goddess, calm and capable, even serene. A serene American person, in 1975? Hard to believe! I was ready to follow her south to Tierra del Fuego. I can see her still. Calmness is a virtue.

A couple of days later I left the guys, and hiked west on a trail that bordered the north side of Lake Thomas A. Edison. Never hike a trail bordering a reservoir, they're always a nasty business of in and out, tracing the shore of an ecological disaster. And I was unhappy to be leaving the Sierra; and my feet hurt. But it had been an epic trip.

Two months later I was up there again, on my first winter trip. More on that one later.

So, these first trips weren't quite as much of a mess as I thought; maybe it was my life in the lowlands that was the mess. They all had many fine moments, and taught me important things. I now knew that the southern Sierra was the heart of the range. And I'd already hiked a lot on snow, and knew that wasn't really a problem. Six trips in two years, and I was hooked.

One thing I remember very powerfully from those first years is the feeling of getting away, driving alone or with friends, usually by night, sometimes all night, up dark roads; then getting out of the car in a black forest, another world, different in its very air, so piney and cold. I would barely sleep, shuddering with the thrill of this translocation, and dawn would slowly illuminate a huge realm of sky and forest, with towers of gray granite all around. Up we would hike into all that, following sandy trails winding through pine needles and broken stone, higher and higher, between tall rough-barked trees that grew smaller and more scattered until we were up into an open immense space unlike anything in my life below: an escape, a trudge up and into a higher realm. It was mind-boggling. It was as if I could choose to visit heaven.

I see now that I began to hike off trail right from the start, on that second day of the first trip, when we crossed the Crystal Range. And that first trip to the southern Sierra was almost entirely on snow, so that too was off trail. I think in those days we didn't even make a distinction between trail and off trail; it was later that this became important to me. The fact that you *can* hike cross-country is another reason why the Sierras are more fun than most of the other mountain ranges of the world, where going off trail is often a recipe for disaster. What that meant in the early years was that I didn't even register the difference.

I first did it on purpose in the summer of 1976, on a trip I planned myself, as Terry was in Costa Rica visiting Bonin. Now that I think of it, maybe I wanted to get off trail because of our Muir Trail trip of the previous fall, when I had hurt my feet hiking long trail miles in tennis shoes. Even a year later my feet were still prone to soreness.

Have I mentioned yet that I don't like the John Muir Trail? The Interstate 5 of the Sierra, the crowd scene, the cliché, the foot killer, the permit sucker? The 212 miles of nonstop human busyness? Probably I'll mention it before I'm done.

Anyway, coincidence or not, it was soon after the autumn foot pounder of 1975 when I began to look into the little Wilderness Press guidebooks to help me design my own trips. And right away I went off trail. That's a sign of what I wanted, even if I hadn't yet fully conceptualized it in those terms.

So that summer of 1976 I went up with my friend Shelby Smith, over Bishop Pass and south on the Muir Trail, but with a plan to cross from the Rae Lakes to Onion Valley by way of a cross-country pass called Dragon Pass. Yes, I probably chose it for the name. Who could pass on a pass called Dragon Pass? From the Rae Lakes one headed east, up into a high trailless cirque filled with the little Dragon Lakes, then up again, to some high ponds; then up a couloir that split a cliff and gave access to the Sierra crest, very near Mount Gould. From there one could descend to Golden Trout Lake, where a trail reappeared and led down to Onion Valley.

This was my first planned cross-country route. A class 2 pass, and over the crest at that. I didn't know then that off-trail crossings of the crest are a special feat, always hard. But this one beckoned. An adventure. Shelby was up for it, and strong. He had been a swimmer in high school, which sets a base layer of strength that lasts for years.

It was a good trip. One day on trail, Shelby told me the story of the first two *Godfather* movies, which I had not seen. His vivid account took about as long as the movies themselves, if not longer, and later on, when I saw the films, I was disappointed; Shelby's version was better.

And Dragon Pass was astounding. We left the Rae Lakes and ascended to the highest pond under the couloir, a pond which luckily had a tiny grass patch tucked among the boulders surrounding it, a patch so tilted that when we lay in our sleeping bags we almost slid feetfirst into the water. We slept under the stars, and the next morning quickly made our way to the foot of the couloir. It was steep! A slot through a cliff, rising at an angle of about—who knew? Plenty steep. The slot was floored by granite rubble, rocks about the size of bowling balls, pretty solidly packed in place. We started up it, and quickly learned that by holding on to the solid sidewall of the couloir, we had a kind of railing to grasp—it was the first time I did that, but it was obvious, no doubt reinvented by almost everyone who tries such a thing.

When we topped out, we were on a band of unglaciated crest material, narrow but not a knife edge. Another road in the sky. We only had to walk a hundred yards south and a few feet up, and we were on a crest peak between Mount Gould and Mount Rixford. It had a great view, all the way from Whitney to the Palisades, with the Kaweahs and Mount Goddard out to the west. I didn't know the peaks' names then, but no matter, there they stood. We were somewhere. Owens Valley lay far below to the east, the usual 10,000 feet, but this too was new to me, and amazing.

The descent to Golden Trout Lake was a talus-and-scree slide, a rock glissade in which every step down onto the loose gravel-size scree slid you a few feet more before you crunched to a halt, by which time you would have shifted to the other foot. A scree glissade, who knew? Down by the lake we found a trail and tromped down to Onion Valley.

A thrilling couple of days, more fun than hiking on trails by — by what? A thousand percent? Infinity? There's no way to put a number to it. It's just way more fun. The navigation, the footwork, they were so much more interesting off trail than on. After that trip, trails were just a way to get to the cross-country stuff. And I wanted more. I wanted the back country.

GEOLOGY (3)

Crests and Divides

ALSO PSYCHOGEOLOGY (1)

Outside and Inside

CRESTS AND DIVIDES

The Sierra crest is like a dragon's back, running approximately southeast to northwest. For over 200 miles, from south of Mount Langley to the northern border of Yosemite, it's continuously high, seldom if ever dipping below 11,000 feet above sea level. The east side drops precipitously into Owens Valley, making that long wall one of the biggest escarpments on Earth. It curves back and forth a bit, in serpentine style, making a particularly big bend at the Palisades, which run almost straight east-west for several miles before turning back northish again in the Evolution group.

So the crest is relatively simple, being just the high line of a watershed border. Precipitation that falls to the west of the crest runs into the Central Valley; to the east, it runs down into the dry basin-and-range country.

This simple story is almost immediately complicated by divides. Like the crest, divides are high ridges. The biggest ones in the Sierra extend from the crest westward. Shorter ridges then often poke out from these big divides. There are also a few divides that are freestanding, usually far to the west of the crest.

The biggest divide is really almost a doubling of the crest. At Junction Peak (named for this reason), the Great Western Divide takes off west from the crest, then turns south, forming an immense wall separating the Kern and

Kings watersheds. It stays high and prominent all the way down to Franklin Pass. The resulting shape, crest and GWD considered together, looks a bit like a tuning fork.

The other big divides, beginning at the crest and extending westward, make borders between the western watersheds in the Sierra, and among other effects, they block the path of the Muir Trail, which stays as close to the west side of the crest as possible. The trail has to get over all these divides at one pass or other. Two of the biggest of the divides bracket the Kings River watershed as it runs west into the Central Valley: the Silliman Crest to the south of it, also called the Tablelands, or the Kings-Kern Divide; then to the north of it, the Monarch Divide and its eastern section, the Cirque Crest. *Monarch* presumably refers to the river's name, but also it is indeed the monarch among the divides, being so long, and often broad across its top, so that it holds many cirques and lakes on its shoulders. Farther north, the Goddard, Glacier, and Silver Divides are named, and are continuously tall and steep.

There are shorter ridges coming off all these divides, often at roughly right angles to them. Basins and canyons are found in the recesses tucked everywhere in this network of ridges.

There are also some isolated peaks east of the crest, a few quite massive, such as Mount Williamson, Birch Mountain, and Mount Tom.

A crest-and-divide description like this can add clarity to any visual representations of the range, either photos or maps. But maps are definitely not the territory, nor are photos. They are all small and flat. When looking at them, the verticalities of the Sierra are hard to remember. In fact you can never seem to fully recall just how up and down it is up there; in the field that tends to come as a perpetual surprise. That's okay: you're up there to go up and down. Or you'd better be.

OUTSIDE AND INSIDE

An affect state that results from this matter of crest and divide is for me a prime example of psychogeology, because there's a powerful feeling that comes over me when I'm up there, having to do with being on the outside or the inside of the Sierra. It's the ridges that make this difference and mark the psychic boundary.

By outside, I merely mean that you are somewhere in the Sierra where you can still see out of it. This includes a lot of places that are wonderful, and fully Sierra-esque, so this distinction is not a matter of quality or exclusion, more a matter of orientation, or one's sense of place. The Sierra being such a narrow range, and so tall, and so much higher than the land surrounding it, you very often find yourself at points where you can see out of the range to landscapes below. This can happen in any part of a trip. The entire crest gives you views outside in both directions, and most of the Sierra on the east side of the crest frequently gives you a view back down to the Owens Valley, and often all the way across that wide valley to the White and Inyo Mountains.

The dry ecologies of the east side add to this feeling of being on the outside. Lower down on the escarpment, you're still in a desert biome, so dry that there's often cactus right by the trail. It's as if you're standing on an upward tilt of the Owens Valley, which in fact you are. Only a few gigantic north-facing basins located entirely on the east side of the crest, like the Bishop Creek drainage, or above Lake Sabrina and North Lake, or the upper Rock Creek drainage under Bear Creek Spire, support life communities that are very similar to those one finds west of the crest. Even those basins often give you a view that makes them still outside, no matter the ecological community around you.

Then, on the western side of the crest, which is so much wider and more gently sloping, there are nevertheless many places where you can see down into California's great Central Valley. The haze by day, the glow of city lights by night: many a high prospect will include a glimpse of that civilized world so far below.

Most places on the crest give a view outside in both directions—you look directly down onto the Owens Valley, and far to the west you can also see the Central Valley. The width of the range is made manifest to your eye. Sometimes it can seem not wide enough, but it is what it is, and since you are up there, and it would take you days to walk across the range (although only hours for certain runners!) it's not really a problem, it's just a fact. That double vision of Sierra and world, both of them in your eye at once, can even expand your pleasure in having gotten up there again.

But it has to be admitted, there's a special joy to feeling you are inside the range. When down in the canyons on the west slope, you can't see out, can't even see the basins right above you; you're deep inside. And in any basin, you can by definition only see out the open end—so if, when you look that way, you see nothing but another Sierra ridge facing you, either nearby or far away, again you're inside. And even when you're up on some of the divides west of the crest, in some of their passes, you can't see out: can't see over the crest to the east, of course, and when you look to the north and south, you can see no end to the peaks and ridges; they extend to the horizon. Sometimes a combination of turns and rises blocks your view westward too: then you're deep inside. The range grows vast; so far as you can tell, it covers the whole world. For the moment, it is the whole world. You're inside the Sierra.

Looking east at sunset, across to Dusy Basin's Columbine Peak and Knapsack Pass: deep inside

SNOW CAMPING (1)
Freezing Our Butts

How we got into snow camping so quickly is a mystery to me. I guess we liked the challenge, and the solitude; very few other people were up there in those months (still true). It had an exotic quality for us, being Southern California beach kids. And in our first round of trips we hiked so often on summer snow that we didn't worry about snow per se. We thought camping on it in winter would be like the snowy trips we took in June. Which was almost true.

My first real winter trip, in December of 1975, made me nervous. I was spooked because I couldn't believe the gear we were carrying on our backs would be enough to keep me warm through the night. I had just spent the previous winter freezing my butt in an apartment in Boston, so it seemed to me that sleeping on snow at 10,000 feet in the Sierra was likely to be even colder. It just stood to reason.

So I skipped an early December week of graduate school and joined Terry and Jeff in Mammoth, but with trepidation. We hiked in over Mammoth Pass on plastic snowshoes, mine bright yellow, Terry's and Jeff's bright orange. They were almost toys. And we had no ski poles, which remained true for all our first snowshoe trips. It puzzles me now that we could have been so clueless, but then again, Robert Scott's expedition members in Antarctica taught themselves to ski using only one pole, a pole about nine feet long at that, so I guess snowcraft is not instinctual. But it is important; Scott's polar group did end up dying, and bad technique was part of that. So ignorance is not always bliss. But the Sierras are considerably warmer than Antarctica, and thus more forgiving. Anyway, the stores selling us gear weren't yet part of a larger culture of outdoor instruction, so we went up and snowshoed without ski poles. Don't do that. Don't even *walk* without poles.

On this first trip we made our way up the canyon of the Middle Fork of the San Joaquin River, which drains the Minarets. We must have hiked by Devils Postpile, but I don't remember it. I was definitely spooked: snow everywhere, forest all flocked white, creeks edged with ice. That first night I crawled into my North Face tent feeling very uneasy. We were sleeping right on snow. My down bag was a three-pounder, but I didn't know how warm those were. Could be I would die that night!

But no. The night was cold but not terribly so. Boston had been worse. I discovered that when I settled into one position in my bag, I would warm up; when I shifted position, that would bring me into contact with unheated parts of my bag, which I would then have to warm up from scratch. Feet were a weak point. A full-length ground pad would have helped, of course, but ours were only about four feet long. So my feet got cold, naturally, and I curled up like a dog to stay on my Ensolite pad. Still, it wasn't a horrid night, and in the morning I felt reassured. I would survive the trip.

The next day we hiked on north. We came to a creek that was too wide to jump over, maybe 15 feet wide. Black water, ankle deep to knee deep, with a few flat rocks exposed midstream, the stream burbling around them. Terry and Jeff stepped large onto these midstream rocks and then jumped to the other bank. With walking poles it would have been quite easy.

When it was my turn I took a big step onto those same rocks, left foot first. Got the snowshoe settled and lifted my right foot forward, and the left snowshoe instantly skidded to the right, so that I found myself laid out horizontally over the water at about waist height, hanging there in space appalled. And the next thing I knew I was sitting on the far bank next to Terry and Jeff.

I wasn't wet. I was sitting on my butt, on the backs of my snowshoes.

Jesus! I said. What happened?

The other two had been checking out the way ahead, and hadn't seen my crossing. What do you mean? they asked. What did you do?

I just fell in the creek! But here I am!

They regarded me curiously. I stood, and we all checked me out. There was a round wet spot about the size of a silver dollar on the outside of my left thigh. I was hiking in blue jeans, yet another sign of how ignorant we were; blue jeans are useless in every situation except cigarette ads.

The guys shrugged. Who knows? they said.

Off we went. But I was stunned, in my mind still stretched out over the stream, about to crash down into the water, get soaked, and then freeze and die. What the hell! How could it be?

I had had a blank-out. There was a gap in the tape, as we said in those days. I followed the other two through the trees, exclaiming at this miracle.

It happened too fast, Jeff guessed.

I said, No way! In sports things happen that fast all the time! And I remember everything, no matter how fast!

After a lot of this on my part, Terry paused and said, Robinson, when you slipped you freaked out, and then when you came down you must have landed on the rock you slipped on, where that wet spot is on your jeans, and then you shimmied like a fucking salmon. Like when they're flying upstream and the bears are standing there catching them out of the air and eating them. Those salmon, they hit rocks, or even just the water, and they bounce away from the bears. Their bodies spring like tiddlywinks. You must have done that.

Maybe, I said. But I don't remember it!

But here you are, they pointed out.

It was a miracle, I said. I translocated instantaneously.

Very doubtful, they replied.

It was windy and cold and ominous. It didn't seem like a day for miracles.

That night I kept thinking about it. The next morning I said goodbye to the guys and headed back home to grad school. I crossed the stream at that same place, stepping on the rocks with extreme care. Even looking at the spot, I still couldn't remember anything between hanging midair and sitting on the bank.

That night, alone in my tent, my first night alone in the Sierra, the absent moment kept troubling me, even frightening me. Terry's explanation struck me as probably right, but why had I gone blank? Had I been so terrified at the prospect of getting soaked on a winter trip that my brain's fuses had blown? That had never happened to me before, even though I'd taken all kinds of falls, been in a car accident, felt a ghost right on the other side of a door I couldn't make myself open. I remembered all those things perfectly. This was weirder than that. It remains maybe the strangest thing that's ever happened to me. Alone in my tent, curled on my stupid ground pad, I shivered more at that memory than at the cold.

More moments from our early winter trips:

In March of 1976 I was back up there, despite my spooky initiation the previous fall. I liked snow camping, I decided, and wanted more. For this trip I invited friends from various parts of my life: Ira from Boston, Webb from Clarion, Darryl from UCSD, Robin from OC. We drove all night past the southern Sierras to get to Meeks Bay on Lake Tahoe. After a long trudge on a snowy Jeep road, we headed up a narrow valley to Lake Genevieve and Stony Ridge Lake, snowshoeing right across the frozen lake surfaces—straight into a south wind gusting about 30 miles an hour. How big the world grows in a wind! By that night the five of us were in four different campsites. An early example of my skills as a trip organizer.

Darryl and Webb bailed, Robin and I relocated Ira, and the three of us had a wonderful time climbing Phipps Peak on my twenty-fourth birthday. We learned that if you have to descend a snow slope so steep that you will slide on your snowshoes down to your death, you can (sometimes) take the snowshoes off and posthole down the slope. We sank to our hips on that slope, we swam chest deep in places, but we weren't going to slide to our deaths.

That was the main lesson from that trip. I somehow missed the obvious one, that I should stop organizing trips.

Once, on the north shore of Lower Echo Lake, the frozen lake too thin to hike on, we were walking the shoreline when a raccoon approached us. We stopped to look at it and it took that opportunity to approach and leap onto Bonin's back, clinging to his neck and backpack such that it was hard for Bonin to get it off. Possibly it was starving, possibly it was rabid, but finally it dropped off without biting Bonin, and on we went.

Later on that trip, we were caught on the Crystal Range looking down a steep icy north face. Terry sat down and pushed off from the top and shot down at speed, catching air a few times and flying down on his back until he slid to a stop on the flat snow far below. I sat down to do the same. Bonin said, Wait, are you going to do that too? Didn't you see what just happened to him?

Yes, I said, and shoved off before he could talk me out of it. It was scary.

We stared up at Bonin. Fuck you guys! he called, and then bombed down after us, laughing like a loon.

Another time, when we were camped just south of Mosquito Pass in Desolation, snow was blowing so hard that I had the door of my North Face tent cinched almost shut, leaving a little round circle for air to get in and out under the rainfly. I was cooking spaghetti on my Bleuet stove, set in the entry with me sitting cross-legged behind it, when my stove ran out of fuel. I unclipped the empty canister, got out a new canister, and clipped it onto the stove's top, hearing a little hiss as the canister was punctured, before it got sealed in place by the rubber seal and the frame's metal clips. Then, just as I noticed that I was performing this whole operation by candlelight, I blew up.

No missing moment here: I had about a second between the sound of the hiss and the explosion, and that was enough time to realize I had just killed myself. So when I blew up, I shrieked HELP! and leaped backward like a grasshopper, pulling my tent out of its stakes and collapsing it onto me like a shroud. I also threw the stove away from me convulsively, and it shot right out of the tent into the snow, even though the round hole in the doorway was only big enough to let it through lengthwise.

Terry and Robin rushed out of their tents to help me untangle myself. You lit up the night! they told me. We thought you were dead!

So did I, I said. In fact all the hairs on my forearms, my eyebrows, and my unshaved beard, and the tent's mosquito net around the door, had been burned or melted away. Otherwise I was okay. Face hot as if sunburned. It took a while to reestablish my tent, and I slept that night dreaming I was on the floor of an Italian restaurant, but next day all was well.

I have never changed a stove canister again without a spike of dread, even though I always do it outside, and the canisters have valves now and don't need to be punctured. I am guessing that this change in canister design is because I'm not the only person to have blown himself up.

That trip was one of several we made in those years to try to get to Lake Doris in wintertime. It was perhaps the first destination we ever set for ourselves to orient a trip, although this one seemed always to be slightly out of reach; in any case we never made it. On the trip when I blew myself up, we only got to the top of Mosquito Pass. On another attempt, from the east, we only got as far as the Velma Lakes.

One time Terry and I tried it in February, so the days were short. We took off from Little Norway, an abandoned roadside stop on Highway 50, and made excellent time, as the snow was like concrete. By the second night we were on the flank of the Crystal Range, on a flat stretch somewhere between Peak 9441 and Peak 9038, and thus only a couple of miles from Lake Doris. We were sure to get there early the following day.

But in the night the winds rose. Gusts whipped over the range and down onto us, knocking our tents around. A Bernoulli plateau, as we later called them; winds really do seem to speed up over such curves. In the morning we agreed it would be best to drop straight into the valley below. We were both folding up our tents to leave when a blast almost knocked us down; we had to turn our backs to it and double our bodies over our tents, holding on desperately as they flapped wildly up and down in front of us, slapping the ground at full length and trying to drag us away like paragliders taking off. There was nothing we could do but crouch side by side and hold on to our tents as they cracked up and down like synchronized swimmers gone mad. We hunched over them hanging on for dear life; this went on so long that we started laughing. Then the blast ended and we quickly crammed the tents into the tops of our backpacks, strapped on the plates, and smooshed down the slope in big glissades, plunging down into a grove of trees that stood in an oxbow curve of the Rubicon.

In this little grove the wind was well baffled. The snow under the trees was old and pocked with black pine needles. We could hear the wind roaring overhead, but down among the trees the air scarcely moved. This phenomenon was new to us and very much appreciated. We put our tents back up, close enough to each other to be heard when we shouted back and forth, and ended up staying there all day, finding water in a little open patch on the iced-over Rubicon.

Next morning the storm was gone, the sky cloudless. The thick layer of soft new snow made hiking much harder; even wearing our snowshoes we sank to our knees, and snow kept collapsing in onto the tops of our plates as we floundered forward. No way could we get to Lake Doris and back to the car in a single day. Time to head home.

Terry led the way. The trees we passed were all flocked with new snow. Melting clumps of it slipped off branches with a whoosh and thump. Rainbows sparked in every dripping drop. When we traded places, I could only lead for a couple hundred yards before slowing to a snail's pace. Sinking thigh deep made for exhausting work. Terry would take back the lead without comment. Following him, I stepped exactly in his deep snowshoe prints, feeling relief at how much easier things became when the trail was broken. In the years that followed, I snowshoed many miles in Terry's prints, but never was I more relieved than on that day. Seemed like he could go forever.

So the pinball years included a lot of snow camping. We went up there every month of the year, at the drop of a hat, and rambled over every nook and cranny of the Desolation Wilderness. But I have to admit, for me in those years it was often a case of escaping my home life and making a break for the hills. Julie and I reunited and broke up, reunited and broke up; then we got married, but this did not seem to help us get along. A few times she went to Desolation with me, and once we went with Dick and his wife Karen, and Vic and his wife Laurie. But mostly it was my thing. I wanted to go with people I didn't argue with, didn't even have to think about. One reason I went so

Hiking out after a snowy night

often with Terry was that we both wanted the Sierras more than we wanted company.

So up we went. For years we kept driving from San Diego past the southern Sierras to Desolation. Then I moved to Davis when Julie started grad school there, and it became a matter of proximity. Terry had moved to Davis too, to work for his dad in Woodland, so we could go at a moment's notice, and we did. We shifted to cross-country skis when we did snow trips, and that got us using ski poles at last. Dick and a couple of his new friends from UC San Francisco joined us a few times, and Terry's housemate Tim. We were in a groove. We went a lot. Sometimes we took both snowshoes and skis, walking on one while carrying the other, to give us versatility on the different kinds of slopes.

All that went on with fanatical intensity, until our New Year's Day trip.

SIERRA PEOPLE (3)
Clarence King

An interesting man, Clarence King. Born 1842, died 1901. Short, energetic, vibrant. And he liked to pretend.

After graduating from Yale with a science degree he set out west with his friend James Gardiner, and they were hired for William Brewer's survey of California, which included a reconnaissance trip into the southern Sierra, in 1864. On ascending a peak that they immediately named Mount Brewer, they saw they weren't on the Sierra crest, as they thought, but rather on a parallel ridge perhaps a dozen miles west of the crest. Far to the southeast, on the true crest, they saw a clutch of obviously higher peaks, one standing well above the rest.

King begged Brewer to be given the chance to make a dash for this highest peak, and with some well-founded misgivings, Brewer agreed. King and their packer Richard Cotter made up knapsacks of rolled blankets holding some food, with loops of rope to go around their arms and shoulders; these weighed 40 pounds each. Off they went. It was the first Sierra backpacking trip.

King's account of this adventure, which takes up the longest chapter in his book *Mountaineering in the Sierra Nevada*, is so vague and supercharged that some parts of the route he and Cotter took can't be determined. Sean O'Grady, who publishes under the name John O'Grady, has convinced me that they said goodbye to Brewer and the others at Longley Pass, descended to the cirque above Lake Reflection, and then headed south over the Great Western Divide between Thunder Mountain and Mount Jordan. This would explain King's hair-raising description of their descent, in which he and Cotter hung by their fingertips and so on; the slope in question, which Joe and Darryl and I viewed in 2012, looks awful.

After they dropped into the upper Kern basin, King and Cotter crossed easy open country to the creek now called Tyndall Creek, and made a camp somewhere under Tawny Point. The next morning they climbed the north flank of Mount Tyndall, finding snow and ice on the summit ridge that gave them moments of high danger. Still they made it to the top, and King writes that he named it Mount Tyndall, ringing his hammer on the very top. He was 22 years old.

It's a classic moment in Sierra history, one that Sean O'Grady and William Tweed have shown is a fictionalized moment. King's field notes reveal that in the real moment, he named the peak they were on Mount Whitney, as Josiah Whitney was head of the California Geological Survey; he named a taller peak to the east (now called Williamson) Mount Tyndall; and the tallest of them all, still six miles to the south, he named Mount Grant (recall it was 1864). O'Grady speculates that it was Brewer who later shifted the names around, to honor his boss Whitney with the big peak, renaming the one that King and Cotter had climbed Mount Tyndall. Williamson, the behemoth east of Tyndall, seems to have been named later still, by Whitney. By the time King wrote his book he was able to match his story to what had been decided by his employers. Strange to have this naming stuff so scrambled right from the start—and useful, too, for anyone who wants all these names reconsidered.

King's description of being on a peak on the Sierra crest is long, repetitive, confused, and magnificent. It's one of the best bits of Sierra writing ever. He tries to recapture his real feelings up there, and to describe what he actually saw, not what one might expect to see. When I've written about being on these peaks, I turn to the analogy of looking out an airplane window; King didn't have that experience, and the sheer weirdness of the view down to the alkaline desert 10,000 feet below, and the infinity of peaks ranging north and west all the way to the distant horizon—it's not like anything he had ever seen. Those great sentences I quoted in my first chapter, about the reversal of ordinary light intensities, captures an aspect of the scene that no one else seems to have even apprehended, much less described, and they are just one part of a feverish attempt to convey the felt reality of his experience up there.

"You look up into an infinite vault, unveiled by clouds, empty and dark, from which no brightness seems to ray, an expanse with no graded perspective, no tremble, no vapory mobility, only the vast yawning of hollow space. With an aspect of endless remoteness burns the small, white sun, yet its light seems to pass invisibly through the sky, blazing out with intensity upon mountain and plain, flooding rock details with painfully bright reflections, and lighting up the burnt sand and stone of the desert with a strange, blinding glare. There is no sentiment of beauty in the whole scene."

In other words, the sublime. Beauty and terror combined. "Silence and desolation are the themes which nature has wrought," King continues. "The one overmastering feeling is desolation, desolation!"

Again that magic word!

King and Cotter went down the southwest slope of their mountain, the ascent from the north having been so dangerous. They circled back to their campsite of the night before (I think by way of Tawny Point Pass) and slept there again. Their return to Brewer's base camp the next day is described in some detail, but again the exact place they crossed the Great Western Divide can't be pinpointed. They crossed this very difficult divide after traversing the upper Kern and coming to "the brink of a precipice which sank sharply from our feet into the gulf of the King's Cañon. Directly opposite us rose Mount Brewer." That means they were almost certainly standing on the Kings-Kern Divide, somewhere between Millys Footpass and Lucys Footpass. "Straight across from our point of view was the chamber of rock and ice where we had camped on the first night." That would match with O'Grady's theory of a first night's camp above Lake Reflection.

The collaborative internet site highsierratopix.com lists a cross-country pass that drops to Lake Reflection from around this spot. The trip reports for this pass, which isn't listed in the guidebooks, match King's description quite well. For sure they must have descended somewhere near this "Little Joe's

Pass," in their case almost slipping over a cliff at the bottom of one chute, then shifting into another chute to continue down, and crossing snow and ice to get around the shore of a lake, probably Lake Reflection. After that they retraced their crossing of the wall south of Mount Brewer, which suggests they crossed Longley Pass again, and rejoined their group. Brewer was of course intensely relieved.

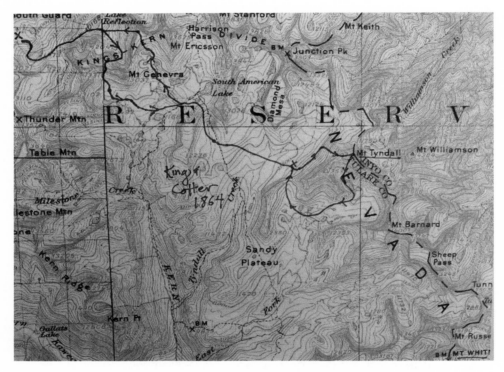

King and Cotter started from the X in the upper left, intending to reach Mount Whitney in the lower right, but missed by six miles to the north. The route interpretation is by Sean O'Grady for the way out, by me for the way back. USGS map from 1907.

A classic: and definitely a candidate for the first Sierra backpacking trip in the modern style, predating as it does Muir's wanderings by almost a decade. What I mean by "backpacking trip in the modern style" is this: they carried all they needed on their backs, and they were traveling only to explore the

Sierra, not to hunt beaver, or herd sheep, or prospect for gold, or find a way to get somewhere else. They set a goal that was in some senses arbitrary, since they had already seen the peak they went to climb. Like backpackers now, they told friends where they were going, and how long they were going to be gone, and they took along just enough food to do it. They had a wonderful trip; they all are; but this one was the first.

For King, it was in many ways the great week of his life. For sure his account of it was the high point of his life as a writer. He never again wrote anything as good; the rest of *Mountaineering* is flat by comparison, and in certain chapters quite bad, like a second-rate Bret Harte. But that one chapter is incandescent.

Even if that was the great week of his life, as I think it was, the remainder of it was by no means a letdown. He was not one of those people who fell in love with the Sierra and then devoted his life to it. In the years immediately after that trip, he did make three more attempts to climb Mount Whitney, once climbing Langley by mistake, as he had Tyndall; thus he missed once by six miles to the north, then by six miles to the south. But all this was only for the glory of being the first to ascend the tallest peak in the nation. As it turned out, by the time he reached the top of Whitney, three fishermen from Lone Pine had ascended the peak, and named it Fisherman's Peak. Another bad name, but funny, and kind of refreshing, especially if you want to make the case, as I do, that the right name has not yet been assigned to this peak.

After those adventures, King went to Washington, DC, and argued for the value to the nation of a good geological survey of the American West; this led to his becoming head of the Fortieth Parallel Survey, after which he was named the founding director of the US Geological Survey. Some years later he detected and revealed a diamond hoax in Wyoming, by traveling out to the site and inspecting the rocks in situ; he became famous for that, and momentarily wealthy. He joined mining ventures, went into debt, traveled to Europe, and joined the Century Club in Manhattan, where he was much admired by people like Henry Adams and William Dean Howells. His club friends and traveling companions felt a real affection for his wide-ranging intelligence, fanciful wit, and ready sympathy. They loved his stories of his mountain life. He lived in a hotel in Manhattan, from which he came and went on his own schedule. People knew him only in part, and it turns out he wanted it that way.

When in Spain he dressed up as a Hispanic dandy, to look for a helmet like the one Don Quixote wore; he wrote up this adventure in a short story that his club friends published after his death, along with their tributes to him. He studied the geology of the Alps in Switzerland and France. In Cuba he spent time with revolutionaries, in Mexico he bartered in markets while wearing local garb. All his life he liked to dress up; once when young he sent out a postcard of himself dressed as a woman. He learned languages by memorizing a thousand nouns and verbs, then talking in infinitives while using English grammar. People enjoyed him. There was something in his character, and most of all, in his Sierra book—especially that one great chapter—that impressed people at the time, and keeps him alive in the American story, and prominent in the Sierra's story.

That mysterious quality, which contemporaries frequently noted in him, was greatly heightened when it came to light that throughout his last 20 years, he lived a double life. By day he worked in Manhattan; at night he took the ferry across the East River to Brooklyn, or walked over the new Brooklyn Bridge, where he became a Black man named James Todd, married in a common-law marriage to a Black woman, Ada Copeland. Copeland had been born a slave in Georgia, and later moved to New York. Their marriage lasted from the 1880s to King's death in 1901, and the couple had five children together, four of whom survived to adulthood. Their two daughters married as white women, their two sons fought in African American units in World War I. King kept his other life concealed from his wife, and told her he was a Pullman porter, which explained his many long absences. His fair coloring and blue eyes apparently did not interfere with his claim of being a Black American. Possibly it didn't occur to anyone that a white man would want to make that claim. In any case he passed for Black when he wanted to. Overtaken by a fatal illness in Arizona, probably tuberculosis, he just had time to write to Ada to give her his real name, beg her understanding, and instruct her as to the location of his bank account. Ada spent some of the following decades trying to get the money from that account, but by the time she won the case in court, the money had been completely lost to legal fees.

We don't know much about this part of King's life. The book *Passing Strange*, by Martha A. Sandweiss, tells what there is to know. Ada Todd, later Ada King, lived on for another half century after King's death, and her family preserved parts of their story. But not much.

There's something sad in this strange tale, in what it says about the culture of that time. In other ways it's quite heartwarming. King loved Ada, as his surviving letters to her make clear. Aside from that one great chapter in his Sierra book, they are his best writing. "Ah, my darling, I lie in the lonely hours of the night and long to feel your warm and loving arms about me and your breath on my face and the dear pressure of your lips against mine. My dearest, I love you with all the depth and warmth of my whole heart and will till I die." "It seems to me often that no one ever loved a woman as I do you.... My whole heart is yours forever."

So he did what he thought necessary to make it all work, becoming James Todd while also continuing to pursue his life as the elusive and charming Clarence King. In the book of memoirs assembled by his club friends after his death, it becomes clear that none of them had the slightest suspicion of his other life, and also, that he enjoyed spoofing them. He played a part for those men as if in a theater. This was puckish, even bizarre, but also, given the affection and regard shown to his memory by his wife and children, as well as by these acquaintances from his club life, there must have been something creative and energizing too, and weirdly ingenious. He felt a need to be two people. And it seems that for the most part, no one was greatly harmed by this desire.

Of course many people live complicated lives, poorly documented and mostly unremembered. The living seldom remember the dead, no matter what they did. King stays part of history because of that five-day backpacking trip, and his intensely engaged, effortful, and honest description of it.

Before that hike, during their time on top of what they immediately named Mount Brewer, his companions bestowed King's name on a peak clearly visible to their north. It turns out to be the finest-looking single peak in the entire Sierra, an actual horn, and it's now flanked by subpeaks named for his hiking partner Cotter, and his particular friend Gardiner. Very often names in the Sierra are bad, but not here. Clarence King was an interesting man.

Mount Clarence King, from the north

NAMES (1)
The Good

The Good, the Bad, and the Ugly: that's how I'm going to structure my discussion of the place names in the Sierra. Possibly there's a missing category that would balance *ugly* on the other side, like *great*; and there are a few great names in the Sierra, maybe; but not so great that they can't just be called good, leaving me free to stick with the spaghetti western's iconic title. There are for sure some quite good names in the Sierra; Mount Clarence King is one of them. But great? That might be going a bit too far.

In fact, what would constitute a great name? They're just sounds. You would need a great meaning. Everest's name in Tibetan, Chomolungma, means "mother goddess of the world." That's maybe a great name. Other than that, not many examples are coming to me. Names are nouns; greatness lies elsewhere. So the triad "the good, the bad, and the ugly" will suit my purposes. I'll start with the good, and hike downhill from there.

All the remaining Native American names in the Sierra are good names, although as Peter Browning, the author of *Place Names of the Sierra Nevada*, notes in his introduction, these are often mistranscribed or misspelled, and misapplied as to place, with their meanings also often confused. But so what: in holding to these names, some European Americans tried in a small way to keep a little faith with the first peoples they were displacing. I've read that there are something like a hundred Native American place names in the Sierra; I don't see that many on the maps, but I hope it's true.

For those places where we still know a Native American name for a place, yet call it by a nineteenth-century European name, I think we should switch back to the Native name, as happened in Alaska with the switch of Mount McKinley back to Denali. One good candidate for this kind of switch would be Mount Sill, in the Palisades. Edward Rowland Sill was no doubt a fine English professor, and I have to admit I like the idea of an English professor from the University of California getting one of the greatest peaks in the Sierra named after him. But still: no Sill. Because there's a known Paiute name for this peak, a very great peak, visible from a broad stretch of the Owens Valley; not the tallest of the Palisades, but almost, and by its position and shape the one that stands over the big valley most prominently, like a plinth. Secor declares in his guidebook, "It is a sacred mountain to the Paiutes: *Nee-na-mee-shee* (the Guardian of the Valley), and is worshipped in their religious ceremonies."

This would be a great start for a substitution. And after that, we should continue returning Native American names up there, when we know them. The Paiute name for Mount Tom is Winuba—that should be the name of that immense pyramid. Birch Mountain, another giant just to the east of the crest, was called P'o'daranwa. Very likely the third great east-of-the-crest monster, Mount Williamson, also had a Paiute or Shoshone name.

The place where Bishop is now located was called Pitana Patu. The Owens Valley itself was called Payahuunadü, "the land of flowing water." That name could be well over 5,000 years old, and should definitely be brought back.

Clearly a naming session should be convened with the Paiute and other Native Americans still living in the shadows of the Sierra. The Bishop Paiute reservation is home to a very active community, including language teachers, and they could be consulted to find names for features in the region. Bringing these back would greatly improve the name situation—especially when we get to the bad names, and even more so, the ugly names. Because good names in the Sierra are few.

In any case, names are always changing, so they are all worth looking at. Good names are those that cast a mood, or even a spell. Granting that most of the names up there will remain as they are, and that most are English names, we can acknowledge there were some good ones given. The Ionian Basin, with Chasm Lake its only named lake, and the peaks towering to left and right of it called Scylla and Charybdis, with the three subpeaks of Scylla called the Three Sirens, and the steep canyon dropping from Chasm Lake called the Enchanted Gorge (in fact it is a black nightmarish cleft): these are all good names, bestowed by Theodore Solomons in his first exploration of the region. The long black ridges bracketing the Enchanted Gorge are named the Ragged Spur and the Devils Crags; these are not quite as good, but they're not bad either. As Mark Twain once remarked, "The Devil was very active in the American West," but if there was ever a hellish-looking ridge, the Devils Crags are it.

I also like, as a name, the Inconsolable Range, near Bishop Pass. And almost as much, the Gorge of Despair, high on the north side of the Monarch Divide, and dropping so hard into the Middle Fork that it can't be climbed or descended, except by climbers rappelling down in wet suits to keep from freezing in the waterfall that pours over them. So even though I doubt that much despair has ever been felt there—and in fact I don't think anyone has been particularly inconsolable under the Inconsolable Range either—still, I like these operatic names.

I love the name Iridescent Lake, as I've said, for the way the lake iridesces. That's a good name, in fact a great name.

I like Shout-of-Relief Pass, because when you come up from the south, the slope is so steep that one fears the north side will be even steeper, as they usually are; but then on top you see the north side is unaccountably easy, and let out a shout of relief.

A good name that doesn't exist anymore, but should, was given by John Muir after his first visit to Kings Canyon. What later got called Bubbs Creek, his map of the region has as the South Fork of the South Fork. A clear winner.

Confusion Lake has an infinity edge, such that if you wander around its shore to its east end, you find yourself looking over a foot-high granite lip, down a 2,000-foot wall into Goddard Creek Canyon.

Walter Starr Sr. came down from his ascent of the peak overlooking Mono

Pass and called it Electric Peak, because of the lightning he and his companion endured up there; that would have been a good name, but the peak eventually got named Mount Starr. Now this name can refer to both him and his son Pete, who wrote the first climbers' guide to the Sierra, and died young in a fall from one of the Minarets. Pete's real name was Walter Starr Jr.; the name Pete he gave to himself, Peter meaning "stone." A fervent Sierra lover, that young man.

Bighorn Plateau was named for the sheep that used to hang out there. Hopefully they will again.

The Black Giant is a good name. It is indeed a black giant. In general, references to odd or distinctive features are pleasing: Milestone Peak, Table Mountain, Red and White Mountain, Red Slate Mountain, Diamond Mesa. Also Feather Peak, because its north ridge looks like a spray of wing feathers poking at the sky.

The highest lakes on each side of Muir Pass are named Wanda Lake and Helen Lake, after Muir's two daughters. Very nice.

The Boreal Plateau is a good name, as it feels very northerly.

Cloudripper is a good name, given by climbers.

Potluck Pass marks the fact that on the pass's east side you have to take pot luck, as there is no obviously best way up or down.

Tunemah Peak is said to have been named by Chinese sheepherders who had to get their herds down the stupendously long steep eastern slope of the mountain. The transcription from Chinese is poor, but it probably means "motherfucker peak."

Seven Gables is good, named by Theodore Solomons in 1896 on his first ascent. As some have remarked, there seem to be considerably more than seven gables on this big square mass, but who's counting? It's evocative, and there are gables. And from its top you can see Four Gables far to the east, on the crest just north of Mount Humphreys. That one really does have four gables, and hidden in the depression at the center of the four is (or was) a little glacieret. I ascended both these peaks in 2013, on different trips, and so called that my Summer of Eleven Gables. That's a good name too. It came about a decade after my Summer of Bloody Accidents, which is also a good name but was not as fun to experience.

There must be more, but right now they're escaping me. I think it has to be said that for the most part, the Sierras are poorly named. Let's do something about that!

Good names: Darryl is standing on the far side of what we call Phil Arnot Pond, and in the distance you can see a bit of Lilliput Glacier — yes, very small.

SNOW CAMPING (2)

Close to the Edge

Terry and I were trying again to make it to Lake Doris in winter. It struck us funny to double down and try to get there on New Year's Day: 1977 turning into 1978.

It began snowing two hours after we took off, and after crossing the frozen Echo Lakes on skis we switched to snowshoes for the ascent to Tamarack Lake, at the top of the Echo Lakes basin. We set camp on a knoll above Tamarack, and quickly decided that the snowfall meant Lake Doris was once again out of reach. We spent a couple of days skiing on nearby slopes, first climbing them in herringbone-ascent style, or even sideways step-up style, and then skiing back down. Half hour up, two minutes down, time after time. Skiing was still new to both of us. We had rented cross-country skis and shoes; the shoes connected to the skis by way of clips that squeezed flat rubber extensions at the toes. Heels were fitted to a slot in the ski, but you could lift your feet to slide on the flats. The skis seemed designed to come off in falls, maybe to keep you from twisting your legs too badly. I fell a lot, so it was a good thing the skis didn't stay on, but I had to do a lot of carefully balanced reconnecting after most of my falls.

In my tent after these sessions I was really wet. Nevertheless I stayed warm. I had borrowed a pair of down pants from Bonin, these were luxurious. And I had finally brought an Ensolite pad as long as my body, obvious and helpful for warmth, even if still horridly lumpy.

The third night it began to snow in earnest. Big gusts of wind struck, up to maybe 60 miles per hour, we couldn't be sure, as it was way off the scale of our previous experiences. Our tents snapped hard in the general roar, but snow was beginning to weight them down, which was a good thing, as it meant they couldn't get blown away. We were both up all night with the noise, and knocking at the tents from the inside to get new snow to slide off to the sides. A few times we shouted to each other.

As soon as there was enough light to see, we smashed down the snow in front of our tents with our snowshoes, and crawled up and out into the dim dawn. Only the top ridges of our tents were still showing above the snow. About three feet had fallen overnight, and it was still blizzarding full-on, thick flakes flying by horizontally on a screaming wind. Visibility was variable but averaged about 30 yards, which was a shock to see—hard to believe there were that many snowflakes flying by, but there were. We crouched in a fast, fluctuating bubble of white.

It was only six miles to the car, so we had the plan without even discussing it—haul up the tents and get our asses out of there. We did that in such a hurry that we didn't eat breakfast or make a water run, and I tore one of the grommets out of the bottom of my tent, pulling at a stake that wouldn't give. Must have been a fair bit of adrenaline in that pull!

We took off on skis. Our packs were bulky with the snowshoes tied on them, and as we took the first drop I was forcefully reminded of how hard it was to ski downhill with a pack on my back. I kept falling, and it was hard work to get back up, reattach the skis to my toe clips, and set off again at what I hoped was a less steep angle. My glasses were caked with snow, especially after my falls. Everything was a blur, cleaned glasses or not. I decided to stop and switch to my snowshoes, because I knew I could walk on them, and getting back up from my falls was taking too much time and effort. By the time I finished putting on my snowshoes, Terry was out of sight. He hadn't noticed I had stopped, and visibility was still just a tight flying bubble encasing me. I was on my own. But glissading sloppily downhill on snowshoes was at least more stable, even with my skis carried crosswise in my arms. I wasn't going to fall.

But then it began to seem like I was lost. The Echo Lakes basin is a simple thing, all I had to do was go down, but there is a gorge cutting through a short set of cliffs right at the inlet to Upper Echo Lake, which we always dodged on the north side, following where the trail went. That dodge was important, but in the falling snow I couldn't see, especially with my smeared glasses, and it was beginning to seem like I was doing too many ups and downs, going too far to the north in my dodge, probably, and thus getting onto the side wall of the valley. The small ups were no fun in these conditions, but if I continued to go east, which was the correct direction, there were more ups facing me, even though there shouldn't have been. I became aware of how few external signs there are to north-south-east-west when you can't see the sun or the horizon, and everything is uniformly white, and you can only see 30 yards in any direction. The wind was strong but I couldn't be positive it was straight out of the west. So I stopped among some trees and got out my compass and map. First and last time I ever tried to use a compass in the Sierra. Hmmmmm. Looked like east, the way I wanted to go, was about 90 degrees farther south than I thought it was. Could it be true? It violated my sense of things so badly that I wondered if the compass was okay. I felt a touch of vertigo, even a little wave of nausea. I kept going in a sort of compromise direction between the compass and my sense of things.

Then came a terrain choice. Left, a white wall. Straight ahead, steeply up. To the right a bit, a tough traverse to get around this up. A bit more to the right led into the top of a ravine going downhill. Or I could go back the way I had come. I decided to go down the ravine. The bottom of it had some discolored flat spots, and I knew I didn't want to walk on those. Obviously a creek would be running there under the snow. So I made my way down one side of the ravine for a decent distance, but then its sides got steeper and forced me toward the low point, nearer the flat spots. I was wondering if I should trust them when I fell through the snow. All at once I was knee deep in water, snowshoes on, pack on my back, skis and poles, which had been crosswise in my arms, now dropped and lying across the snow, giving me something to hang over. Snow had collapsed in from the sides onto my legs such that I was now waist deep in new wet whiteness, and I could not see my legs down in the creek. NO! I shouted.

My panicked squirm to leap out of the cold water got me nowhere. I was stuck. Shoes filled with cold water. A bad moment. I tossed the skis and poles onto the left wall of the ravine, shoved my arms down through snow into the water to undo my snowshoes. When my feet were free I lifted my legs out of the snow. Sitting there on my sinkhole in the snow, I dug down again to get the snowshoes out from under the snow and water. When they were out, I stuck them rear-end first into the steep snow of the left wall, and pulled myself up using them. Climbed slowly out of the ravine, until I could kick into the snowshoe straps far enough to shuffle on them up the edge of the ravine to the first clump of trees above me.

There I dropped my backpack and dug in it, whipped out the tent, and strung it loose between two big trees, one tie at each end. With those secure, I threw my pack into the tent and crawled in after it. Set this way it was just a nylon bag strung between two trees, but still very welcome. I was cold, for sure, but neither shivering nor feeling the cold anywhere except in my feet and hands. That numbness was enough to have me working fast. I felt like I should be cold, and my hands were definitely numb. My fingers were moving poorly.

I got the stove out, balanced it the best I could on the uneven floor of the flapping tent, lit it, huddled over it. I got out of my clothes in a kind of acrobatic writhing, to avoid burning myself. When my feet and legs were bare I positioned them around the stove as close as I dared, just an inch or two from the blue flames, my hands cupped over them even closer. Frequently wind gusts would knock the tent around, and I'd grab the stove and hold it upright. Ate some candy as I sat there, and snow too. Should I stay there for the night? Well, no, it was probably about 9:00 a.m., maybe 10:00 at most. Well, heck. I was getting warmer, and I had my dry-ish night clothes to change into, including Bonin's down pants. On with the show, I declared to myself after an hour or so, feeling generally recharged, and if not warm, then at least not freezing.

I dressed in another acrobatic performance and struggled out of the tent back into the storm, feeling pleased with myself for my recovery from the bad moment. But back out in the storm, looking around in the white roaring forest, I could only find one snowshoe! Bright yellow plastic—but only one of them. After a mad search, including a look back down the ravine, I had to give up. The other one was nowhere to be found. Another blank-out! This was intensely frustrating, and mystifying too—probably a sign that I was colder and more freaked out than I thought I was. But there was nothing to be done. I slung the other snowshoe away in disgust, changed back from my dry boots into my soaking wet ski shoes, and clipped the damn skis back on.

What followed was about an hour of grimly careful skiing, as I sought out the least steep way downhill, no matter where it led me. That first had me headed back the way I had come, keeping well to the right of the ravine, and noting with alarm that my earlier tracks were already completely snowed over. When I came to downward slopes I felt I could handle I skied down them, angling at the gentlest lines I could find. I wanted slopes of like five degrees or less. This required some serious zigzagging. I fell a few more times, but it wasn't as bad as falling in a creek, so I just got up, re-skied myself, and continued on.

Finally I slid down an easy slope onto the surface of what had to be Upper Echo Lake, it seemed so big. Sometimes in my bubble of white there appeared brief glimpses of distant trees, just blurry dark triangles far away and at my level, confirming this sense of size. For sure I was on a frozen lake surface. Huge relief.

After that it was just a slog over the two Echo Lakes. Easy to balance, just keep going, wind at my back. It was colder in the full wind, very cold in fact, and the lakes were stretching out on me, but I knew where I was, and I wasn't going to fall again. Still windy, still snowing like crazy. Sometimes a gust would hit me so hard I got carried along on my skis for a ways, feet together, sliding as if going downhill, simply from the push of the wind on my back; this never lasted for long, and it was so weird while it was happening that I didn't really appreciate it.

Eventually I came to the little lodge above the dam at the outlet of Lower Echo Lake. I unclipped from the skis and climbed the stone steps and opened its outer door. Terry was in there, sitting in the enclosed porch foyer. He was relieved to see me. There was a woman there in the lodge, doing some kind of writing retreat, she told us. She seemed quite annoyed with us for interrupting her writing day. We promised her we would leave shortly. I told Terry what had happened to me, and he said he had had adventures of his own, having been blown by gusts of wind into big snowdrifts on the lee side of the Echo Lakes, time after time, until his clothes were soaked and it became a case of walk or freeze. He said he had to take off his skis and walk for five miles straight, and had barely had enough warmth and strength to make the short climb up the slope to the lodge.

We said bye-bye to the disgruntled writer and trudged up the snowy road to Julie's VW, which was deep under snow; dug it out with Terry's snowshoes; drove it in reverse back down the snowy road, until we were stopped by a stuck truck that completely filled the snow-walled lane. We took refuge from the continuing storm in the truck owner's cabin. He had a shoe box of marijuana steaming on top of his wood-burning stove, and welcomed us to burn some of it with him. We waited there, steaming ourselves, until 11:00 p.m., when the guy's truck and then Julie's VW were pulled down the lane to the highway by a big white Caltrans truck. Why Caltrans was clearing that little side road at that hour I'll never know. Then on Highway 50 we found that the bug's head-lights didn't work, but wait, the brights did; so I drove us at ten miles per hour down the mountain through the unrelenting storm, chains on, then chains off, finally reaching Davis at 3:00 a.m. A trip that ordinarily would have taken us about 4 hours had taken 21. We went through the drive-by window of Jack in the Box, then over to Terry's place. I fell asleep before I could even eat my food.

Thus our New Year's Day blizzard. It changed us a bit.

For one thing, Terry began making gear. During our disaster day he had been wearing a jumper he had bought at an outdoor goods store, made of a 60–40 mix of rayon and cotton that was supposed to be the latest and greatest outdoor fabric. Why anyone would think that about rayon and cotton, in any mix whatsoever, I have no idea, but Terry had been quite pleased with it when we started the trip. So the way it had failed him when push came to shove shocked and angered him. How can they sell shit like that? he demanded. He borrowed his mom's second-best sewing machine, and began to design and sew all his own gear. The blizzard trip was a watershed in that regard.

Four months later we were back up there zooming around. Nothing quite as desperate as that ever happened to us again, at least in terms of weather. Without knowing it, we had begun a shift to the next phase. The pinball years were not quite over, the '70s still had two years to go, but Terry was beginning to make our gear, and I was beginning to look at weather reports.

MOMENTS OF BEING (1)
A Sierra Day: Morning in Camp

I fear that the pinball years and all their learning curves are leading me astray here, in my goal of demonstrating to the reader that backpacking in the Sierra is a safe and peaceful thing to do.

It is safe and peaceful, I swear, but one's memory tends to fixate on the adventures, meaning the misadventures—those times when things went awry and we had to scramble. As in novels, one looks for a plot, and a plot is the story of something going wrong. And indeed in the '70s a lot of things went wrong. But also, since we survived them, they struck us as funny. And I like funny.

And yet still, these events were exceptions. The ordinary Sierra days were active but mellow, stimulating but contemplative. There's a serenity to the ordinary Sierra day that can't be conveyed by focusing on the adventure days. Nine days out of ten, or at least four days out of five, the day unreels like an exercise in Zen walking meditation, and that's a precious thing. It's an iterative experience, or what Gérard Genette called the pseudo-iterative: variations on a theme. I have to try to convey those pseudo-iterative days too in this account, even though, in truth, there are still more adventures worth telling. But the ordinary Sierra day is not like that.

One thing I'm going to try, in pursuit of conveying the ordinary experience up there, is to write up a Typical Sierra Day, leaving out geographical and other particulars, to focus better on what we usually do up there on a backpacking trip, and how that usually feels. I'm going to split that account up and distribute it through the other chapters, in the hope that this will extend its spell over all the other kinds of experiences.

There is a characteristic Sierra backpacking day. It's beautiful; it's what we're trying for, and when we get it, we're happy. If they all turned out that way, it would be great. Maybe a little less dramatic—less epic, more lyric— but that's not something to be concerned about, since drama is going to intrude itself no matter how careful we are. Exposed to the elements, you're going to get some weather drama, no matter what you do. And sometimes you're going to get lost, and perhaps then have to deal with difficulties of terrain or orientation. Always we try for that Platonic ideal of the peaceful great day, and then cope with whatever the Sierra gives us.

So I'll do this by dividing the paradigmatic day into parts spread through the rest of the book: Morning in Camp, Rambling and Scrambling, Sunset and Twilight, Night in Camp, and Under the Tarp. First up, morning in camp. Dawn is a feeling, a beautiful ceiling...

When the sky gets light in the east I often wake. Pleased that day has almost arrived, I sometimes snuggle back into my sleeping bag for a last snooze; other times I put my glasses on and lie on my back and watch the stars wink out. The dawn sky is gray before it takes on the blue color. Sometimes peaks to the west of camp have a dawn alpenglow, more yellow than pink. It's cold, but often I'm done with sleeping, and things are visible, and very likely I have to pee. Once up and about, I seldom climb back into my sleeping bag and lie down. Easier to sit on my scrap of egg-crate foam that serves as butt pad, hip belt, and pillow, and pull my sleeping bag across my legs, and brew up my coffee and sit watching the morning happen. If the sky is clear, the first blast of sun over the mountains to the east will immediately warm things up. Between coffee and my warmies, and the bag draped over me, it's usually warm enough. Although for sure I am also waiting for the sun.

Packing up gets intermingled with eating breakfast. Pour dried milk powder carefully into water bottle, shake. Pour milk onto my cup of cereal. Nice to feel a little hunger. Same breakfast as at home. Quotidian reality. Pack up whatever is at hand that needs packing. Things go into my backpack in a certain rough order, mainly just hard things away from my back, soft things stacked horizontally against my back. Nicer that way. No need to hurry, not usually; all the chores and pleasures of the morning can be completed in about an hour and a half. Two hours is leisurely, an hour is not hard. It's best not to hurry, not to look at one's watch.

Definitely one of the great hours of the day. A chance to see where we are in a different light. And morning light is so beautiful. Water noises are the only thing breaking the silence, little clucks from the nearby stream, sometimes more if there's a waterfall or a bigger stream; liquid clatter. But quiet. The time of day when you're most likely to see the local birds going about their business. They flit from tree to tree, they cheep, they fly hard in the thin air. They seem busy. Sometimes we see Steller's jays, like my scrub jays at home, but with a jaunty black crest at the backs of their heads, quite a handsome flourish. More usually finches or swallows or robins, or their Sierra equivalents. Clark's nutcracker is a substantial bird. Crows flap by and swoop around in the treetops. Occasionally water ouzels, now called the American dipper, I'm told; and rosy finches, bold camp robbers with their subtle rich wing color, a dusky rose. Chickadees, more heard than seen. I whistle their song back at them, one note high, two low and syncopated, and they will reply in a kind of conversation, although they always say the same thing, as far as I can tell. I only recently learned that those three notes are made by chickadees, and that the name of the bird is supposed to be a transcription of their call. I'm not that happy to have learned this; before, their three notes were pure music to me, like clarinet notes. Now that I know it's a chickadee making the notes, I find myself annoyed with that name: there is no "chick," there is no "dee," it's a terrible transcription, which only messes up your ability to hear the actual call. Bad lyrics, instead of a good instrumental; Nashville instead of Brahms. I would just whistle to designate those little birds, and call them that.

Often the main business of the morning becomes waiting for the sun. This can be mesmerizing. Very often there are ridges above the camp to the east, which means that almost every camp is in a little bit of a hollow—although there are those rare camps that overlook the Owens Valley, and the sun cracks the distant horizon before it even comes level with you: you are higher than sunrise. But mostly you're in a hollow, and thus in the shade for a while, sometimes a long while. And there are ridges and slopes to the west of you too. So sunlight strikes the peaks to your west, really all across the westward semicircle of your horizon, from the highest peaks on down. All that is quite visible to you, and it means there's a shadow line, usually uneven, as it's being cast by an eastern ridgeline that can be very jagged, onto a western slope that is sure to be lumpy. But no matter the topography, above this shadow line it's bright and sunny, and obviously warmer than where you are, if it happens to be cold, as it so often is; and you are down in the shadows below, waiting for the sun.

And the line moves, down and down and down. This is the speed of the planet rolling under your feet. It's slow, but not so slow that you can't see it. If you watch a boulder near the sun, but still in shadow, and keep watching it, then the sunlight will hit the top of the boulder, then move down the boulder—also the whole slope—slowly, slowly, but not imperceptibly, not quite—you can see it, if you watch. It doesn't even require that much patience. It's moving. The Earth is rolling under you, at that slow stately pace. At the pace of time itself, it seems. You can see time.

Of course at every sunset you can also see the speed of our planet's rotation, but you're used to that, and blinded by it physically and conceptually. This indirect vision, of sunlight moving down a mountain slope, feels different. It's natural, it's eerie. It's beautiful but disturbing. This particular morning is passing at this very speed, it won't come back. The rocks will be here for millions of years, but not this moment, which creeps down and down at you, even if you hold your breath, even if you suspend your usual busy stream of consciousness and just look at it, be with it. Time passes.

If you're camped by a lake, as we often are, the lake surface can be perfectly still, and reflect the opposite shore as if in a mirror, everything upside down in it, an effect very striking, surreal but real. The Sierra as God's art gallery.

Then a peak or ridge to your east flares at one brilliant point, and the sunlight hits you, radiant and warm on your skin. You can go from almost shivering to too warm in five minutes. Ahh. The day begins. Time to finish packing and start hiking.

A calm morning by Green Lake

MY SIERRA LIFE (6)
Crossing Mather Pass

By the end of the '70s I felt like everything was falling apart. My marriage, my grad-school career, the country, the world. Of course the world had been chaotic for the entirety of the '70s, and my life in those years a pinballing from one home to the next, one mistake to the next, but now it was all ending with a whimper. Ronald Reagan was about to become president.

So naturally I took off for the Sierras. It wasn't a popular decision at home, but I was past worrying about that. I took a Greyhound bus from Orange County to Independence and walked west out of town, past Mary Austin's place. Looking at that neat little house gave me a shiver; I felt all of a sudden as if I had walked into a freezer. A premonitory chill. At the time I knew nothing of her life, but I did know that writers' lives were often strange. That little house chilled me.

West of town I started hitching but no one stopped. Despair struck far deeper than the usual despair of the hitchhiker when no one stops. Ever since Boston I had been making huge life mistakes, and now here I was, alone on a desert road, thumb out for no one. Something was cracking in me. I was walking out of my life.

Finally near sunset a van stopped and four guys welcomed me in. When they dropped me off at the Onion Valley trailhead, I hustled post-sunset up into the dusk. I camped by the first small lake; its inlet stream, a small waterfall, was noisy and I slept poorly. A mouse ran over my face and woke me.

Next morning I crossed Kearsarge Pass, feeling better. I was in the Sierra, on an autumn hike. It felt strange to be alone, but good. I turned north on the

Muir Trail, crossed Glen Pass, and got down to the nice campsite at the north end of the Rae Lakes just before a thunderstorm struck. I read Proust in my tent. Delicious incongruity of Proust in the Sierra; I had sliced *The Captive* in half to save weight. Proust's melancholy observations stuck me like knives. I marked passages as I read. Which ones? I still have that sliced volume, so I can look and see. Opening it at random, I find this marked: "It seems that events are larger than the moment in which they occur and cannot confine themselves in it. Certainly they overflow into the future through the memory we retain of them, but they demand a place also in the time that precedes them." Marcel! He was helping me see my situation, my fate. My future was pressing in on me, I could feel that as a tension in my stomach. Next marked passage: "Resigning myself was no longer possible in this new universe bursting with green leaves, in which I had awaked like a young Adam faced for the first time with the problem of existence, of happiness, who is not bowed down beneath the weight of the accumulation of previous negative solutions." My God! That too struck a nerve. It was not me reading Proust, but Proust reading me.

Next day I hiked north down the long canyon to the Woods Creek crossing. The bridge there was gone, or hadn't yet been built, and in crossing the creek downstream over a fallen log I lost the Muir Trail, not easy to do. I worked my way up the north bank until I stumbled across it again and continued on my way. Up toward Pinchot Pass I ran out of daylight and swerved off to the left, onto the rise overlooking the trail. Again it was windy and stormy through the night, again I read Proust.

The next day was stormy from the start. I put on my green Gore-Tex jacket and pants, sewn by me under Terry's direction. Dressed in them I felt like I was in a space suit, warm in the west wind, which began to include more and more flying snow as I hiked over Pinchot Pass and up Upper Basin. This was the day I described in my poem "Crossing Mather Pass," and it was just like that; as I hiked up into the dark low storm cloud capping Upper Basin, a kind of euphoria came into me. I was going to take off like Albertine and hope for the best. And I was so very comfortable in the Sierra; sun or storm it was my home, I knew what I was doing there and did not need or want my friends.

Better to fly solo and do what I pleased, to be in these mountains just them and me. I felt so very much at home.

Crossing Mather Pass

At the turning point of my life
I hiked toward Mather Pass.
With each step clouds thickened
Till the world was roofed in gray.

Thunder rolled from west to east
Like barrels over a floor
And as I crossed great Upper Basin
It began to snow.

I walked inside a white bubble,
Mounds of slush on every rock.
Warm and dry in pants and parka
I felt my old life slip away.

I gave it up. Fly away!
I'll never go back!
Each step up was a step away.

A shattered slope of stone,
The pass on top, unseen.
Trail swept up without a switchback,

Right to left in a single shot,
The Muir Trail crew's one touch of art.
It cost a life; I passed a plaque
And read the name: Robinson.

Then I was in the pass.
Snow flew up one side and
Down the other. In the lee
I sat but started shivering. Go.

Easy clumping down the trail
A white line on the northern slope
And then I saw the two big lakes
So far below. The sun came out:

White lace on wet gold granite.
A new world, a new life,
A new world I'll make it new!

I passed two hikers setting camp.
Did you come over in that storm?
Yes, I said, I left my life on the other side
And now I'm not afraid.

SIERRA PEOPLE (4)
Mary Austin

So, who was the Mary Austin who lived in that foreboding little house in Independence?

She was one of the first nationally known women writers to come out of the American West, and her autobiography *Earth Horizon* is one of the great American memoirs. Born Mary Hunter, in 1868, in Illinois, she moved with her widowed mother to California, after finishing college. She married Wallace Austin at age 22 and with him moved to Owens Valley, around 1891. The following year she gave birth to a child, a girl with developmental problems. After a few years and a temporary move to Los Angeles, she separated from her husband, placed her daughter in an institution in Northern California, became part of the Carmel artistic set, and got her first book published by Houghton Mifflin, one of the premier publishing houses in America. They marketed her as a writer of the American West, which she was, and for the rest of her life she made her way in the world as a prolific woman of letters, and a first-wave feminist. After years of travel, some spent in New York doing theater work, she ended up in Santa Fe, New Mexico, where she played an important part in the formation of the artistic community there, founding a theater that still exists, and collaborating with Ansel Adams, among other artists.

The book she's best remembered for is that first one, *The Land of Little Rain*, published in 1903. It's been reprinted many times and is still in print, deservedly famous as a smart and soulful portrait of the people, animals, and plants of the Sierra's east side. In 14 short essays (the book in its Dover edition is 70 pages long) she explores aspects of a landscape utterly unlike the one she and most of her readers had grown up in. The essays keep circling back to the land and its indigenes. Two are about the American mining culture that had recently arrived, but the rest are about the Shoshone and Paiutes still living on the margins of the valley, in "campoodies" by the streams exiting the Sierra canyons. Austin's sympathies are with the Native women, and the Hispanic women living in the towns, and she is skeptical and dismissive of the men recently arrived to look for gold or silver. There are two essays specifically about the Sierra itself, one about riding up to the passes, another about the water cycles. She writes, "Never believe what you are told, that midsummer is the best time to go up the streets of the mountain...for seeing and understanding, the best time is when you have the longest leave to stay." This from someone who could usually only get away on day trips. She goes on to say, "It is a pity we have let the gift of lyric improvisation die out. Sitting islanded on some gray peak above the encompassing wood, the soul is lifted up to sing the Iliad of the pines." In other words, she recognized the god zone. She writes, "You of the house habit can hardly understand the sense of the hills.... The business that goes on in the street of the mountain is tremendous, world-formative. Here go birds, squirrels, and red deer.... Whoever has firs misses nothing else. It goes without saying that a tree that can afford to take fifty years to its first fruiting will repay acquaintance."

Even better than *The Land of Little Rain*, for me, is her autobiography *Earth Horizon*, written near the end of her life. She mixes "I" and "Mary" in careful ways to make distinctions about herself. She is frank about marrying young to a person with whom she had nothing in common: "The third year of Mary's marriage was largely devoted to the discovery that between being born with intelligence and behaving intelligently there is a gulf fixed." That one made me laugh. In your sixties (which is how old she was when she wrote her memoir) you can laugh; in your twenties it's not so funny.

Animals and places often spoke to her. John O'Grady writes of her belonging to a tradition of "Transcendental Mediumship," and she writes of feeling these communications from the natural world "between my shoulders in the back of the neck." Maybe when I walked by her house in Independence, on my way out of my own early marriage and into the next life, that downdraft of frozen air that I felt was a message from her. There was definitely something uncanny about that house, as if it were still a little bolide of unhappiness and trapped fervor.

Austin tells some wonderful Sierra stories. Once when at home—not at the Independence house, but at a rented ranch nearer the Sierra escarpment—she went out with her baby girl to collect some of the trout that washed down "George's Creek" (George was a Paiute Indian chief) in the flash floods that followed thunderstorms high on the peaks. When Mary spotted a large trout flopping in the shallows of the creek, she put her baby under a sage bush while she got the trout out of the water. By chance a bald eagle had been going for that same trout, and when Mary chased the eagle away, it went right for her baby; as Mary leaped to drive it off her child, it clawed her on the arm before flapping away.

Human existence in her tiny desert town interested her too, and she sketched many neighbors with bold strokes. She wrote of the men who lived there, "There was a spell of the land over all the men who had in any degree given themselves to it, a spell of its lofty and intricate charm, which worked on men like the beauty of women. It was proof against all prior claims, and required no justification."

She cared more about the desert than the mountains, but that might be because she knew the desert better. She explored the Sierras mainly on horse-back, starting from her various homes on the valley floor. Riding up the east-side canyons, principally the big canyon leading to Kearsarge Pass, but also sometimes up George's Creek, and Symmes Creek, and Lone Pine Creek, she would come into the high country in mid- to late morning, then usually have to return home in the late afternoon. This is what she could manage, as far as getting up to altitude. It means she was always on the eastern slope. She never got inside the Sierra, that we know of; that might have made a difference in terms of her affections. As it is, she's really always writing about the Owens Valley, a province of the great American desert, and an antechamber to the Sierra. Although she later traveled widely, in pursuit of a bohemian life wild enough to raise eyebrows even now, she ended up in Santa Fe because it had all that she wanted most in a home: desert; artistic community; Indigenous people holding their culture together; mountains nearby. She had to work to make that artistic community in Santa Fe real, but it was a group effort, joined later by D. H. Lawrence and his wife Frieda. Over time it became a magnet for artists and intellectuals from all over the world. Nothing like that would have been possible in Independence, which even before the great LA water grab was a tiny village, and is now even smaller than it was when she lived there.

Seeing her house in Independence, on the road to Onion Valley, is always for me a poignant thing. It's a compact house, nondescript, but neat and well built; Mary designed it. It's got a state historical marker out front memorializing her time there. Her house in Santa Fe is also on the National Register of Historic Places. So she left a mark by way of her homes as well as her books, and since she was a writer of place, and of regional cultures, that seems appropriate. She was famous in her time, and she led a free life. But there's something lonely about that little house.

Her consistent advocacy for Native Americans, and Hispanic culture, clearly came from a feeling of solidarity. Her advocacy for those oppressed or forgotten in American society was an aspect of her feminism. Among the American writers of her generation she stands out for this ability to imagine and feel with people from other cultures.

There's a Mount Mary Austin, over 13,000 feet tall, just north of Onion Valley, to the east of the crest, overlooking Independence. The name was suggested by Norman Clyde. Could those two isolatoes have hit it off, I wonder? It's hard to say. Unlikely, I'd guess. But it was a thoughtful gesture on Clyde's part. It suggests he read her first book, at least, and recognized a fellow solitary, a fellow mountain lover.

I like to imagine her riding a horse up the dirt road to Onion Valley, and then going farther up the eastern slope on the old Native American trail that she called the mountain street, getting higher and higher above the broad valley, and finally stopping to get the big view, maybe even in Kearsarge Pass itself. She would feel elevated up there, and, if not at peace, then visionary with purpose. In any case she came back down from her Sierra ascents and changed her life—took hold of her destiny, wrote hard, got lucky in publishing, had friends and affairs, and a life in theater and letters—had the wild life of a bohemian artist of the early twentieth century, a woman writing her way through the world. I wonder if she saw it all one day up on Kearsarge Pass, all of it spread out below her—an unhappily married person conceiving a plan, after which she went back down and took the plunge toward freedom.

Mary Austin

PSYCHOGEOLOGY (2)
Altitude and Foreshortening

This is both psychogeology and physiology. The rocky mountain high that many of us feel—could it have something to do with altitude? I mean, you're high. Less than 6 percent of the Earth's surface sticks up more than 3,300 feet above sea level, and far less than that, more than 10,000 feet. High mountains are rare, and hardly anyone lives year-round above 15,000 feet, even in the Himalayas and the Andes. The Sierras are a remarkably high and narrow range.

Driving from sea level (Davis, California, lies at about 50 feet above sea level) to a Sierra trailhead, ranging from 5,000 to 10,300 feet, can be hard on the body. Arriving at a trailhead midday and hiking up to a camp even higher can be harder still. When I was young this only manifested itself as a reduced appetite. Then in my late forties I began to feel sick in the middle of the first night up there, if I was camping above 10,000 feet. I was suffering from altitude sickness, and when I figured that out, which took a couple of repetitions, I began to take Diamox for the first night. It works. The peculiar tingly feelings I sometimes feel as a result of taking it are well worth it for the elimination of any nausea. Over time I've calibrated the dose that is right for me. If the first night is under 9,000 feet, I don't need it; above that, I do. Maybe. More aging may have made me less susceptible, but I haven't experimented enough to be sure.

After that adjustment to altitude: What's it like? Is it different up there, is that part of the mountain high?

It's hard to say. The air is thinner, and thus clearer, and cooler. Warm in the sun, cool in the shade. The sky is often a darker shade of blue. The clouds tend to be lower in the sky; some float right at your level, or you're even in them, in a fog or a mist. Even cirrus clouds look lower, because they are. Or rather, you are higher.

So you can tell you're higher than you are at home. If you're on the outside of the range, where you can see down to the Owens Valley, or down to the Central Valley, you can see your altitude by way of the distant horizon, sometimes looking slightly curved. And the steep drop to the Owens Valley is a common east-side view. An airplane view, as I've said.

There is less air pressure up there; I've read that at 10,000 feet the air is about 70 percent as thick as at sea level. One effect of that is the stars at night are amazing. For the body, the less dense atmosphere means there is both less oxygen to be taken in, and less partial pressure to push that oxygen into your lungs' cells. The body adjusts with a slightly quickened breathing and heart rate that you can't notice or control. This is the cause of altitude sickness; that quickened breathing blows off more CO_2 than is normal, and this reduces the acidity of your blood. That change in your blood's pH, becoming more basic, causes the various symptoms of altitude sickness, which can include headaches, nausea, and lassitude. Bad cases are called "acute mountain sickness" and manifest as edema, meaning trapped water in cells. Both pulmonary edema and cerebral edema are very bad for you, and can be quickly fatal, as in, over a matter of hours.

Ordinary altitude sickness is an adjustment problem, and your body will reacidify your blood by natural means, usually within a day or two. Diamox speeds up that process in ways not fully understood. The side effects of Diamox, mostly its diuretic effect (lots of peeing) and its central nervous effect (tingling and numbness, especially in fingers and lips) are apparently not directly related to the desired reacidification of your blood.

One mild altitude effect is a lessened appetite. Some people get ravenous up there, but others don't get as hungry as their exertions should have made them. I'm in the latter group, which can be useful when packing food for a trip. When I'm up there I can only eat about a pound of food a day, minus its water weight.

But back to altitude itself: Why do we say *I feel high, I'm going to get high*—why *high*? Is it the extensive view when we are high? But that's so cognitive. Why should *feeling* high be a good thing? And if you don't go to the mountains, which many don't, how would you know that it feels good enough to use that phrase?

Probably it's just a metaphor in which height equals goodness, as if graphed on a chart. Lakoff and Johnson, *Metaphors We Live By*—a good book on this matter of the hidden spatial metaphors in language, orienting us to reality.

As for the reality itself, all I can report is that when I'm in the Sierra, I feel different, and good. It's physical and spiritual. That sense of elevation, of being raised up (again phrases assuming height equals goodness), gives me an underlying calm, humming like a continuo beneath my thoughts. By now it's somewhat associational, I'm sure; I feel good in the mountains because of all the previous times I've felt good in the mountains. Contentment, happiness, bliss. Being high is more than physiological, it has to do with wildness, with beauty. You couldn't take an elevator to the top of a high tower and feel it, and you don't feel it in an airplane, where the air pressure is set to the equivalent of 8,000 feet above sea level. No; it's an effect of history, and a manifestation of the sublime; the reduction of oxygen may not have anything to do with it.

Although the Sierras are high, they are to a certain extent a high plateau, as I've said. It's a tilted and deeply etched plateau. Many mountain ranges give you much greater heights to contemplate. In the Sierra, the ridges around you are often only a couple thousand feet higher than you are. If you're in Fort William, near sea level in Scotland, looking up at Ben Nevis, you're seeing a slope twice as tall as that. Sitting on Kala Pattar, in the Khumbu region of Nepal, you're looking up at Everest, only a few miles away, and it's 10,000 feet higher than you. And so on.

But strangely, there is an effect called foreshortening that makes these differences between heights less apparent to observers. The truth is, when you're looking up at terrain on a tilt, you can't see it very well. There's an optical illusion that comes into play that is simply the result of seeing the vertical part of a slope without being able to judge the horizontal part of it very well, so that things tend to look much steeper than they are when you actually get on them. Also, partly as a result of this exaggerated vertical effect, slopes seen from below all tend to look roughly the same height. The closer you are to one, the more this happens. You look up from the foot of Half Dome, it looks about the same as it does when you're looking up the west side of Rockbound Pass, or the north face of the Eiger, or even the southwest face of Everest. I'd say they all look to be roughly a thousand feet tall. Even when you know better, you can't make the adjustment. You need to get back a good distance to make distinctions between one height and another. You can't get far enough away from Tehipite Dome to see it as 5,000 feet tall, for instance, but in the Alps, you can do it; underneath it, the Eiger looks the same height as any other prominence, but from the lakeside town of Thun, about 20 miles away from the Berner Oberland, you can see that that famous north wall is simply enormous. They say it's the same with Everest, that the Kala Pattar in the Gokyo valley, about ten miles farther away from Everest than the one over Everest

Observation Pass from Amphitheater Lake

Base Camp, reveals how tall Everest is in a way that being on the closer Kala Pattar can't. (Kala Pattar means "black hill.")

This effect, or these two effects—slopes seeming steeper than is actually the case, and quite different heights looking about the same—both get called foreshortening. In the Sierra as anywhere else, this foreshortening effect can be really deceiving.

I offer as an example the north side of Observation Pass, as seen from Amphitheater Lake. Oh my God. Looks vertical, an awful prospect if you're thinking of going up and over it. My backpacker friend Djina tells me that she and her hiking partner Julie looked at it and said no way, and went east and took on something much worse instead. Because as it turns out, Observation Pass is quite easy. The clue in the photo on the left is to notice the slope to the right of that awful snow cornice at the low point, the part that looks speckled or slightly furry—this indicates scree or small talus, which means that slope has to be angled at less than the angle of repose, or else that rubble would have

Joe and Darryl high on Observation Pass north side

slid off the slope, leaving it clean rock. So that's a clue to the actual steepness, and despite how it looks from below, and I'd say it looks like a nasty 60- or 70-degree angle, if you hike up to that point, you'll find yourself on a narrow band of slope you can handle. See the photo of Joe and Darryl on that slope to get a sense of the angle as it really is when crossing it.

Another example: look first at Split Mountain as seen from the north (from Ed Lane Pass!). Steep, right? Although again, the slightly furry look of the slope is a little clue that it might not be so.

Split Mountain from the north

Then look at a view of that same slope from the west. We just walked up that rise on the left, to one of the best views in the Sierra.

A trick to deal with foreshortening, sometimes described by mountaineers, is to tilt your head to the side and look at the slope with your eyes stacked

Split Mountain from the west

vertically; this is said to apply more depth perception to the angle of the slope. I find this of limited effectiveness, because the parallax you gain is so very tiny, but it's always worth a try.

This is also a good situation in which to look at topo maps, to help gauge what you're seeing. And it's also a good situation in which to have some faith in your fellow hikers, and the general Sierra community. If a Sierra slope is listed as being class 2 in the Sierra Club system, it almost certainly will be; so there you go. It might turn out to be horribly strenuous, but isn't going to be dangerously steep.

So, yes, the thrill of the purely unknown is much reduced in modern Sierra hiking. Not that you can't find many a slope never described in the guide-books. But I don't deliberately seek out those nondescripts, except for very occasionally, and I don't go up there without maps to see how that feels. Snow camping's erasure of trails is maybe as much as I need in pursuit of that kind of return to unknown wilderness.

Although it is fun to try a slope never described in the literature; and going out without maps is not a bad idea. David Brower used to claim he could be dropped blindfolded anywhere in the Sierra, and take the blindfold off and within an hour determine where he was. Sounds impressive, but all real Sierra lovers could do that, because the range is narrow, and has such highly idiosyncratic ridges and peaks that you would soon see where you were. I could definitely do it, and I don't think I'm at all unusual in that.

But getting lost is a topic for other chapters. As for foreshortening, it's going to happen whether you're new to the mountains or know all about this unshakable optical illusion. It's part of mountain life, one of the immutable facts of psychogeology.

SIERRA PEOPLE (5)
Mapping the Territory

The map is not the territory, this is always true, but it's extra true when the maps you have are wrong. Why mapmakers feel compelled to fill in their blanks with fictional features is an enduring question, and maybe the answer is always right there: It's embarrassing to have blank spots on your map, even when there are blank spots in your knowledge. Maybe especially then. Maps don't like blanks because people don't like ignorance. So *terra incognita* becomes *terra errores,* and as for the effect of these maps on users of them, another Latin phrase is useful, as always: *Caveat emptor.*

This gold rush era map is blissfully ignorant of everything about the Sierra except its general location and its crest-and-divides structure.

The Sierra hikers of the 1880s and 1890s were therefore exploring a range that was not just imperfectly known, but improperly mapped, and their joy in discovering what was really there is palpable still in their writing. The first ten years of the *Sierra Club Bulletin* are filled with modestly exuberant articles by people who went up into the range, usually from the west side, and found new things. Many people were part of this project, but I'll only mention a few of my favorites here.

One was a sheepherder, better remembered than the other sheepherders because he was the most forthcoming about where he had gone and what he found there: Frank Dusy. In finding good summer pasturage for his sheep, he went up the deep canyon of the Middle Fork of the Kings Canyon, starting right at the confluence with the South Fork. Thus he was the first European American to see Tehipite Dome. He took a camera back with him to document the find, and after that, people wanted to see it. Then, by going up the canyon of the Middle Fork farther, he got first to Simpson Meadow, then to Grouse Meadow, another great place for sheep. His entire route out-yosemited Yosemite in several respects, including beauty. But not ease of access. For a while in those first decades, people made the effort to see Tehipite Dome, including Muir, as I said; then it was forgotten, as being too much trouble to get to. It's the tallest dome of all, but the stretch from the confluence of the Middle Fork with the South Fork up to Tehipite Valley is a wicked bushwhack, with lots of rattlesnakes. So—forget about it!

As for Dusy, though it seems strange that he wanted even more forage for his sheep than he had already found in Simpson and Grouse Meadows, they say Sierra sheep numbered in the tens of thousands back then; and also, it seems Dusy was interested in seeing places for their own sake. In any case, he ascended the easy canyon wall east of Grouse Meadow, came up over the Lip, and found himself in what we now call Dusy Basin, the most beautiful basin of them all. Lucky man! Though we have very little writing from him, still, the sense comes down through the years of a happy Sierra explorer.

Recently I discovered that this same Frank Dusy lived in Fresno, and was the inventor of a precursor of the modern earthmover, used in his time to dig irrigation ditches. That's a strange combination of interests and occupations, but I guess that's what happens when one lives a nomadic two-season life. Another interesting Sierra bundle of contradictions.

The greatest figure of this early mapping era was Joseph Nisbet LeConte Jr., often called Little Joe LeConte, and usually signing his articles J. N. LeConte, to distinguish himself from his famous father Joseph LeConte Sr., an early UC professor who traveled across the Sierra in 1870, and helped found the Sierra Club. LeConte Sr. is a problematic figure to be discussed elsewhere in this book, but his son was a Berkeley kid, who later also became a professor at UC, in mechanical engineering. He's another person who fell in love with the Sierra and devoted his life to it thereafter. From now on I'll call him Joe, and I'll call his dad Joseph.

Joe particularly enjoyed mapping the range, making many systematic explorations with surveying tools, and completely overthrowing the bad maps from before his time. Very active in the Sierra Club, he married a fellow member he met during club outings, Helen Marion Gompertz. The two of them were Sierra Club royalty for their entire adult lives. They summered up there together, even after their children were born, and Joe was instrumental in finding links in the route for the Muir Trail, as well as getting the basic geography of the range sorted out. By the time USGS professionals like George Davis got into the game, Joe had established the layout of the range and many peak elevations, making the work of the USGS cartographers much easier. Between 1890 and 1907, maps of the Sierra shifted from mostly wrong to almost completely right, and Joe made a big contribution to this effort, which he thoroughly enjoyed. He took along heavy cameras and glass plates, and Ansel Adams later collected an album of his photos, praising them for their clean expressive style. He was also a bold climber, and his first ascent, with three friends, of North Palisade is a classic of early Sierra climbs, well told by him in the pages of the *Bulletin*.

Another great early explorer was Stanford art professor Bolton Brown. He was a fin-de-siècle rebel in his professional context at Stanford, often in trouble for his belief in nude life studies as being crucial to drawing classes. When in the

Sierra, he was an active and wide-ranging explorer and climber. Like Joe LeConte, he married a woman who also loved the Sierra, Lucy Fletcher, and they took their infant child up there on horseback and fed her on chocolate and trout for entire summers, rambling daily from base camps, and also, before the baby came, backpacking together. Lucys Footpass was just the start of a day for them that remains awesome to contemplate, including a first ascent and traverse of Mount Ericsson, a gnarly peak that they named for a friend of theirs. Their first ascent of the class 3 west side of Mount Williamson was the capstone of that same trip. Brown's solo first ascent of Mount Clarence King has been called the finest climb of the nineteenth century, and he also pioneered winter backpacking in the Sierra, dragging a sled east over the Tablelands and in the process destroying two sets of boots. He reported that 50 pounds of gear would keep you comfortable on a week's trip up there in winter—this in the 1890s.

All these explorers and others are well described by Daniel Arnold in his excellent book *Early Days in the Range of Light*. Bolton Brown in particular is revealed by Arnold as a complex man with a poignant life story; his devotion to the Sierras took him up there so often that eventually he lost both his Stanford job and Lucy, who divorced him. Another case of loving the Sierra too much.

The last of that generation I'll mention here is Theodore Solomons. One clear winter day, as a boy growing up outside Fresno, he saw the entire snow-covered range forming his eastern horizon, and the idea came to him of establishing a trail that ran as close to the crest of the range as possible, from Yosemite down to Kings Canyon—the whole stretch that he could see. That became his project for a decade of his youth, before his interest turned to Alaska. In his Sierra years he made several pioneering backpacking trips, one with Leigh Bierce, the son of Ambrose Bierce. Always he was searching for a best route for a John Muir Trail, as he named it. Although he didn't finish that job, he did a lot of good work on it, and obviously had a lot of fun.

My favorite story from his life is almost like an Ambrose Bierce short story. He and his companion warmed themselves one cold night by setting a fire against the side of a tall tree. They went to sleep in rolled blankets, and woke when the tree fell on them.

It was one of those old-growth monsters of the forest zone, so, not just its huge trunk but any of its many massive limbs could have crushed the men dead. As it turned out, they were both able to stand up out of their blankets. They found the tree's fallen trunk lay between them, so tall that they could barely see each other over it. Major branches trapped them in the spots where they had lain, such that it took a while for them to work their way free. By a great stroke of luck, they had slept in two of the only places they could have been situated without getting crushed. After they had freed themselves, they were so freaked out that they ended their trip, turning downhill and taking whatever route seemed easiest to get themselves out of the Sierra as soon as possible.

Desperate and even irrational retreats like this one ended every Sierra trip Solomons ever made. Maybe that's why he headed for Alaska. And maybe it's this ragged aspect of his career that makes me fond of him. Mount Solomons is the first peak west of Muir Pass, at the midpoint of the Muir Trail: a nice memorial. Another lucky man!

GEOLOGY (4)

Fellfields

PSYCHOGEOLOGY: THE GOD ZONE

All these people who go up into the Sierra and are so smitten by it: Why? Which part of the experience causes such appeal, such powerful surges of affection? To people who've never been there it probably seems mysterious, as it does also to those of us it's happened to. And it's no doubt a little different for everybody. But I'm going to make a simple first cut, and say it has to do with the part of the Sierra that lay under glacial ice through the ice ages.

That means a big percentage of the high part of the range, of course, so the answer doesn't explain much. How is a formerly-under-ice granite landscape so different from anywhere else? And different in ways that make some people love it?

Well, it's rock. Granite, in this case, that has been smoothed, burred, polished, and so on, by the immense weight of ice that lay on it and slowly slid downhill. Everything portable got taken away in that action. So it's mostly granite after glaciation. There's only been 10,000 years since the ice left, so often what you're seeing is still simply big slabs of exposed bedrock. And across a lot of these highlands, above say 10,000 feet, not much has grown since the ice left.

And yet it's not barren. It's not like the nearly lifeless deserts of this world, like the Dry Valleys in Antarctica, or the desiccated ranges east of the Sierra, out there in its big rain shadow. The Sierra catches a considerable amount of rain and snow every year, refilling a dense hydroscape of lakes and ponds, and streams both permanent and seasonal. The only things life needs to flourish are heat, water, and some minerals. So there's lots of life in the high Sierra.

What has happened, therefore, at this particular combination of altitude, latitude, precipitation, and rock forms, is this: big rumpled areas of bare granite, slightly furred or garnished with life. Very often, when we are hiking up out of the forests below into this higher land, seeing the highest trees grow dwarfish and twisted around us, turning into a kind of bonsai ground cover that is often no higher than the typical snowbank heights in winter (the snow having protected these plants like a blanket), we look around and say to each other, Now we're in the god zone.

It can be thought of by way of the life zones model, as first proposed by Alexander von Humboldt, following his studies in the Andes and elsewhere, and now a commonplace among ecologists. As you rise up a mountainside you move through life zones that, if distributed on flat ground, would be the equivalent of moving many latitude lines to the north (or the south, if in the Southern Hemisphere). Going 200 meters higher is somewhat like moving a latitude line nearer the pole (a little less than 70 miles); thus ascending the eastern

The Sierra's east side, a 10,000-foot-tall escarpment, is a living example of Humboldt's life zones concept—note the layer of pines across the middle, happy in their comfort zone.

escarpment of the Sierra is like moving about 1,000 miles to the north. The heights thus form a local sub-Arctic, you might say.

In the mountains, when you get above tree line, much of that higher land is what some ecologists call fellfields: *fell* is Gaelic for "stone." These are stone fields, where the land is more than half stony, the rest covered by low-lying cushion plants with strong roots and the ability to withstand both months of drought and months under snow. Because of the rumpled nature of the land itself, small communities can form in hollows that are like little meadows, with grasses and sedges and taller plants beginning to shade out the cushiony ground-cover plants. When these plants die, their bodies become part of the soil that nourishes the subsequent generations of the same species, and also of different plants that need richer soil to thrive. Thus the meadows grow by accumulation, composting themselves and welcoming newcomers that, when their seeds float in on the breeze or get transported by birds, can survive. But big bare rocks still obtrude everywhere, so the little life communities are small. And as the seasons and years and centuries pass, the rocks break apart into talus, then scree, and then sand, partly because the lichens and little plants that can live in gravel are eating parts of the rock itself, which then breaks up. The rocks get weathered—meaning hit by rain, brushed by wind, and struck by photons from the sun—also eaten by living things—until they crack. The living things die and turn into the soils in which more life can live.

It's a slow process, too slow to be seen in action, but it can be understood and described. *Land Above the Trees*, by Ann Zwinger and Beatrice Willard, does this very beautifully. Their detailed explanations of what they call sky islands—a great illustration of science as devotion—helped me to understand the Sierra's fellfields better, after which I saw them better too. That's how seeing works.

The experience of being up there in a fellfield is not so easy to convey. All the other elements come into play: the altitude and light, the long views under the big sky. Underfoot, the variety of forms is part of the glory—a few steps, when moving up in what I call a vertical meadow, meaning really a tilted or terraced meadow, take you past different types of plants, mosses, grasses, flowers, and lichens, all clustering in different kinds of microbiomes, and always intermixed with big chunks of rock. Hiking along, upstream especially, keeps bringing surprises; oh, here's another perfect garden! This couldn't be improved by moving even a single rock or blade of grass! Look at that set of concentric terraces, as on rice-growing mountainsides in Indonesia—solifluction did that, sunlight and melted snow and gravity, and the plants' roots, together making long curving dams, as if miniature farmers have been industriously at work for centuries—which is basically true. And look, there's a buckwheat—I think—there are so many different kinds of buckwheat. And saxifrage, after which I named my terraforming scientist Sax, in my Mars trilogy: Latin for "rock breaker." Which that plant does. Now that's a good name. So are most of the lichen names, all those different kinds plastering the granite like living paint, their names usually metaphors, tiny poems. Battleship-gray lichen, eggyolk lichen, bloodstain lichen, rock pimple lichen, peppermint drop lichen, sulphur lichen, map lichen, witch's hair lichen—on and on it goes.

But this is to turn the experience into language, and the commentary in my head. Often it happens so fast as I walk that there is no time to think, I'm too busy seeing it, taking it in, making sure I don't trip on something as I look and walk.

Comparisons to other places, or even to art forms, are often circular. Fell-fields look like Persian carpets, because Persian carpet makers were trying to convey the look of the fellfields in the Zagros Mountains towering over Tehran (this is Zwinger's observation). Then also they look like Zen gardens, because the Zen gardeners in Japan were trying to convey the look of Japanese mountain landscapes, in gardens down at sea level (Gary Snyder told me this). Millefleur tapestries in France were repeating patterns that had been seen in the Alps. And so on. This imagery from art helps those who've never been up there to see it. Photos can help too. But this is one of the many aspects of the Sierra where pictures can't capture the experience of being there. Muir's written raptures tried to convey the impression by direct linguistic enthusiasm, and my friends and I do that too, with our talk of being in the god zone, of reaching cosmicity.

Rock and gravity. Sunlight and scree. And water. Water follows the path of least resistance, it pools in depressions, including depressions filled with sand, after which it seeps or falls over the low point in that depression, down to the next flat place. And life follows water. More water, more life: around every pond grows a verge of moss and lawn, a garden. And even a little water, even sporadic water, even very infrequent water, will be enough for certain tough low plants. Penstemon is a tiny flowering bush, for instance, so tough it can live in broken rock almost as well as lichens can; and yet its flowers are as big as a fingernail. Any little protected spot is enough to let these plants grow, right up to the highest peaks in the range. So you get flowers springing right out of the rocks.

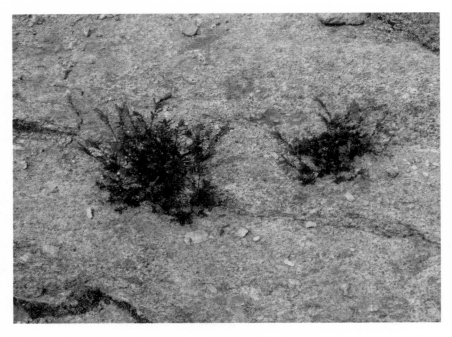

Penstemon happy in granite

The higher you go, the greater proportion of stone to flower, until at the highest elevations you are in a rock garden, but even there, some of those pebbles are alive.

I know the names of rocks and animals, I don't know the names of trees and flowers. Every few years I learn some of these names and forget them again. Sometimes I've learned some plant names in order to write a scene in a book, then written the scene, then forgotten the names. But up there, in fell-field terrain, in the vertical meadows, I never lose the sense of walking in a miracle.

On the Sierra crest at Granite Bear Pass

SIERRA PEOPLE (6)

Common Neighbors

There are animals up there that I know pretty well. We see them often, and always with delight. There aren't all that many of them, either of individuals or species. I'll speak here first of the common neighbors, the ones we see all the time. Rare sightings I'll get to later.

Most common are marmots. God bless them. Rodents, like woodchucks and groundhogs, or giant prairie dogs. Not seen in zoos, typically, I don't know why. They hibernate in winter. Like big cats in size, maybe a little bigger. Blond and brown and auburn, with streaks of black and white, and black noses. They're comfortable around people, they even show off it seems, sitting on rocks and tilting their heads to let you know they see you and don't care. They eat plants, including grass seeds. Once I watched a young one wandering slowly across a meadow, reaching out with a rather human-seeming arm and hand to pull nearby grass stalks to its face, thus bunching the seeds at the top of the stalks, so that it could munch those seeds off in a few bites and then chew reflectively. Looking across the meadow I realized that during that week, anyway, this person's food supply was effectively infinite.

They have some predators, including raptors from the air, coyotes and foxes, bobcats and pine martens; but the raptors seem not that numerous, and the hunting mammals seem rare at the very highest elevations, where marmots often hang out (we've seen marmots on top of Whitney); they really like talus slopes and bouldery fellfields. They often perch on boulder tops to have a look around; they like a good view, just like anyone else. You can be sure of that because you see them perched on a good prospect looking around; and also, whenever you get onto a big boulder yourself, say to get a good view of the sunset, that boulder top is almost sure to be covered with marmot turds. Also there's a kind of lichen that likes nitrogen, called red jewel lichen, and down the sides of these marmot lookout-post boulders, this red lichen tends to spill, thriving exactly where marmot urine would run off the rocks. It's very clear: marmots enjoy watching a good sunset. This I find moving.

Their alarm signal is a high whistle cut off at the end, like a cheep. The young ones will startle at this watchman's cheep, and galumph across the grass to get under a rock. Their homes are under big boulders, in crevices presumably too small for anything larger to get down. Predators, like foxes and coyotes and bobcats and wolverines, back when there were wolverines, also mountain lions, can't usually get down into marmot homes. And so the marmots live their lives without too much hassle. You see older individuals, in the same way you can spot dogs who are older: grizzled muzzles, some gaps in

Marmot posing

the fur, some loss of sheen. Youth too is easy to spot. Gender, no. You can never tell. Quite a few of them like to show off for the camera. They pose on top of rocks quite patiently. They respond to voices, and look back at you. They're used to humans and do not fear them. They are great people.

Deer: What can you say? They're everywhere on this continent, and there are often more of them than the land can support; they surge and crash in population. Their main predator is the automobile. They don't seem very smart; not as smart as marmots, for instance. But they are very beautiful.

In the Sierra, they don't fear people. Not in the national parks anyway. They eat grass and all kinds of leaves, looking up at you from time to time, aware you are there but unafraid. Occasionally one will walk right into camp, or right by us on the trail—once, we could have reached out with our bare feet and touched one passing by.

It all combines to mean that you have to remember they are wild animals, getting by in the world on their own. That fact is always enough to make me love them. That they are common is all to the good. Although letting their predators live on this continent would be good for them too. What's good is what's good for the land: Leopold's slogan is the ultimate rubric, the highest morality. What that means in the Sierra is that we need to help the wolves and wolverines come back. As we do everywhere.

Quite often we see more deer than people on our trips. We stand, resting our chins on our walking poles, and watch them eat, sometimes for half an hour at a time. A bunch of mammals together in a meadow, at peace. Or spotting one across a lake at dawn. They get by in this world without our help, without any technologies, surviving by way of expertise and endurance alone, unclothed in the world but competent in it.

They squat like a dog pooping if they want to scare you; perhaps they think this makes them look bigger, and thus harder to bring down. It's not a good look for them.

The bucks walk over the rocks with magnificent posture and movement, with flow. Sometimes the guys seem as self-conscious as marmots, or fashion models. Maybe carrying that heavy rack of antlers makes them aware of their magnificence. Of all the deer, these bucks are the ones most likely to get spooked and run off. They are very fast.

Bears are up there for sure, although they don't seem to go very often up into the god zone; there's less for them to eat up there. They're down in the forest, looking for food. Seeing them always gets our fullest attention, and I notice none of our photos of them is quite in focus, as if we've taken them on the verge of running away. The bears look and move like people in fur coats, or like a cross between people and dogs. It's obvious they don't see well. Once a giant cinnamon-colored one followed us up the Bubbs Creek Trail all day, and that night knocked our bear canisters around in frustration. That racket woke us, but I was so deeply asleep that as I came to the surface, and saw the bear walk right by my head, I immediately fell back asleep.

Another time we saw a movement in the forest, and then a young bear skulked by us in a hurry, looking guilty to be seen. Abashed.

Often by the side of the road they run away from our car, sensibly.

Unhappy youth

Last year we saw a black bear that was truly black. More on him later, but here I'll say this one was demolishing a pine cone to get at the pine nuts inside, and as with the young marmot eating grass seeds, I realized that if pine nuts were on his or her menu, this bear's food supply was also effectively infinite.

At the opposite end of the size scale are pikas. We see more pikas than bears. They are about the same shape, but pikas are the size of mice. They're more closely related to rabbits than to mice, and knowing that helps one to see them better; they are odd-looking mice, but great-looking tiny rabbits, with big translucent ears. Their look is a lot smarter than rabbits', I have to say: very observant, industrious, indomitable. They look like living pebbles. Two or three times I've seen them with grass stalks clutched in their mouths, 10 or 20 neatly arranged such that their mouths bite the stalks right in the middle, so they extend like green whiskers, twice as long as the pika's body. Nest building, or food collecting. They bite off grass and flower stalks and lay them in the sun to dry, then take them into their holes for winter food. They have an active subnivean life in the winters, and live on stored seeds and berries and leaves, and the stalks they've dried.

Pikas' little bodies are sensitive to rises in air temperature beyond what they're adapted to, and if exposed to prolonged excessive heat they will die. (We are like that too, at a wet-bulb 35 temperature index.) They are thus endangered creatures, moving higher and higher on sky islands that will eventually top out and give them no more relief. We're like them in that also. The Earth is our sky island.

There are also lots of squirrels and chipmunks. Belding's ground squirrels live in grassy hills like little prairie dogs; we only see them occasionally, but the typical squirrel or chipmunk camp robber is very common, and has to be guarded against, as they are fearless and have sharp teeth that can cut through not just plastic bags, but backpacks.

Some of my ecologist friends tell me the high Sierra is relatively depopulate when it comes to animals. They'd rather sit in a marsh, where the fecundity is great. There just isn't enough food up in the god zone to support much of a community, they say. It makes sense. But there are animals up there. So I like it for that, as well as for other reasons. My friends can have their marsh.

Seeing the animals up there used to be kind of a side thing for me, exciting but incidental, but as the years have passed each encounter has become a deeper and deeper thrill. I've realized how bad the situation is for wild creatures everywhere, and I feel the awful dread of the oncoming mass extinction event we are creating. We need to make room for these people. The vast stretch of the Sierra as a single habitat corridor, where humans are visitors only, and the local animals are left to live in peace, is now more precious than it's ever been. In fact the whole idea of wilderness has been transformed and redeemed by the necessity of making adequate living room for these fellow citizens of ours. Protected areas like the high Sierra of California are now wildlife refugia, serving as early parts of the Half-Earth project, which is becoming a life-or-death thing, the ultimate existential test for our species and our biosphere. Without spaces like these we are doomed to cause a mass extinction event. So they are not just playgrounds, but sanctuaries.

These days I keep my eye peeled, and when I see animals in the Sierra, even marmots, even deer, I pause and feel blessed. These wild creatures are sacred. As Muir put it, they are our horizontal brothers and sisters.

MOMENTS OF BEING (2)

A Sierra Day: Rambling and Scrambling

Most Sierra days, after packing up and taking a last look around the campsite to make sure we haven't left anything behind, we take off and hike cross-country, off trail, because that's what we're trying for. That's what we're up there to do.

Carter and Darryl on an easy morning ramble down to Woods Creek, looking across at the Castle Domes

Anyone who can walk without pain could enjoy hiking cross-country in the Sierra. It's not a skill sport, or to put it more precisely, it's not a specific sports skill having to do with eye-hand coordination. Eye-foot coordination, maybe. Balance and the like. But we evolved as a species by walking; we evolved in order to walk better. Natural selection was selecting for that skill, so, barring a physical problem, we're good at it. This is central to the joy of backpacking, making this discovery. We're born to walk!

Not that it doesn't help to be in shape. Now that so many of us sit all day, and get around in cars, we're not as tough as people used to be. Coleridge and Wordsworth used to walk ten miles to visit each other, and then walk home that same night. They were not athletes, they were humans in the eighteenth century. These days, those of us who do physical work for a living are still strong, but back then even writers were strong, because it was walk or get nowhere. So they walked.

With some preparatory getting in shape, anyone can still do that. If you're young, you're already strong enough for the Sierra, no matter how much you sit around at home. Youth itself is a kind of strength.

What I am advocating for here is not mountain climbing. Sierra scrambling is nothing like any of the extreme sports, it doesn't share their mentality, or partake in the brutal tests-to-destruction that appear to dominate contemporary culture's idea of what people are supposed to do in mountains. Hang off cliffs, fall and die; get caught in storms and die; climb Everest and die. Thus mountaineering in our time.

Rambling and scrambling are not like that. We try not to get onto any slope steeper than a staircase. This means the hardest stuff we hike over is rated class 2, using a classification system that was developed in the Sierra by early Sierra Club climbers. In this system the scale goes from 1 to 5, where 1 means walking, and 2 means getting on slopes where you might use your hands for balance, or as an aid up, and if you fell, you could only sprain an ankle or the like. Class 3, which we try to avoid, is hands-on for sure, partly to help yourself up or down, partly to hold on to the slope, because a fall, though unlikely, could in theory kill you. Classes 4 and 5, even more so. For both 4 and 5, ropes are advised for protection in case of a fall, and 5 gets divided into decimals, though it no longer stops at 5.10—it goes up to 5.15 now, to indicate levels of technical climbing difficulty. Class 5.5 and above is really gecko land, but all the terrain in classes 4 and 5 is steeper than you want to fall from, as the result would be fatal.

This brief stretch of class 3 we crossed on hands and knees.

These distinctions are easy to make in the field. In fact we have found it impossible to avoid noticing the border between class 2 and class 3, because it's quite vivid, often even a bit traumatic. On class 2 you're having fun, on class 3 you're scared—this is an easy distinction to make! And in fact I've crawled on my hands and knees over a good percentage of the class 3 terrain I've crossed. By and large we stay on class 2. And the Sierra Nevada of California is the great class 2 playground of the world.

The game we play up there—mainly a game, but with an aesthetic, philosophical, or spiritual aspect—is partly like walking through a great art museum, partly like orienteering, and partly like fooling around on a jungle gym when you were five years old. Mostly we ramble, sometimes we scramble. Scrambling is very simple monkey fun, and the rambling over such a landscape is beautiful.

So our days up there are occupied by a kind of game. It's not a return to nature, not exactly; in the Anthropocene it isn't even clear what nature is, and maybe that was never clear. Our activity is supported by many kinds of high-tech products; this has always been true, right back into the Paleolithic. Ötzi the Iceman's kit was extremely sophisticated.

However you think of it, backpacking won't save the world. It isn't virtuous, although it's true that the carbon burn involved, once you start walking, is extremely low. Backpacking is not dangerous, and often it isn't dramatic. Still, there is something deeply attractive in it. Central to the attraction is simply the act of walking. Walking is key. If you go backpacking mainly to enjoy your time in camp, and only endure the time you spend walking from camp to camp, then backpacking ultimately will not appeal to you. Because it's mostly about walking.

The Baier waltzes across, Joe waiting his turn.

Admittedly, scrambling is a bit different. When we were kids, my friend Steve and I would be taken by our moms to Corona del Mar beach, near Newport Beach, California. One game we played was to race each other out to the end of the jetty bordering the beach. The jetty is about 300 yards long, made of giant boulders dropped in place to make a pretty neat causeway, the boulder tops roughly flat or just slightly tilted, the gaps between them ranging from an inch to three feet. We were eight years old, barefoot, and running at full speed over these giant rocks. We got pretty good at it. Thinking of it now, I shudder, and if I see it clearly in my mind, I feel a little sick to my stomach. It was crazy. If I tried to do it now I would kill myself. Maybe my lifelong battle with plantar fasciitis had its origins in this game. But we enjoyed it thoroughly. And now, in the Sierra, when we get into similar territory, created by glaciers rather than people wielding a crane from the back of a railcar, I curse like anyone else, and take it slow; but I enjoy it too. I call it boulder ballet. It's a vivid callback to my innocent childhood, when so many dangers were danced over like that. And I remember Steve, with love and regret. To die at 16 is a miserable fate. In his last six months he saw it coming, and as we played board games together at his house, he looked at me with a look I can't quite characterize: distant and remote, gentle and wise—as wise as any human ever gets. And a little hungry. He was protecting me from knowing too much, and said little about what he was going through. But from his look, I know this: he would not have risked his life for any game. This may be part of what's behind my lifelong revulsion at the idea of climbing.

Sierra walking is not risking one's life, not even close, but there can be a bit of adrenaline when scrambling comes into play. It's problem solving, keeping your balance, not falling down, and heading somewhere.

The main problem is, which way to go? This is cross-country hiking in a nutshell. Choosing your way, step after step. Some find this wearying, and it is effortful—just as any game is effortful.

In San Diego we would go see surfing films, and the audience would hoot in approval or laugh scornfully, depending on the line the surfers on the screen took. Busywork to show one's virtuosity was scorned by the crowd, but just staying inertly on the wave was not approved either. What they liked to see was a surfer shaping his ride organically to the wave's surprises, and getting through problems with style and ingenuity—a nifty fitting into the evolving givens of the situation, accomplished decisively. That would get a hoot.

That's what cross-country hiking is like. You're surfing a wave that is stuck and motionless (or moving extremely slowly compared to you!), so that you have to provide the locomotion yourself; but the principle of where to go is the same. When you look up a complicated slope above you, or across one, or down at one, it's always rumpled, and often there are parts of it that are out of your view. Can you deduce or intuit a line that looks good? I'm always looking for some give-and-take with the opportunities and blockages. If you pay attention, there often appears a sort of staircase inlaid into the granite, revealing itself for your convenience as you find it. That's the clean line on that slope. Reinhold Messner once remarked that his climbing lines are his true sentences. I like to find a clean hiking line in just the same way I like to write a clear sentence.

Joe finds a line up Midway Mountain.

*   *   *

We start hiking after breakfast. If the day's hike demands it, we can be off early, but on normal days, having gotten up soon after sunrise, we depart at more like 9:00 a.m. Pack on back, feeling a bit lighter than the day before, very nice. Lighter by the weight of a dinner and breakfast; that means about a pound lighter, sometimes closer to two.

Typically we've camped at ponds near tree line, usually between 10,000 and 12,000 feet in altitude. Campsites in this zone have the best views combined with the most comfort. So the morning hike is likely to consist of going either up or down. That's pretty much a given in the Sierra, of course, but what I mean is, we are usually either continuing up to some pass, or going down into a canyon before making a rise to some farther pass. Rare is the day we don't go over a pass, and two in a day is not unusual. This comes from going cross-country, and hiking in areas where basins are high and small. These clusters of basins are what we seek out.

Typical days cover from 5 to 15 miles, depending on the terrain and our desires. When we are on trails we go about two miles an hour, with downhill being not much faster than uphill. Hiking cross-country, the average is perhaps half a mile an hour, but this is only an average, and says little. In some off-trail places you can walk almost as fast as on trail, while in others you get caught in various versions of Zeno's paradox. Bushwhacking in particular is very slow. These slowest days are lamented, but in the way one groans at puns. Getting up to a pass is celebrated as a moment of expansion and exhilaration. One of the high points of the day, so to speak.

Wild basins have no trails in them—that's part of what makes them the god zone, that absence of trails. In some senses, they're wilderness.

Of course we have detailed topographical maps with us. But basins are often not smooth, nor do they have regular patterns in their rumples, unless you think of a broken maze as regular. You often can't see all of what you would need to see to determine a route very far ahead. The result is a lot of unavoidable up and down.

Going uphill, you often can't see what's above you past a horizon that can be quite nearby; just 50 feet above there can be a temporary skyline. The implication is that the slope above that skyline is less steep than what you're on now, or else you would see it too. When going down, on the other hand, you can usually see quite a long way below, but steeper drop-offs in that downslope can create lips you can't see over; so even though you might be able to see what's 300 feet below, the unseen in-between could include a cliff or cliffs that you can't get down. It only takes about a 20-foot cliff to be a complete stopper. So going down can hold some suspense, as you don't want to get stranded at the top of any such cliff. Not that you can't retreat, but such retreats are both effortful and unstylish, so it's better to avoid them.

So going uphill or downhill creates different kinds of unknowns. Going up, what you can't see is likely to be easier than what you can; going down, what you can't see could be much steeper than what you're on. Either way, you can't see enough of the terrain to be entirely sure which is the right way to go. It's a little exploration.

Going up I tend to zigzag, to create a less steep path. Going down, I try to intuit drop-offs I can't see, by way of my knowledge of previous similar slopes, and I traverse to avoid these suspected drop-offs, even though sometimes it turns out the obstacles don't exist. Secor in his guidebook's description of Kaweah Pass warns hikers descending the north side to "beware of the invisible cliffs," which always makes us laugh: invisible cliffs would be a real bummer! But he means one of those cliffs that by a congruence of slopes creates an optical illusion from above, in which the cliff can't be spotted. Only when you come to the edge will it appear and then be quite visible indeed, as in: Oh no! A fucking cliff!

Even mainly level terrain turns out to include enough up and down that you often can't see forward very far. Still, since almost any horizontal way will go, more or less, you end up persisting forward in the general direction you want. And on you go.

The immediate constant problem is where to put your foot next. You can't be looking in the distance and assume that your feet will be okay under you,

Coming to the edge of a drop-off: cliff or slope? I'm checking left, Darryl is going to check on the right.

because a stone blocking your foot at the wrong moment can trip you fast. Sometimes walking poles can save you from one of these falls, other times not. So you have to attend to your walking. It all happens in slow motion, so you can stop to think things over, make slow-motion changes of plan. Like dance, or maybe tai chi. A devotional exercise, a form of Zen.

There is time enough for a stream of consciousness that flows at the pace of walking. All the parts of your life, all the time scales, smoosh together. This pace is a mode of being: the walking pace, pedestrian and prosy. Thinking is pedestrian. Aristotle's *Peripatetics:* they talked things over while walking around the Lyceum, and their walking helped them to think. They felt that.

I like the sweaty huff and puff of the uphill slogs, and the meticulous stepping of downhill, and every other part of walking. Of course I also like the rest stops, and setting camp, making dinner, wandering around, watching the sunset, lying down at night; I even like insomnia if it happens to strike me. I like it all. But what you do most of the day up there is walk. And I like that most of all.

*   *   *

Then you come to slopes so steep that you have to start scrambling. In fact we seek these out, it's true. The transition can be an eye-opener. Oh my God: hands on rock! Collapse your walking poles and stow them away in backpack; put it back on, and here we go. Not rambling, but scrambling. Class 2! Oh dear, oh my. Here we go again!

When scrambling, proprioception is very much involved: that means awareness of one's body in space. This is partly physiological, partly cognitive, and partly emotional, in that you have to trust your judgment and balance to get into the scrambling flow state. Once recently while scrambling up a talus slope, I accidentally pulled down a big boulder and had to dodge it and scream *ROCK* to my friends below; it cut my thumb a little as it passed, but it could just as easily have snipped that thumb off like a paper cutter. The rest of that day my scrambling was tentative and clumsy.

Scrambles range from easy to hard. The easy ones involve steepish slopes that are nevertheless stable under foot and hand. Ledges of bedrock, or massive interlocked boulders — in any case, solid rock, but at an angle steep enough to require hand work. Sometimes these steep slopes can even be vertical meadows, as I call them, because they are loaded with moss and grass and flowers, which tend to stabilize the rocks they're growing in. These scrambles are easy. Often I keep my walking poles out for these.

It's looseness of rock or sand, combined with steepness, that make for hard scrambles. There are a lot of those too.

In fact, talk of class 2, and that whole class 1–5 system, doesn't account for an aspect that would be nice to know in advance, which one could call the brutality factor. Our scrambles are all class 2, but we've become very aware that there's a huge variance among these slopes, not in terms of danger, but in terms of the physical exertion required. This is partly just size and distance, but also, going up loose scree is effortful; if you have to go up 2,000 vertical feet of it, that's brutal. Loose talus likewise, either up or down. So, a scale for that kind of effort would be helpful in any complete guidebook. I believe British mountaineering used to have such a scale. It could be expressed as something like, class 2/effort 2, or class 2/effort 8. Like 2/5, 2/8—thus adding a 10-point scale for effort, which sometimes, in the usual Spinal Tap way, will go all the way to 11.

Then again, a complete guidebook is a bad idea. So let's just say class 2 is a big category, and doesn't tell you anything like the whole story.

A very common class 2 pass is one that gets you over a ridge between two basins. Often these passes are found at a low point in the ridge, but what is crucial for such a pass is not how low it is on the ridge, but rather how laid-back the slopes are on each side. Sometimes this meeting of two relaxed sides will occur higher than the lowest point on a ridge, the low part having a cliff on one side or the other. But very often it's true that the meeting of the two easiest slopes will come at some low point.

Many a class 2 slope is covered with broken rock, which is still lying there because the slope isn't steeper. The angle of repose defines the angle at which stuff will hold on a slope, and this differs for different materials; for broken rock it's said to be about 35 degrees, but if the slope that the broken rock is on has corrugations in it, as often happens in the Sierra, the angle can get a bit steeper. When it gets steeper still, to a tilt of about 45 degrees, maybe, the broken rock tends to slide off, leaving the bare slope itself.

Some people say the steepness of class 3, having shed all loose rock by being so steep, makes it preferable to class 2, because you have only hard bedrock to grasp as you climb, and you can count on it to stay in place when you grab it or step on it. Maybe so, but I don't like the steepness necessary for that to happen. Like the absent loose rock, if you aren't grabbing on to it, you too will fall.

This means, for us, sticking to class 2. Thus we are often scrambling on angled slopes of broken rock. The rocks are mostly stuck there, and without a person coming by and stepping on them—or a little earthquake—they would sit there for a very long time. The freeze-thaw cycle has caused them to shift around every winter until they are wedged in a position where they can't be moved any farther by more freezing and thawing. Even when they're resting on points and edges, like hugely magnified pieces of gravel, the individual weights of the bigger rocks on such slopes are such that a mere human's weight on them is not going to shift them.

Then you step on the one-in-a-thousand rock that happens to be balanced precariously, and it tilts under you. That kind of rock needs to be watched for. You can never assume that rocks, no matter how big, will hold their position. I call the rocking ones Tom Sawyer rocks, but you have to have been on Tom Sawyer Island in the California Disneyland of the 1960s, before the age of liability, to catch this reference to the artificially tippy rocks they had on that island for kids to play on. The high Sierra still has Tom Sawyer rocks, so you have to take care.

When the rocks on a slope get small enough, say the size of ordinary gravel, they will slide underfoot when you step on them. This is safer than boulders shifting under you, but effortful to walk up. Walking down this can sometimes be easier, because of the short little slides I first discovered on the descent from Dragon Pass, rock glissading as it's called: it can happen.

So the size of the broken rocks resting on class 2 slopes matters. This is how I understand the words used to describe these different sizes:

SCREE is sand and gravel that will slide under your feet.

TALUS refers to bigger rocks, sized from say softballs to refrigerators, with smaller fragments joining them or not. Talus will mostly hold under your foot, but not always.

BOULDERS are, yes, boulders, sized from refrigerators to houses. They will almost never move under you, but occasionally one will.

So, class 2 slopes can consist of these various sizes of rock in a uniform way, or be a mix of all of them; or it can be clean hard bedrock. It's generally around 30 to 35 degrees off the horizontal, which doesn't sound so bad, but in fact class 2 slopes often feel much steeper than that, and occasionally they really are.

Going downhill on steep talus can be especially tricky, because as you descend you can't help your foot landing hard sometimes. That can cause rocks to move under your foot. Often it's best to keep three of your limbs fixed to the rock, and move just one hand or foot at a time, testing the newest perch. You have to go completely quadruped in these moments if you want to stay safe. Often you can still stay upright over your feet in these maneuvers, meaning you keep your weight over your feet in the normal way, and use your hands for balance only. Other times you have to lean in and shift your weight onto all four limbs, and be ready to crawl up or down for a while. It's best to stay upright if you can, as that takes much less energy, but sometimes you have to latch on and crawl like a gecko.

A mistake and injury on class 2 terrain could be catastrophic for your trip, and maybe for your long-term recovery—it would depend on the injury. Mostly if you slip you'll fall the length of your body or less. But landing on rock, or even worse, falling into a hole between rocks—or getting in the way of a moving rock—all could be bad. The chance of breaking a limb is clearly there, right under your feet as you walk. If you did that, it would be painful, and suddenly you would be stuck there, mostly unable to move, in some very inconvenient place. Often only a helicopter lift would be at all possible, and first your companions would have to get out and tell people you needed help, and then relocate you; and maybe the helicopter could not easily lift you off. You might have to crawl or be lifted down to a place where a helo could land or hover. Small GPS devices with 911 buttons are a great new innovation, and could be really useful after an injury, but still: it would be bad. Better to avoid that.

So, scrambling is a sport with some risks. Here the museum walking, the continuous inhalation of beauty, gets forgotten. You go primal. You are back to being a primate, putting your hands on rocks and scrambling with all four limbs engaged. That effort becomes all-consuming. The problem solving of one move after another gets repeated literally hundreds of times, so that patterns emerge, and certain physical solutions get applied over and over. An expertise builds; one can become a good scrambler, in part by learning to trust one's judgment, which has to be honed. One learns never to make a leap of faith, but also, to trust one's sense of balance, and one's ability to walk on edges and points that are above or below you, but not by too much. Firm boot treads help a lot with this. One learns to stop and look ahead, to rest while planning the next couple of steps. Then off again, in a start-and-stop flow that doesn't lead to imbalance, that can be sustained for as long as you need to sustain it. That's a fun feeling. The whole thing is really a lot of fun. But there's an edge to it too. More than most activities, it causes you to *pay attention*.

*   *   *

Sometimes when you're coming down from a pass on a steep slope, scrambling hard, it's possible to see the place where you will throw off your pack and rest. Maybe it's by water, maybe you will take off your boots and stand in the shallows, maybe you will take off all your clothes and dive in. Likely you will eat food, drink water. Soak feet in the lake. So that green patch of lawn by a blue pond becomes a kind of beautiful island in the day, and coming down on it from above, you can see it well in advance of your arrival. It's somewhat like seeing into the future. In half an hour, in an hour, I will be there. Now I am not there; but I can see there now.

Oops! Almost slipped! Watch where you're going! Fool! You can rest when it's time to rest. For now, you have gotten yourself into a world of crazy fun.

MY SIERRA LIFE (7)

Owls in the Blue

Twin Lodgepole Pines *by Tom Killion, 2010*

By the time I got together with Lisa I was 28, and had been going to the Sierra for seven years, in perhaps 25 trips, in all seasons, but always as an escape from the world, a scramble to hold my head together despite my many mistakes, and a general sense of flailing ignorance. Maybe this is the way many people's twenties feel. Not that mine were bad, indeed lots of the time they were great: a huge adventure, free to do anything, carve a life, fumbling along day to day, year to year, feeling time fly by, things disappearing in the rearview mirror, childhood that once had been remembered in full now drifting into nothingness; trying new things with very few responsibilities, go go go, go go go.

Well, youth. White American middle-class youth, a young man, one of the most privileged people of all time, and in the 1970s. A baby boomer, in other words, part of that accidental aristocracy of all world history—the crown of creation, as Grace Slick sang so memorably. But wasn't the end of that lyric: "And you've got no place to go!" Existential angst belongs to everyone, but it strikes so hard in youth; it's not just the bedrock of adult consciousness that it becomes later, but a new feeling, fresh and so very intense. Angst!

So, right on Grace and the early Jefferson Airplane. Never let it be said that the rock music of the '60s wasn't one of the great moments in musical history. It was a good time to be young, taken all in all, and I lived that period to the full, the crazy good and the deep weirdness.

And then I met Lisa. At first she was just one of a dozen swimmer gals in the lanes of Davis Aquatic Masters. I loved these naiads, their cheerful work ethic, their athleticism, their sleek bodies around me in the pool. Most of them were stronger swimmers than I was, which I liked. These were good people.

Then I got in the habit of lunching midafternoon, in order to have enough energy to sustain the Dave Scott happy-death workout that was coming that evening. It was 3,000 yards of intense effort, no matter how hard I tried to dodge it, every evening sloping in at 6:30 after work at Orpheus Books, thinking damn I'm tired, why did I come, I'm going to lowball it tonight for sure, I'm going to go last on every set, do the absolute minimum necessary to get through this, why did I come, damn damn damn; and then half an hour later

I'd be killing myself to do what Coach Dave was asking of us, all my negativity forgotten, bodysurfing a wave of adrenaline and endorphins and group solidarity. That was Dave Scott: six-time Hawaii Ironman winner, master psychologist, he could turn lap swimming into a game you wanted to play. Which is magic, really, because in fact it isn't that much fun. I report this after 20 years of lap swimming, now happily 20 years in my past.

Anyway, there at that same late lunch, many days, in a sandwich shop near the bookstore where I worked, was Lisa, fueling up for that same workout. At first I didn't even recognize her, because she was dry. She had to say hi to me for me to figure out who she was. Then we kept crossing paths there. You had to eat around 2:00 p.m. in order not to be too full or too hungry when the evening workout put its demands on you. It was a fine balance, and Lisa and I had both come to the same timing in regard to that. Then in the pool that evening we'd either be in the same lane or the next lane over, as the lanes were organized into beginner, intermediate, experienced, and advanced, and we were both in the biggest grouping, experienced. Four people per lane. I was faster on the sprints, she had more endurance over the long haul.

So we'd say hi as we got lunch. She always went to the salad bar and loaded up on cottage cheese, I always got a sandwich.

Then once or twice we sat down at the same table and chatted over lunch. I only had a 20-minute lunch break, so these were brief conversations. But they added up. I learned about her roots in Massachusetts and Maine, her year in Africa, her work in environmental toxicology at UC Davis. I didn't learn much more. I knew her better in the pool. She was a hard worker, very steady. Her fastest and slowest speeds were almost the same. And she could kick using a kickboard faster than some people in the club could swim, because she had a bad shoulder and kicked a lot. She pushed herself. She looked good in the pool.

So all this was thought-provoking, and after two years in Davis, when Julie and I returned to San Diego, we broke up for the last time. After that I lived in my office on campus at UCSD, often sleeping out on Blacks Cliffs. I called Lisa after a while and told her I was single now, that I was getting a divorce. Sorry to hear, she said. Then she added, There's a conference on fish oxygen in San Diego next month, I was thinking of going to that. And she did, and we got together. I still don't know what fish oxygen is, but I have the poster for that conference tacked up in our garage, well chewed by mice. In fact I just went out to look at it, and it now teaches me that I've misremembered what Lisa said so long ago: that conference was actually on dissolved oxygen, but the poster for it features two fish, which is probably how I got confused. When I mentioned to Lisa that we first got together on the occasion of her coming down to a conference on fish oxygen, she laughed pretty hard. Fish oxygen? What would that be? She laughed for quite some time.

After that, we could have become a couple living at a distance for a year or more, but my faculty advisor Donald Wesling, a wonderful advisor through thick and thin, saw my situation and arranged a dissertation fellowship for me. That meant I could stop working as a teaching assistant and write my dissertation anywhere, so I returned to Davis and moved in with Lisa, and wrote my dissertation there, while working at Orpheus Books on the side.

Tucked into a tiny duplex at 321 D Street, life was suddenly good. I was surprised. An unexpected turn of events, for sure—almost like a flip turn in the pool. My plan for my life was working, and that startled me; it had never happened before. But it was very welcome, and all because of Lisa. We were a good match, and that made all the difference.

Soon after we moved in together, I took her to the Sierra. First to Desolation, then to Dusy Basin, almost back-to-back, as had happened for me in June of 1975. This was just a coincidence, but it's true these were still the places I liked most.

In Desolation, a fire had closed the Wrights Lake road, so we took the Ice House Road to Van Vleck Ranch and started from there. I had never used that trailhead before and got lost immediately by following a ranger's lame directions, but found the trail again without too much bumbling around in the forest, and off we went, up to Lake Nine or Five. I had equipped Lisa, and she had bought some gear, and she was just like she was in the pool: stronger than me over the long haul. How I loved that. She had leg strength to die for, and as for cardiovascular strength, Dave Scott had seen to both of us. There's no walking on Earth as hard as a Coach Dave swim workout. And she liked it. That was what really mattered.

Next day we went by Top Lake, which is divided by a moss dam into higher and lower sections that are about a foot different in height. From there we went right up Top Lake's steep headwall to the top of the Crystal Range. Down to Lake Lois, around to Lake Doris. Then we tried something I'd always wanted to do, which was to camp right on the edge of the Crystal Range, just north of Peak 9038. Lisa was fine with that, so we carried bags of water up with us, and there was indeed room for my tent up on top; views incredible, sunset awesome.

On the Crystal Range near Peak 9038

We got back to my car by way of the Rockbound Pass trail, and resupplied at home, and a day or two later drove south and hiked over Bishop Pass from South Lake. Dusy Basin, glorious as ever. Then over Knapsack Pass to do the Palisades Basin cross-country ramble, deservedly famous. I botched the approach to Knapsack, taking too high a traverse and getting us into the giant boulders under Columbine Peak. Lisa didn't care; it was all the same to her, being new. From that pass over to the Barrett Lakes, and then through the Palisades Basin over Potluck Pass, I hit a clean line without trouble. This was my first time crossing the Palisades Basin, but all was well, and more than well; after a day's superb ramble, and a clean drop down the potluck side of Potluck Pass, we camped on the crab-claw peninsula sticking into Cirque Lake, and had the whole world to ourselves.

Next morning we went up and over Cirque Pass. Although the ascent proved easy despite its steep look from below, in the last part of the descent I again blew the line. My Wilderness Press guidebook map had a dotted line showing the cross-country route, and I tried to follow that line on the map, rather than eyeballing the landscape myself. A rookie mistake, but at that time I still hadn't learned definitively that you need to trust your eye over the map. This day was a big part of that lesson. In fact, the drop to Lower Palisade Lake is very easy if you go to the right as you descend from Cirque Pass. But we went left instead, traversed onto a cliff face, and then had to do chutes and ladders (meaning really ledges and chutes) to squeeze our way down to the lake.

There we displaced a deer and had the campground to ourselves, where these days there are typically 50 people every summer evening, because of the Muir Trail mania. The next day we went north on the Muir Trail to Grouse Meadow, then up the great wall to Dusy Basin again, and out the day after that. At the South Lake trailhead we were given a ride by a nice older couple in a pickup truck; we sat on their truck's bed looking backward for the mile down to Parchers. There we retrieved Lisa's car, took showers, and drove down to a night in Bishop, seeing a movie about Pelé and sleeping in a motel, a huge extravagance. In the morning we ate in a restaurant called Huk Finn's (sic!), and ran into the couple who had given us a ride the day before; they didn't recognize us, we were so cleaned up. That day we drove across California by way of Tioga Pass, and got to Santa Cruz to meet Lisa's sister Kate, Kate's husband Denis, and their new baby Jim. A new world, a new life—

Owls in the Blue

I remember our night on the ridge.
I saw a nook some years before,
Flat sand in broken granite,
Right on the crest so I thought I could find it,
And you were game for anything.

We hiked up late one afternoon
Carrying water in our packs.
Up in the shadow of the Crystal Range,
Up shattered granite all patched with grasses
Until we stepped back into the light.

We found the nook and pitched the tent
Between two gnarly junipers.
The sun set in the big valley's haze.
The light leaked out of the sky.
We leaned against rock cooking our supper.

And in the last electric blue,
The richest color in all the world,
We jerked at a flash in the air above
And jerked again as out of the night
Black shapes dove at both our heads.

In the dark we could barely see them.
Their quick dives made no sound at all.
Too big for bats, too quiet for hawks,
We ducked it seemed at an onslaught of owls
Out hunting in a little pack.

A strange disjunction of the senses:
Wings baffled to damp their noise

We heard nothing except the stove
Yet saw the steep black strobe approaches
The sharp glides turning away.

Then one came close, we sensed the talons.
I picked up the stove and held it aloft,
A Bleuet canister with blue flames burning
Bright in the dark blue expanse of space
Beyond it black wings flitting away.

We laughed with just a touch of a shiver
Actually to be considered as food.
Above the stars popped out all over
Netted in the Milky Way
And afterimages of blue flame.

Then we lay in our blue tent.
The moon rose and our air turned blue.
A blue still in us
It will always be with us
All the color of the twilight sky.

All the time and space we travel
The years pass so many now
Falling asleep owls twirl over us
I feel the granite under our bed
We soar in the blue without a sound.

SIERRA PEOPLE (7)
The Sierra Club's Women

The Sierra Club was not Muir's idea, as I've said, but rather the invention of an actor network of men interested in protecting the Sierra from destruction by loggers and sheepherders. It was one of the earliest nongovernmental organizations devoted to land protection, founded soon after the National Geographic Society, and part of that expansion of civil society which is said to strengthen democracy by making it into more of a polyarchy. It's also a great example of how actor-network theory includes the nonhuman, because one of the principal players in the Sierra Club was the Sierra Nevada itself, inspiring the love of people who then put a lot of work into advancing its interests in the human world.

Recall that the originating group included prominent citizens of all kinds, all of them men. But there were women members of the club, and William Colby, the club's longtime executive secretary, had the idea that the club ought to organize annual "high trips" during which members for a moderate fee could go up as part of a large group, up to 200 people, and spend a month in the high Sierra, camping together and making excursions from a slowly moving base camp. And right from the beginning he insisted this should be open to all, and that women should be encouraged to go. Wives were urged to come, and he made sure some of the sororities at the University of California and Stanford knew about the trips, and knew that women were invited. Many of the first women to join these high trips were Berkeley undergraduates, and word of mouth spread through the Bay Area that these were wilderness trips where women, married or single, were welcome.

The *Sierra Club Bulletin* also welcomed women writers, and served from the start as a lively forum where members could learn what other members were up to, both in exploring the range and advocating for it in Sacramento and Washington, DC. I recommend reading the earliest years of the *Bulletin* in full (but only the articles that interest you) to get the best feel for the group, and for West Coast culture. In that moment of the 1890s America's East Coast dominated the nation's cultural life, and the local movement sometimes called "imperial San Francisco" felt a desire for a California culture with its own emphasis and style. In that project, the Sierra Club was one node in an even larger actor network.

The annual high trips bonded the core of the club membership, and gave hundreds of people an introduction to the Sierra that pulled them into the magnetic grasp of the range, and influenced their lives below. Later the high trips were widely mocked for their glamping style, but when you read the accounts of participants, you can feel the love the trips engendered, not just for the Sierra, but for each other, and for the group as a group. There were many marriages that came out of these trips, and even more friendships. For many of the participants, these trips were the best part of every year.

The Sierra Club as feminist organization: whether this was an accident or by Colby's design, it was very real. Because as soon as women got into the high Sierra wilderness and did what men were doing up there, it became clear that they were just as strong as men. For many of the men, and maybe some of the women too, this was news. It wasn't trivial news either. Recall the Victorian "cult of true womanhood," in which middle-class women were considered creatures of the house, weak and in need of protection, their four cardinal virtues "piety, purity, submissiveness, and domesticity." Getting out of this system for a month every year was a huge relief, even a euphoria. Women wrote in the *Bulletin* of "true democracy," meaning everyone washed the dishes, no matter what their status was at home. They described the trips in rapturous terms, using words like *equality* and *socialism* and *utopia* with the utmost seriousness.

That the high trips were feminist ventures had mainly to do with the women in the club seizing the opportunity. Whether walking, scrambling, or climbing, they excelled. And they knew how to run the logistics of camp life too. The loyalty to these trips, people returning year after year, and the exuberance of the trip reports, often written up by women as comedies of relief and role reversal, as during Carnival, shine out of the early *Bulletin*s like rays of sunlight. It must have felt somewhat like an annual release from prison, a scheduled escape to freedom.

So: William Colby, with his Buster Keaton stone face and a little twinkle in his eye, as secret feminist? Who knows? Quickly it became the ethos of the whole club, including most of its men—among them Muir, who urged his daughters to join the high trips, which they did for many years.

Some of these women wrote and published enough to be still visible to us. They were not professional writers like Mary Austin, but they were writers, and they were much more devoted to the Sierra than Austin was.

HELEN MARION GOMPERTZ LECONTE

Helen Marion Gompertz was an early Sierra Club member, and one of the best writers in her era of the *Bulletin;* her trip reports are funny and insightful. She met Joe LeConte in the Sierra in 1896, when they were up there in a group of mutual friends. They made some tough climbs, fell in love, and soon got married; this was clearly a big event for the Sierra Club, announced and reported in the *Bulletin*. After that they went up together for many years. When their children were born they took them almost immediately to the Sierra for most of every summer.

Their favorite place, a lake in the Lakes Basin just off Cartridge Creek, became their annual summer base camp. They would lead burros carrying a summer's worth of supplies up the old route of the Muir Trail, and settle in at this lake, which was fed by a glacier tucked above it, adding a dash of glacial silt that made its water an opaque, creamy cobalt. Joe named it Lake Marion,

Helen's middle name; whether this was his private name for her, or her preferred name when not writing, or a substitute for Helen—because Muir's daughters had recently had the two lakes on each side of Muir Pass named after them, so that there was already a Lake Helen pretty nearby—I don't know, I can't find out. Beyond her early writing for the *Bulletin*, there isn't much easily found information about Helen. We know they kept taking their two kids to the Sierra, and doing the high trips, and working for the club, until a cancer killed her in 1924, when she was 59. Joe outlived her by 20 years. A year or two after her death, he was joined by their kids and a club group in a trip back to Lake Marion, during which they bolted a bronze memorial plaque to a triangular boulder facing the lake. It's still there.

Once I was looking around in the summit registers in the Bancroft Library, and in the register for Goat Mountain I saw the signature *Helen LeConte*, but this was for the year 1926, two years after Helen had died; that gave me a start! Looking into that was how I learned that Helen's daughter had been given the same name as she had. So her daughter was still going to the Sierra, even in the immediate aftermath of her death. It must have been a bittersweet thing.

From her article about going up University Peak, referring to the scree slide under University Shoulder (on which more later): "Much to our dismay, each step upward seemed to carry us downward." Exactly.

MARION RANDALL PARSONS

Parsons's story began somewhat similarly to Helen LeConte's, and the two must have been acquaintances at least. Marion Randall was younger by 10 or 15 years, and had been homeschooled in Berkeley, and was said to be shy. Now I always wonder about people described like that; very possibly we would be calling them "on the spectrum." She was said to be able to play all Beethoven's piano sonatas, but only when in a room by herself, without listeners. She also painted, in a strange style all her own. These might be signs.

In any case, she somehow came to know Wanda Muir, and Wanda invited her on the first of the Sierra Club high trips in 1902, and she went up there and flourished. Four years later she was married to Edward Taylor Parsons, one of the founders and directors of the Sierra Club, 20 years her senior. She began writing trip reports for the *Bulletin*, soulful things, unafraid of trying to express the rapture of being up there.

Seven years later Parsons died. Marion Randall Parsons remained a widow for the rest of her life, in effect staying married to the Sierra and to the Sierra Club. The club quickly named a peak in the Sierra after her husband, and she made the first known ascent of it a year later, in 1931. She became a serious mountaineer in those years, and made over 50 ascents around the world, including major peaks in the Canadian Rockies and the Alps, and many in the Sierra, including tough ones like the Black Kaweah; she was a bold and accomplished climber. She joined the Sierra Club's board of directors, and served on it for 22 years, traveling to Washington to lobby Congress on behalf of the wilderness. She was said to be an unusually effective lobbyist.

She wrote of the high trips, "You make the discovery that you yourself look as queer as your neighbor. You are a Sierran by that time, body and soul, ready to find your place in the socialist's Utopia which you inhabit for a few short weeks."

She wrote two novels, one called *A Daughter of the Dawn*, published in 1923. She continued to paint, focusing mostly on old houses in Northern California; her work reminds me a little of the contemporary painter Jessica Park. Colors were clearly very important to Parsons, so the paperback edition of her book *Old California Houses* is disappointing, as the reproductions of her paintings are in black and white, greatly reducing their impact, and even making them hard to see. In her renditions, these historic houses tend to sway, as in van Gogh or Munch, which gives them a naive-art quality, a Halloween hokiness sometimes, but their coloration, which can be seen online for one or two of them, makes them interesting and pleasing to the eye.

At the end of Muir's life, after Louie had died, and Helen and Wanda had married and moved out, Muir lived alone in the big Martinez house, occupying just a couple of rooms of the place. Marion Parsons became his assistant, and visited every day to help him arrange his papers and finish his book *Travels in Alaska*, the last one he completed for publication. Her account of that time with him is filled with admiration and pleasure, and it seems certain that he felt likewise about her.

So this was a life centered on the Sierra Club, and the Sierra. Getting involved with the Sierra was a great move; if she began as a shy person, she found her work-arounds up there, and pursued life intensely. Once when representing the Sierra Club in testimony to Congress, she wrote, "Those of us who have learned to know the uplifting of spirit, the renewal of bodily strength and activity of mind which accompanies every visit to these wonderful alpine regions, feel that we owe it, not only to the present, but to future generations, to do our utmost to preserve in its natural beauty some portions of the Sierra wonderland for the enjoyment and benefit of the public."

PEGGY WAYBURN

Peggy Wayburn's account in the 1975 *Bulletin* of her first high trip, after marrying Sierra Club president Edgar Wayburn in 1947 and joining him on the trip in 1949, is a beautiful piece of writing. Later she became a well-known nature writer, author of *Edge of Life* and *Adventuring in Alaska*, and she worked with her husband in various Sierra Club campaigns to protect wilderness, campaigns that were among the most effective (and yet least celebrated) of the club's achievements.

Her essay in the *Bulletin* about her first trip captures the conversion moment in its essence, when as a Barnard graduate just moved to California, she met and married an outdoors guy, and went up to the Sierra entirely unaware of what that would entail. She's very funny on that greenhorn experience, and her essay gives a better sense of what high trips were like than any other description I've read, including a brief and affectionate portrait of those "ladies of an uncertain age" who joined the trip year after year, and made a happy gang of anarchic single women. In the final paragraph of it she wrote, "As I expect it did for many other people, it changed my life. When we made our way 6,000 feet down from Granite Pass to Zumwalt meadows on the trip's last hot day in July, 1948, I had never felt more alive or free. I could skip over talus and walk a log across a stream. I had drunk the waters of cool, clear mountain streams, skinny-dipped in an icy mountain lake and sun-dried beside it. I had seen the Sierra's pale granite peaks stained apricot and gold and blue as the sun's afterglow swelled and faded. I had awakened to the song of mountain birds. The love of the wilderness had entered into me. I was, and forever would be, one of John Muir's disciples."

SIERRA PEOPLE (8)
The Fresno Crowd

Another nice illustration of how actor-network theory can help us understand human affairs, especially when it comes to explaining the Sierra Nevada and its interactions with humans, is to notice that the Sierra Club was not the only organization to have gathered around the Sierra to defend its interests in the human world. Coming from charismatic San Francisco, the Sierra Club was by far the largest and best known of these, but there was a smaller and looser group of people working for the Sierra based out of Fresno, and they deserve to be remembered too.

Fresno itself is on the whole forgettable; for people who don't live there, it's mainly the place you pass through to get to the Sierra. Ursula Le Guin told me that she once gave a reading at Cal State Fresno, and began by apologizing that in the novel she was going to read from, *Always Coming Home*, the Fresno area was under 300 feet of water. The audience cheered.

But naturally it had its prominent citizens in the early years, and naturally some of these had given their hearts and lives to the Sierra, after going up there when young. Frank Dusy was one of those. Another was George Stewart, not the writer of *Earth Abides*, but the Fresno newspaper editor of the same name, who campaigned tirelessly and effectively for the protection of the giant sequoia groves, and the southern Sierra more generally. It's great that one of the most striking peaks in the Kaweah group is named after him; he deserves it.

Another Sierra advocate from that area was the writer Stewart Edward White, well known in his time as a popular chronicler of the American West. His best book for Sierra people is *The Pass*, a description of his summer-long attempt to find a horse route over the Kings-Kaweah Divide, accompanied by his wife Betsy, a friend of theirs, some horses, and a dog. Their adventures are entertainingly told. When they eventually discovered what he named Elizabeth Pass, they celebrated by setting a tree on fire. Many rattlesnakes died in the making of this memoir, but you can't help enjoying the book. I was really pleased to discover that the camp at the confluence of Deadman and Cloud Canyons, which was their base camp during that summer of exploration, is still called Stewart Edward White Camp, the sign announcing this almost worn away.

The Fresno figure I most enjoyed reading about is Judge William Wallace. For many years Wallace hiked all over the southern Sierra, often with his companions Wright and Wales. The three *W*s now have three lakes up in the Wallace Basin named after them, just under the cosmic jewel of Tulainyo Lake. A nice memorial to what was obviously a fun hiking trio.

Wright was a terrible mapmaker, one of the worst of the fill-in-the-blanks-with-anything cartographers. His maps formed part of Joe LeConte's problem to solve, they were so wrong. Yes, Wright was wrong. And Wales was from Scotland (I'm making that up).

Wallace, however, was truly funny: very obviously a Sierra nut of the first order, but also a prominent judge in Edwardian America. He had an important and respectable job, and he seemed to feel that it didn't sound quite right to tell people he was going to disappear every summer into the Sierra to fool around for a month or three, even though that's exactly what he did. So he told them he had a mine up there. Which he did; he took out papers, he spent money, he hired people and bought mules, all to go up to his copper mine. Really it should be written as "copper mine," because this supposed copper mine is actually a cabin-size knob of copper-bearing rock, sticking out of the ridge at the top of Deadman Canyon.

The single shaft of the mine in this knob is about six feet in diameter, and cuts down into the rock about ten feet. It's like a big marmot hole. Also, it's located on a ridge 12,000 feet above sea level, with steep drop-offs on both sides. For whatever reason, the trail for the workers and the burros who carried the copper ore off the ridge did not descend Deadman Canyon, which

The "copper mine" at the top of Deadman Canyon; it's the black dot in the biggest patch of snow in the distance.

would have been dead easy, but instead ran east on the ridge, up to the top of Peak 12345, then down in steep switchbacks into Cloud Canyon, a name bestowed by Wallace; he was very insistent it not be called Cloudy Canyon, writing to the Sierra Club to insist that they take that mistake off early maps. Men leading burros, mules, and horses visited the mine using this trail, then took their loads down Cloud Canyon to the giant bench of high ground overlooking Kings Canyon on its south side. There the ore got carried west to the start of a stage road at Big Meadows, where wagons could haul it down to Fresno. No doubt tens of dollars' worth of copper was produced by this effort. But Wallace had his excuse for spending every summer up there. Yes, a real miner. It went on for years.

One time, Wallace and a friend decided to descend the gorge of the Kings River, downstream from the confluence of the South Fork and the Middle Fork. Now parts of this gorge are drowned by a reservoir. He and his

Wallace's copper mine in its entirety. The hole to my left is about six feet deep.

companion intended to take a day for this exploration, but they disappeared and did not come out, only emerging five days later, after everyone assumed they had somehow died. Only after our 2019 trip down the Muro Blanco did I understand how such a delay could occur.

After that adventure, Wallace's feet were shot, and he spent his declining years riding a tricycle around downtown Fresno, no longer able to walk. He had given not just his life to the Sierras, but his feet. I think it might have been a case of plantar fasciitis gone very bad, so he has my utmost sympathy. But he had fun while he lasted. Now, if you are standing on the shores of Wallace Lake, you are in a really good corner of the god zone, and can skip a rock over the water in his memory, and thank him for his good work. Or you can visit his copper mine, which has some beams and tools and chunks of green rock laid out before it, and laugh.

That reminds me to add: there are two Coppermine Passes. Some people think this pass is simply the old route over the top of Peak 12345, because that's where Wallace's mining trail goes, still quite visible as a phantom trail. I'm in that camp myself. But there are others who insist that a peak can't be a pass, by definition, and that the pass of that name crosses the ridge extending north from Peak 12345, about half a mile from the peak. I think this other pass might be easier for skiers crossing in the wintertime. In the absence of snow, it seems to me that going over the peak itself is much easier. But I haven't been over the more northerly Coppermine Pass, so I should really go check it and see.

Meanwhile, the thing to remember is not to be confused by competing claims as to the location of this pass, as if one claim is right and the other wrong, put forth by people fooled by some kind of mapping error. People do argue about it in those terms, including Secor in his guidebook, but in fact there are two Coppermine Passes. I think Judge Wallace would have been pleased at that.

ROUTES (1)
The Four Bad Passes

There are no roads crossing the Sierra between Tioga Pass and Lake Isabella, far to the south of Mount Langley. This 220-mile-long stretch of roadlessness is crucial to the feel of the range; it's a really big wilderness, about the same size as Switzerland.

Because of that immensely long roadless stretch, you are forced to come at the Sierra from either east or west. On the west side, the trailheads are mostly pretty low in altitude, from 5,000 to 7,000 feet. On the east side there's more variety, the trailheads ranging from 4,500 to 10,300 feet. That spread in altitude makes a huge difference in how they feel to hike, because the rise to the high country is going to happen on your first day, when packs are heaviest, and your body has had the least amount of time to adjust to the altitude. Low trailheads mean you have to walk up more, and that's hard. So high trailheads are popular, and the east side has quite a few of these. Low trailheads are correspondingly unpopular. That's one of the reasons I like them.

The east side of the southern Sierra, that great escarpment, has the spur-and-gully form one sees on the great canyon walls of Mars, or in many a Terran desert. From Langley to Mammoth it's a corrugated wall featuring steep canyon after steep canyon, parallel variations on a theme. The lowest trailheads all start on the floor of Owens Valley, where the Sierra escarpment begins its big jump to the sky. That means they're all around 5,000 feet above sea level. Since all the passes over the crest are between 11,000 and 13,000 feet high, when you start from the lowest trailheads your first day will ascend about 6,000 vertical feet. Yikes! These are real humps.

The four trails that have these low trailheads I therefore call the Four Bad Passes. It's my name for them, recalling the Chinese mania for numbered sets. They are, from south to north: Shepherd Pass, Baxter Pass, Sawmill Pass, and Taboose Pass.

We've done them all—it was a goal—and they were hard. It's likely we won't do a couple of them again. But they're worth doing. They're not crazy, like some of the cross-country passes that we've taken across the crest. That's something to add, before I describe these four trails: any time you cross the Sierra crest where there is not a trail, you are in for some serious work, and probably some suffering. Not that that should discourage you! It will be a memorable day, or possibly two days.

ONE: SHEPHERD PASS

This one is important, because it gets you into the upper Kern, at the eastern end of the huge arc made by the crest and the Great Western Divide. It's also a quick way to the west side of Mount Williamson, the second-tallest peak in California at 14,386 feet, and so it's a trail that is often used, despite its big vertical leap.

The trailhead is located at the end of a dirt road running west from Manzanar, the World War II internment camp for Japanese Americans on Highway 395. The road ends where Symmes Creek debouches from its canyon onto the Owens Valley floor. Unusually, the trail ascends in the bed of Symmes Creek for a short distance, then rises 4,000 feet on that canyon's south wall, before crossing a ridge into Shepherd Creek Canyon, after which it traverses downward about 500 feet until reaching Shepherd Creek. This loss of 500 feet on the way up, or the 500-foot ascent on the way down, is sometimes said to be a heartbreaker, but in fact, in the larger picture of this trail, it's scarcely even noticeable.

There are a couple of small campsites perched on the ridge dividing Symmes and Shepherd Creek Canyons, which can be useful if you want to break the ascent into two days. Anvil Camp, on Shepherd Creek, wooded and extensive, is also a good place to camp, again dividing the ascent of the pass across two days.

Upstream from Anvil Camp there's a meadow called the Pothole, a green depression from which a trail used to run northward up a sand gully to Junction Pass; this was the original route of the Muir Trail, before Forester Pass was dynamited into existence during the 1930s. This was the only place the Muir Trail crossed the crest, and twice at that, to sidestep the steep divide now crossed by Forester.

Bill Tweed's book on trails says that the Shepherd Pass trail was built by a crew of volunteers from Lone Pine in 1913, after it had become a known route to the back side of Whitney, and to Mount Williamson. The reason they located the lower part of their trail in the Symmes Creek drainage is that the lower section of Shepherd Creek Canyon is a tight brushy gorge, obviously difficult and maybe even impassable, at least without a Judge Wallace–like effort. Critics of the trail makers' route haven't looked closely enough at either the map or the territory; in fact the trail is very smartly routed, solving a nasty problem by taking an elegant and ingenious line, which in some sections, in particular the high traverse from the Symmes-Shepherd ridge down to Mahogany Flat, is startling in its audacity.

The pass is a monster to ascend in a single day, and yet nowadays there are people who use it to climb Williamson and return to their cars in one day, so obviously this feeling of monstrosity is relative. In the summer of 2020 we encountered almost a dozen young people trying for both Mount Williamson and Mount Tyndall in a single day. That would entail 10,000 feet up and 10,000 feet down, over a horizontal distance about the length of a marathon. When they were failing in this goal, as they often cheerfully admitted they were, it was for lack of time, not energy. Some of them were therefore running; some had even planned to run. They were using their phones as maps, and were obviously part of an adventure culture, intent to bag all California's 14ers, or perhaps just ascending peaks often mentioned on the internet. They had to be endurance athletes to do what they were doing, I judged: soccer players, swimmers, cross-country runners, and so on. They were beautiful to see.

When you go at slower speeds, carrying a backpack with the intent to stay out for a week, two days to cross the pass might be best. The two little ridge camps, or Anvil Camp, or a little campsite at the last stream crossing before the headwall, would all work well to break the task into two parts. In two days it's easy; although it has to be added, there's usually a brief unavoidable snow crossing just under the top of the east side, a steep tongue of snow that is the last snow to melt every year. This can be really nerve-racking to cross. If you slipped on it, you would slide a long way.

The best thing about Shepherd Pass is that after you cross it, you are immediately in the heart of one of the greatest parts of the range. The upper Kern is a kind of superbasin, or a broad fan of basins spread out next to each other, all of them opening southward and draining into the deep gorge of the Kern. This broad upland was home to one of the biggest ice sheets in the ice-age Sierra, a true *mer de glace*. You could spend weeks up there exploring this high region, which I think of as the Sierra's Mongolia.

TWO: BAXTER PASS

Baxter Pass has a paved road running to its trailhead, which features a big unpaved parking lot where the north fork of Oak Creek emerges from its steep canyon. Despite the great road leading to it, it's an unmaintained trail. The USFS trailhead sign is peppered with bullet holes left by some hikers disgruntled by this lack of maintenance. A message taped to the sign lets everyone know how upset these people were.

The trail is fine at first, but a problem crops up where it crosses the canyon's creek, a couple miles up from the trailhead. The creek here is so overgrown with alder and willow that you have to fight your way through the brush, then find a place to cross the considerable stream as it rushes down its slot. People accomplish this awkward crossing in various places, which makes it hard to pick up the trail on the other side. We didn't find it after we crossed the creek, and had to bash up the steep slope for quite a distance before running into it again.

Far up the creek, at around the 10,000-foot level, there's a small campsite in a stand of trees clustered by the creek. One time we set up our tents in this grove just two minutes before rain hit; that was nice. From there, the next morning, we lost the trail again, because it leaves the creek and heads north up a steep rubbly slope where an avalanche appears to have knocked down a full-grown forest, leaving a maze of bare tree trunks. Picking a way up through this mess, we eventually ran into the trail by accident, and continued up a good set of switchbacks to the pass. There's no low point in the crest to mark the pass; it's just a place where the slopes on each side are more laid-back than elsewhere.

On the pass's inside there's a high basin with a big lake tucked into its top. The trail drops from the pass at an angle down to the east end of this lake, then circles the lake and heads west down the basin, toward the deep canyon holding the Muir Trail. The drop from pass to lake crosses a colorful stretch of roof-pendant rock, a slope of intense red-brown stained by giant splashes of yellow and white. It looks like the surface of Jupiter's moon Io.

The inside of Baxter Pass

The trail from that highest lake down to the Muir Trail is definitely not maintained, and looks to be seldom used. It drops through forest, and quite often disappears for a while under fallen pine needles and bark and branches. When it goes away, you have to hope to run into it again. Trail ducks sometimes helped us rediscover it, and in a couple of places hikers, perhaps frustrated by this elusiveness, have monumented big boulder tops with 15 or 20 trail ducks stacked together, making handsome goldsworthies in the forest.

More people need to hike this trail to keep it alive. We heard coyotes at night, we saw deer by day. The Io patch is unique in the Sierra. The trail eventually emerges from the forest onto the great wall of the canyon of Woods Creek, near where the Sixty Lakes Basin drops in from the other side. This makes Baxter Pass the perfect entry for a circumambulation of Mount Clarence King, if you are so inclined. We did that and it was wonderful.

THREE: SAWMILL PASS

Sawmill Pass begins at a trailhead in the middle of nowhere on the Owens Valley floor, a dirt parking lot with no cars in it. Nevertheless it features one of the standard Inyo National Forest trailhead signs, and from there you take off on a trail that makes a gigantic traverse of the Sierra escarpment itself, southward and slightly up for three full miles, until you reach the opening of Sawmill Creek's canyon, which is perhaps a thousand feet higher than the parking lot. There the trail turns right and off you go, steeply up another Sierra east-side canyon. Given how many random dirt roads there are on the western side of Owens Valley (who built all these, and why?) it's a bit mysterious why the road to the parking lot didn't continue to Sawmill Creek, but it doesn't. Hiking back down this part of the trail is like coming in for a landing in a small plane, in slow motion.

Once in the Sawmill drainage, however, the trail makes a nice clean run past a long vertical ridge in the canyon floor called the Hogback (in glaciologist's terms, a riegel), past the site of an old sawmill and up to a small lake at the 10,000-foot level. Then with a right turn the trail climbs to the crest, which again, as at Baxter Pass, is running east-west in this stretch, such that you ascend a south-facing slope. Reaching the pass feels easier than reaching the other Four Bad Passes. Then only a short walk down the gently sloped north side and you're into a sweet basin just south of Mount Cedric Wright. Wright was a famous landscape photographer and early Sierra Club regular, like his friend and mentor Ansel Adams. He played his violin around the high trip's nightly campfires for more than 20 years. Peggy Wayburn reports that he called their portable toilet system the Straddlevarius.

The trail running from this high meadow down to the Muir Trail is again seldom used, and it's overgrown in wet places such that some guesswork and luck, and the occasional help of well-placed trail ducks, are necessary if you are to avoid losing it. Soon enough you hit the Muir Trail, but in a rather unhelpful spot, in terms of making any quick loop trips. Still, of all the Four Bad Passes, this one gave us the easiest first day. We slept in the lonely parking lot the night before, which might have had something to do with that; we got off with an actual legendary early start, very rare for us—they are usually more legendary than early—and thus avoided the heat of the day for much of the ascent, and were in our first campsite, unexhausted, by 4:30.

FOUR: TABOOSE PASS

This one is a beauty, and puts you right in another sweet spot. It's no surprise that it was a major pass for Native Americans crossing the Sierra, because from Owens Valley it appears as a truly enormous U in the crest, so big and low that it seems it must be an easy way over the range. And so it is. The clear view of it from Owens Valley, and all the obsidian chips scattered in the pass and the meadow west of it, make it obvious that the first peoples used it regularly. On its west side they would have gone straight down the Muro Blanco to Kings Canyon, or popped over what we now call Pinchot Pass and descended the far easier Woods Creek drainage.

The current version of the trail starts at the end of a dirt road that has no parking lot. It rises on the north ridge of the canyon, then contours into the canyon itself and continues up in a steep ascent of only six miles from car to pass, crossing the creek several times. A little more than halfway up there is a knot of trees by the creek, sheltering a good campsite (but the trees drop their sap on you!), if you prefer to split the ascent in two, which, from now on, we do. We camped there once on a descent, a welcome break in that direction too. This campsite almost got burned over in a wildfire in 2018, but seems from the fire maps to have been spared by a couple hundred yards. The cliffs backing this campsite are like ivory cathedrals in the dawn light. And indeed the whole canyon is more glacially chiseled than the other canyons of the east side, a steep twisting half-pipe of solid rock. The final ascent of the canyon is flanked by sheer walls of orange granite, marked by some dikes running vertically through them like black lightning bolts. It's quite magnificent, and when you finally top out, you find yourself in one of the biggest passes in the Sierra, in every way. The peaks to each side are a full mile apart, and a thousand feet higher than the trail; the pass is also long east to west, very unlike those many passes that are like crossing over a roof beam, or even the top of a fence. Ice very clearly filled this pass during some of the ice ages, which is an unusual thing to see evidence of at the crest.

Now a number of small ponds dot the broad granite expanse of the pass, and as you continue westward, a quick descent leads to a west-facing meadow, a little green hanging cirque, which overlooks the wide canyon of the South Fork of the Kings River.

The hard orange granite and expansive views make Taboose a special pleasure, but it's a hard first day, no doubt about it. Both times we did it, we ascended in a single day, and made camp in the high meadow exhausted. The first time it was midsummer, and we fell asleep before it even got dark. The second time we felt thrashed for two or three days afterward, and decided as we staggered along that if we ever go up it again, we'll use that halfway campsite. Which I hope we do. It's a superb pass, among the most impressive in all the Sierra. Too bad, though, about that 6,000 feet. No matter how much you want to ignore it—I mean, how hard could it be, only six miles, right? Sure to be over quickly, right? Just do it! But it kicks your butt.

* * *

Thus the Four Bad Passes.

Aside from the cool name, the use value of such a grouping is to see patterns, and thus to find projects. Of course once you see these four as a group, you have to do them all. And indeed, carrying this thought further, starting trips from all the east-side trailheads would be another very worthy goal. Goals like these help in designing new trips, and in making new discoveries.

So, what about crossing the crest in as many places as possible? Would that be a good goal? This I wondered for several years.

But no. There are many non-trail crossings of the crest, in theory they could number in the hundreds, and they're always brutal. Turn the dial to 11. You will suffer, and for me, it's often felt like we made a mistake to go over some of these. Sometimes it was literally a mistake, as when we got lost trying to go over Lamarck Col and discovered, or invented, our own personal Lysenko Pass—more on that later.

I used to be happy to make such mistakes, but now, no. And no matter what your age and fitness, it's just very hard. University Pass, for instance, is a cross-country pass that gives you access from Onion Valley to Center Basin in just three miles, right over the crest south of University Peak and steeply back down, boom boom—whereas taking the trails would get you to that same spot after about 12 or 14 miles—but the trail route would be easier. Same with my first such crest crossing, Dragon Pass (which these days is the name of the next pass to the north of the one I took, which has been renamed Gould Pass), going directly from Onion Valley to the Rae Lakes, rather than taking the trails over Kearsarge and Glen Passes. The trails would be easier, even though four times as long, and crossing two passes. Although I loved Dragon Pass.

As for Ed Lane Pass, well, this is a chapter about the Four Bad Passes, not the Half Dozen Stupidly Bad Off-Trail Passes that we have crawled over in our time. Trails are easier than cross-country, and when you're going over the crest, it's especially true. So even the Four Bad Passes are by no means the worst options up there.

That said — go for it. Do the Four Bads, and then just pick some random class 2 pass over the crest, or even a likely place on the map, or as viewed from Owens Valley, or on Google Earth, and go for it! You will both regret it and not regret it.

MOMENTS OF BEING (3)
A Sierra Day: Sunset and Twilight

In the evening comes an hour of peace. From a good campsite you can see a long way, and often a lake floors the basin below you. Dinner eaten, camp set, legs tired, you can pour two ounces of single malt into a yellow plastic cup bought at a dollar store in 2005, which weighs nothing or maybe even less than nothing, and sit on a rock and just watch the sunset. Again the speed of the world comes clear. It's slow but it goes too fast.

If there are clouds, they turn orange and pink, bronze and gold, mauve and magenta; or stay gray; or do all these things at once. Nature doesn't believe any colors clash; anything can happen. If there are clouds in the west, the sun sends god rays in a spray that makes no sense astronomically speaking. It doesn't matter, there they are, spangling the sky. Glories, the English called these bursts of light through cloud.

Distant peaks may still stand in the light of day when you have been long in shadow. A moment comes when the lake under you seems to be lighter than the sky above. This must be an illusion of contrast, the rocks being dark now. Silhouetted trees are black on the bluing sky.

We sometimes laugh at the photos we keep shooting in this hour. They are both over-the-top and not adequate to the reality. Pointless to try, and yet many a sunset has been caught by dozens of photos. Is there something about being in the mountains that makes the sunsets so spacious and florid? Or is it just that when we're up there we are by necessity outdoors at sunset, and therefore see it? It's occurred to us from time to time that at home we're usually indoors at that hour, and thus we don't see what the sky and clouds do in that late light. So much is lost by living indoors.

On the other hand, it could be that the sunsets up there are just better. For sure the heights expand one's view. And things happen having to do with the immense verticalities revealed. Clouds overhead can go dark while the land under them is still caught in a horizontal fan of sunlight.

Shambhala Pond, sunset

Other times clouds stack up, and with 2,000 vertical feet of peaks standing around you, it might be easier to see that some clouds reach up 10,000 feet or more, catching the late light of day.

Sometimes lenticular clouds form over the Owens Valley, displaying their French curves like alien spaceships.

Other times the nearby lakes go still, and reflect the slopes on their other sides like a mirror.

An Owens Valley lenticular

Finally even the highest peaks lose the direct light of the sun. Then comes alpenglow, and after that, the Earth shadow. Alpenglow is intense and some-times breathtaking: the granite to the east blushes apricot, glows pink, shades to rose as it dims. Any snow on these peaks will turn pink as well, a very pure pink, finer than any watercolor. The colors infusing the snow and granite are so pure that it can take your breath away.

Earth shadow is a phenomenon visible in the air to the east: the lower air is in the Earth's shadow, and thus a dark dusty blue; then you can see, above a quite distinct horizontal line, that the upper part of the sky is still lit by sun-light, and glowing the usual sunset colors. That horizontal line is the mark, standing on a sphere as we do, of the Earth's shadow cast eastward onto the atmosphere. M. Minnaert's fantastic *The Nature of Light and Colour in the Open Air* will give you the angles for this phenomenon in precise detail. The sun-light above the line has just missed the Earth, Minnaert reminds us, and now will fly across the universe unimpeded, more or less. So: dusky dark blue below, pale rose above. Earth shadow. It's very hard to catch this on camera, but as clear to the eye as one's own shadow on the ground. It's a version of the

Mount Darwin from the Darwin Bench

Spectre of the Brocken (also well described by Minnaert), with the Earth making the shadow rather than your own body.

Then comes the best moment of all. If the sky is clear to the west, then as the light of day dims, twilight deepens, and the stars begin to pop into existence overhead, where the sky is turning from blue to black. In the western sky the blue of day persists for quite a while, and deepens in color. This is the Earth shadow again, at a different angle: the air to the east, and also overhead, is no longer lit, but to the west you're seeing air that is still hit by some sunlight. This blue air becomes a color somewhat like lapis lazuli, but transparent. And it's cut very sharply on its bottom edge by a border of mountain ridge, which by this time is a pure black silhouette, jagged against the blue. Pure black and pure blue, divided by a jagged line so sharp and clean that often the border between the two colors vibrates a little, and the blue that lies just over the black, the lightest part of the blue still there, seems to pulse. It's an electric lapis lazuli, darkening above to indigo, but at the horizon itself, still glowing the bluest blue ever seen. The pulsing of it is maybe in your optic nerve, or perhaps it's your own pulse, your body quivering as it soaks it in. The blue inside of blue, electrically crackling from its own oversaturation.

As that light leaks out of the air, and dusk comes fully on, the blue shrinks to nothing more than a narrow ribbon between black Earth and black sky. Then it's black velvet below; a strip of glowing lapis lazuli across the middle; above that an obsidian sky, pricked with stars. When that last band of lapis slips away, the day is done. The beauty has not gone away, but shifted. It's beating inside you. You're in the dark, and have to wonder if you remembered to put your headlamp in your pocket, or if you're going to have to dig for it. It doesn't matter, you can see in the dark. Finish your Scotch, start getting ready for bed. It's been a good day.

Note on back of map, 6-28-20

Above Steelhead Lake
We crawled on hands and knees
Over tilted snow—
Fingers stayed numb for an hour
But we did not skid down.
Great views from the pass. Then
Coyote. Osprey. Bald eagle. Osprey again:
An hour like that and you know you are
Deep inside.
Around Desolation Lake, so big.
West wind strong. Colder.
How big the world grows in a wind.
Mt. Humphreys just lost alpenglow all at once:
Topaz to rust. 8:05 PM.
Why do I love it so much.
Can I say in the moment itself.
Wind on lake. Snow on peaks.

Sun and shadow. Alpenglow.
No I guess I can't explain it.
The spaciousness. The rock. That blue. The birds
Calling at sunset, the wind gusting
Through my heart.
The totality. The connection with my
Past, my young self. That romantic fool,
God bless him. God blessed him.

Desolation Lake and Mount Humphreys, sunset, June 2020

MY SIERRA LIFE (8)

Robbie You're Wasting Your Precious Youth

Robbie you're wasting your precious youth.

This was something Terry said to me many times in the '80s. It was a jest, a reproach, a kind of slogan. And he was right: I did waste my precious youth. At least I did if getting up to the Sierra had been my only goal. But it wasn't, because there were other things going on in those years. I was busy.

Still, readers reading this, if you are young: don't waste your precious youth! It only comes once, and it goes fast. And in the Sierra, youth is a real asset. So get up there as often as you can, and see what happens.

Ironically, for me, having gotten through the pinball years, and ended up in Davis with Lisa, I got to the Sierras a little bit less than I had been going before. Maybe that says something about that first period of immersion. Escaping a fate, getting back to the true home—sure. Now home was Lisa.

We still went up there pretty often, among our other activities, which included going to San Francisco to see our friends Dick and Karen, and to Santa Cruz to see Lisa's sister and family. My beach life started up again in Santa Cruz, bodyboarding in a wet suit, great fun. And down to Southern California to see my parents, and traveling to science fiction conventions, and so on. Teaching freshman composition at UC Davis. And writing novels, very absorbing, very time-consuming. I was getting published regularly now, I was a new science fiction writer. Damon Knight had given me my start, and editors Ed Ferman and Terry Carr and Beth Meacham had followed that start with the editorial encouragement crucial to a new writer, and now I was on my way.

And the science fiction community likes its newest writers. A very friendly crowd, a different kind of hometown.

So life in Davis was busy for both of us. For four years we lived the same week every week. Lisa finished her PhD, I taught freshman composition on campus, and wrote my first few books, and a lot of stories. We swam in the Masters club with crazed enthusiasm, inspired by Dave Scott and our fellow swimmers. I played softball with Lisa's department's team. Taken together, as a set of habits, it was wonderful: one of the sweet spots in our life together, and the first one, which is naturally the one with the biggest sense of surprise in it. Being the same week every week, it now seems like it only lasted a week. And then we moved to Switzerland.

Still, even as busy as we were, I got up to the Sierras pretty often. They were nearby and we could go on a whim, and we did. Lisa and I went snow-shoeing up the Echo Lakes one Easter weekend, mushing right across the frozen lakes, then up past my blizzard ravine, though I had no way to tell which one it was. We snowshoed into fierce winds both going in and then coming out, the wind having shifted 180 degrees while we were up there. I wore some new warm bunting pants Terry had sewn, not windproof, and that was my first and only experience of penile frostbite, which I have since taken care to avoid. The snow was so deep at Tamarack Lake that we had to fish for our water, because the open patch at the exit stream was at the bottom of a 20-foot-high funnel of snow. I tied a water bottle to a ski pole with a length of tent line, and we bobbed it around down there until it picked up some water.

And Terry and I went up often. We would get together in Davis to run, or swim a Masters workout, or have dinner with him and his girlfriend Ann, and our talk would often turn to plans for the next trip. Mainly these were quick getaways to Desolation. Two hours to the Wrights Lake trailhead, then any-thing from an overnighter to three days; these were easy and fun, and hap-pened in all months of the year, except midwinter. I shifted entirely to skis for the snow trips. We ran around every corner of Desolation.

One time after an unusually steep descent off the Crystal Range, we sat at the bottom of it, looking up at what we had come down, like a wall with a slight overhang at the top, class 3 for sure, and Terry lit a cigarette and said Fuck we could have gotten killed doing that, and I said Well, it would be better than dying in a hospital bed of lung cancer, which had happened to Lisa's dad the year before I met her. About a month later Terry stopped smoking tobacco, cold turkey, without saying a word about it.

The southern Sierra was always harder to get to. Once Terry and I went north from Whitney up to Glen Pass, where we got caught in what is now called an atmospheric river. Then it was known as the Pineapple Express, but on trail we had no way of knowing that; it could have been the usual afternoon thunderstorm, except it kept raining, for hour after hour. Terry's tent was the latest in his continual line of gear experiments; this one was like a hammock of nylon sewn to the underside of a rainfly, the whole thing to be tied between trees. We had stopped where there were some dwarfish junipers Terry could hang his tent between. It rained all night, and the next day it was raining so hard we spent the day in our tents waiting it out.

My North Face tent was as good as any commercial tent of that era, but in a storm like this it didn't matter; water was an inch deep everywhere on the ground, something I had never seen before. Inevitably it began to leak in through the seams in my tent bottom. I got my sleeping bag perched entirely on my Ensolite pad, and was thus on an island the size of my ground pad, in the little shallow pool that my tent interior had become. Nothing to be done about it. It would only have to rise a bit more to soak me in my down bag, so I watched with trepidation, and marveled at the immense quantities of rain pounding my tent fly with a heavy percussive patter.

During a slight misty break, Terry came over and crouched outside my round tent door (no mosquito net, of course) to look in and say hi and see how I was doing. Oh wow, he said. Your tent is really dry!

That made me laugh. Of course I then had to go take a look at his. He had made a little platform for its bottom, using his backpack combined with some sticks and rocks, hoping to get the floor of it to drain a little from the seams, but despite that he was lying in a pool about three inches deep. This might have been the origin of his conviction that tarps should never have bottoms, that tents are just bags of water waiting to happen; that there should be no such thing as tents.

When we hit 48 hours of continuous deluge, and all our gear was soaked, and we were too, we decided to bail. As in leave, having already been bailing for some hours. We turned around and left by way of Kearsarge Pass and Onion Valley. Of course the moment we began the ascent from the Muir Trail to Kearsarge Pass the sun poked through racing clouds. We knew that in full sun we could dry our stuff in an hour, but we kept on going. Leaving early: that's the only time I ever did that with Terry.

From my arrival in Davis until Lisa and I left for Zurich in 1985, Terry lived in a room he rented from another DAM swimmer, Russ, and also spent a lot of time at the house of his girlfriend, Ann, who also swam in DAM. Ann was a nurse who owned a house in North Davis; the four of us spent a lot of time there. Ann was smart and capable, strong and funny; she loved Terry, and understood that his trips to the Sierras were part of him. She went with him quite a few times, and they told me about one time when they were crossing a log over a rushing stream, and she slipped and fell, and hit her head on the log on her way down into the river, which then carried her off downstream. Terry raced down the bank and pulled her out by her hair, and then spent the rest of that day and night drying her off, warming her up, drying out her stuff, and through the night waking her on an hourly basis to make sure she was not concussed. Quite a drama, which she recounted cheerfully enough.

But as those years passed, she got interested in settling down. Lisa and I married in the last hours of 1982, and I asked Terry to be my best man, but he backed out after first agreeing to it, partly because he thought it might give Ann ideas. He wanted to hold to their original agreement that they stay only boyfriend and girlfriend, with separate households. They went to Nepal together, and came back very enthusiastic about the experience, but Ann's job meant she couldn't go to the Sierras as often as Terry. Things got a bit tense.

In 1984 they returned to Nepal, and it seemed like that might change things. Which it did; on her return (he had stayed longer), Ann broke up with him.

Lisa and I were sad to see it. The four of us had had a lot of fun together, and when friends break up it's always sad. For Terry it was much more central: a crushing blow. For years he brooded over it. Why had it happened?

Who can say? I would reply when he asked me this. There was no answer to that one that he would hear. I said all the useless things that I had often said to myself in the '70s. Learn and move on, etc. But ultimately there was little one could say.

Then in the fall of 1985, Lisa and I moved to Zurich, where Lisa had gotten a postdoc. On the way there we visited the Himalayas and trekked to Everest Base Camp, a huge adventure. And then it was time for the Swiss Alps. Time to learn a different range! Or not learn it.

THE SWISS ALPS (1)
Kistenpass

Lisa and I took the long way around to Switzerland, visiting Thailand, Nepal, Egypt, and Greece before we finally got to Switzerland. And in this book about the Sierra Nevada of California, I'm going to include quite a few thoughts about the Swiss Alps, because my experiences there helped me to understand the Sierra better, and also many of my mountain experiences there were thrilling for me, and worth recounting.

Geologically, the two ranges are pretty similar. Psychogeologically, they are dramatically, sometimes drastically, different.

Both ranges have the usual origin, of one tectonic plate diving under another, melting in the mantle, and cooling as a big blob of granite, wrapped in metamorphic rock of various kinds and later on obtruding high into the sky. One significant geological difference is that when Italy dove under Europe, it didn't get very deep, being a terrane of land rather than ocean bottom. This kind of collision is now described by the old word *orogeny*, which is not quite the same as subduction. In this particular orogeny, Italy quickly bent in the mantle under Europe and tipped back upward, giving the Alps a strong banding of parallel ridges that the Sierra doesn't have. But for the most part they have similar origins, ages, altitudes, and sizes.

The differences between them that are geological include rock types, latitude, and climate, including both glacial history and current weather. But the crucial difference is really psychogeological, created as it is by human history and culture.

*   *   *

After Lisa and I got settled in Zurich, I went up into the Alps often, excited to see this new range. And at first I was very confused. It wasn't just that the range ran east-west rather than north-south, and consisted of several big crests running in parallel. Weirder was the fact that between these giant ridges lay a dense network of roads, rail lines, and towns. Where was the alpine wilderness? No matter where I went, civilization was there.

And where were the alpine basins, lakes, and ponds? There were none to be found. No ponds; no wilderness; and (therefore?) no backpacking. When I asked my Swiss baseball teammates if it was legal to sleep out in the Alps, they didn't even know, because they had never heard of anyone doing such a thing. When I asked them to circle their favorite places in the Alps, they all circled towns and villages, eventually covering much of the country. And fine country it was, but I remained confused.

It was probably at this point in his brief postwar exploration of the Alps that David Brower, a Sierra Club luminary who had recently finished his leading stint in the US Army's Tenth Mountain Division in World War II, wrote an essay for the *Sierra Club Bulletin* called "How to Wreck a Wilderness." It's a classic example of seeing the Alps exclusively through a Sierran lens. He didn't see that there were 3 million people living in this mountain range, which covered most of a country that was about twice the size of New Jersey.

I stayed longer than Brower, and thought about it more. The Swiss hadn't wrecked a wilderness; they lived in it. This wasn't that easy to do, because the range itself is really steep and wild. As I rambled over it I saw that it was seriously wild, without being wilderness. This was an idea that took some getting used to.

So, in my ongoing attempt to understand this new range better, I bought a wonderful plastic 3D map of Switzerland. In the evenings I would place it flat on our dining-room table and stick my face down among the peaks, squinting in search of likely day trips. Day trips, how lame! But Lisa was working hard and couldn't get away for more, and besides, camping out seemed not to be done. And because of the dense rail and road and cable car system, you could get almost anywhere in a morning, hike over a pass to a different spot, then go back home. My 3D map made it clear how these trips could happen. Roads and rail lines were marked on it, also cable cars and chairlifts, which were scattered everywhere. The map was like the Google Earth of its time, and in some ways better, in that it stayed a single size, and you could see all of it at once.

I started out by looking for areas 10,000 feet or higher, hoping to get into the god zone. This was a mistake in itself, as I discovered after a few traumatic ascents to that height. Turns out, in part because of the latitude = altitude effect, the god zone in the Alps begins at more like 7,000 feet. At 10,000 feet in the Alps, I found myself passing out of the god zone into the death zone. One can always retreat from such situations, hopefully — scurry back down to transport and a return to Zurich — and I did that more than once. In our first summer there, I would often trudge along Hochstrasse from the tram stop to our apartment at sunset, thoroughly defeated, and pull myself up the stairs and collapse at our kitchen table and tell Lisa about my adventures.

Stan: I got into this absolutely wild pass, and there was a stone restaurant up there!

Lisa: Of course. They're in a competition to see how unlikely a place they can put those things.

Another time, Stan: I got onto this glacier, and it went from total sun to complete fog in five minutes! I had to crawl off it. I didn't want to fall in a crevasse and die, and get shoved out the bottom of the glacier 50 years later. I figured you would be annoyed with me for coming home that late.

Lisa: Yes, I would have been annoyed.

Another time, Stan: I saw the Spectre of the Brocken! It's your own shadow, cast down onto a cloud below you! I was the Spectre!

Lisa: Didn't you climb the Engelberg today? So really you were the Spectre of the Engelberg.

Another time, Stan: The map showed there was a trail running down the cliff right next to the glacier, so I took it, but it turned out it was an abandoned trail, and all its wire handrails had rusted off and were lying on the ledges trying to trip me! They were worse than useless. I had to crawl like a gecko.

Lisa: Maybe you should research these hikes a little more before you go. That plastic map might not be enough.

Stan: Well of course! I buy the topo maps of the area I'm going to before I take off, they're great.

Lisa: But maybe not enough.

Lisa's point was well taken, though in fact I didn't take it. I kept using my plastic 3D map to plan my trips, and using that method, I spotted another likely day trip over a pass: Kistenpass. It would get me over the big ridge separating the Upper Rhine Valley from a canyon on the north side of the ridge. Cable cars were marked on both sides, rising from little villages located at the ends of roads that led to train stations. A plan was born! I went downtown and bought the relevant topo map.

Off at dawn from Zurich's Hauptbahnhof. By 7:15 we were in Chur. The next train was made of little old cars. The Rheinische Bahn, I discovered: it had laid its narrower tracks in the 1860s.

Up the Vorderrhein, an immense glacial U valley with a deep river gorge snaking along the bottom of the U. The river was the Rhine in its highest reaches, S-ing from sidewall to sidewall so that the little train had to cross bridges and viaducts, go through tunnels, and struggle up sharp curves. It seldom got up to a speed of 50 kilometers an hour. The other passengers conversed in German that sounded Italian, which I realized must be Romansh.

Two hours up the valley we stopped at a tiny station and everyone got off. A conductor came through my car and conveyed to me that I too had to get off. *Erdrutsch;* sounded like "earth rush." A landslide must have blocked the tracks ahead.

The conductor nodded at my look of comprehension. He told me a postal bus would carry passengers past the blockage to Trun, where another train waited.

But I want to go to Danis, I said, and then up to Breil.

The conductor nodded and led me off the train to a schedule posted on the station wall. Apparently we were in Tavanasa, and a bus would leave for Breil at noon.

While I was still pondering this the conductor got on the postal bus and they all drove off. The train backed down the valley and disappeared. I stood alone in the empty station of Tavanasa, 500 meters below Breil, and 2,000 meters below Kistenpass. It was now 10:00 a.m., and I had thought I would be in Breil by 9:00. And the noon bus wouldn't make it there till 1:00.

I decided to run up the road to Breil, my only chance to get back on schedule. But quickly I saw that this part of the northern wall of the Vorderrhein was steep and smooth, and on such slopes the Swiss like to grade their roads in long gentle traverses with hairpin turns. At every switchback I could look down on the one below: a run of half a kilometer had netted me a vertical gain of about 20 meters. So although it was only 2 kilometers from Tavanasa to Breil as the crow flies, if you followed the road it might be more like 15 kilometers.

I began to hitchhike. It had been years since I had done that, and in Switzerland it felt a little crazy. People in the cars that passed me, often guys in their Swiss Army uniforms, stared at me in a way that made it clear I was right to feel that way. Possibly hitchhiking was illegal, but probably just not done. As I trudged up the road I recalled a Swiss friend trying to explain Swissness to us. On the night before Christmas, she told us, Samichlaus came to the door accompanied by his sidekick the Böögen, a tall creature dressed in a black bag and carrying a smaller black bag. Samichlaus consulted with the parents about their children's behavior that year, and the parents produced an account book of their kids' good and bad acts. If the children had been good that year, they would get a gift from Samichlaus; if bad, the Böögen would snatch them into his bag and take them away. The children were brought to the door to witness this consultation. "And that," our Swiss friend concluded, "is why I hate Switzerland forever."

So I had given up hope of catching a ride, and wasn't even trying, when a Mercedes slowed ahead of me and stopped. I ran up to it; the driver was a woman, with two kids in the back seat. I thanked her as I got in and off we went.

My driver was blond, good-looking, sympathetic. In my hitchhiking days whenever women picked me up I was so grateful I pretty much fell in love with them immediately. Now that was happening again. She was saving my day. She asked me politely where I was going, and in my broken German I told her about my disrupted plans.

"Kistenpass!" she repeated, surprised. ("Keesh-tee-pahsss!") But, she said, the cable car above Breil was a ski lift only. In the summer it was closed. Very few people ever hiked over Kistenpass.

That is bad news, I replied. Again I had to admit to myself that my plastic map probably wasn't giving me enough information.

The woman turned left far below Breil, and stopped at a small building called the Hotel Alcetta. She suggested I use the PTT phone booth in the hotel to call a taxi down to me from Breil. I thanked her and tried that, telling the man who answered my call where I was and where I wanted to go. Then I went back outside and started walking up the Breil road again, figuring I would see the taxi coming down for me.

No taxi passed. In desperation I started hitching again.

Another farmwife stopped for me. I got in her Jeep feeling really fond of the women of the Vorderrhein. I repeated my story, and she too exclaimed "Keee-stee-pahss!"

She dropped me off at the door of Breil's tourist office. It was obviously not a tourist town, but the door opened when I tried it, and a surprised young woman looked up from her book. She too heard out my story. Her English was as bad as my German, but between us we confirmed that I had wanted to take the cable car up toward Kistenpass, and already knew it was closed for the summer.

She suggested I call the village's taxi and ask him to take me up the farm roads above the village—these went all the way to a dairy located a little higher than the cable car's upper station. The taxi fare would be about 30 francs, she guessed, and the vertical gain, I saw on my map, would be about 800 meters. Such a deal!

I conveyed this to the young woman, and she called the taxi for me. A few minutes later it rumbled into the square: a big black pickup truck, with huge snow tires and radio gear sticking out all over it. This vehicle had in fact passed me as I had walked up from the Hotel Alcetta, but I hadn't recognized it as a taxi.

The driver got out and shook my hand. He was a big man wearing blue jeans and a plaid shirt, with thick black hair, a round face, and a cheery manner. He spoke no English at all. I explained in German where I wanted to go, and he nodded and made a gesture: *In you go!* And off we went.

The steep one-lane road we ascended ran in switchbacks past the kind of farmhouses you see dotting the high alps. The taxi driver, whose name was Mario, talked about these houses as we drove by. His German was amazingly clear to me, probably because he was from Ticino and his first language was Italian. The big farmhouses were attached to even bigger barns. Dairy farming at such altitudes was hard, Mario said, but they had been doing it for centuries. The alps themselves were huge lawns, in effect, having long before been cleared of their original cover of forest and rock. The labor needed for that transformation was mind-boggling to contemplate. We agreed that this was part of what made the Alps feel strange: a pretty park that in half an hour could turn nasty and kill you. I mentioned Muir's description of the Sierra as gentle wilderness, and suggested it could be matched by a complementary description of the Alps as savage civilization, and he laughed and agreed. All this in German.

At these altitudes, Mario went on, dairy farming wasn't profitable. The government subsidized it, paying more the higher the farm. But it wasn't enough to keep the young people at home. These houses were mostly maintained by husband-and-wife teams. They were like millionaires' mansions, much too large for their occupants. People thought that would be great, but it wasn't so. It would be sad.

Too much money makes you sad, I ventured. Having a conversation in German was making me feel like a philosopher. Watch out Immanuel Kant!

I wouldn't know, Mario replied with a laugh. I'm very happy myself! I live in a suitcase! I live in this taxi!

He had lived all over since leaving Ticino, including Zurich. His German was fluent, but he didn't seem to care about or even notice my grammatical blunders, which were many. As he said when I mentioned it, if you get your meaning across, the rest doesn't matter. This made me even more comfortable, and I damned the torpedoes and sped full ahead. And I suppose that I had finally crossed some threshold in my miserable German. Lisa and I had been going to night classes twice a week for over a year, and now it seemed I could hold up my end of a real conversation. We talked about Zurich, about what I was doing in Switzerland, about our wives' work, about where he had lived, about Ticino and the Vorderrhein, about the German Swiss as opposed to the Italian and French Swiss. I confessed that I had been the one to call him from the hotel below Breil, but had failed to flag him down because I had been looking for a cab like one from Manhattan or London. He laughed at that and said it didn't matter, as we had finally met in the end.

It was the best conversation in German I ever had, and when Mario dropped me off at the dairy barn at the upper end of the road, shaking my hand and taking off with a wave, I was really happy. All those dull classroom hours had finally been put to use! And not only that, but it was only noon! Between the kindness of Swiss farm women and the professional help of the tourist office worker and Mario, I was not all that far behind schedule.

I took off up the trail and immediately lost it. This is hard to do in Switzerland, where trails are obnoxiously oversigned and often brown trenches across green alps. But this alp was contoured by many narrow dirt trenches, either cow trails or erosion patterns, and I had apparently taken off on one of these false trails. Assuming I had headed out too low, I traversed up the grass, hoping I would soon intercept the real trail.

I didn't, and my climb began to steepen. And apparently it was fly season here. There were hundreds of flies, even thousands, all buzzing around me. I had never seen flies in the Alps before, and these were big ones that bit. I climbed slapping at my legs and cursing; the slope steepened yet again, and I found myself on a grassy wall, using my hands to pull myself up from grass clump to grass clump—this only ten minutes into my hike!

Finally I intercepted the trail, and ran. The flies pursued me through a number of little pastures, all with barns as dirty as any buildings I had ever seen in Switzerland. The spotlessness of the tourist zone, and of the German Swiss cantons generally, had here given way to a grubby working landscape, hot and glary and dusty and flyblown. It looked like a ranch in Nevada.

I turned to look south. The gap of air between me and the spiky white range where Italy began was so immense that I thought I could detect the curvature of the Earth. Well okay maybe it wasn't like Nevada.

I hiked up a hill into rocks and felt like I was finally getting down to business. It was about one. The trail rose toward a notch in the ridge above me. Granite burst out of the grass in forms big and small: sand, scree, talus, boulders, bedrock. Soon there was more rock than grass, and the little meadows that remained were covered by the full array of Swiss wildflowers, including moss campion, which is like a pincushion of dark moss stuck by a circle of tiny pink flowers. Moss campion and blue cornflowers, scattered over dark orange granite, fine-grained and handsome—yes, I was finally getting up into the god zone: and yes, I had reached about 2,500 meters. Finally I had figured that one out. But also, I was headed higher.

Soon I reached a small granite bowl where the rock was half covered with snow. The far rim of this bowl was Kistenpass itself. The pass! I tromped happily up old snow and was soon in the pass. Up there I discovered, as one often does, that the landscape on the other side was very different from what I had seen so far. I was looking north along the snowy western side of a long steep ridge, called the Muttenbergen. The west-facing slope of this ridge dropped very steeply into a lake called the Limmerensee—1,200 vertical meters in less than a horizontal kilometer! But this steepness was not continuous; between cliffs above and below there extended a band less steep, a band about the steepness of a church roof, still covered with snow, and at my current height. The pitch of this band's slope looked uncomfortably steep, but because of the cliffs above and below, it was the only way. The trail crossing the band was apparently still under snow.

Kistenpass below, Muttsee above. Quite a day.

A line of boot prints ran over the snow and I followed them. The Kisten-band, this slope was called on the map: a good name. The Swiss long ago gave good names to every feature you could possibly name, right down to individual boulders. Ötzi the Iceman could have named this band.

The line of boot prints ran closer to the top of the lower cliff than I would have liked, but it was a bit flatter there, and the untrodden snow above it was much slippier, so it seemed best to stick with the boot prints. They were only semifrozen now, and had a tendency to collapse down to the left when I stepped in them. The cliff I was skirting was so steep and tall that I couldn't see the lake at its bottom, and only knew it was there because of my map, which showed it to be a long narrow reservoir, a thousand meters below. Walking poles would have been great here, crampons and an ice ax even better, but I had not expected snow. It was August 12, and I was only at 2,700 meters on a west-facing slope. In the Sierras—well, the Alps were not the Sierras. I was learning that yet again. All I could do now was slow down and pay really close attention to my footing, staring at the snow under me until the world took on the look of a photo negative.

This went on forever, although the Kistenband is only a kilometer long. But it's a big world at times like that. Every time I slipped to the left, chunks of ice clattered down and disappeared over the cliff. I found myself holding my breath a little. When I came to the north end of the Kistenband, where the slope laid back, I stopped and took a breather. There was a spur just below me to my left, jutting out over the Limmerensee, and to my surprise a little roof-top poked out above the flat top of the spur. I walked over and found a tiny locked shed tucked under the spur. No signs on it. A storage shed, maybe. In any case there it was. The flat top of the spur above it was clear of snow, and had a big airy view. And I was past the crux of the hike, which I now could admit had been scary as hell. Now I was relieved, and suddenly hungry. I sat down to eat my lunch, feet kicking over the edge.

I got out my map and checked it as I ate. To my right I could see that the ridge of the Muttenbergen curled like the top of a question mark, curving from the Muttenstock to the Ruchi, then around to a different peak called the Rüchi. Tucked in the arc of the question mark was a snowy basin called the Mutten, filled for the most part by an icy lake called the Muttsee. A high Alpine lake! By now I knew these were rare. I could see the next section of my trail as a line of boot prints running across the snowy rib that held the Muttsee in place, and there on the rib stood a little square dot. My map identified this building as the Muttseehütte SAC (Swiss Alpine Club). When I got there it would be *kafi fertig* time for sure, coffee *finished* by way of a big shot of brandy.

Under my feet the space over the Limmerensee looked like an enormous roofless room, long and narrow, with the lake as its blue carpet. The wall on the other side of the lake was a horizontally banded cliff, rising sheer from the water to my own height; above that it lay back in a wild jumble of snow and boulders, ending in a jagged skyline that ran from peak to peak—from the Vorder Selbsanft to the Selbsanft to the Hinter Selbsanft to the Vord Schiben to the Hinter Schiben. *Vord* and *hinter*, fore and aft: all these names made sense from my vantage point, as if they had been named from here.

The Muttsee and the Limmerensee were both blue, but the blues were very different. The Muttsee was the brilliant sky blue of shallow water filled with ice. The Limmerensee, being a reservoir in a watershed with two big glaciers, was stained by suspended glacial silt to the opaque weird blue of radiator anti-freeze. The reservoir flooded a valley that must have been quite something before it was drowned. The mapmakers had retained the contour lines of the submerged area, and these showed the area had probably been meadow and forest, with the Limmerenbach running down the middle. It must have looked a bit like Yosemite Valley, but this had not stopped the Swiss from damming it. In their drive for hydroelectricity they had dammed and drowned many of the deepest gorges in the Swiss Alps. I suppose you can't afford to regard 65 percent of your country as an untouchable wilderness, but I was still a little shocked whenever I saw how relentlessly they had altered their landscape. No doubt a hidden valley like this one never had a chance.

And yet it was still a great space, and the Muttsee at least was still beautiful. I pulled my *bahnhof* sandwich from my daypack, pleased with my lunchtime prospect.

As I began eating I heard a buzz from below, and spotted a helicopter the size of a mosquito. It rose in slow spirals, working hard to gain altitude. No doubt climbing to resupply the Muttseehütte. I had seen other SAC huts resupplied in this manner, it was going to be interesting to watch.

The helicopter rose in a spiral that used the entire space of the gorge. It took about ten minutes for it to ascend, giving me a new sense of just how deep the gorge was. Foreshortening had gotten me again.

Eventually it completed its climb, and banked in a final spiral that brought it under my part of the cliff. I was going to get a good view of it. Its two circles of blades blurred, big one horizontal, small one vertical. The engine noise, which had started as a mosquito buzz, was now a roar. It was really going to pass close to me.

Then it rose to my level and hung right before me, making an incredible racket. It turned toward me, and I found myself looking into its bubble windshield, eye to eye with the pilot. He was wearing mirrored sunglasses and big earphones. I waved at him, but his hands were busy and he didn't wave back. I saw his forearms shift on his controls, and the helicopter tilted forward and began to drift straight in at me.

"Whoa!" I said. What the hell? The helo was still closing, the pilot's face was still blank. I scrambled to my feet, turned and retreated quickly over the spur's flat top. I looked over my shoulder and was shocked to see the helicopter topping the spur and dropping onto me, louder than ever.

I bolted up the hill in terror, a blast of wind buffeting me. In the horrible roar I dared look over my shoulder again—

The helicopter was landing on the flat spot behind the spur.

I stopped running. Aha: I had been sitting on his landing pad. It was the only flat spot around. Restocking the little shed, no doubt.

Well of course! I had not dropped into a horror movie after all!

I stood there feeling my heart blast blood through me.

The pilot killed the engine and climbed out of the cockpit. I walked back down toward him, intending to apologize for not getting out of his way.

He saw me and said something before bending to his cargo door, but there was still a lot of noise and I didn't hear him. I came closer to yell that I didn't speak much German, and all of a sudden he straightened up and shouted, "ACHTUNG!"

I stopped in my tracks. He pointed up at the blades still thwacking overhead. In that instant I saw that as helicopter blades slow down they become visible from the inside out. What I had assumed were the ends of the blades were actually just the ends of their visible part. Looking more closely, I saw the faint blur of sky that marked their real ends; the blades were about twice as long as I had thought. Not only that, but as they slowed they drooped a little, and I was descending onto the landing flat from above. So the actual tips of the blades, now quite visible to me, were at my head level, and about 15 feet away.

I turned and walked off. The pilot was busy anyway, and I had lost all interest in talking to him. I got out of there.

Several minutes down the trail I noticed that my half-eaten sandwich was still in my hand, squished to a ribbed tube of dough. I nibbled it as I hiked, noticed I was too deaf to hear myself chew. I looked back once or twice without intending to. I came to some of the deepest suncups I had ever seen, skidded this way and that on snow that had lost all structural integrity. It didn't matter; I wasn't really there.

When I trudged up the final approach to the Muttseehütte I was very ready to sit down and have a *kafi fertig* or two, or three. After that I would continue over a nearby rise called the Muttenchopf, and descend to the cable car that would drop me to the road at Tierfed.

The hut keeper was standing on the porch outside his door. He greeted me as I approached: "Grüüüüt-zi!" It was the Swiss greeting at its most Swiss.

He was short and bald, barrel-chested and suntanned, with immense forearms. He asked me where I had come from and I told him, reentering that zone of competence in German that I had magically occupied during my time with Mario. The hut keeper asked questions about snow conditions on the south side of the pass, and I described what I had seen, and all was clear. I didn't attempt to tell him about my encounter with the helicopter, which was beyond my German to express, so the conversation proceeded well. At one point, enjoying my ability to do so, I asked him how long it would take me to hike over the Muttenchopf, and when the last cable car of the day left Galbchopf for Tierfed.

The question startled him: Why? he asked. Did I want to take it?

Exactly, I said. *Genau*. I did want to take it.

He walked across the porch to me and said very firmly, "Du muss schon gegangen sein!"

You must already gegone to be.

I thought it over; yes, that was what it meant; most of the words were utterly simple, and I knew very well that *schon* meant "already," because that was what I used to yell at my Swiss baseball teammates when they did something good, intending to yell *schön* like they did, a mistake that had given them no end of amusement. So:

You must already be gone!

"Whoa!" I said. The hut keeper nodded as he saw I understood. He took me by the arm and walked me down to a trail sign just below the hut. In rapid but still magically comprehensible German he told me that this trail, which went down to the dam and then through a tunnel to the cable-car station, was a much faster route than the trail over the Muttenchopf—so much faster that it was my only hope of catching the last cable car, which left at 3:45.

It was now 3:05 p.m. I got out my topo map and he nodded approvingly and traced with a thick finger the trail I should take. "Vierzig minuten," he said emphatically. Forty minutes. And then he stepped back and cried, "Fliegst du!"

Fly you! Yikes! No more than five minutes had passed since my arrival, and here I was waving goodbye to the hut keeper and running down the trail, over the lip of the Mutten and down a steep green bowl to the shore of the virulent Limmerensee.

The trail was snow-free, and dropped down gullies and over grassy humps, and most of the time I could run it. Where the trail banked against rock walls there were cable handrails bolted into the rock, and these helped me maintain a good speed even when things got quite steep.

After about ten minutes of this I paused to catch my breath and look again at my map. As soon as I calculated the altitudes and distances involved I took off again, running down the trail faster than ever. Forty minutes! He was crazy! The drop to the lake was 650 vertical meters, and the tunnel looked to be about three kilometers long! No way!

But way. He had said it was possible, and he wouldn't have said it if he hadn't been sure. He had done it. Those Swiss Army guys passing me in their cars could do it, each chased by his own personal Böögen no doubt, but they could. If they couldn't the hut keeper would have told me to forget it, that I should stay the night at his hut, where there would be a radio phone I could have used to tell Lisa what had happened. Then I could have relaxed on the hut's porch drinking *kafi fertig*, or just the *fertig*, finishing myself while watching the evening alpenglow light up the Muttenstock. That was a good idea, now that I thought of it, but instead here I was hauling ass down the trail like a Keystone Kop, cursing the Swiss with every leap. Have a nice day in the Alps! I shouted as I plunged. So relaxing! God damn you guys! God damn your cable cars, and God damn you for closing the fucking things eight hours before dark! When you bother to keep them open at all! It's ridiculous! But I was going to do it anyway, and without any Böögens to chase me either—just a determination to get home that night, and because the hut keeper had said I could do it.

So I descended 650 meters in 25 minutes, certainly my all-time record. I panted along the shores of the radioactive Limmerensee until I was stopped by a cliff that dropped straight into the water. The trail ran right to a black iron door in this cliff.

The tunnel. God damn it one more time. I don't like tunnels.

I approached the door and looked at a page taped to it. The printed message, in German of course, had words so long they crossed the whole page. I couldn't understand any of it. Apparently my streak of German had ended in the great exchange with the hut keeper. *Fly you!* I had flown.

I turned the handle and pulled the door open. There was a light button just inside the door, and when I pushed it a line of bare bulbs came on overhead, illuminating a tunnel about nine feet high and not much wider. There were metal tracks, like tram tracks, laid on the tunnel's stone floor.

I stepped back out into the sunlight and tried to read the sign again. No way. Inside, a simpler note by the light button told me that the lights would stay on for 20 minutes after I pushed the button. Back outside I checked my map again. Yes, the tunnel was between two and three kilometers long. Say a mile and a half. I could run that in less than 20 minutes. And I would have to, not only to beat the lights going off, but in order to get to the cable-car station at the other end of the tunnel before 3:45—because it was now 3:31!

I banished my distaste for the tunnel and stepped inside the iron door and let it clang shut behind me. I hit the light button one more time and started jogging along the stone floor between the tram tracks.

Quickly I was far enough down the tunnel that I couldn't see the door behind me. In both directions the lightbulbs ran together into faint lines, which eventually disappeared entirely in the gloom. There were leaks in the rock ceiling, and occasionally I ran under little curtains of dripping water; often I stomped through puddles between the tracks. Getting winded, I checked my watch; I had been running three minutes. My initial pace had been too ambitious.

Very low creaks echoed down the tunnel, as if the rock around me was stressed. Maybe by the weight of all that radiator fluid. If the dam were to burst the tunnel would get torn apart. If an earthquake struck it would collapse. I ordered my mind to stop conjuring such events, but I have a fear of tunnels, and the infinite regress of dim bare lightbulbs in both directions was creepy. I kept pressing the pace, my boots splashing in the puddles, my daypack flopping on my back, my breath beginning to whoosh in and out. My watch showed 3:35 — but then I recalled that I had set it five or seven minutes fast, to help me keep up with Swiss timeliness — to help me in situations just like this, in fact. So I had a bit of leeway. And hopefully I was around halfway through the tunnel. It seemed to me that I was running at a nine-minute-mile pace at the very least, despite my boots. It all should work.

Twice I passed open black side tunnels to my left, the lake side, and I hurried by them and their wafts of cold air, wondering if they ran out to the dam, or under it. Once as a child I had gone with my parents and brother to Parker Dam on the Colorado River, and we had taken a tour through one of the big turbine rooms, and that night I dreamed we had been locked in there by accident and they let in the water and it rushed over us, causing me to wake up filled with a deep dread. There aren't that many dreams you remember your whole life. Now I seemed to be running in that dream, and the side tunnels scared me. I suppose in many ways I am still eight years old in my mind.

Thus when I heard a faint roar behind me I first put it down to morbid imagination. Then it got louder and was obviously real. A very definite roar in the tunnel behind me — and getting louder! I looked down at the tracks in the tunnel floor: tram tracks. A tram was coming!

I redoubled my speed. Swiss tunnels are often sized just a few inches wider and taller than the vehicles that pass through them. I glanced over my shoulder, in what was getting to be the day's signature movement, like in a poster for a Hitchcock movie, and saw two pinpricks of light. Little headlights under the string of lightbulbs, quickly growing bigger, filling the tunnel as the roar got louder. I turned and ran like a bunny.

Suddenly the tunnel widened and split into three. I ducked left, away from the tracks, and pulled up tight against the wall. An old VW van with a bad muffler sputtered past me.

Its driver had not seen me, and he drove on. I took off after him, guessing as I ran that the sign taped to the door at the other end of the tunnel might have announced the van's schedule to people wanting a ride. No doubt its last trip of the day was timed to take people out to the last cable car of the day.

The van came to a halt so suddenly I almost rear-ended it. We were at the end of the tunnel, it seemed. I had made it in time for the last cable car down.

The driver of the van (he had carried no passengers) turned out also to be the operator of the cable car. I followed him into a concrete chamber with a big gap in its floor and got in a cable car with him, not even trying to explain why I had run through the tunnel rather than wait for a ride. He did not seem interested in any case. Right before our departure (he was checking his watch to leave at the first second of 3:45), we were joined by an elderly couple in the full regalia of Swiss mountain walking: heavy leather boots, long wool socks, wool knee pants, plaid long-sleeved shirts, varnished walking sticks, old leather rucksacks. The man wore suspenders and a jaunty green cap with a feather. The woman's white hair was perfectly coiffed. No doubt they had timed their arrival so closely because they knew they could; the driver would only leave at precisely the designated time.

When they were in, the driver closed the door and latched it, punched at his control panel, and the car jerked out of the station and dropped like a boulder hung on a clothesline. Down we sailed. Tierfed was a thousand meters below, and watching the cliff shoot by I was very glad I had hurried to make the last car. Without it there was no way I would have made it home that night.

When, I asked the van driver hesitantly, suddenly self-conscious about my German, when did the bus leave Tierfed for the train station in Linthal?

He looked quickly at me, surprised. Bus? There was no bus.

I stared at him, appalled. I had never heard of such a thing. All the cable cars had bus connections to the nearest train station! It was over ten miles from Tierfed to Linthal, there had to be a bus!

The van driver shrugged. No bus. The elderly couple stared at me. I was still sweating from my tunnel run, and in fact I had broken a sweat several times that day, some of them hot sweats, some of them cold. I could taste the salt on my lips, and feel the sunblasting I had gotten; I knew from past experience that my face would be a flamboyant red, and in the window of the car I could see a faint reflection that showed my hair spiking out as if I had been electrocuted.

So when the van driver suddenly asked the elderly couple if they would give me a ride to the Linthal train station, I blushed an even deeper red. We still had a fair distance to descend, and this certainly put them on the spot. They didn't look like it was their kind of thing, and I was pretty sure they wouldn't have offered on their own. Some Swiss like their *Ausländer*, but others don't. There were political parties that wanted to kick all of us out, and their membership came mostly from mountain cantons.

A quick discussion between them and the van driver dove immediately into the deepest *Schwyzerdüüütsch*; I couldn't understand a word of it. But after a bit of back-and-forth, the husband turned to me and made the offer himself, very stiffly, in *Hochdeutsch*. I nodded gratefully and said *Danke*, at this point the only German word left to me.

We clanked into the Tierfed station and got out. I thanked the van driver and trailed the couple to their car, a big square Mercedes. Gingerly I got in the back seat. The husband drove us down the curving road in a dead silence.

There were so many things I wanted to say, stuck on the tip of my German tongue. Your country is so beautiful. I love the Alps. I'm only going to be here another few months, and I want to see everything before I go. Your transport system is really quite amazing. Although the bus component in this case has let us all down, forcing me to ask for your assistance. A helicopter almost chopped my head off at lunch. It chased me. I'm also scared of tunnels. I thought that VW van in the tunnel was a tram that was going to squish me like a bug. Even before that I was unhappy. I'm sorry you've been forced to do me this favor. I hope I don't smell too much, but I was terrified twice today. That rarely happens even once. If it weren't for the kindness of Swiss women I wouldn't even be here. Your farmwives are so nice. But a lot of you are mean to hitchhikers. And your cable cars stop way too early in the afternoon. I think many of you must have been traumatized by the Böögen, wouldn't you agree? It's a Swiss theory. It explains a lot, you have to admit.

I said nothing. None of it was sayable. I could hear all the sentences in a sort-of German in my mind, but I could not make my mouth say them.

In the front seat they were just as quiet. It was too bad, really; we had just spent the day up there in the same mountains, after all. I focused my mind, ignored my insecurities about tense and word choice and sentence order, about whether it would properly be *wohin* or *woher*, *tag* or *morgen*, *die* or *der* or *das*... I had made so many mistakes. How do you play baseball? You take nine human beings...my teacher had grinned at that one, he couldn't help himself. But if you got your meaning across, Mario had said, that's all that matters.

Where to today did you wander?

Rüchi, the wife replied.

Rüchi! The mountain?

Yes, the mountain. Rüchi is a mountain.

Wow, I said.

They had gone up there for lunch, she explained.

I got out my topo map, and she twisted around to show me their route. From the cable car they had traversed the Muttenwandli—then climbed the south slope of the Nüschenstock at the end of the question mark—then run the ridge from there up to Rüchi. What they had done was probably harder than what I had done, and they weren't even ruffled. *Ah genau*, I said as she named every point, *genau*. Exactly. This was what my Swiss teammates always said when other people were telling them things. It was something like our uh-huh, or I see, or yeah yeah, or you bet. *Genau:* it's a word the Swiss love to say and to hear. It may be the national anthem all by itself.

Pretty? I asked, being careful not to say Already?

They both nodded. Very pretty, the wife said.

Then she said, And where today did you go?

Kistenpass.

Keesh-tee-pahsss!

That must be what one always said. Some kind of surprise about it. Well, maybe that was right. Yes, I said. Keee-stee-pahss.

And was it pretty?

Very pretty. The Alps, I said, are very, very pretty.

They nodded again, glowing with quiet pride, with love. *Genau*, the husband murmured.

The train for Ziegelbrücke was leaving when I walked in the station, and in Ziegelbrücke I had to run to catch the Zurich train. My legs were sore. On the Zuri train I relaxed. I was going to make it home that night. Zürichsee, Hauptbahnhof, a number 6 tram; up the hill, up the stairs, into our apartment, flop into my kitchen chair. It was 7:15 p.m.

"How was it?" Lisa asked. "You look kind of wasted."

I opened my mouth, but nothing came out. I gaped like a goldfish.

She pointed a spatula at me. "Did you have another adventure?"

"Genau."

SNOW CAMPING (3)
The Transantarctics

The maps of ice coverage in the Sierra during the last ice age are rather amazing. Glaciologists like Francois Matthes did a lot of fieldwork to determine how high the ice piled up in the range, and their results are quite detailed, and ever so evocative.

Big sheets of ice covered large expanses of high upland such as the upper Kern, Tuolumne Meadow, and Humphreys Basin. These were ice seas, *mers de glace*. But for most of the range it wasn't like that. The highest ridges always stuck out of the ice, either as ridges or broad ramps. So the more typical ice cover consisted of many glaciers, big and small, starting high and then merging downward like the veins in a leaf, or the twigs and branches of a tree, all flowing downhill until the biggest dozen trunks poured down in long runouts to the west, or short drops to the east. How I wish that some computer company would make an Ice Age Sierra the way Google made a Google Mars, so that we could virtually helicopter over it, seeing in miniature what it would have looked like in that period. That would be a lot of fun. In the absence of such a digital glacio-paleo-psychogeological cartography, what we have are these glaciologists' maps, and our imaginations.

It must have been awesome. Of course there might not have been any people around to see it; but then again there might. Humans were in the Americas then, including in the basin-and-range territory, so some of them could have seen it. They probably did. Some little band of ice age nomads, or even an individual, or a pair or trio or quartet, might have even conceived some reason for crossing the range while it had its ice cover. Probably it would have been best

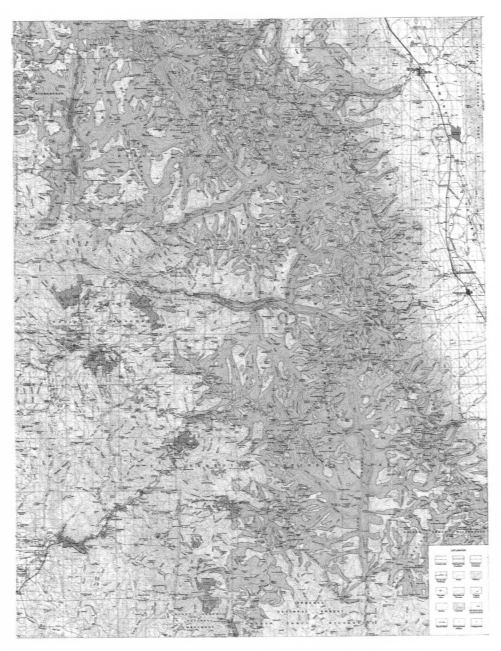

Ice age maximum, southern Sierra, based on work by Francois Matthes et al., USGS

accomplished in the late summer, or maybe in the spring when many crevasses would be filled with snow. Taboose Pass would always have been obvious from Owens Valley, and the easiest way across. On that route, ice would have covered the entire width of the range, from the floor of Owens Valley over the crest and then down and out through the gate of lower Kings Canyon. Crevasse fields would presumably have been frequent and awful, but if a route through them could be threaded, which is usually possible, it would have simply been a matter of walking on tilted ice. That would be hard, of course. But it would have been possible. These were ice age people, glaciers were everywhere in their time; ice would not have been unfamiliar terrain. They might have occasionally made forays similar to those of Scott and Shackleton and Amundsen, hiking up the big glacier roads through the peaks of the Transantarctic Mountains—

And suddenly, thinking about this one day, while writing this very book in fact, I realized I *had* seen what the Sierras must have been like back then! I had seen it in Antarctica!

That was a happy thought.

The Transantarctics are a mountain range quite similar to the Sierras and the Alps, geologically speaking. They are quite a bit older than the twins, but have been well preserved by their freeze-dried life. As Reinhold Messner once remarked, in his book about crossing Antarctica on foot (he had promised his mother that he would stop climbing after he finished ascending all the world's 8,000-meter peaks without oxygen aid, so after he did that, he set to walking the Gobi, then skiing [pulled by kites!] across Greenland and Antarctica, etc.)—he said, the Transantarctics are a mountain range like any other, but buried to the neck in ice.

That's how the Sierras were 20,000 years ago!

That realization has given me a new way of thinking about my time in Antarctica, especially my visits to the Dry Valleys, and to Roberts Massif in the Transantarctics. About 25,000 years ago, the Owens Valley might have somewhat resembled the Dry Valleys today, the big east-side Sierra glaciers pouring down out of their canyons onto the valley floor, and there melting or subliming away in the dry desert air.

Canada Glacier and Lake Fryxell, Taylor Valley, Antarctica

And Roberts Massif, located where the Shackleton Glacier pours off the great polar ice cap, is a rock island in a sea of ice—a nunatak, as the Inuit call them. It sticks up only a little above the ice flowing around it. Against its south shore, that ice forms the edge of the big polar cap, the biggest ice sea on Earth by a long shot. Ice slowly accumulates up there and falls off that cap under the pressure of its own weight, and in that slow fall it flows around the rock island of Roberts Massif, in gigantically wide glaciers that meet again on the downstream side of the massif. So it's a low square island, several miles in diameter, in an ice sea as big as the United States. The ice flowing around its red dolerite shore is either white, or a creamy turquoise. In places the ice rears up over the rock like big ocean waves, flash-frozen just before crashing onto the land. One day we hiked under one of these frozen waves for an hour, marveling at the blue ice hanging over us. In other places we could look offshore from low bluffs, and see the ice broken into a cross chop, or forming a smooth pour, seeming to rush by without moving.

Roberts Massif on the right, Shackleton Glacier in foreground, latitude 86 degrees south. This photo was taken from a helicopter piloted by someone a bit too enthusiastic to show me how huge the crevasses were. We almost flew down into one.

Although Roberts Massif is bigger, its shape reminded me of Diamond Mesa, in the upper Kern; when the upper Kern was covered by an ice sea, Diamond Mesa would have been a nunatak sticking up out of it.

Diamond Mesa surrounded by the upper Kern, Junction Peak behind it to the right, Shepherd Pass to the far right

Imagining what it would have felt like for the people living back then, living next to land iced over in such dramatic ways—well, that's hard. I tried to do it when writing my novel *Shaman*, and I concluded it couldn't really be done, but was worth trying anyway. It would have been awesome, of course; the whole world was awesome then, a vast mysterious unfolding; and the thing is, it still is. You just have to go outside and look. Walking also helps.

In terms of psychogeology, this glacial history of the Sierra is the key fact. As I said when describing the fellfields, you should go where the ice was. Of course this means most of the high Sierra, so maybe the point needs to be reversed: don't go where the ice didn't go! Those lower places, okay, they aren't terrible; nice forest, etc.; but compared to the glaciated high country, they are mundane, which is to say worldly, unexceptional, and unfriendly to walkers.

Now the Sierra's glaciers are almost entirely gone. There are said to remain around 100 little glaciers and around 400 glacierets, glacierets being glaciers

Palisades glaciers from the northeast, airplane view

so small that the ice in them no longer slides downhill. I now think many of these are already gone. Once while flying from Sacramento to Phoenix I caught a photo of the biggest remaining glaciers in the range, lying in a line under the northeast wall of the Palisades. The range was snow-free at the time, so this photo illustrates very well how close to ice-free the range now is.

Part of the Sierra's current glory, even most of it, is attributable to the scouring of the great glaciers and ice seas, carving hollows for water to pool in. There are other glorious factors, such as the cleanness of the ice-burnished granite, in broad rumpled gorgeous expanses still treeless and easy to walk on. But the crucial effect was the creation of so many ponds, lakes, and small streams. Here's where the Sierra's history of *light glaciation* matters so much: there are literally thousands of little ponds and lakes in the high Sierra. I once read that there are 6,000 ponds and lakes in the range, but the number would depend on your definition of what to count. No matter the exact number, the light glacial scraping of the granite resulted in an immense number of lakes and ponds, and of course when they're filled with their annual snowmelt, they spill over at their lowest points, and that water then runs down the path of least resistance, usually down a set of cracks in the granite, into a lower pond or lake. Through most of every summer, every non-drought summer I should add, these streams are everywhere. It's not just the system drawn on the maps, already very extensive; it's also the seasonal streams pouring out of every miniature pond, down through every tilted meadow and tiny alluvial fan. Because there is so little soil, what water there is tends to run over the bedrock surface into some lower catchment. Thus everywhere water is in visible motion; in the summers you almost can't camp in a place where the sound of moving water won't be part of your lullaby that night.

And everywhere there's water, there's life. Even if the water isn't there year-round. Many kinds of life, including lichens and mosses, can be desiccated for a long time, then get resuscitated by a new spate of snowmelt. Year after year these plants revive, and then they add to their terrain as they grow. Slowly but surely, life has spread over terrain that lost the bulk of its ice 10,000 years ago, exposing a nearly barren rockscape.

Scenes like this are scattered everywhere.

What this means for backpackers is really profound. Everywhere you go there will be water; you don't need to carry more than a few mouthfuls with you as you hike, as Terry so often insisted, because by the time you get thirsty, another stream or pond will be there to help you.

And you'll always have somewhere beautiful to camp. A campsite 20 or 30 feet higher than a nearby lake is one of the most beguiling landscapes to spend time in, as the watery part of the scene will always be changing with wind and weather and time of day. Having these expansive mirrors inlaid into the rock around you, reflecting the stone and the sky, is a very beautiful thing.

This is what the glaciers of the ice ages gave us: a sculptured, burnished, watery, vivid landscape. From a range like the Transantarctics, to the Sierras as we have them now: it only takes ten thousand years.

SIERRA PEOPLE (9)
Norman Clyde

Norman Clyde (1885–1972) was one of the clearest cases ever of a man who fell in love with the Sierra and then changed his life to act on that love. But for him it was a second marriage, so to speak; he was a widower. The Sierras were his consolation.

He married Winifred Bolster when he was 30, she 25. She worked as a nurse in a tuberculosis ward in the Bay Area, and almost immediately became ill with the disease, and died of it four years later. Clyde cared for her through her illness. After her death, apparently her mother somehow blamed him for her getting sick. He took off for the Sierras and never came back.

He had been educated in the classics at Geneva College, in western Pennsylvania, and all his life he carried Homer in Greek, and Virgil in Latin, in his backpack. People called him "the pack that walks like a man," and noted frying pans, cobbler's anvils, and similarly heavy items in his gear. Once his pack was weighed on a horse packer's scale, and came in at 75 pounds; the men there offered him tin cans of free food, to see how much more he would add to his pack, and they say he added about 20 pounds before he walked off. He was a short man and weighed about 140 pounds.

He worked as a high school principal in Independence, until scaring off some hooligans on Halloween with gunshots, after which he was fired. From then on he worked as a winter caretaker for various lodges around the Sierra, and spent his summers climbing in the range. For a long time he lived in an abandoned ranch house near Big Pine. He made first ascents of 117 Sierra peaks, a record that can't be beaten, and pioneered multiple routes to the top of many of these. He went up Whitney 50 times.

He helped in the search for Pete Starr when Starr went missing in the Minarets, and stayed on after the rest of the search party had given up, until he finally located Starr's body two weeks later. It was clear Starr had taken a big fall. Clyde went out to inform people, and returned with Jules Eichorn to climb up and inter the body in a cleft at the back of the ledge where Clyde had found it. Eichorn reported that Clyde wouldn't touch the body — that he himself, a 21-year-old kid, as he later put it, had to get the body into a canvas bag and build the rock wall over the cleft. All the while Clyde wept.

Pete Starr, the man they found dead up there, was another Sierra lover, dying at age 32 after spending his twenties running around the range at a tremendous clip (120 miles in an extended weekender, etc.), climbing every peak he passed. Clyde had hiked and climbed with him many times, and sitting there while Eichorn got Starr's body into a bag, Clyde must have remembered not just his friend, but his wife. All these deaths. The Sierras may be a place of solace, but they are not a place of forgetting. As you look down from that high perch, the world can seem so strange, so awful. If only you didn't have to go down; if only you could live up there forever.

Clyde basically did that. I think he might have spent a larger percentage of his days in the high Sierra than anyone, even the rangers, even the Native Americans. He lived up there; thus the frying pan, the anvil, the volume of Homer.

After he died, Eichorn and some other climbing friends cast his ashes from the top of Norman Clyde Peak, a Palisades peak visible from Glacier Lodge, where Clyde had often lived as winter caretaker. His friends had suggested the name for the peak 40 years before, after he made first ascents from both sides in June of 1930.

He climbed solo most of the time, so he must have had some close calls. He must have been careful, and good; quick, nimble, clear-sighted, resourceful. Every peak summit register from the 1920s and 1930s that I've looked into at the Bancroft Library in Berkeley has his signature in it, usually several times.

Clyde used a rope sometimes, but solo climbing is solo climbing, rope or not. Maybe he had an attitude like that of Dougal Haston, Chris Bonington's great lead climber, or the Mallory generation on the north side of Everest, most of whom were World War I veterans: something so bad had happened to these men in their youths that it made them fearless, because they didn't quite care if they lived or died. And on a hard climb you can't think about anything else, it becomes all-absorbing. You get taken away from your thoughts and your memories, and the present moment becomes all. On a rock wall the world goes away. So Clyde spent a lot of time on rock walls.

He hiked with the Sierra Club's high trips often, but got banished more than once, for yelling at men he thought were behaving badly. He wouldn't be reprimanded by anyone, not even David Brower. So years would pass when he was banished from the club, or he banished the club. Then he would come back. During one of the last of the club's high trips, in the basin above Lake Sabrina, he showed up in camp coming down from above, which suggests he came over the crest to get to them—that would require crossing either Echo Col, or Blumlein Pass, or Darwin Col—all very difficult and strenuous cross-country passes. He was 82 at the time. His last campsite was in the Fourth Recess, which means he crossed Mono Pass at age 85, a year after an operation to remove a cancerous eye. Melanoma of the retina, after lots of sunny Sierra days, for a Sierra lover not inclined to wear sunglasses.

His favorite lake was Tulainyo Lake, which I'm sure spoke to him as an image he liked: a simple oval, very removed from anywhere else, with no outlet stream. Austere and mysterious.

His articles for an automobile magazine are completely bland and without distinction. His camp journals read like Homer jotting notes by the fire: hungry and cold, cold and hungry.

For most of his life, no one knew he had once been married. He didn't tell even the people who knew him best, his fellow climbers. Late in life he was visited at his home by Walt Wheelock, who was reprinting an old book made from his magazine articles; Wheelock had been a police investigator, and after a few hours of questions, Clyde told him about his youthful marriage. He asked Wheelock to put a dedication to his wife at the front of the reprint of his book, but somehow it didn't happen. A few editions later, long after Clyde's death, and Wheelock's too, Wynne Benti of Spotted Dog Press put the dedication in there.

"To Winnie, Norman."

Norman Clyde: sometimes the camera really does capture your soul.

NAMES (2)
The Bad

Bad names are simply too plain, or too obvious, or somehow wrong, or just lame. Often all these at once.

Matterhorn Peak, for instance, is a stupid name. The peak looks nothing like the real Matterhorn from any angle, nor is it a horn. Lincoln Hutchinson, in the *Sierra Club Bulletin* for 1900, wrote, "That the name is a poor one there can be no doubt."

That name should be changed to Snyder-Kerouac Peak, to honor Gary Snyder, who took Jack Kerouac up this peak in October of 1955. Kerouac should be added to the name, because if he hadn't written up the ascent in his novel *The Dharma Bums*, we wouldn't know about it; and his account of the climb is very fine. His big lesson from the climb, shouted ecstatically: "You can't fall off the mountain!" is one of the great examples of false generalization from a true particular. Gary Snyder could somersault his way down the east slope of this peak, because it's a grassy hillside. But you can still fall off the mountain—even that one, on the other side. That silliness aside, Kerouac's careful observation, good memory, and precise soulful writing make for a very lively account of a Sierra trip 1950s style. There were many more Sierra trips like theirs than there were the curated expeditions of the Sierra Club, even though the latter tend to dominate the written record of the range. So Kerouac's account is very valuable, and as with Clarence King, the description of a Sierra backpacking trip ended up being the best writing of Kerouac's life.

On Matterhorn Peak, 1999: Terry, me, Victor, Darryl, Dick, Joe. The summit register box was
stuffed with tributes to Snyder and Kerouac.

Easy to find more bad names: Bubbs Creek, for instance, which is named for a guy who descended the creek with a group in 1864. It was lamented as a name for this canyon many times by Sierra Clubbers, who thought Bubb sounded too low-class. I don't want to be snobbish like that, it's no worse than any other name memorializing some random guy who once passed by the place, like Joe Devel Peak farther south, but I do want to point out again that it had a much better name before, to be seen on John Muir's map of Kings Canyon, published in a magazine article of 1890, a name Muir almost certainly bestowed himself: the South Fork of the South Fork. He must have laughed as he jotted that one down, and it is a good joke, and a great name, not to be lost!

*   *   *

Then there are all the many names that come from physical features too obvious to make a name. Granite Dome, Granite Pass—of course, I know just the one you mean! Or Round Lake. Or Rock Creek (two of them). Or White Mountain (four of them). Or Twin Lakes, of which there are many; and they're never really twins.

No no no. Grass Valley, Deer Meadow, Pine Creek, Granite Park, all these ultraobvious names are bad. Really, when you add up all the various kinds of bad names, there are many more bad names in the Sierra than good names. Sorry to say it, but it's true. There's work to be done here, people. The job is not finished. After first draft comes revision, and hopefully improvement. There is no reason why a single generation, with questionable taste and dubious values (i.e., much like ours), should get to name the features of this range for all time.

All the names that memorialize people who never saw the Sierra or even gave it a thought—people who were prominent at the time, or simply rich—they are all bad. "I always get a little tired of the way Professor Whitney named everything after himself and his friends," someone in the 1910s wrote to the *Sierra Club Bulletin*, but that was only the start of the badness.

In fact, that thought leads directly to one of the worst of the bad names, which is Mount Whitney itself. Josiah Whitney was an undistinguished professor and bureaucrat, and in the only meaningful geological controversy of his life he was wrong, and rudely condescending to boot. No way does he deserve to have the tallest peak in the range named after him! And named by his employees no less, in a kind of kiss-ass gesture. Of course the peak in question is just the tallest bump on the crest, but it is a rather magnificent bump at that, and it is the tallest.

What should it be called instead? The answer is obvious, and by a nice coincidence, the right name is already there on the south shoulder of Whitney, bestowed on one of the four needles poking out of the peak's south ridge: Mount Muir. So everything can be made right with a simple reversal of the names of two peaks located only about a mile from each other. Call Mount

Whitney, Mount Muir, and call Mount Muir, Mount Whitney. The real relationship between the two men and their importance to the world will then be made manifest in stone.

The justice of this simple correction would be very satisfying. I expect the act of Congress making this switch will be written and passed the very moment it gets suggested.

Another bad habit: notice how women tend to get features named after them by their first names only, while men get remembered by their last names, or even, if it was a common last name, by their full names. Lake Doris, Lake Lois, Martha Lake, on it goes. It's a widespread problem.

It leads me to propose one redress for this, which would also deal with the cluster of bad names found in Pioneer Basin. Pioneer Basin itself is a bad name, because the people honored with the names of the four peaks surrounding the basin, the supposedly eponymous pioneers, are Huntington, Hopkins, Stanford, and Crocker. So the basin's real name should be Robber Baron Basin. Not a bad name in itself, really, and it's what I've been calling that basin for more than 20 years. And I recently noticed that the great online Sierra map at caltopo.com has an informal name added to a fifth peak overlooking this basin, called Robber Baron Peak—someone was thinking along the same lines I was.

But that name for this basin is kind of a downer, bringing up as it does the question of why we remember men like that with peak names. It's like naming the four peaks Mount Jobs, Mount Gates, Mount Musk, and Mount Zuckerberg. Does anyone think that's a good idea? I hope not! Although some of these men are rather unobjectionable compared to some people with money—but that's irrelevant. It's a bad idea no matter which billionaire you choose, and it was just as bad an idea a century ago as it is today. Not that they thought so back then, and of course some people still idolize our rich men, but enough is enough. There's no rule that says we have to stay saddled with the past's lame taste forever. A change is in order, both in our mountain names and in our culture more generally.

So, we could call it Robber Baron Basin, and shift the names every century to the latest generation of rich business leaders. But let's be more positive about it. We have a basin surrounded by four peaks that make a set, and they all need new names, being named after unremarkable rich guys of an older time. And those old names were given at a time when women were being systematically disadvantaged and oppressed, such that distinguished women of that time are now under-remembered in our culture, and under-represented in the Sierra's names. Just a tiny little aspect of the damage done by patriarchy, but now some gestures can be made to make the range itself a better place, and maybe our culture too, by reflecting a more gender-balanced outlook.

One way women get left out of the record is by the creation of our literary canon. We don't remember the great women writers of American literature very well, no matter how good they were. So I propose those four peaks be renamed Mount Willa Cather, Mount Edna Ferber, Mount Zora Neale Hurston, and Mount Edith Wharton. You could use just their last names if you want, people would get it—Mounts Cather, Ferber, Hurston, and Wharton— nice quartet! But they look good with their full names too. Either way would be fine. And then Pioneer Basin could remain the name for the basin, and become appropriate at last, because these women were pioneers for real. *O Pioneers!* as Cather put it in one of her titles. That would make it such a nicer place. Because names do matter.

If you would prefer women writers more connected to California and the American West for the Sierra, fine, good idea; let's do that too. I'll get to that in the chapter called "Corrections and Additions."

Yes—in case you are wondering—I am playing a game here. But I'm serious when I say that this is a game we should be playing. Michel Foucault, by way of Margret Grebowicz: "We must think that what exists is far from filling all possible spaces. To make a truly unavoidable challenge of the question: What can be played?"

Naming itself is a kind of game. And while it's true that there are some truly ugly names in the Sierra, which I'll get to later, and which probably should engage our initial attention and efforts at repair, the merely bad names are not made much better by the presence of the ugly names. Let's change them all, until we have nothing but good names up there. Native American names where possible, and where it's not possible, improvements in our language, in an ongoing process of revision. It may be a game, but it's a good game. Let's play it.

ROUTES (2)

The Six Good Passes

If the east side of the Sierra has its Four Bad Passes (and it does), are there also Four Good Passes? Good, in the sense of having a high trailhead, a quick trail to the crest, and lots of interesting places just over the pass?

Immediately I would guess that there are more than four, even keeping to the east side only. After some consideration, I think there are in fact Six Good Passes on the east side.

ONE: NEW ARMY PASS

I'll make the list south to north, as with the bad passes; so the first is surely New Army Pass, leading to the Miter Basin and places north.

The trailhead is Horseshoe Meadows, at 10,300 feet one of the highest trailheads of all. The easy hike up to the Cottonwood Lakes is about five miles, and the broad plateau holding the Cottonwood Lakes is set right under the crest.

New Army Pass and Old Army Pass are both fine; if there is no snow, I'd recommend taking Old Army, as in the first chapter of this book. Snow complicates both of them, but New Army, facing south, loses its snow quicker, and has more options when a residual snowpack is still cornicing the top. Depending on your party's speed and strength, if Old Army Pass is clear of snow, you can be in the Miter Basin at the end of the first day, and even add an ascent of Mount Langley if you like. Definitely one of the Six Good Passes, counting the two alternative routes as one.

TWO: KEARSARGE PASS

The road to the trailhead is great, the parking lot at Onion Valley is huge, you're already at 9,000 feet when you get out of your car, and after four or five miles up the overly graded trail you're in Kearsarge Pass, which is at 11,900 feet. It's a quick and easy up.

On the inside there are a lot of good places to go. Drop directly west to Bullfrog Lake and the Muir Trail, and you can head either north over Glen Pass to the Rae Lakes, or south toward Forester Pass. Center Basin can be accessed to the south, and Gardiner Pass off to the northwest. You could also drop farther west, and make left turns into Vidette Basin, or up to East Lake, or even drop down to the Sphinx Lakes trail, or all the way down to Kings Canyon. This last, a complete traverse of the Sierra, was one of the main trans-Sierran routes for Native Americans, and for good reason, being one of the easiest.

THREE: BISHOP PASS

My first and favorite. This is a Very Good Pass, maybe the best. You start from South Lake at 9,300 feet, and Bishop Pass is at 11,900 feet, some five or six beautiful miles away. The trailhead has a parking lot not big enough, so you might have to park on the road below, but whatever. Parchers is down there, and they're great for renting a hiker's cabin, and for overflow parking.

And on the other side of Bishop Pass is Dusy Basin. There's no basin I love more. I would go there every year, happily.

FOUR: PIUTE PASS

This one leaves from North Lake rather than South Lake. Again the trailhead is around 9,300 feet, and Piute Pass is at around 11,400 feet, five miles up an easy trail. This also was a Native American crossing, as you can drop down to the west and emerge in the western foothills by way of curving easy canyons.

Immediately west of Piute Pass is Humphreys Basin, a single huge slope tilted down toward the west, with any number of nice ponds scattered over it, and on its northern side the gigantic Desolation Lake, one of the biggest high Sierra lakes of all. Mount Humphreys looms over the basin with its jagged colorful charisma, a beast of a peak, made of old roof-pendant rock stuck right on the crest. Class 2 crossings can be made out of Humphreys Basin into French Canyon to the north, and Darwin Canyon to the south. And at the bottom of the basin runs the Muir Trail.

So Piute Pass is an excellent pass, now made even better by the fact that on the way up you pass between Mount Emerson and our Mount Thoreau, previously Peak 12691. This is a very fitting reminder of how those two men and their transcendentalist love of nature helped us invent a new sense of sacred space, to enable European newcomers to better feel their relation to the land. Adding Mount Thoreau to Mount Emerson makes for a gateway pair of peaks, a pair to equal the gateway in the Ionian Basin that leads downward between Scylla and Charybdis.

FIVE: PINE CREEK PASS

Not a good name, by the way. It should be called the Tungsten Mine.

The road to it leads to the abandoned tungsten mine still there rusting in place (though the cleanup is proceeding, slowly but surely). The trailhead has a little parking area, at about 7,200 feet. Pretty low for a Good Pass, but it's worth that extra verticality, because the trail takes you up to two wonderful passes, Pine Creek Pass and Italy Pass. Pine Creek Pass is low and easy, and leads into French Canyon, a very pretty glacial canyon with an apron all the way around its upper end, said apron covered by a number of lakes. You can descend French Canyon to the Muir Trail, or cut up and over into the Bear Lakes region using Feather Pass, on the Roper High Route.

Italy Pass is higher, and is like Lamarck Col, in that it isn't trailed on its inside slope. Even on the east side, the trail peters out just below the pass. On the west side everyone takes a different way over rough rocky terrain, but the routes down to Jumble Lake, or through a sandy slot to White Bear Lake, are self-evident. And the entire region between Italy Pass and the Muir Trail is marvelous. There's a trail running from Lake Italy down to the Muir Trail. Toe Lake, by the way, next to Lake Italy, should obviously be called Sicily Lake. Hard to figure how they blew that one, given the shapes involved.

The Bear Lakes are little gems, scattered over a rumpled white granite massif; and the Seven Gables Canyon, at the western foot of this massif, is magical. It's simply a very great region of smooth white rock, broad and high; loops of all kinds can be made up there that will get you back to the trailhead in a week.

I noticed just now that I skipped Lamarck Col, also out of North Lake. I guess it's a great pass without being a Good Pass. Even though it's not on the maps, there's a continuous trail from North Lake to the col, which is at 12,880 feet, or so someone with a GPS has scratched onto the sign in the pass. But on the Darwin Canyon side, the trail disappears and you have to descend the sandy south-facing slope on your own. That's easy, but then Darwin Canyon, which you also have to descend, has some bouldery sections you can't avoid. By the time you get to the triangular Darwin Bench, a sweet inside perch, it feels like it's been quite a workout. From Darwin Bench there's now an excellent use trail leaving the south side of the outlet stream, just above where the stream plunges into the immense depth of the canyon below. The use trail leads left on a descending traverse to the Muir Trail, meeting it right where the Muir Trail finishes switchbacking up the big east wall of Evolution Valley. A perfectly routed use trail, the natural genius really nailing it, and you don't want to miss it—we have, and I can certify that going higher or lower is a big mistake.

So, Lamarck Col is a great, but not a Good Pass. The next Good Pass is surely…

SIX: MONO PASS

Out of Rock Creek. Speaking of bad names, there are two Mono Passes, and two Rock Creeks, but putting that aside, this one is a Good Pass. The road to it goes up from Tom's Place, on Highway 395, to Mosquito Flat; the parking lot is at 10,400 feet, the highest trailhead of all. Mono Pass is just three miles away, at 12,000 feet. Then you're at the top of the Mono Creek drainage, which drops west in a straight line, with the four Recesses to the left of the creek, and Pioneer Basin and Hopkins Creek, and then Laurel Lake's creek, rising on your right. All great. From Second Recess you can cross over Gabbot Pass to Lake Italy; from Laurel Lake you can cross easy passes to the colorful metamorphic drainage west of McGee Pass. Both of these form parts of Roper's High Route. Lower on Mono Creek you come to the Muir Trail, running low again, as so often. Somewhat awkward loop trips are possible in all directions, but going down Mono Creek and exploring sideways up both sides, and then returning back the way you came, is not a bad trip; and the whole region is very nice. It's maybe the most modest and limited of what I am now thinking are the Six Good Passes, but still, it's good.

North of Mono there are okay passes, like McGee, or Agnew, or Mammoth; but none of these rises to the level of the Six Good Passes. You can drive over the crest near Mammoth Pass, for one thing; the road quickly stops over there, but still, this is weird and unsatisfactory, part of the general weirdness and unsatisfactoriness of the entire Mammoth region. Roads, streets, town, ski lifts, cable cars to tops of peaks, it's all a kind of plywood Switzerland, catering to a ski crowd from LA. Not a real Sierra place, sorry. The whole area is less impressive than the high Sierra anyway, which ends, for me, a bit to the south, around Silver Pass and McGee Pass. Indeed McGee Pass has a nice trailhead and parking lot, just off 395, and over McGee Pass is the colorful glory of the Red and White Peak complex, a red roof pendant all mixed with white granite, making for a fine stretch of Roper's High Route. McGee is therefore a Pretty Good Pass.

North of that, this book will seldom go. Yosemite has enough enthusiasts to make up the lack here. Did I mention I don't like Yosemite? Maybe I shouldn't.

GEOLOGY (5)

Canyons and Massifs

CANYONS

Once upon a time, there were three beautiful and accomplished sisters who grew up together in a cottage in the forest. One was crowned queen, one was murdered, and the third was completely forgotten. The end.

This is the fairy-tale fate of the Sierra's three most famous canyons, Yosemite, Hetch Hetchy, and Kings Canyon. They are all three glacial canyons of the kind that Muir tried to name yosemites, so that people would understand that they were all formed in the same way—part of his case against Whitney, but also a valid observation, and the noun *yosemite* a nice idea, not taken up.

What follows from Muir's observation is that these three big yosemites are by no means the only ones in the Sierra. You could easily tack on a dozen more glacial canyons like them on the west side, and a few on the east side. Some of these other yosemites have also been drowned under reservoirs like Hetch Hetchy, the murdered sister in the fairy tale. Vermilion Valley was famous in its time for its eponymous color; that's now the Courtright Reservoir. The point of drowning Hetch Hetchy was precisely to destroy the idea that beautiful canyons should be saved for their own sake, and the point was taken. Any canyon with a narrow gorge at its lower end would make a fine reservoir, as Hetch Hetchy showed; the fact that lower watersheds in the foothills could impound much more water behind lower and cheaper dams was effectively obscured. The Bureau of Reclamation eventually dammed many of these foothill opportunities too, but while the idea of glacial canyons as reservoirs held, a half dozen or so were dammed in the Sierra. When Kings Canyon National Park was established, cutouts in the park boundary were made to allow for the hypothetical possibility of dams on both the South Fork and the Middle Fork of the Kings River. Only after the impulse to drown glacial canyons subsided did these canyons and their dam sites get folded into the park.

This deep canyon forest would be under water if Kings Canyon had been dammed, as planners in the 1940s hoped to do.

This is a relief, even retrospectively, because it would have been a real tragedy to repeat the drowning of Hetch Hetchy in the two forks of the Kings River. Both these canyons are superb, and in different ways. Kings Canyon proper (the South Fork) is vast, and more V-shaped than U-shaped, so there's no one place where you can get a good view of the whole of it. You drive in from the south on a winding road that cuts into the side of the gorge where the canyon debouches onto the foothills, a gorge so narrow it's hard to believe your eyes as you drive by, even given the inevitable foreshortening effect, because at that point it's one of the deepest canyons in the world—deeper than the Grand Canyon, while also being much narrower.

As for the canyon of the Middle Fork, it's narrower still, while being just as deep. It twists like a snake as it runs uphill, first northeast, then east, then north, then at its very upper end, northwest. All the while its ice-smoothed granite walls curve together like synchronized swimmers. A hidden treasure, a lapidary masterpiece, maybe the greatest Sierra canyon of all.

And there are many other glacial canyons almost as fine. The Hilgard fork of Bear Creek, Evolution Valley, Piute Creek canyon, Woods Creek, the South Fork of the South Fork, the Muro Blanco, Rock Creek south, both forks of Lone Pine Creek, the Kern-Kaweah canyon, East Creek, Cloud Canyon, Deadman Canyon, Palisade Creek, Cartridge Creek, Goddard Canyon, Goddard Creek Canyon (speaking of bad names, these two take off in opposite directions from Reinstein Pass)—French Canyon, Seven Gables Canyon, Mono Creek south, Kern Canyon (a monster)...as with the high basins, this list could be extended in a fractal fashion, until you get down to little capillary canyons, as Muir did in his discussion of Twenty Hills Hollow.

Thus the canyons. When I was young, they were just roads to get us to the high country. We hurried through them on trails and then burst up into the trailless high country like grouse exploding out of brush into the air.

Now I don't feel that way. Things happened to change me:

—Hiking up the Middle Fork all of one long day, astonished at the beauty rearing up on both sides, the creek bouncing in its muscular green rush through a chiseled granite channel.

—A sunset down in the shadows of Evolution canyon, watching a water ouzel stand on the bottom of a stream eating bugs.

—The polished walls of Bear Creek canyon, gleaming like marble in the rain.

These and other days have taught me to see that Sierra canyons are beyuls, as Tibetan Buddhist mythology calls them—mystical hidden valleys, like Shambhala or Khembalung. You can only recognize beyuls when you have achieved the proper mindset to see them. Now I see them.

Even the Muir Trail gets redeemed, almost, when you see it that way—as a long interlocking set of canyon walks.

Grouse Meadow, in LeConte Canyon, on the Muir Trail

MASSIFS

A derivative effect of the deep glacial canyons dissecting the Sierra batholith is that they cut the range into massifs, which are, in one definition, "a mountainous mass or group of connected heights, more or less clearly marked off by valleys." The southern Sierra is therefore like a rough jigsaw puzzle of contiguous massifs. Whether these massifs are individual pluton tops, separated from each other by the glacial scouring and deepening of the depressions between them, I am not geologist enough to say. One massif seems isomorphic with what geologists call the Cartridge pluton, which is what gave me that idea. Whatever their geological origins, these massifs definitely exist.

The clearest examples are the Mount Clarence King massif, and the Arrow Peak massif just to the north of it. For the Clarence King, the canyons bordering it are the Woods Creek canyon to its north and east, and the South Fork of the South Fork on its south. The massif's top is not a level plateau, they never are (except for the Table Mountain between Lake Sabrina and North Lake); it's scored by Gardiner Basin, Sixty Lakes Basin, and the unnamed basin dropping from King Col down to Woods Creek. Sometimes when basins open onto the deeper canyons bordering their massifs, they become hanging valleys, and their exit streams plummet down the big canyon walls. A few hang so hard you can't even get up the exit stream, as at Gardiner Creek's drop into the Muro Blanco, or the Gorge of Despair's drop to the Middle Fork. Other basins cut down to the canyons they debouche into and meet them "at grade," as they say in the Grand Canyon.

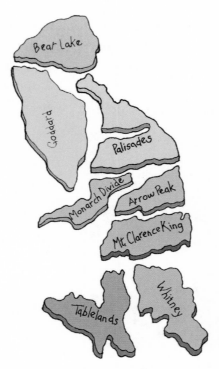

Some massifs of the southern Sierra. Drawing by Elizabeth Whalley.

The Arrow Peak massif has the Muro Blanco on its north, the Muir Trail canyons on its east, and Woods Creek on the south.

A bigger massif than these two is also a triangle of sorts, a long isosceles triangle: the Monarch Divide, on the northern side of the Kings River. Just north of the Monarch Divide massif is the Palisades massif, which includes the Cartridge pluton, and farther north again, the Bear Lakes massif, which is bordered by French Canyon, Hilgard Canyon, and the Granite Park.

The Tablelands are another long triangular massif, with Kings Canyon to the north, Kaweah River canyon to the south, and to the east, the other side of the Great Western Divide.

The idea of massifs feels important to me, because it helps identify backpacking routes. A weeklong trip needs a loop that will get you back to your car. One way to conceptualize such a trip is to imagine getting up onto a massif, and exploring things up there. The circumambulation of Mount Clarence King is a good example of this, and going out onto the Tablelands is another. What staying up on a massif saves you from are the deep drops and rises necessitated by going down and then back up the sides of any of the deep canyons. Even though the Sierras are human-scale, still, 3,000 vertical feet is a lot. So once you get high, you should try to stay high. That's what exploring one massif per trip can do for you. If you do that, every day's walk will be glorious, every campsite great.

MOMENTS OF BEING (4)
A Sierra Day: Night in Camp

The Milky Way is a moraine of stars.

—Muir

Sleep out. Don't sleep in a tent unless it's raining. This is important: I advise this most sincerely. It's not that cold in the Sierra, you don't need the slight extra warmth of a tent. If it's windy, your tent will just make noise with its flapping. Your sleeping bag is itself a tent, and a quieter one. And sleeping out, you are out there. Night in the Sierras is a magic time.

It's true that inside a tent, or a tarp tacked down to the ground, it will be about five degrees warmer than sleeping out. In the Sierra this doesn't usually matter. Temperatures at night rarely drop below 25 degrees Fahrenheit in summer; and in spring and fall, even winter, rarely below 15 degrees Fahrenheit. Down bags will easily keep you warm in those temperatures.

However, just to give you an extra feeling of security, you can do what I've often done: set up the tent, stick the foot of your sleeping bag into it, and leave your head outside so you can see the night sky. To be clear, the sleeping out is mainly about seeing the night sky. Although sleeping outside on the ground is itself a real value, being such a primeval thing. But with the tent up, its door open, your feet inside, you can capture a little bit of warmth for your feet, which are likely to go cold first; and if in the night you happen to feel too cold, you can easily shift under your tent, zip the door closed, and warm up.

By tent I mean tarp, of course. More on this in the gear chapter, but as this is a nighttime question, it can be said here: Don't take a tent into the Sierra. Maybe anywhere. Just a single-sheet tarp, nothing more. The ground under you is a great part of the experience. You don't want to be in a bag. No point in going up into the mountains and then getting into a nylon bag configured like a little house. The whole point is to get out of the house. And the saving in weight is considerable.

So, darkness falls. No campfires are allowed in the high Sierra, so it's time for bed, being dark and quickly getting cold. I've taken little half-pound artificial fire logs up there with us, but they are so lame I've given up the practice. And besides, when it gets dark you're already sleepy. Can you stay awake till 9:00 p.m.? Maybe, maybe not. And it's getting cold. So, into your sleeping bag. With modern sleeping bags and ground pads, you're comfy. Which is a blessing, I want to add with real fervency, and love of tech, given my decades of nighttime discomfort in the Sierra. These days, not a problem. You're comfy. Lying out on the ground, hopefully on a good slope, etc. Never lie on a tilt side to side; also, of course, never with your head lower than your feet. A fairly large tilt of head above feet can be accommodated with no problems. Your pillow is a stuff sack stuffed with your day clothes and other soft stuff.

So there you are, lying down, and comfortable. Oh my God. Got up early, big day. Often you're out like a light.

Then you wake up. Wonderful sleep, feeling rested, look at your watch (or if there's a moon up, and you've remembered how to use it to tell time, the moon). Wait—midnight!? Oh my God. It's only midnight! So there you lie, awake.

That's when it helps to be used to it, and know that it's okay. Time to put your glasses back on, if you wear glasses, and lie on your back, and get comfy, and look at the night sky.

Oh my God again. You never see anything like it where you live, this I can guarantee. Not one person in 10,000 lives in a place where the stars are visible like they are in the Sierra at night. Dark skies (meaning away from cities), 10,000 feet above sea level: that means thousands of stars. Watch for half an hour and see several meteors streak across the sky, sometimes at cosmological speeds, faster than anything you'll ever see by day. Also satellites: and hope like hell you aren't looking at the sky crawling with satellites in a few years, more satellites than stars. With luck the astronomers will kamikaze those foolish plans.

For now, a real sky, black as can be, spangled with stars. As you're likely to be up there in summer, the Milky Way will be stretched across the sky north to south, actually a touch northeast to southwest, looking like a cloud. Often I've mistaken it for one, it's so obvious and articulated; but with some looking, you can see it's not a cloud. You can see various darker patches inside it, and diffuse bands of whiteness. You can wonder where the center of the galaxy is, and if you have friends who know, they will tell you. Not in the middle of the night when they're asleep, but maybe the next night, if you remember to ask. (It's in Sagittarius, and yes, I needed help finding that too.) For now, you have the world to yourself.

Gary Snyder once taught me a Zen saying, maybe from Dogen: What now is lacking?

In these insomniac moments, nothing is lacking. You can give up on the desire to sleep, the worry about not sleeping. You can't do anything about that anyway. For now, be awake, and rest in the reality of being up in the Sierras at night. Not cold, not hungry, and you don't have to pee. If you do, get up and do it. Then lie back down, on your back, and get comfy. There you are, somewhere in your life. A moment of rest. Whatever has happened, whatever will come later, for now, it's just this. It's quiet. If there are sounds, they are water over stone, or wind in pine needles. Oh my. Feel your breathing for a bit, not in any meditation-exercise way, just feel it. Resting, at peace. The mountains at night. At some point you'll feel sleepy. That little cycle of waking and falling asleep might even happen more than once through the night, but if it does, it's just more to enjoy. That's the Sierra at night. Serenity, and the stars.

Thinking about this, I've realized that when I crossed that watershed in my life—when night in the Sierra went from an endurance contest and even a mild form of torture, to starry hours of peace—that was when I became a whole person, and the god zone seemed to extend out to everywhere. That was thanks to good ground pads, and to Lisa.

Night Poem, 1988

Writing by starlight
Can't see the words

Fill a page
Nothing there

Waterfall distant sound
Tree against stars
Milky Way
Juniper Jupiter white rock
Wind dying my heart
At peace a Friday night

Big Dipper sits on the mountain
Friends lie in their tents
I sit against rock
Star bowl spinning overhead
Feel the movement
And soar away

Who knows how many stars there are
All those dim ones filling the black
Until it seems no black is there
And then you see the Milky Way

The sky should be pure white with stars
That's black dust up there
Blocking the view
Carbon and hydrogen
All of us flung together
In just this way

A blank white page
I write and then
A blank white page
Story of my life!

ROUTES (3)
Some West-Side Entries

Most of my high Sierra trips have started from the east side, so I don't know much about the west side. But we've had some great trips that started on that side, and I want to share what I've learned about the few west-side entries I've tried. South to north, same as on the east side.

MINERAL KING

This trailhead requires a 25-mile drive up a paved road that is almost single-laned. It contours up the north flank of a long twisty canyon to a tiny ranger station at the end of the road. There are said to be 800 turns in this road, but it feels like more. The canyon is so big it reminds me of the Himalayas' foot-hill valleys.

The trailhead gets you in at a decent height (7,800 feet), on the west side of the southern end of the Great Western Divide. I've only used it to go over Sawtooth Pass, directly east of Mineral King, but one can also head south over Franklin Pass, and north over the Timber Gap, and on that route you can reach the Farewell Gap and Black Rock Pass. Immediately east of Sawtooth Pass is an east-facing basin with a lovely series of lakes—paternoster lakes, as they're called when they appear to be on the risers of a giant glacial staircase. From them you can drop into the deep slot of the Kern, or head north toward the Kaweahs. It's big country down there, and like the Miter Basin, it has a Mediterranean look.

WOLVERTON

This is my favorite west-side entry. Wolverton is the name of a vast parking lot built to provide parking for a ski resort that never happened. Now it rests just off Highway 180 near the Lodgepole ranger station and campground, on the south ridge of the canyon of the Marble Fork of the Kaweah River. That puts it at around 7,000 feet, pretty high for the west side. A trail built by the CCC leads quickly up to the Tablelands, a wonderful high plateau with views and routes in all directions. You can also cut over the Panther Gap to the High Sierra Trail, a masterpiece overseen by Sequoia National Park superintendent John White. The High Sierra Trail runs east through the Kaweah Gap, a deep pass in the Great Western Divide, and from there, all the glories of the Kern and Kaweah are immediately at hand.

The Tablelands is a trail-free plateau, east of the Pear Lake ranger hut. At the northeasternmost point on the Tablelands' north ridge, five miles beyond Pear Lake, you reach a little pond right on the ridge overlooking Big Bird Lake, protected by a low wall from south winds; all of which makes it a campsite with one of the best views in the Sierra.

I first discovered the Tablelands from the air. I was flying north from San Diego, sitting on the right side of the plane and looking down at the Sierra, in late spring or early summer, and saw a long wedge of snow extending far to the west from the Great Western Divide. This snowy triangular plateau, I saw as the plane flew over it, formed the southern ridge containing the immense gash of Kings Canyon; it was the equivalent of the Monarch Divide on the great canyon's north side. Staring down amazed, I said to myself (aloud), What the heck is that? When I got home I consulted my big Sierra map, and was pleased to find it was named the Tablelands. That's a good name. And it turns out to be part of a famous trans-Sierra cross-country ski route.

Since then, we've taken backpacking trips on the Tablelands in all seasons. It's perfect for snowshoeing, and great fun any other time of the year. That pond on the rim that I spoke of is about ten miles from the trailhead, and stands at around 11,200 feet. I read about the pond and its great view in Phil

Arnot's wonderful guidebook *High Sierra*, so from our very first visit we always called it Phil Arnot Pond, and I think that name should stick, because Arnot's guiding career, and his books, are inspiring. And the Tablelands, and the area to the east of it, form one of the great massifs in the Sierra.

KINGS CANYON

This canyon is so big, deep, and wild that it holds quite a few trailheads, but I'll focus on the one I know, which is at the very end of the road, called Roads End.

The drive into Kings Canyon is almost as convoluted as the Mineral King road. The canyon is the forgotten sister in my fairy tale in part because of this long winding road. Once the road gets onto the canyon floor, it meanders back and forth on bridges over the South Fork to Roads End, passing a couple of nice but often nearly empty car campgrounds, featuring a small motel and restaurant. It's like seeing what the Sierras looked like in the 1920s.

At Roads End there's a ranger station, and you can start hikes up Copper Creek, or up the South Fork to its confluence with Bubbs Creek (meaning the South Fork of the South Fork). Going up either of those creeks leads to many great places.

Copper Creek Trail is one of the oldest trails in the region, and leads up and over the Monarch Divide by way of the Granite Basin, then down to Simpson Meadow on the Middle Fork. These days it's also the start of the Roper High Route.

John Muir visited Kings Canyon in the late 1870s, and loved it. He wrote about it at length for *Century* magazine in 1891, and he made sure William Colby sent some of the earliest Sierra Club summer high camps there, starting in 1902. His articles, and the club's high trips, helped make Kings Canyon famous. Later David Brower and Ansel Adams led the Sierra Club's effort to create Kings Canyon National Park, as a northern extension of Sequoia National Park, in 1940. They wanted to call it Muir National Park, but right-wing interests blocked that idea, as they did the idea of renaming North Palisade as Brower Palisade, two generations later.

Now these trails aren't as famous or as much used as they once were, with the single exception of the Rae Lakes Loop, a triangular circuit that starts at Roads End and goes up either Woods Creek or Bubbs Creek to the Muir Trail, then uses the Muir Trail to go by the Rae Lakes and Glen Pass, then back down to Roads End. This is one of the most popular hikes in the Sierra, and deservedly so, even though it stays in canyons most of the way.

The thing about Roads End is, although you are already tucked far inside the high Sierra, you're also in the deepest depths of a great glacial canyon, and thus only 5,200 feet above sea level. That's low; and everything around it is high. So there's going to be a very big first day of uphill, no matter which way you go. Still, it's worth it.

WISHON RESERVOIR

This is a slightly higher west-side trailhead, about 7,100 feet high; another long winding drive gets you there. It's as close as you can get to Tehipite Dome, which makes it worth at least one visit. From the trailhead it's about 15 miles of forest walking, gently uphill, to the rim overlooking the Middle Fork, with Tehipite Dome to your immediate left. The trail then drops in switchbacks down the immense sidewall of the Middle Fork. The almost vertical canyon scoring the opposite wall is the Gorge of Despair. After a few hours you're on the floor of Tehipite Valley, a small oval area; the trail then runs up the canyon ten miles to Simpson Meadow.

FLORENCE LAKE

Florence Lake is a reservoir that expands a smaller lake that lay in this valley before the dam was built. This is a great west-side entry. It starts at the dam of the reservoir, where there's a little store.

The road to Florence Lake extends 25 miles beyond the last good road, which is already many miles of mountainous twists and turns from Fresno, so it's really slow to get there. The last 25 miles is like a paved trail, basically single-laned, and even slower than the Mineral King road. But worth it anyway. The trailhead, at 7,300 feet, has a good parking lot, a mini store, and a ferry that takes you five miles across the reservoir (don't take the trail along the west shore if you can help it!), and then you're just five miles of flat hiking through meadows to Blayney Hot Springs, on the Muir Trail. This hot spring is surrounded by a little walk-in cabin resort, also a post-office drop with lots of supplies for thru-hikers. So many people have mailed food here and then not picked it up that you could supply a complete trip just from the giveaway barrels. Although it would be a weird selection.

Heading north on the Muir Trail from there, you soon cross Selden Pass, and are on the high region west of Seven Gables. Before reaching that pass, you can go cross-country up Senger Creek, and get over a cross-country pass I call Sharp Note Pass, unlisted, class 2, a very fine direct route to Seven Gables.

Going south on the Muir Trail, you pass a couple of major canyon confluences, then rise to Evolution Valley and then Evolution Basin; or you can cut up Goddard Canyon, as we once did, to Martha Lake. There you can cross to Wanda Lake by way of the Davis Lakes, or go in the west entrance of the Ionian Basin by way of a slot that our boys called the Mordor Gate.

As for farther north: I don't know. There's Yosemite Valley, of course. I leave that for other books. And there's Hetch Hetchy, which has, right at its dam, an excellent trailhead for the trail running along the north side of its notorious reservoir, and the fine country east of it.

Lastly, Cherry Lake, west of Hetch Hetchy: this entry gives you the southern end of Emigrant Wilderness, an exposed pluton top of beautifully burnished granite, an unexpected patch of high Sierra set low, like Desolation. Upper Cherry Creek is definitely worth a visit: it's astonishing to find such beautiful stone so far north and west of the high country.

Upper Cherry Creek

MY SIERRA LIFE (9)
Gear Talk

Go light.

Backpacking is a game in which you wander in the mountains with everything you need on your back. Maybe it's also a religion, or a primal nomadic urge, prehuman in its provenance; but whatever it is, the goal is to settle in after the day's walk and pull a comfortable home out of your bag, and good meals. That makes it a gear game. This has been true from the beginning. Ötzi the Iceman's gear resembles the modern array in every respect, and he was very well outfitted. He lived around 5,000 years ago, but all of his gear except for his copper ax no doubt was being made to similar designs and with similar materials for at least 50,000 years.

When my friends and I began in the 1970s, much of the thinking about backpacking equipment resulted from a basic category error, which imagined that what you needed in the mountains was a lightweight version of your house. Ray Jardine was a pioneer in writing against this notion, and he had a big influence on some hikers, including Terry. After Terry's supposedly state-of-the-art clothing failed him in our New Year's Day blizzard, he read Jardine and other sources, and permanently borrowed one of his mom's sewing machines, and set to work teaching himself to design and sew his own gear, then to test it out, including concepts like vapor barriers and R-values and the like. We were the beneficiaries of his experimentation, and became early ultralite practitioners. Everything we took up there, except boots, was made by Terry or could have been, and he was always working to make things lighter. Backpacks, sleeping bags, tarps, clothing, water bags, gaiters—all this and more came flying off his sewing machine, with each year bringing new refinements and efficiencies.

Decades later, when the Pacific Crest Trail and the Appalachian Trail became a one-season goal for many thru-hikers, as they call themselves, the weight one carried became crucial to one's success. Where people had previously obsessed over ounces, thru-hikers obsessed over grams. Hiking a marathon's distance every day for four months will stimulate that kind of close interest. Terry himself became an enthusiastic thru-hiker, partly as a new way to exercise his gearcraft.

People like me, usually out hiking for about a week at a time, are now the beneficiaries of the thru-hikers' obsession with lightness, and the cottage industries that have resulted from it. Gear these days is really good; not quite as light as Terry's, usually, but close, and often demonstrating features for comfort that Terry didn't care about. One way Terry made things light was by making them so small that you had to wrestle into them: clothes, sleeping bag, tarp. A little leeway can be a relief. Pockets can also be nice. And now, new materials he never worked with are adding to the possibilities for improvement.

So now a point has come where you can say, if you want to, "I'm light enough." The rubric Terry used, having read about it and tested it, was to get your backpack's weight down to 10 percent of your body weight. When it's that light you're not going to be impeded by it, or even notice it much. This rubric has felt right to me when I've achieved it. So I recommend using it as your goal: try to keep your backpack weight to a maximum of 10 percent of your body weight.

Does that include your food? Yes, try for it with your food included. That will make it harder to achieve, but these days it can be done. It takes paying attention, and using some of the newer materials and products. In this sense, backpacking is not a back-to-nature primitivism, but rather a high-tech game.

First some basic principles:

1. You don't need to reproduce your house. In summer and fall in the Sierra, you don't need much gear to be comfortable. So: don't take what you don't need.

2. Incidental dampness is not fundamental wetness, and incidental dampness doesn't matter. This is a distinction the 1950s designers didn't acknowledge: you don't have to stay as absolutely dry as you typically do at home, in order to remain both warm and comfortable. Realizing that makes a lot of gear unnecessary. Condensation on the inside of your tarp? Not a problem. The only thing you really need to worry about is fundamental wetness, which ultimately comes down to your sleeping bag being too wet to work, so that you will perhaps freeze your butt. That you want to avoid.

3. For every item, all of them, take the lightest version that will still function for its purpose.

4. Try for dual use, meaning more than one function for the stuff you take with you—as in puns, where the crux word means two things and makes you laugh. Why are pirates so bad at playing cards? Because they're standing on the deck! In a similar way, there are some items with two functions. Note this began all the way back with Clarence King and Richard Cotter, who used their sleeping blankets to make their backpacks. These days, walking poles can be your tent poles at night; backpack cushioning can serve as your pillow; your tarp can serve as a rain cape by day; your down vest is a mobile part of your sleeping bag; your empty backpack can serve as a short ground cloth, or a foot bag (Gary Snyder says that in the Pacific Northwest this last practice was called siwashing). And so on.

With this kind of thinking, it's not materials driving the change in gear, but philosophy. We change our desires, then make things accordingly. Thus ultralite as a design ethic becomes suggestive when we go on to think about the rest of our lives. Because we always carry our houses one way or another.

I'll briefly discuss the gear piece by piece. Gear talk can quickly get obsessive, but it's important to go up there as light as you can, so it's worth a little attention. I should also reiterate that this entire discussion is about summer and fall in the Sierra Nevada of California. Other seasons and other ranges may make different kinds of demands, but that's not the topic here.

First, your tent. Recall the 1950s category error of reproducing your house. Thus tents had to have roofs, walls, and a floor—of course!

But oh dear; the roofs of nylon houses have seams, to make them look houselike, and those seams will leak. So a second roof, made of a single water-proof sheet, had to be put over the first roof. Thus the rainfly, strung over the tent proper. Tent poles and lines and stakes had to be added to hold all this up. And it being your house, you had to be able to sit up in it, and standing would be better. So make it tall. And big enough for two or three people, with their gear. Result: weight. It isn't at all unusual to see nine-pound tents, and tent makers are really proud to offer tents weighing four pounds.

But all you ever really need is protection from the rain. So you could liter-ally have taken the rainfly along and left all the rest of it behind. I did that with my old North Face tent's rainfly for several early trips, and it worked fine. Now they're called tarps, and they're cut so they can reach the ground all the way around.

You do need to have room to sit up, and that can be created under an A-frame made by one's walking poles. You also need to be able to lie down, and to cover all your gear. So this tarp can't be *too* small; a bivy sack, which doesn't allow you to sit up—or a tarp that's too short in length, or doesn't reach the ground all the way around—these are not okay on the stormiest nights. Which could last three or four days. So there are limits to how much you can shrink your tarp and still be comfortable. Bivy sacks in particular, when the going gets rainy, suck. A bad design, not good for any conditions whatsoever.

This idea of *enough to do the job* illustrates another important general prin-ciple. There's an x axis and a y axis to this game, resulting in the usual scien-tific graph; lightness is x, comfort is y. Although it has to be said that lightness *is* comfort, when it comes to the whole package on your back. But if you make lightness the only rubric, as some tend to do (Terry included), you could in theory just hike up there naked and you would have won the game. Ray Jar-dine was a bit like this; to deal with storms, he advised that you hike down to lower altitude. That's not always possible, and besides it's not the game; you want to stay comfortable no matter what happens up high, which means dealing with storms where they hit you. But in the case of shelter, a full to-the-ground tarp and your walking poles will do the job just fine. They are better than a tent, and not just because of weight; suddenly the floor of your little bedroom becomes the ground itself, which in the Sierra means it's beautiful. Everything becomes nicer—you're no longer stuck inside a nylon bag for hours on end.

Also, before moving on: remember to just sleep out! Bring the tarp in case it rains, but if night falls and there are no clouds, don't put that tarp up! Sleeping out under the stars is one of the main reasons for going up there in the first place. Many days, even entire trips, can pass without my tarp ever leaving its tiny little stuff sack. Always sleep out!

But when an afternoon thunderstorm strikes, or a rainy night comes, you really do need that tarp. You need a dry place to lie down, which means a roof over your head.

Good tarps are made by several small online companies. The one I use now is made of a newish fabric called Dyneema. This synthetic fabric was invented to make lighter and stronger yacht sails for America's Cup races. It's kind of a miracle fabric, such that you can make a one-person tarp out of it that weighs only a pound, stakes and stuff sack included. And it's more windproof and waterproof than nylon. So look for a Dyneema tarp.

Backpacks: a simple backpack can weigh a pound or less. A bag, basically, with shoulder straps and a hip belt added, simple as that. My favorite Gossamer Gear pack weighs ten ounces, and I still use an older pack of theirs that weighs eight ounces, though the duct tape holding it together probably adds an ounce or two. The thin blue nylon they used to save weight for that earlier pack was too thin, and the bags would rip when just brushed against a rock, or even when looked at wrong. They had to be treated like eggs. Gossamer Gear was forced to give up on them and shift to stronger materials; when they announced that, I quickly ordered two more while I could still get them. Gossamer sent them to me in a flat 9-by-12 Express Mail envelope. That made me laugh; it was a joke, or a boast. I've used all three of my blueys often since then, and they're all taped up. On summer trips, if we aren't going to be doing any bushwhacking or hard scrambling, they're still great. Although there are now quite a few good backpacks out there weighing around ten ounces. So the monstrous backpacks still sold by the outdoor-adventure stores, often coming in at four or five or six pounds, are a bad mistake. They are the SUVs of back-packing.

Your tarp and backpack are two of what Terry used to call the four big-ticket items. The other two are sleeping bag and ground pad. Can these also do a good job at a pound or less? Yes.

Sleeping bags: these should be made of 900-fill goose down, the warmest and lightest insulation there is. Then also, very important, Terry's idea was that the down under you gets crushed and becomes useless as either insulation or padding; all the down in a sleeping bag should therefore be located over or beside you, not under you. He sewed accordingly. The undersides of his sleeping bags were simply nylon sheets, there to hold you, and maybe your ground pad, in place under the down-filled blanket that formed the upper part of the bag. A great plan! And occasionally some companies have agreed enough to give it a try.

It's true that you have to roll over in such bags without rolling the bag too, or you'll get the down under you and the sheet of nylon over you, which will quickly chill you. This internal roll takes some care, and a lot of people don't like to bother with it, so this design has always been rare, and appears to be getting rarer. For a while Western Mountaineering, my favorite down gear manufacturers, made this kind of bag, and I bought one that weighs exactly a pound. They don't make them anymore, so I grabbed one more while they lasted. I'm sure some small companies will soon be making bags in this style again. A heavier bag is not needed; I've been comfortable in my bag at 15 degrees, by wearing all my clothes to bed. This is another example of dual use.

Ground pads? They have gotten fantastically good. I appreciate this more than any other gear improvement. In the old days we slept on Ensolite pads, as I've mentioned, beige or blue closed-foam things that felt almost exactly like sleeping on the ground. Their insulation was great—you could lie naked on one of them set on snow, and you would still stay warm, or I should say, not get chilled from below—but as for comfort, no. I suffered. I lost many hours of sleep lying on those things, squirming by the quarter hour in the movement we nicknamed the rotisserie. I became an early seeker of a better ground pad. I bought thick pads of foam and rolled them into giant rolls tied on top of my pack. I bought the early Therm-a-Rest foam-filled air mattresses, quite an improvement, although so thin that to keep off the ground you had to blow them up as hard as a board. I combined those with foam pads, becoming quite "princess and the pea" about it, never satisfied, always insomniac, always uncomfortable.

Finally I bought a thing called Stephenson's Warmlite, an inflatable air mattress with a bit of down trapped inside it to make it warm; this compensated for air mattresses' notorious weakness, which was they were always as cold as the ground under them, and worse yet, convected your heat down into the ground, in a battle for equalization that you were always going to lose. Some goose down inside an air mattress captured your heat in the mattress and solved that problem. The first night sleeping on one of these, I woke up and it was still light, so I figured it was around 10:00 p.m. and groaned, but actually it was 6:00 a.m. Amazed, I became a devotee.

The insulating ability of anything can be measured by an R-value, an index of heat retention that comes from the building industry's insulation codes. With a bottomless sleeping bag like mine, you need an R-value of at least 4 in your ground pad; I found this out just last week, freezing my butt while trying a new air mattress with an R-value of 2.3. It wasn't enough, and I ended up curled on my pillow like a dog.

So, for many years I loved my Stephenson's Warmlites. But they're bulky, and just recently the newest generation of Therm-a-Rest air mattresses, some of them called the Neo-Air, have become the best yet: warm, light, tall, comfortable, easy to blow up, and compact when packed. You can be about as comfortable as you are at home in bed. Always take one that extends from head to foot, of course. The new ones can be that long and still be very compact in your backpack, which means also that you can take a smaller and thus lighter backpack.

So over the course of my hiking career, ground pads have gone from bad to good, or even from terrible to great. And thank God for that, because if there's one place I'll carry some extra weight for the sake of comfort, it's ground pads. You lie on them all night.

Clothing should come next after the four big-ticket items, because without your paying close attention, clothing can quickly get out of hand in terms of weight on your back.

You wear your day clothes during the day, fine. Don't carry extras, this isn't a fashion show. Recently I've realized, by way of skin cancers, that sun can be bad for you, so now I wear long nylon pants, and a long-sleeved nylon shirt, both with an SPF element. I thought hiking in long pants would drive me mad, but it turned out not to be true. I was stupid to resist them without testing them out.

At night you need a completely different set of clothes, because your day clothes will be sweaty and get cold — they are only good for pillow stuffing at that point, but they do serve for that, so again, dual use. At night, for my legs I wear long underwear made of polypropylene, and for my upper body, a long-sleeved undershirt of that same material, which is fuzzy and breathable: wonderful blue things, a matched set bought for my Antarctic trip in 1995. I loved them down there, and have loved them ever since. They feel like heaven.

Then Thorlo socks, at trekking thickness; the same kind night and day, but dry ones at night. On the last day those can become your day socks, and you hike out fresh. Most trips you need just two pairs. If your feet are going to get wet by day, in streams or snow, maybe three pairs.

Then something warmer than your underlayer for your core. In the Sierra in summer, this can be a down vest. Like all the rest of my down gear, my vest is made by Western Mountaineering. In the spring and fall, a down jacket from them feels good. Remember you can drape your sleeping bag over your shoulders as a cape in the evenings, so don't bring too much in this regard. In general, your down bag and down vest or jacket should be considered two parts of one system, in a mountain range that doesn't get very cold. Don't bring too much, especially in the summer. Dual use works.

Then also, something warm for your head. In theory this should be a parka hood that is sewn to, or snaps onto, your vest or jacket; in practice, this excellent design feature has in recent years somewhat gone away. It's a victim of the arms race in the gear industry to make and announce the lightest version of whatever the item is, for thru-hikers and other ultralite fanatics who are buying things online. Arms races like these can tweak design in a bad way. Even though a parka hood is always appropriate, gear companies can't add one without making their vests or jackets heavier than their competitors', and people are buying the lightest of whatever they see on the internet. So now you have to provide for your head at night by adding something to your other clothing. I've used the detachable down hood from my ancient North Face down jacket, or a wool cap, or one of the new down hoods for sale online. Terry made me one of his felt head covers; it has a medieval look, as it features a strap that goes under my chin and covers my ears. On summer trips this cap is enough, and weighs two ounces. One of Terry's finest products, and mine has grown thin from long use. I can see from photos that I look like a character from Brueghel when I wear it. But those northern Europeans knew how to stay warm, and again, fashion is not the point.

Although it's true that Terry did like to look fashionable in his way. He had a distinctive sense of style, and in that sense was very stylish.

That's clothing. It's warmer and more comfortable than in the old days, while weighing less than one-third as much as the old stuff. We lie around our twilight campsites like pashas in silks, radiating body heat into marvelously fine goose down, enjoying meals and then a nightcap. Then we sleep in comfort about equal to our beds at home. It's very pleasing.

Rain gear: you need it. For sure take a waterproof windbreaker and wind pants, the lighter the better. Don't bother with Gore-Tex or similar breathable products, they don't work well enough in rain to matter, they're best in snow. Zippers are seldom needed, a pullover in the old anorak style is fine. Hoods are not optional, and indeed are almost always included with windbreakers because of that need. Terry sewed the same nylon he used for tarps into simple pants and windbreakers; the combined weight of both clothing items was seven ounces. The commercial industry has not yet caught up to him on that one, but there are little online companies now making these things out of Dyneema, so look around and do what you can to stay light there too. Go light; but you need these items, for sure.

Boots: go for comfort! And that's a very personal matter. I use low-top hiking shoes, with strong bottoms but flexible tops. I don't believe the high tops of high-topped boots actually work to support your ankles when you make a mistake bad enough to hurt yourself.

I also buy shoes that are two or three sizes bigger than what shoe stores say my foot size is. The shoe industry's notion of what size shoe you should wear is arbitrary and crimping. So I buy larger than they advise, which allows my toes to do what they want; they are never crushed or confined, it's almost as if I'm barefoot in that regard. I fill that extra space in the boots with thick socks. When I combine Thorlo trekking socks with Salomon hiking shoes, I'm good to go. Given my early years of horribly heavy boots or too-light tennis shoes, resulting in all those years of blisters and plantar fasciitis, my current foot protocol is again a very wonderful development.

I'm told that each shoe company uses a different last, which is the foot-shaped block they use to build their boots around; it's their default human foot. So you need to try different companies' boots until you find the company that uses a last that most resembles your foot, and then stick with that company, even if they keep shifting styles to create fashions. With good boots and socks, you can take a potentially big problem completely off the table.

One of my favorite gear innovations concerns the stove, or rather the lack of a stove. Of course very light stoves exist now, and on snow trips it's a joy to have one along, their flames like an arc welder's torch. But the stove itself and its gas canister, and the compressed gas inside the canister, in combination add up to a dense chunk, weighing at least a pound. And some years ago there appeared for sale little white cubes that burn hotly, one trade name being Esbit cubes.

Their white waxy material is said to be a product of DARPA research, commissioned by the Army, and it reeks of weird futuristic chemicals. Each cube of it will boil two cups of water. So if you choose to use these for cooking, you can dispense with a stove (metal) and fuel canister (metal), and carry only the naked fuel itself. I love that idea! And constructing a little rock stove to hold the white cube while it burns is a childish pleasure. One game I play is to make a rock stove using only the rocks I can reach from where I'm sitting. A lazy game, but the Sierra being such a rocky place, it almost always works. Watching one of these cubes burn is like seeing what it might be like to live on a slightly more oxygenated planet. They're like Sterno fuel but hotter, like candle flames but fatter. And your cup of water eventually boils.

The titanium cup that also serves as my pot weighs only three ounces, and my plastic spoon barely registers on the scale. Same for my yellow plastic cup, brought along for my Scotch. Those three items and a cigarette lighter now

My kitchen in its entirety

constitute my entire kitchen. That's four ounces, plus the weight of however many Esbit cubes I bring for the trip, each weighing about an ounce. With a single cube I can heat my coffee in the morning and blow out the flame, then use that same cube to heat the water I need to hydrate my dried meals at night. I balance my titanium cup-pot on the rocks of my little ad hoc stove, and if I remember, I bring a sheet of aluminum foil to cover the titanium cup; that definitely helps the water boil. There I sit, sipping my Scotch and watching the pot boil (so it never does). It's absurdly satisfying.

Important to remember: we are quadrupeds.

Not really, but put it this way: we were quadrupeds for a lot longer than we've been bipeds. Like, millions of years longer. And everything in the brain gets conserved. Roughly speaking, we have a lizard brain in our cerebellum, a mammal brain in our temporal lobes, and a human brain in our prefrontal cortex. Even if we don't use them, all the parts of the brain that evolved long ago are still there inside us, waiting for their chance. And so: walking poles.

They are tremendous fun. And they help a lot too.

Their use value comes in reducing the impact on your legs and feet, and in saving you from falls from time to time. They aren't surefire in that last regard, but when they do save you from a fall, it's a blessing. And with every step, they are distributing the load. Your upper body gets a workout, which means your shoulders feel better under the backpack straps, and your hands don't swell up from blood getting caught in your arms by those same straps. So the use value of walking poles is very high. I note that all the thru-hikers use them now, which is pretty good proof of their utility. The thing that got me to try them in the first place, in 1999, was seeing a photo of Reinhold Messner using them while hiking in to one of his Himalayan climbs. When I saw that I thought, if it's good enough for Messner, it's good enough for me. He's the great walker of our time.

It's also very nice that at night, your walking poles become your tent poles; this means you don't have to carry tent poles on your back all day.

And then there's the fun. Think of yourself as a quadruped who can't do it anymore, because of a peculiar elongation of your spine. You could get on your hands and knees, but no. Your knees don't like to be feet, and it just doesn't work. So your quadruped days are in your past, speaking as a species, and that big part of your brain just sits up there in you, unused, and probably feeling kind of neglected and grumpy.

And then you pick up the sticks and start walking cross-country. Quicker than you might think possible, you're good at poking the ground and getting in a rhythm, swimming uphill, lofting downhill. In effect, your forelegs have been given prosthetic extensions that get you back on four feet again. That part of your brain wakes up and shouts HURRAY! It quickly figures out that your new forelegs are long and double-elbowed, articulated in a triple system much like a praying mantis's forelegs. And suddenly you're back on the ground, like all the rest of our horizontal brothers and sisters. Glorious fun! More fun than just walking, and less painful too.

Set the poles long, so that they are chest high on you, not waist high. This is important; when they're set too low, your wrists are awkwardly bent and the poles do you little good. So the higher the better, really; almost shoulder high is fine.

Sometimes you have to put the sticks aside, either by holding them bunched in one hand, or collapsing them and carrying them in your backpack. (Only use the poles that have exterior clamps to adjust their length, by the way, a system originated by Black Diamond, called FlickLock in a silly marketing ploy. Never use the poles that have interior screw cams, which can fail and leave you with no tent poles. The exterior clamps are so superior that interior cams are quickly going away, but keep an eye peeled.) Using the poles can be deceptive in boulder fields to the point of making said boulders more danger-ous rather than less. But even there, if you're careful, and never trust them completely, they can help, or at least, not hurt. And for the rest of the time, they're a joy. Don't go without them.

So, putting it all on the scale, every big-ticket item can now weigh a pound or less, and minor items typically weigh only a few ounces. Clothing can come in at just a couple of pounds total, or a tad more. Kitchens need weigh hardly anything. So the same kit that weighed 40 pounds in the 1970s now weighs around 8 pounds (some thru-hikers will snort and claim 5 pounds), and yet it all functions better. In your ditty bag, minimal weights for every little thing are easy to find; one-ounce headlamps, traveler's tubes of toothpaste, etc. Even there, paying attention can make a difference. So, do you have to cut the handle off your toothbrush, as people used to joke? No. But there are these little traveler's toothbrushes…

Then, to that excellent base weight, you must add food, which these days I try to keep to about a pound per day in dry weight. As I usually experience a bit of appetite suppression at altitude, I've learned to believe that that amount will keep me full. But food is very personal, and some people get hungrier up there, rather than less hungry. So I won't say much more about it, except to add, don't carry water weight on your back, even in your food, if you can avoid it. Freeze-drying is another tech that has become the backpacker's friend. Regular food drying also. There's all the water you'll ever need up there to rehydrate things.

Speaking of that, to reiterate, as Terry always warned us, with a shocked, religious intensity: *Never carry water!* It's fucking heavy! And there's water every half mile in the Sierra, and humans were meant to go without water, just drink some in the morning and you'll be fine, those CamelBak water bags with tubes you can sip from as you walk are the stupidest most bogus rip-off in the history of the world—

You get the picture. In fact, carrying about a quarter of a liter of water is not a bad idea, just in case. Beyond that, I must bow to the maestro, because he was right; no water in your backpack, it's a mistake. Two pounds per quart, and not needed—no. No way. Never carry water.

And for holding your water around camp, dispense with those thick Nalgene bottles, four ounces each and never really clean inside. Buy disposable plastic sports-drink bottles of the same size, at only two ounces each, and recycle them at the end of the trip. Take two for convenience and for redundancy in case of loss. Net gain four ounces. Thus sayeth the Baier.

People ask about water quality in the Sierra, and what we do to purify it: nothing. The water in the Sierra was snow the previous winter, and *Giardia lamblia* is almost nonexistent up there. There's a good article online, written by a climber MD, which describes Sierra water as cleaner than what comes out of the taps in San Francisco: http://californiamountaineer.net/giardia.html. The park rangers advise purifying water up there mainly out of liability concerns, plus a bit of public safety overkill. And it's true you wouldn't want to drink water from streams where horses cross, or where hordes of humans camp, as along the Muir Trail. Human shit is by far the main source of giardia up there, so a little care needs to be taken. But we've never purified our water, except in some unusual situations where it seemed like a good idea. If you are still really worried about it, do like we do in those situations: use iodine tablets. Easy, effective, light. Tastes just like Nepal.

Since our typical trip has usually been a week long, that means my backpack when I take off on a summer trip now weighs around 18 pounds, food included. Starting at that weight, on day 2 it drops to that goal of 10 percent of my body weight, which does seem to be a weight one scarcely notices. Halfway through a trip, carrying only 10 or 12 pounds, it can feel almost like not carrying a backpack at all.

After the many years of humping a big load, this is a golden feeling. Also, given that we are getting older and yet still trying to do this wonderful activity through our sixties, and hopefully through our seventies too, it's become a safety issue, and indeed the basic enabling device. Last year I went hiking with three younger friends, guys in their early forties, and they were interested enough in weight to have a hand scale in their car, which told us their packs weighed between 38 and 41 pounds. I was amazed. It was almost as if they were being polite and handicapping themselves to make me feel less slow, but no— it was just their style. I had been concerned to keep up with them, so I had cut everything in my pack to its absolute minimum, and it weighed 17 pounds. I could barely lift their packs, and yet they hiked from North Lake over Lamarck Col that first day, no problem. Same throughout the week of the trip. They were strong guys, and experienced backpackers, but still, it taught me things, watching them. In my twenties I too had hiked with weights that heavy, and could do it back then, it seems, hard though that is to believe now. Now, I couldn't do it. I don't think I could make it two miles carrying what they did.

But I don't have to. Neither do they, of course, but they don't have to worry about it either, young and strong as they are.

And they had a different style: they cooked together, slept in one big tent, read to each other at bedtime. It was beautiful to witness, and also kind of shocking. Trained in the Baier's strict method, I could hardly believe it. I realized (again) that I had had a very intense guru. I hadn't even known there was any other way, it had all made such sense at the time. Of course you hike light, have your own kit and food, never share, never carry water, hike from sunup to sundown every day of the trip: How could you not? There's only one way!

In fact there are many ways. But in all of them, going light is a good thing.

You can't find ultralite gear in backpacking stores. They can't carry it or they wouldn't sell anything else they have on offer, because the other stuff would be revealed as ridiculous; indeed often crap, conceptually speaking; and profits would plummet. So in the big brick-and-mortar outdoor-equipment stores of America, all the backpacking equipment is still supersized. The down gear would roast you in Antarctica, the padded backpacks could hold 80 pounds and you wouldn't feel a thing (in the store); the tents could accommodate dinner parties. You could ride down the Mississippi on your ground pad. Bigger is better! As this is a universal truth of capitalism, ultralite is contrary to logic.

So if you're interested, you have to go online. On the internet many little companies specialize in one product, or more typically, offer a small range of products that constitute their part of the larger endeavor. As I said, Western Mountaineering is my favorite for down gear, Gossamer Gear for backpacks, Mountain Laurel for tarps. Ground pads from Therm-a-Rest. Socks from Thorlo, boots from Salomon. But for all these items, other companies are also making very good gear (Zpacks, Big Agnes, etc.), as are individual makers who set up online and do great work.

I find the sight of hikers in the Sierra Nevada still humping monster packs somewhat depressing. Older hikers using the beloved gear of their youth I can understand; I too keep all the gear I've ever owned. I just don't use it. That would be silly.

It's the younger hikers who have simply gone into the adventure stores and bought whatever is offered that I find depressing. I wonder about them as consumers and as critical thinkers. I suppose they're strong enough to carry the extra stuff, most of the time, so it doesn't really matter to them; and they get the joy of doing something hard. But it could be more fun for them if they distrusted American commerce and thought it through. There they are on the Muir Trail, staggering under enormous backpacks, hustling along to keep to a timetable, having somehow managed to turn backpacking into a job. They are the equivalent of commuters in SUVs on the highways of America. A national weakness for overkill, even for conspicuous consumption. That they suffer for it when hiking uphill on their first day is often very evident when you pass them on the trail, sweaty, red-faced, dismayed, getting desperate, about to cry, even actually crying. We've seen it all. But they haven't twigged that there's a better way.

Technology is the expression of a culture, and it changes over time with our desires. Now there are many reasons for us to want to go lighter in every way. When I see articles about 300-square-foot houses, I think to myself, that's the ultralite ethos, reversing the 1950s error; back then they tried to make tents like houses, now they're trying to make houses like tents. Good idea!

This may lead to other types of going lighter. Tiny cars made of carbon fiber, tiny houses that are self-powered; tiny cars that are also tiny houses! And so on. This would not be a regressive return to nature, or even some kind of voluntary simplicity, but rather a more sophisticated and stylish high tech, achieving more comfort with lower costs for both people and biosphere. It's a design ethos, a way of being in the world, a style. Higher tech for lower impact; the most sophisticated civilization yet. A lightweight permaculture. Such stylish design will make us more alive—no longer cocooned in crap, which very much includes being cocooned in fossil fuels—and also more skillful and comfortable in the world, while harming it less. In a world of 8 billion people, this kind of tech ethos will be crucial to living well while passing along to the generations to come the same Earth that nourishes us. So both in this particular case of backpacking, and in life in general, throw that monster off your back and go ultralite!

THE SWISS ALPS (2)

My Ascent of the Matterhorn

Iwouldn't have done this one on my own. I kind of tricked myself into it. Lisa and I had been to Zermatt and seen the Matterhorn in person, and maybe it is unnecessary to say it, but it is one steep mountain. Having seen it, I had not thought further of hiring a guide and going up it. I knew that was possible, but it wasn't the sort of thing I did.

So when our friends Brian and Brad showed up at our place, and expressed an interest in climbing the Matterhorn—

But the thing is, I must have been the one who mentioned the possibility to them. Maybe I was using them to pull me into it? They were biking around Europe, so it isn't something that would necessarily have been on their minds. I was the one who knew about it. Maybe I was just trying to think of fun things for them to do in Switzerland. Or maybe I was using them as a way to get myself to do it.

Brad and Brian are my friends Dick and Karen's younger brothers, eight or nine years younger than I am, both excellent athletes. We had hiked together before, on a Sierra trip with Dick out of Mineral King. Now they were excited by the idea of the Matterhorn, and insisted I would have to join them, so they would have a German speaker along, and a guide in the ways of the Swiss. Neither would have been necessary, but I agreed to go. I did know more about Switzerland than they did.

Including about the Matterhorn, and so I began to worry. In the Sierras when we strayed onto class 3 terrain it could get traumatic pretty fast. In fact, for us it is somewhat the case that class 3 = trauma. But the easiest route on the

Matterhorn—the so-called *Normalweg*, which goes up the Hörnligrat, the ridge running down the middle of the mountain in the classic photos from Zermatt—is rated class 4, and some sources say its hardest pitches would be rated class 5.5 if they were in the Sierra.

I warned the guys it would be expensive. I called the Zermatt Bergführer-verein and inquired about prices, and was told it would cost us each $300, as each client had to hire an individual guide. Brian and Brad said they would be willing to cut their Europe trip short to be able to afford it. So it seemed I was stuck with it.

My lifelong armchair climbing, reading all those thrilling books on the edge of my seat, began in my childhood with James Ramsey Ullman's *Banner in the Sky*, a boy's book based on the early Matterhorn climbs. After that I sought out and loved similar books, especially *Pursuit in the French Alps* by Paul-Jacques Bonzon. When I began hiking in the Sierra, I continued to read the climbing literature, and somewhere along the way consumed Edward Whymper's classic *Scrambles Amongst the Alps*, in which he describes his group's first ascent of the Matterhorn in 1865, which ended with the deaths of four of the seven men in the group.

Despite all this reading, I had hardly climbed at all. My brother Chris was a rock climber, and he taught me the basic rope techniques in a day of bouldering at Tahquitz. I had used what he taught me once in Switzerland, on a short wall climb with a friend from Lisa's lab. But my interest was in walking. The only ascents I had done on my own were walk-ups in the Sierra, including one with Brian and Brad to the top of Sawtooth Peak. Lying down to stick my head over the northern edge of that peak, I looked down a thousand-foot drop and felt my stomach trying to clench onto the rock like a limpet. It's not the part of mountains I like.

But now I found myself driving Brad and Brian across Switzerland to do a couple of preliminary hikes, then go to Zermatt and hire guides to climb the Matterhorn. Me and my big mouth! Me and my sneaky secret ambitions!

We parked in Zermatt's parking lot and trained into town. Zermatt doesn't allow cars in the village, although there are lots of little electric carts humming around its narrow streets, pushing through the pedestrians. We joined the throng and walked past the many perfectly appointed shops to the Bergführerverein headquarters. There we were greeted politely by a young man, who ushered us in to have a conference with the senior *Bergführer*.

The *Bergführer* was a retired mountain guide, a portly man who spoke English well. We all stood as we spoke, as his office wasn't big enough for the four of us to sit.

He told us that the usual plan for people hoping to climb the Matterhorn would be to make a preliminary guided trip up an easier peak, usually the Rimpfischhorn, to see if they were capable of doing the Matterhorn.

This hadn't been mentioned to me during my inquiries over the phone. I saw Brian and Brad looking concerned, and told the *Bergfürhrer* we couldn't afford the time or money to make a preliminary climb. I added that we were used to the mountains. We were all wearing shorts, and suddenly I was inspired to grab Brian's knee, lift his leg until his foot was on a chair, and point at his thigh.

All is good, I said in German. We can do the mountain. *Wir können den Berg steigen!*

The *Bergführer* laughed. Brian's thigh was about as big around as my waist. Meanwhile Bradley was a PE teacher, wiry and tough. Both the guys were endurance athletes in their prime.

So the *Bergführer* nodded. My speaking German was part of it, I think. Okay, he said. I will let you directly go.

He called in his young assistant and scheduled us for the next day. Then he gave us instructions on the proper shoes to rent next door, as he judged our hiking boots inadequate.

Necessary to have boots that the crampons like to grip, he said.

He helped the young man take our $900 in traveler's checks, and then wished us good luck and sent us off, saying that everything else we needed to know would be explained to us at the Hornlihütte, where we would be spending the night. This was the stone lodge located high on the side of the Matterhorn. Apparently our $300 also covered our night's stay in the hut.

We went next door to a ski shop and rented shoes that looked almost like ski boots, also crampons, but not helmets or ice axes or harnesses. With our rented gear in our daypacks we walked south to the end of town and took a cable car up a few thousand feet to a station near the Schwarzsee, then spent the rest of the afternoon walking up a steep trail to the Hornlihütte. We got there around five, and spent the end of the day on the terrace outside the big stone lodge, in the shade of the great mountain. The Matterhorn's eastern wall loomed over us like a gigantic version of the Transamerica building, its highest part seeming to tilt our way. It was definitely intimidating.

East face of the Matterhorn, from the Hornlihütte

The hut was a stone hotel, quite big considering how far it was from any road. Some young women were working the desk inside; they had us on their list, and knew we were climbers for the next day. They showed us where we would eat and sleep. We ate at a picnic table in a dining room, with other guests at other tables, while the guides ate at an inset booth reserved for them. After the meal the guides got up and went around the room asking for names and telling people who would be guided by whom. It was like being tapped out for the Boy Scouts' Order of the Arrow.

My guide was named Max. He was a burly man, older than the other guides, perhaps in his late forties, with long brown hair and a big handlebar mustache. The young women running the hut called him Mad Max. Possibly as an older climber I had been assigned the older guide; Brian's and Brad's guides were about the same age as they were. One of them told Brian or Brad he had climbed the Matterhorn 83 times; after hearing this, I asked Max how many times he had climbed it. Max just laughed and shook his head.

I asked him in German, because it turned out Max had less English than I did German. I was surprised at this, because my German was poor, and with most Swiss people I ended up conversing in English, especially if they had any involvement with tourism or foreigners. Maybe I had been paired with Max because I had said those few things in German to the *Bergführer*. In any case, after I realized the way things were, our interaction shifted into German and stayed that way for the rest of our association. Just what I needed.

We were told to go to bed and get some sleep, that we would be awakened at 4:00 a.m. to eat a quick breakfast and then be on our way. It was important to get up and down the mountain as early as possible, we were told, to avoid rockfall, and also the very frequent afternoon thunderstorms.

In the dormitory-style bedroom that night I slept poorly. It felt very different from the insomniac anticipation I experienced before my hikes in the Alps; even when those went a little nuts, like over Lötschenpass or Kistenpass, they only made me laugh.

This wasn't like that.

Soon after I fell asleep a clanging cowbell woke us, and we all gathered and ate in the dining hall. I was surprised they served us a formal sit-down breakfast, but I shouldn't have been, because this was a Swiss hotel, and no matter its unusual location, order and comfort had to be maintained.

After breakfast we went out into a cold darkness all cut by flashlight beams. Max and I found each other and he tied a rope around his waist and then mine, stifling yawns as he did so. Tying the rope around our waists was another surprise, as I knew that wearing harnesses was the modern way. A simple waist wrap was a nineteenth-century technique, and any substantial fall while using it could break your back. So this arrangement did not reassure me.

Nor did Max himself, half asleep and entirely without English. The language thing still seemed odd to me, given that he was a person whose job required communicating with international customers. I was sure I was going to have questions for him through the course of the day, and I didn't like it that I was going to have to marshal my German to do that.

After getting roped up the guides led their clients off into the dark, pausing to create a little separation between parties. Our sextet took off together and quickly came to the foot of a cliff that blocked the ridge entirely. That was a bit shocking; was it all going to be this steep? Could this really be the easiest way?

Max climbed the cliff first, and when he was sitting on top, I followed. I needed both hands to climb, but I had been carrying my flashlight in my hand. Luckily it was a square flashlight with a wire frame to prop it on picnic tables and such, and I found I could hang the wire over my lower teeth and let the flashlight swing below my jaw, where it illuminated the rock quite nicely. This felt ingenious but also bizarre. I was without question climbing the Matterhorn at night with my flashlight hanging from my mouth.

Above that first cliff it got easier. As we ascended I soon learned that the route up the *Normalweg* was extremely convoluted. We turned left or right every few feet. Max clearly knew every turn, even every step, and he set a fast pace. Following him was like hustling up a twisty staircase. In my flashlight's beam I saw that the way we were taking had been worked out in such detail that it was almost a trail, marked on the rock by dust and grit, and scratches that might have been inflicted by hobnails. Thousands of ascents had given the guides the chance to refine the route to perfection.

The frequent turns always stayed close to the ridge, but whenever it got too steep or jagged, which was pretty often, we moved onto the east face. Out there we exploited cracks and declivities allowing a way up. The dark rock of the Matterhorn breaks in blocky ways, making for many irregular troughs with stepped bottoms, like staircases incised knee deep or even waist deep into the surrounding rock. I liked that very much, as I could feel that the darkness behind us contained nothing but air. The troughs felt even better after Max turned right and led me briefly back onto the ridge, where we could see across the north face. This great wall was just visible in the darkness, but was clearly much steeper than the east face; almost vertical, in fact, with a dim white glacier flaring away from its bottom, far below. I was happier when we got back onto the east face.

Around us the sky lightened, but sunrise somehow never happened. Eventually it became apparent that we were climbing in a cloud. For a while we could see across the east face toward Italy, but then the cloud thickened and we could only see a short distance in any direction. This happened so fast it felt like a surprise, although I had been in Switzerland long enough to know that clouds should never be a surprise.

We kept weaving up the foggy east face, then came to the bottom of a rough wall 30 or 40 feet high. Three iron pigs' tails emerged from the rock, marking the line of ascent. I did my best to belay Max as he free-climbed to the pigs' tails and looped the rope around each before ascending farther. If by chance he had fallen, I would have belayed him from the highest iron twist the rope was looped to; also, if I fell following him, which was much more likely, he would hold me from the highest iron twist I had reached, and I would be less likely to pull him down.

As I climbed past the pigs' tails I unwrapped the rope from them, and aside from those brief delays I scampered up at speed; the wall had many holds I felt good about, and the belay also was very nice. If I fell, the rope might squish me a little, but it would also save me from anything worse. And besides the holds were big and solid.

After that we continued up more nicely incised staircases, and surmounted a couple more short walls, each with an iron twist or two sticking out of the rock. Fog or not, it was becoming fun. Possibly the fog even helped. We couldn't see anything but our immediate surroundings; the six of us climbed in a kind of dim white bubble, moving fast on rock that was challenging but did not vary much.

We passed a few teams that had started ahead of us. Despite these encounters, the mountain did not feel particularly crowded. For one thing we were in our fog bubble, but also the spacing being done by the guides had its effect. Also this was 1986, and the climb was not as popular then as it is now. In 2003, for instance, a section of the lower route collapsed, and 85 people were trapped above the break and had to be helicoptered off. (It's interesting to think there was no alternative route down.) On our day it seemed we were mostly alone.

Throughout the morning, however, there was a solo climber following close behind us, a friendly young man named Ueli. He was sticking close enough to us for Max to think he was using us to show him the route, without of course paying for the service. At one point they got into a sharp conversation in *Schwyzerdüüüütsch* about this, far too quick and Swiss for me to understand, but the import was clear: Max thought Ueli was ripping him off; Ueli thought Max was ridiculous to think so. Ueli was just following us because he was taking the right way. Max was disgusted by this assertion, but Ueli didn't care. He was really enjoying himself, calling up to us in English from time to time, and singing the song "Wooden Ships" by Crosby, Stills & Nash. He kept repeating the lines, "Wooden ships, on the water, very free and easy / Easy, the way you know it's supposed to be," and so on, always belting out the final line, "Talking about very free, and easy." He seemed to be doing this partly to annoy Max, but it was also obvious he was in truly high spirits.

So we wound our way up through the cloud, which blew thicker and thinner, brighter and dimmer. We saw nothing but the battered rock in our immediate vicinity, until we came up to a little wooden hut, perched on a flat spot right on the ridge. This was the Solvay Hut, a wooden cube located about two-thirds of the way from the hotel to the peak (2,400 vertical feet from hotel to hut, 1,500 feet from hut to peak). The hut looked slightly bigger than the spot it was perched on, with the balcony outside its door only three or four feet wide.

We paused there to put on our crampons, but did not go inside, or even look in the door. Brian or Brad's guide told us that sometimes as many as 20 people had been forced to overnight in the hut. If so they must have been packed in like sardines, but of course in a lightning storm that wouldn't matter. It was hard to imagine how the thing had been built, and later I looked into it and read that the materials had been hauled up on a temporary cable strung between the Hornlihütte and the ledge, and it only took five days in 1913 to build it, though it's been rebuilt since. I wonder if the people who built the thing were also hauled up and down the cable.

Crampons on, we continued up into the white fog, which grew thicker as we rose. The crampons felt odd: scratchy on the rock, sticky on the snow that now plastered every crack. We could only see 10 or 20 feet in any direction, and it almost looked like we were moving upward on a kind of slow downward escalator, as nothing else in our white bubble ever changed.

Then suddenly Max stopped. He had hardly said a word to me all morning, but now he said something like, It will stay cloudy all day, you won't be able to see a thing from the top, it's pointless. Let's go back down now, and I'll only charge you half your fee for the day.

Dismayed, I wanted to say something like, Seeing the view is not the point, climbing the mountain is the point! But between my poor German and my sense that this was a delicate moment, I kept that thought to myself.

Above us Brian and Brad and their guides were disappearing into the mist. Politely I pointed this out, and suggested that Brian's and Brad's guides did not seem to be turning back.

Max scowled at this and looked away.

Seeing I had him on the defensive, I said, You are my guide, the decision must yours be. I will do what you think right is.

This did the trick: He winced, rolled his eyes unhappily, stared for a while up into the cloud. Finally without a word he continued up the mountain.

For a few moments I was vexed that this delay had taken Brad and Brian out of my view, but quickly the climb recaptured my full attention. We were now ascending the big shoulder high on the Hörnli Ridge, visible in all the classic photos. This section is called the Moseley Slabs, because an unlucky Englishman of that name died there in the 1870s. Now that some 500 people have died on the mountain you don't get a spot named for you if you die on it, but in the early days it was different, so now we were on the Moseley Slabs, and they were much steeper than the east face had been. Confronted with this new verticality I forgot my friends and concentrated on the work at hand.

Then as we rose above the slabs we came back to the ridge proper, and could again see across and down the north face, which had been out of our view for the previous couple of hours. The cloud still enveloped us, but it turned out there was a slot of clear air between the cloud and the rock which ran down the entirety of the north face, all the way to the glacier, now 5,000 feet below, glowing in sunlight.

I wanted to look away from this vision but I couldn't, because I had to see the rocks in front of me to be able to grab them. So for a time my visual field was split vertically down the middle: to my left, black rock inches from my face; to my right, glowing white ice a full mile below me.

Okay, this was stupid. This was mountain climbing. This was what mountain climbing looked like, surreal but undeniable. This was what they meant in the climbing literature when they talked about *exposure*; now it was obvious that the exposure was to death. They had left that last part out, as being perhaps something that went without saying; it was mostly a British literature, after all. But there it was.

On we climbed and the ridge steepened even more, adding to my feeling of mild electrification. Then a thick fixed rope appeared, running down the middle of the ridge from one giant iron eyebolt to the next. Gratefully I grasped this rope, carefully I set the points of my crampons. Above me Max was doing the same thing. He kept our rope taut between us.

After a while the fixed rope on the rock came to an end, which I was sorry to see. Worse yet, Max now left the ridge and veered out onto the north face itself. I was shocked at this, but then I saw that the north face had laid back enough to hold a blanket of snow. So I followed Max out there onto the snow, as of course I had to, being tied to him.

Quickly I learned to appreciate my crampons, which spiked in and stuck very firmly in the crunchy but not rock-hard snow. I also appreciated being roped to Max. I knew that now we were on the fatal slope; this was the section of the north face where Whymper's team had come to grief. Later I read that this section, which they call the Roof, tilts at a 40-degree angle, very much less steep than the huge north wall under it. But I was discovering that 40 degrees is still quite a steep angle. It was like being on a roof, yes—the roof of a church.

We ascended slowly. We could walk, but I only needed to reach out to touch Max's boot prints before me, and it was very easy to stick my forward-pointing crampon teeth deep into the snow. I stomped up trying not to think about Whymper. This was where their rope broke—the wrong rope, as it turned out, the skinniest rope they had with them, which I have seen in the museum in Zermatt and which looks like a clothesline. It broke between the upper three and the lower four men tied to it, after which the lower four slid off the Roof and fell down the north face to their deaths on the glacier 5,000 feet below. I tried to ignore this knowledge, but it was like the blur of sunlit glacier in my right eye earlier, impossible to look away from.

Suddenly Brian and Brad and their guides appeared out of the mist above, headed down toward us. Grinning, exhilarated, they told me I only had five minutes to go, and after the briefest of pauses headed down. Max and I continued up.

Then the cloud brightened to an incandescence around us, and at the same moment we reached the summit, we also emerged from the cloud into clear air. It was as if we had breached the surface of a white ocean and were on some kind of low island.

All I could see of the Matterhorn's top was a ridge of snow about the width of a saddle, running east to west for about ten yards, just barely poking up out of the cloud. It was like the view out an airplane window when the plane descends into a cloud.

As I swung my right leg over to sit on the snow ridge, I slipped a little toward the Italian side. With a jolt of fear I caught myself, and Max, standing right beside me on the Swiss side, warned me to be careful. He said something like, Getting to the top is only half the way.

I sat straddling the summit, my left foot in Switzerland and my right foot in Italy. The sea of cloud swirled just below my boots, extending as far as I could see in all directions. There was a small red flag stuck in the snow next to me, I think a Valais cantonal flag. I twisted around to look west, but the rest of the summit ridge, which I knew was well over a hundred yards long, was enough lower than us to be lost in cloud. Only our part of the peak emerged from the sunny white swirls.

We took photos of each other with my camera, had another look around at the blue sky and the cloud tops, and then headed back down.

During the descent I led and Max followed, belaying me from above. Again we were in the cloud and could see very little. Again I found myself aware that I was on the slope where the disaster had happened. The skies had been clear on that day, so they would have been able to see where they were. The least experienced climber among them, young Robert Hadow, had slowed so much that the guide Michel Croz was reduced to moving his feet for him one step at a time. Whymper was at the top of the rope and didn't see exactly what happened, but later had the impression that Hadow had slipped, knocked Croz off his feet, and started the fatal fall. If the rope hadn't broken, all of them might have been saved; or all seven might have slid down to their deaths.

In my white bubble I could see nothing but the slope under me. It was steep, but the snow was consolidated in a way that allowed me to stomp deeply into it. I stepped down sideways and felt the crampons bite. The rope from Max tugged at my waist. Even given the sharp downward angle, even given my unfortunate awareness of the first ascent, I felt pretty solid. Although I was grateful for the cloud.

We came to the fixed rope on the ridge. I turned in and grasped the rope, moved downward one limb at a time. My crampon points usually stuck in cracks pretty well. Down through the mist we toiled.

Sooner than I expected, we were back at the Solvay Hut. Brian and Brad and their guides were sitting on its balcony, taking off their crampons. Max and I sat and did the same. We drank water, ate granola bars, had a look around. It was midmorning now, and below us to the east the cloud was beginning to clear away.

We took off down the ridge, once again a group of six. Our descent went on for what seemed a long time, because we were getting tired, and it was a long way. But it felt easier too. It was certainly less exposed, which was nice, because we were now under the cloud and could finally see where we were. There were peaks in every direction—also cliffs, glaciers, snowfields, and alps—but most of all, miles and miles of open air. Everything seemed a huge distance away. At each pause we marveled, but while moving we kept our eyes on the rock.

Brad and Brian and their guides, looking down at the Hornlihütte

We retraced the tricky route, using the iron pigs' tails to belay us down the short walls. Max even taught me how to rappel, belaying me as I turned in to the slope, held the rope, and stuck my legs straight out and bounced down as he paid out the rope from behind his back through the highest pig's tail. This was another thing I had never done before.

I was leading, and had to be, but I didn't know the way, and time after time I missed turns in the route. When I did Max would quickly correct me. *Nei, rechts! Nei, links!* This happened many times. Often I was surprised to learn from him what the proper way was, finding it counterintuitive, and I would say "Wow, hard to believe," then go down and make another mistake. *Nei, rechts,*

rechts! Nei, nei, links! Or most emphatically of all, *Nei, gerade aus!* which I knew meant "Go straight!" as the phrase had been taught to me by Lisa's German colleague Ursula, as she sat in the passenger seat of our rented car and directed me with some asperity through the streets of Zurich to a restaurant.

Nei, gerade aus!

Okay okay! *Gerade aus* it is, *genau!*

I would drop a bit more, take what looked like a right—

Nei!

Oh sorry, *enschultegung, gerade aus* it must be—

Nei! Links!

Vraiment? Links?

Genau. Links.

I could hear Max growing suspicious that I was going the wrong way on purpose to tease him, and so I began to do that, banging down any old way and turning whenever I felt like it. It was part of my growing good mood. I would have done it even more, but I was too tired. Also my ankles were getting a little frayed by the upper edges of my big rental boots.

The cloud had dissipated, the sky was clear, the views stunning. The descent became easier still, while remaining hard to discern. The little wall right over the Hornlihütte proved to be just as steep as it had felt seven hours before, when I was climbing with my flashlight clenched in my teeth. This time I thoroughly enjoyed it. One last downclimb and then we were on Earth again, and walking rather than climbing.

At the Hornlihütte we went briefly inside, and Max had me sign his guest book. I wrote something hearty and grateful, in English. I didn't really care about the delay he had caused; the peak had not proved to be a place I wanted to share with others. For one thing, there hadn't been room. And now I was down and had done it and was in a good mood. I had climbed the Matterhorn.

The guides gave us diplomas in Wizard of Oz fashion, and we sat out on the terrace looking up the mountain. It was still topped by its cloud. Then Brian and Brad reported headaches, and I suggested we descend immediately, assuring them they would feel better in Zermatt. They didn't quite believe me but we hiked down the trail to the cable car anyway, and by the time we got down to Zermatt they felt so much better that we stopped for pizza. Again I saw what a rich, even luxurious town Zermatt was, and all because of the Matterhorn. As we walked to the train station we took one last look at it, its peak now almost 10,000 feet above us. The summit was still balled in its little cloud.

We took the shuttle train down the valley to the parking lot, and I drove the rental car home to Zurich. In the car Brian began to bounce in his seat and exclaim, "I want to do it again! I want to do it again! I want to do it when we can see what we're doing!"

I had to laugh. In the years after that, Brian and Brad both went on to become accomplished mountaineers, especially Brad, who still does technical climbs in the Scottish Highlands and elsewhere. I never did anything like that again.

Here's why: Because it's dangerous. You could get killed.

Okay, I climbed the Matterhorn, and I'm glad I did. It was a memorable day, and it taught me things. But the exposure—meaning *exposure to death*, let's keep that clear—was shocking and ridiculous. If I had made a mistake bad enough, being tied to Max would only have meant he too would have died. Two people tied together without a belay connecting them to the mountain doesn't make you twice as safe, and even if it did, twice as safe as extremely dangerous is still very dangerous.

That's climbing, people will say when I make this kind of comment. Yes, exactly. Which is why for many years, for most of my life in fact, despite all my reading, I felt that rock climbing in the mountains on class 5 faces was a foolish thing to do, an activity sought out by decadent or jaded people, who couldn't manage to get their thrills from activities that wouldn't kill them if something went wrong. It seemed to me that doing things like that indicated a profound irresponsibility resulting from a blunted sensibility, or even an insensibility—a mind that couldn't get off on lesser thrills.

Yes, I was quite judgmental about it. And none of the many climbing books I read in my armchair managed to convince me that the activity had any justification that would hold water. In Chris Bonington's generation, many had died, indeed sometimes it seemed like most of them, including some of the best climbers in the group: Mick Burke, Pete Boardman, Joe Tasker, Dougal Haston, and so on. Writing about these losses, the surviving climbers were regretful but inarticulate. They gave a paragraph to the deceased and moved on. Even the philosopher among them, Reinhold Messner, anguished over the death of his brother on Nanga Parbat, couldn't do much more than mourn and move on. It's who I am, he writes. I have to climb. Although he was the only one in that group of writers who had the guts to write honestly about the moment when he had to tell his mom about his brother's death. That's a scene all the rest of them leave out.

Not so long ago, when Dick suggested we all climb the Matterhorn again, as a twenty-fifth-anniversary celebration of the climb that he had had to miss the first time around, I went on the internet and began to watch videos of people climbing the *Normalweg*. It looked even crazier than I remembered. Admittedly the head cameras that many climbers wear now have a bit of a fish-eye lens, which distorts perspective in a way that makes the fixed-rope section of the upper ridge look even narrower than it is, but still, it is fucking steep. And the drop down the north face goes on forever.

No. Not only was I not going to do it again, I also realized I took no pleasure in the fact that I had done it. It was quite a bit stupider than taking psychedelics of unknown provenance in the '70s. And really, all I'd done was follow someone I was tied to. What kind of accomplishment is that? I am much prouder of all my ascents in the Sierras, even though they have all been walk-ups, easy as pie. I did those myself, and they were navigational problems, even scrambling problems, and gave me great views, and the satisfaction of being on a mountaintop, for whatever that's worth, without me risking my life.

So, well: more on climbing later. It took something new, much later in my life, to add to my opinions about it. I'll get to that in its time.

What I want to say to end this section, and wrap up my account of our beautiful two years in Switzerland, is maybe obvious from everything else I've said already, so I won't linger on it. The two ranges are similar in some ways, but very different in the way they feel. In the Alps I was always getting in trouble, going too high, having adventures, meaning misadventures: running around in Keystone Kops style. The people were great, always so very friendly and encouraging; and all my best German happened up there too. But to spend nights in the Swiss Alpine huts was just a waste of a mountain evening, as far as I was concerned. Once I walked out of a steamy clangorous dining room at sunset, and there were the Dent Blanche and the Obergabelhorn towering over the glacier we were on, all of it tinctured pink with alpenglow, cold and quiet, and I was shocked to see it; I thought, if we were backpacking this would be the great evening of the year. And that night in the close-packed dorm a French guy forgot he was sleeping on an upper bunk, and when he got up to go to the bathroom he plunged headfirst to the floor with a clonk like a coconut hit by a hammer, and all of us were awake for an hour wondering if he would live or die. He came to and said "Qu'est que ce passe?" and we all heaved a sigh of relief and tried to get back to sleep.

Grand Mountet SAC Hut, Dent Blanche in background, Lisa, Brad, and Brian on the patio

No. Not for me. It's a different culture, a different style. I may not have made these differences clear enough, because in writing about the Sierras I've often tended to focus on the days that somehow went wonky and involved us in some kind of adventure. But those kinds of days in the Sierra are the exception; and also, those misadventures tend to be wilderness events, like bad weather or getting lost. Our typical day is more like walking through a giant open-air art museum, past masterpiece after masterpiece. In truth the Sierra is as Muir named it, a gentle wilderness. We go up there to relax, even if the relaxation can include very vigorous forms, and sometimes go wrong. The ordinary day up there is delightful, and filled with a very particular kind of peace: exciting peace; peaceful excitement. That's the experience I want to have and to describe.

As for the Alps, God bless them. Such beautiful peaks, such friendly generous people, such crazy days. I hope to walk in them again someday.

Now, back to the Sierra, to my home ground. I'll have a bit more to say about climbing itself later on.

MY SIERRA LIFE (10)

Return to the Sierra

After our Swiss years, Lisa and I moved to Washington, DC, where she spent four years working for the FDA, and we had baby David join us. By the time we moved back to Davis in 1991, I had already begun a pattern of high Sierra trips that persisted for most of the next 20 years. While we were in DC, I made arrangements twice to fly back to California and go on a week-long Sierra trip. Naturally I called my old friends still living in California, and we gathered at the trailheads and went up together. After Lisa and David and I returned to Davis in 1991, and baby Tim joined us in 1995, we kept doing that. Joe flew in from Hawaii for these trips, and Robin sometimes came over from New Mexico. Soon we began to add shorter spring and fall trips to our central summer week. That we managed to do all this despite busy home lives was a sign of our commitment to it. We were enjoying it.

My two years of dashing about the Alps had given me a new appreciation for Sierra qualities I had never really noticed before. The feel of days 2 and 3, for instance, when you know you're going to be out for a week. The quiet mornings. Sunsets. The rhythm of walking all day. The nights out. Wilderness as experienced while walking in it, traversing a space so above or beyond our ordinary world. The sense of being on a quest; the exploration of unknown territory, wild and remote from the world. The slow devotional practice of it. The harmless fun.

All these qualities now stunned me. They were like enormous gifts from the Earth, from Gaia or however you want to think of this planet and its biosphere; also from the people who came before us, who protected this high place from exploitation. Oases of calm in a sometimes frantic life. Possibly these were the same qualities of Sierra reality that had been impressing me all along, including during my chaotic youth, but now I saw them better, felt them more. I recognized them for the gifts they were. My time in the Alps had caused me to love the Sierra more than ever.

This feeling, as it strengthened and became more articulated, began to infuse my fiction as well. Through the first half of the '90s I was writing my Mars trilogy, and everything I saw and felt in the Sierra got translated into that project, sometimes quite directly. Indeed the process of terraforming Mars, as described in my novel, was really a matter of turning the Red Planet into something more like the high Sierra. Then in the second half of the '90s I went to Antarctica, seeing it as a kind of Martian analogue; but here again the Sierra served as my psychogeological benchmark, adding perceptions to my Antarctic experience and my Antarctic novel, and to much of my other fiction from that time.

Joe was a major force in getting us up into the Sierra so often. Having moved to Hawaii soon after our graduation from UCSD, he had missed a lot of trips in the '70s and '80s, and when he rejoined us in the early '90s, he wanted to make up for lost time. He joined every trip from then on, and instigated our resumption of spring snow trips, and in general was always pushing for more. Darryl and I were always up for that, Vic and Dick and Robin came when they could, and a few times some other friends and family joined us. It became a big part of our lives, not so much in terms of days per year up there (maybe 25) as in the space it occupied in our minds.

Even so it was by no means enough for Terry, who went up there much more often than we did. I would guess he spent about three months of every year up there. He did the Muir Trail at least once a year, and many other trips besides. He and his partner Melody were joined by baby Cory in 1991, and soon after that they married. Most of the time he lived with them at Melody's house in Davis, and so I saw him often, as in my previous Davis life. But he also bought some land next to Highway 80, high in the Sierra foothills, and just as he had taught himself to make his own backpacking gear, he now taught himself to build a house. Over the course of a couple of years, he built his place from the foundation up. Except for the pouring of the foundation itself, and when he needed someone to help him hoist a beam, it was a completely solo effort. When he was done he had a very neat and handsome two-story house, overlooking the great gorge of the North Fork of the American River. He lived up there a lot, and skied from there every winter day that he wasn't in Davis.

When he was in Davis, he and I would go for runs, and also we ran our Frisbee golf course with Neil and Bob. For our runs together we soon settled on a regular Wednesday morning excursion, alternating between his place and mine. When we were both in town we did that weekly for almost 20 years. We talked as we ran, and talked some more afterward as we drank smoothies and cooled down. Mainly our talk concerned the politics of the day, Buddhism, science, friends, family, books, and potential Sierra trips. As for backpacking, in the summers I sometimes joined him for sections of his Muir Trail trips, and he was involved in the planning of all our group trips, indeed we minced the possibilities very finely during our winter runs in Davis. Darryl and Joe were also involved in these off-season planning sessions, and we all had to coordinate our schedules and find a week when all could make it. This wasn't always possible, but it happened more often than now seems plausible, since for whatever reason it keeps getting harder to do, even now that the kids are grown. Life just keeps accelerating.

But we got in a lot of trips. And the trips were getting good. Weeklong loops became our norm; the few experiments we made in hiking from point to point wasted too much time arranging cars, time that was better spent hiking. So we went out in big loops, and never repeated ourselves; the southern Sierras are bigger than one suburban hiker's life can exhaust. At the rate we were doing it, it would have taken maybe 60 or 70 years to see the whole range in full.

Through these years, we developed a kind of routine. I would pick up Joe at the Sacramento airport, often with Darryl. Many times we would simply drive south from the airport to a trailhead, sleep by the car, and be ready to hike the next morning. This felt slightly manic, but also fun, and it maximized our Sierra time. Dick and Vic would drive up from Southern California; Terry was often already up there. Meeting at some high trailhead, a car campground or just an empty parking lot, was a pleasure: back in the cold high dark forest, piney and windy and starry, about to embark on another adventure. On the first days of these trips, we would struggle up a trail and over a pass, taking it slow, chatting as we walked and catching up on the previous months. As the days passed we slid into the feel of the trip, relaxing in many ways. Navigational problems took over as our main concern. Could we find our way? Would we get back to the car in the time we had allotted ourselves? Were we lost? Could we make it up that unexpectedly horrid slope of broken rock? The week would expand into a felt time of about two months, while at the same time it was over too soon. A pocket epic. The treks usually ended with a long tramp back down to the car, dirty and happy. Drive home to real life. Another good trip.

So I always wanted more. There was never a problem finding new and interesting places to go. I spent many winter nights looking at maps and guidebooks, and flying around in Google Earth when it arrived, doing what Darryl and I called armchair backpacking. Over time we became somewhat better as armchair backpackers, meaning more realistic as to what could really be walked, and although some trips were badly conceived, even those were huge adventures. We would return home full of the desire to go back up. In the 52 weeks of every year, that one week, or three at most—five for me, with the family trips included—always stuck out as among the most memorable. East side, west side, see something new. And if it's new to you then you are discovering it, and the perpetual cognitive dissonance between map and territory will always cause a little bit of getting lost, a little bit of orienteering and finding a way. Class 2 routes and trail-free basins added hugely to that feeling of exploration and discovery, of nomads poking over a ridge to see what lay on the other side. And so we had our method.

As the years passed, problems in our group dynamic developed or revealed themselves. Terry was often impatient with our slow speed, and with our choice of routes, even though he was always involved with the latter. He also disliked our desire to stop early every day, with all of us gathered in the same campsite. He liked to hike till dark, and he felt there were looser group styles he would have preferred, although since he never hiked with anyone but us, these styles were hypothetical at best. He often went missing up ahead. I felt the strain of that sometimes, and did some hustling on some days to keep Terry in view, while also doubling back to indicate to the others where he had gone. A little dashing back and forth, a little diplomacy, was often needed to get us into the same camps at night. There was in fact an early trip where it was just Terry, Darryl, and me, during which Terry had zoomed ahead and Darryl had fallen behind, with me in the middle scurrying back and forth. I caught up to Terry in Italy Pass and told him we needed to camp ASAP, as I had lost sight of Darryl down below in the Granite Park. Improv at sunset, note left in pass, high bivouac just over the pass, etc.; but even so we lost Darryl for two days, mainly because he followed the directions in the note we had left in the pass, and went ahead of us in the dusk down to Toe Lake, which we examined from a distance the next morning without spotting him. Two days spent entirely in search mode, zipping back down the trail to look for him where he wasn't, and so on. It turns out that searching for someone in the Sierra is not an easy thing. On the second morning of our wandering, we encountered a tent that had appeared overnight while we were asleep, and thinking it might be Darryl's new tent, I went to it expecting him and shouted a hello, because there's no doorbell to ring on a tent; and out popped my friend Carter Scholz, whom I hadn't seen since we had backpacked together five years previously. That was one of the biggest surprises of my life, just as surprises go. Carter joined us in our hunt, and after we finally ran into Darryl, who of course had been looking for us too, we all hiked together for a while, before Carter went off on his planned route.

What that trip demonstrated was that it is easier to stay together through the day, and end up in the same campsite at night, than it is to lose someone and go into search mode, worrying that something bad might have happened. But this lesson did not seem to impress itself on Terry. Possibly he was always slightly hoping to lose us, and thus be free to ramble at his own speed.

So I did some running around in those years, but mostly it all went fine. We did lose Terry a couple of times overnight, but those were exceptions. The strain I felt in all this diplomacy and go-between work was completely overmatched by the joys of the trips, and I figured it was mainly my problem.

The great thing was that we managed it, and kept coming back. Exploring new parts of the Sierra; occasionally walking up a peak; visiting several new basins per trip, by way of class 2 cross-country passes: these were really fun weeks. We had a lot of them. And the years flew.

On the High Sierra Trail

MOMENTS OF BEING (5)

Close Calls

Our trip over Ed Lane Pass in 1996 was a botch, although in truth we had fun anyway. When we got to the crest just west of Birch Mountain, late on the second day of intense uphill scrambling, even including a rare glacier ascent, we saw the view down the other side, and groaned: parallel vertical gullies, angled at the steepest pitch possible to still get called class 2. Maybe it was even the mythical class 2/3, although by definition this hybrid should be impossible. I had read somewhere that this pass had once been used by mules, but no. Winged mules, maybe. So we spread out—there were nine of us on this trip—so, our largest gathering for our stupidest trip—and we took a few separate gullies to make our descent, keeping a good distance above or below each other, so as not to knock rocks onto those below.

About halfway down, Victor, well above us, felt a big rock shift under him and yelled out a warning. We looked up; he was in Joe's gully, I was one gully over. Victor had dislodged a rock about the size of an old television set, now tumbling down at Joe with startling acceleration.

Joe regarded it. I saw this clearly: he watched the rock come at him, on point like a hunting dog, waiting till he was sure which way it was going to go. Only when it hit a big rock and spun as it went airborne did he dart to the side. It flew by him, close enough for him to feel the wind of it, he said later, after which it crashed down a long way.

Now that was presence of mind, I thought. Quick thinking indeed! Probably one of the reasons Joe was such a good wrestler in high school, along with his strength. Quick and decisive.

Disaster dodged, we continued down the gully forever. Late in the day we found a campsite among small ponds, at the very upper end of a little basin tucked above who knows where. We could see that no one ever came here, not since Ed Lane anyway. There are hundreds of dead-end high basins like this scattered around the Sierra, all gems. We sat there exhausted and watched sunset fall on us like a starry blanket. It had taken us two days of radical scrambling to cross the crest. Not unusual when you cross the crest off trail, but still—Ed Lane Pass? No. Not really a pass. Only do it if you have an interest in Sierra curiosities.

Tulainyo Lake on the other hand is a beyul, that Tibetan Buddhist concept of a hidden sacred valley that you can only find if you look for it in the right

Tulainyo Lake is center-left in this satellite photo, still frozen, overlooking the long drop to Owens Valley; Wallace Lake is below it to its left, a kidney shape, also frozen. Photograph by Planet Labs PBC.

spirit. Everyone should try to get to one. This particular beyul sits right on the crest of the Sierra: a big oval lake, half a mile long and almost as wide. Bizarre to see it right there on the crest; from its east retaining wall, which is at most a hundred feet higher than the lake, you look directly down onto Owens Valley, 10,000 feet below. On the west side a small plateau holds it in place over a steep drop to Wallace Lake.

The name Tulainyo derives from the fact that the lake sits on the border of Tulare and Inyo Counties. A lame mash-up if you ask me. The lake deserves a name more like God's Eye, or the Heart of the World, or some Elvish name a lot more suggestive than Tulainyo, although admittedly that could be Tolkien on an off day. Better to call it Gandalf's Fastness!

Kenneth Rexroth visited it and wrote about it as the culmination of his yearlong Guggenheim-sponsored voyage around the world, in his book-length poem *The Dragon and the Unicorn*. Norman Clyde declared it his favorite lake in all the Sierra, and that's interesting—yet another indication of Clyde's well-hidden soulfulness. Clyde's Favorite? Rexroth's Culmination?

Ironically, from its north shore you can see the top of Whitney poking over a ridge. (You can see Whitney in the photo at left, center.) And yes, this means that from Whitney you can see an arc of Tulainyo Lake—not enough to let you grasp how big and weird it is, but it's visible. And so the two spots regard each other—Whitney famous, crowded, pointless—Tulainyo unknown, empty, radiating some kind of calm power that is even a little ominous. The sublime and the ridiculous; and America being what it is, the ridiculous is what everyone queues up for, to the extent of joining a lottery and crossing fingers that their number gets chosen for a permit to climb. Take a number for the sake of a number: 14,505 feet above sea level, the tallest peak in the United States— not counting Alaska. If you win that lottery, you get to hike a long trail to the big broad summit of an abstract idea ("The TALLEST") and marvel at the stone building on it, and the giant summit register like an old hotel's guest book. You get to listen to people on their cell phones calling friends and family to tell them about their great climb. The day we were there, I watched the seated Baier hunch his shoulders further and further as a guy behind us crowed into his phone, "You didn't think I could do it but I did! I win! You lose!"

Literally his words. With 50 people milling around trying to ignore him so they could make their own triumphant calls.

I pointed out to Terry the visible arc of Tulainyo Lake, a couple thousand feet below us and maybe three miles north as the crow flies. I said, We'll be there tomorrow.

Good, he said, and stood up to leave.

So we got to Wallace Lake, below Tulainyo, late the following afternoon. Dick joined Terry and me on the steep scramble up to it, while Joe and Darryl made other explorations in the area. A great afternoon.

The next morning Terry took off early on his solo Muir trek, this time headed north. He always left us like an arrow leaving the bow.

The Baier takes off.

Now there were four of us, Dick, Joe, Darryl, me. Darryl decided he wanted to see Tulainyo Lake after all, and would run up to it quickly and then rejoin us for the hike down to the Muir Trail, then around to Shepherd Pass. Dick and Joe didn't want to wait for him, so I said I would, and they took off.

Darryl returned around 11:00, and we got going soon after. At that point he had done five miles of difficult cross-country, with a tough climb to the mystic lake.

As we descended Wallace Creek the clouds bunched and thickened, and it began to rain. We geared up and forged on. In one downpour we stood under a grove of pines and stayed protected, feeling good when the rain turned to hail.

Then we reached the Muir Trail, turned north, and hiked hard. It was raining less, but thunder rumbled as we started across the Bighorn Plateau, which is a vast high exposed space with an awesome prospect in all directions. But now this expansive view allowed us to see bolts of lightning touching down around us. Usually in Sierra thunderstorms, you first see the clouds flash white, and then you hear a rolling boom. Now, under a low ceiling of black cloud, little crackling lines of pure white were snapping between cloud and ground, sizzling our retinas and then smacking us with a crack like a rifle shot, announcing the bigger crashing boom that quickly followed. Seeing lightning bolts is always a dreadful sight, a jolt of fear; seeing them hit the ground near you is terrifying. Green afterimages bounced in our vision, scorching our view of the dark high plateau. But we had to hike on, as there was no shelter anywhere to be had. Talk about the sublime! Beauty and terror were bound into one galvanizing surge, and our blood turned to pure adrenaline.

Bighorn Plateau is home to a few isolated foxtail pines, standing bravely here and there; now as we ran by them we saw that every one of them had been blasted black at its top by lightning strikes. Oh my God. We ran hard, or to be precise, we hiked in huge haste, at whatever gait you might call it when you're going as fast as you can with a pack on your back. We hauled ass. Again the question of whether aluminum walking poles would attract lightning occurred to us, and again we couldn't answer it (apparently they would). Since our walking poles were also our tent poles, it wouldn't do to cast them aside and run like a bunny. But damn, they did seem to be humming in our hands. The eye-slicing brilliance of the lightning bolts continued to shock us, no matter how far away. They were very clearly hitting the ground—little elbowed lances of pure sizzling white, appearing out of nowhere and seeming to cause bursts of earth and vegetation to fly wherever they struck down. We could only keep scampering.

At the end of that terrorized transit of the high plain, and an added mile or two of forest that we scarcely noticed, we came to the intersection of the Muir Trail and the Shepherd Pass trail. We sat down under some trees to catch our breath. Trees are said not to be protection against lightning strikes, and the blasted foxtail pines back on the plateau served to confirm that, but it definitely felt better to be among them than to be out on the bare plateau.

Perversely, now that we had some shelter, real or not, the lightning relented. Thunder rumbled in the distance. It was still raining, but lightly. The dark cloud bottom formed a flying ceiling just over us. We could still see a long way in all directions. The upper Kern resembles Mongolia at the best of times; now it looked like we had been transported to some bigger planet.

Darryl was looking beat. He had already done a 12-mile day, including a tough ascent to Tulainyo Lake, and now our mad dash across the Bighorn. And yet we were still 5 miles from Shepherd Pass, up a steady grade.

In those years Darryl was an advocate of the Atkins diet, a true believer, such that even in the Sierra he ate nothing but salami and cheese and nuts and I don't know what. He was going into ketosis right before my eyes.

Big D, I said: carbs. Fucking carbohydrates. Now is the time. Just this once. And I held out my gallon bag of Cheez-Its to him.

Warily he eyed the weird industrial orange of those great crackers. Salt, flour, oil, cheese flavor extraordinaire, color like a sun-damaged life jacket. The bag glowed in the dusky light.

He ate some. It was like giving communion. Probably many a person who has taken communion has been hungry more than spiritually. And some carbo-loading never hurts. It's always a little bit religious, eating, but especially when you're hungry. I felt very pastoral. Then we heaved our packs back on our backs and carried on.

The trail from the Muir Trail to Shepherd Pass is always magnificent, but never more so than on that dark day, under that storm cloud rushing up the slope faster than we were. Diamond Mesa, well named for its shape, looked down on us from our left, providing a way to gauge our progress; you start well below it, you end up well above it. The ridge to our right steepened and displayed its ice-beveled vertical ribs and chutes, silvery when wet: the superb north wall of Mount Tyndall, curved like a Frank Lloyd Wright building. The trail steepened then laid back, steepened then laid back, on and on for five miles, and all the while the entirety of the upper Kern darkly visible around us.

We traded the lead as the spirit moved us. Wearing Baier's tarps as capes, we grasped the shoulder corners under our hands as we gripped our walking poles, and draped the rest of the tarps over our heads and backs so that they almost reached the ground. Dressed like that under his dark blue tarp, flowing up that slope, Darryl appeared to me like a giant manta ray. He was moving well, smooth and relentless, in a rhythm. The carbs had kicked in, I could see that in the way he was moving. I felt it myself, that second wind that sometimes can fill you. Maybe it was even the rare third wind. We could have gone all night.

As it was, we got to the pass about half an hour before dark, and quickly set up our tarps, got water, and sat down to make and eat dinner by headlamp. Joe and Dick were happy to see us. We traded tales of the Bighorn Plateau, babbling in that goofy way that happens when you have dodged a fate and are immensely relieved. The next day we would plunge down the great escarpment and eat hamburgers in Lone Pine's Whitney Café. All would be well. We would live to make other trips. But there would be few days as memorable as that one. Hopefully there will be more like it—except for the lightning.

ROUTES (4)
Desolation

It's like looking through the wrong end of the telescope, my father once said to me when talking about his past.

Maybe that's how Desolation is in me now, even though it was my heart's home in the early years; even though, when I went up there again last month, snow camping for the first time in years, it bloomed in me like Proust's madeleine in the tea, and was the same as ever.

How to describe it? It's a postage stamp in the northern Sierra, a rectangle 8 miles wide and 12 tall, or so I read, though that strikes me as ridiculously small; surely it must be bigger than that! A kingdom bound in a nutshell, as in those fantasy novels like *Lud-in-the-Mist*, where once you cross the fairy border you're in a universe larger and more charged with meaning. Or, as in Tibetan culture, a beyul, a hidden sacred valley. Although not so hidden.

My backyard? That's not right. But I have spent something like eight months of my life there, and some sections of it I know rock by rock, tree by tree.

My heart's home—but that's not right either. It's the southern Sierra I feel that way about. In fact, were I asked to designate some small patch of granite as my heart's home, that would be Mount Desert Island, that other magic patch of the Sierra Nevada, torn out of the range and thrown into the Atlantic just off the coast of Maine—talk about magic! A topic for another book; enough for now to say, I love that island very much.

Desolation as a previous reincarnation? Maybe that's right. And more than one previous reincarnation at that. First the '70s, crashing around like a crazy person: the pinball years. Then the '90s, the family years, with Lisa and our boys, and some close friends and their kids. Those peaceful lovely weeks—a different kind of Sierra life—they went on for many years, year after year, as if they would always happen. But now that the kids have grown, those too are gone.

It's part of the Eldorado National Forest, southwest of Lake Tahoe. Protected as wilderness since 1899. Its eastern border almost touches Emerald Bay on Tahoe.

It's more proof of my contention that any granite that lived under glaciers is going to end up good for backpacking. Desolation was almost entirely covered by an ice cap, which over the centuries scoured its granite and meta-

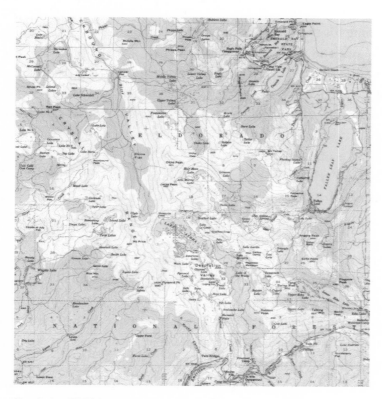

Desolation Wilderness, USGS

morphic rock into small basins. It looks higher than it actually is, partly because it's farther north, but mainly because of that ice-on-granite scouring. Soil has not yet grown back enough to cover large stretches of it, so its tree line is far lower than the tree line that gets created by atmospheric pressure and summer low temperatures.

Now Highway 50 runs by the bottom of Horsetail Falls, giving access to trailheads on Desolation's west and south sides. Highway 89, which runs up the west side of Tahoe, gives access to the east-side trailheads.

There are about 130 lakes in the once-glaciated area, and a vertical span of about 3,500 feet. A low transverse ridge between Jacks Peak and Mount Price is the watershed between the north-running Rubicon River, and the south-flowing broad flat granite maze that drains down Horsetail Falls into the South Fork of the American River. This strange high flatland was completely covered by an ice sheet, and the usual rock maze resulted. It was dammed in 1875, and the shallow Lake Aloha now fills the lower parts of the maze in a weird patchwork that doesn't escape the usual reservoir ugliness.

The main ridges make a big H shape, although it's more complicated than that, as usual. Glaciers flowing down westward from the Crystal Range cut the Lyons Creek and Silver Creek drainages, and east of the ridge that runs from Ralston Peak to Phipps Peak, there are a number of steep east-running basins, including the one that holds the Echo Lakes.

It adds up to what I call a "pocket high Sierra": a single pluton top, full of quartz crystals, and marbled in places with an irregular roof pendant of black rock, and some orange granite too. All the various kinds of Sierra rock are there.

I've said Desolation is about one-sixth the size of the high Sierra, but this is mostly psychogeological; what I mean is that where in the high Sierra you make a 3,000-foot ascent, in Desolation you'd be facing around 500. Horizontal distances are similarly reduced. This is a crucial difference when you are hiking with young kids. It's the best Sierra for children, and like certain Pixar movies, adults can enjoy it just as much as kids, while also enjoying their kids' enjoyment.

It's also well run by the US Forest Service, which has always maintained very helpful policies regarding wilderness permits for Desolation, making it possible to show up at their ranger stations on the morning you go in, to get day-of-entry permits for a visit (this may no longer be true). Because it's safest to be at the ranger station a bit before it opens, to get the permit you want, we were often done with that and on the last part of the road early, and hiking by 9:00 a.m.

In the '70s we tried all the Desolation trailheads and ran all over the place, but by the '90s I had come to feel that the best entry is Wrights Lake, in the southwest corner of the park, eight miles north of Highway 50. That entry leads to the most beautiful area with the least effort, and with young kids that's important. Both my boys started hiking there when they were two, although we carried them in baby backpacks whenever they requested a ride, until they were four or five. It's a beautiful feeling to have a child on your back, archaic and parental, and Tough Traveler made a good baby backpack, with room under the kid's butt for a full load of other stuff. That was not ultralite, but it didn't matter.

At Wrights Lake's southeastern corner, where its inlet stream meanders through a meadow, there's a small parking lot located next to the trailhead. From there one can head north to Rockbound Pass, five easy miles away, but usually we went straight east, up to Twin Lakes and Island Lake. Two miles and 800 vertical feet bring you to Twin Lakes, the first of several great campgrounds in this basin. It's a wonderful area of very clean granite, deeply etched and burnished by its icy excavation. The not-so-twin lakes fill the lower lobe of the basin, at 8,200 feet; Island Lake lies right above them in a slightly higher cirque. Standing over the north shore of Island Lake is Peak 9441, a high point on the Crystal Range. South from 9441, the Crystal Range runs east of Island Lake up to a spiky shoulder we called Snaggletooth, then up some more to Mount Price, almost as high as Pyramid Peak, which is the culmination of the Crystal Range, a couple of miles farther south. A divide drops west from Mount Price and forms the southern arm of the Twin Lakes' classic glacial horseshoe shape, which opens to the west, allowing for late and long sunsets. Even some early cell phone coverage. When flying into Sacramento from the east, planes often descend in a path that gives passengers a view down onto Desolation, and what always strikes me is how big the Twin Lakes–Island Lake basin looks relative to the rest of the region; it doesn't seem that way on a map, but from the air it's obvious.

Desolation expands after you enter it, and you never run out of new things to see. The crack patterns scoured out by the ice left horizontal ledges everywhere, also little ponds tucked in holes. From Twin and Island Lakes there are quick ascents in all directions to overlooks, higher ponds, peaks, and ridge runs to neighboring basins. The lack of soil created since the ice age means it's still mostly exposed rock, its scattered trees isolated, small, wind-sculpted. Very picturesque; the Zen garden effect is strong.

After Lisa and I moved back to Davis in 1991, we started going up to Desolation again, first with David, then with David and Tim. In that period we went to the Twin Lakes basin almost every time. Tim and I had regular paired sleeping spots overlooking lakes or ponds, and I lay on the side that would keep him from rolling off cliffs into the water while he was asleep.

We were joined by new friends from our neighborhood in Davis, Village Homes. A group of kids met early at the Rivendell day-care center, after which their families became friends, so it was natural to go backpacking together. That lasted for most of 15 years. Often it became a kind of rolling back country party, in which some families would go up first and stay for a while, then other families would join later, while some who had been up there would go home. I always stayed with the boys the entire time, with Lisa joining us as her work schedule allowed. What this meant was that often the boys and I would be up there for ten days or two weeks at a time, and this went on for years.

Almost every day we moved our camp. This was mainly for the fun of it, but it was also my backpacking habit asserting itself. Of course you have to move! We would pack up camp at Twin Lakes, get our backpacks on, and then hike up to Island Lake, just a mile away, and set a new camp there. And in fact the new camp did have a completely different feel to it, so it was worth doing.

Over time we found other favorite campsites. Some of these were by ponds

Our Village Homes family at Twin Lakes

so small they aren't even on the map, including our favorite, the most glorious of them all. Our names for them reflected our feelings. Rangers in the '70s had told me they called the V-shaped pond above Island Lake Shangri-La, so we used that name for it. Then the nicest pond we found and liked we named Shambhala (this was the older kids' idea). We also had Dale's Ponds, discovered by our kids' tennis coach when he was trying to follow our directions to Shangri-La. Another pond was called the Pool, or the Swimming Hole, or Our Pond—small, secluded, sun-facing, and warm.

Sometimes we had quite a big group up there; this was fun, though a little too crowded for wilderness. I suppose our maximum size once reached 20 people from six families, with two wilderness permits to make it nominally legal. More typically we would only have eight or ten in camp at any one time.

Our little adventures were as common as the chipmunks that were always dashing about, doing their camp-robber thing. Once when crossing the little old Island Lake retainer dam, Tim started running ahead of me and I chased him, thinking I might need to snatch him from the air if he fell; instead I stepped on a block of the dam's masonry that broke off and cast me forward onto him, so that I knocked him into the lake to the left, while I crashed down into the brush below the dam to the right. By the time I struggled back up to the dam's level, alarmed at what might be happening to Tim, who was about four at the time, he had pulled himself up onto the dam and was hanging on to it with both arms, utterly soaked. We hung on the dam from opposite sides, faces about two feet apart, staring round-eyed at each other. He was always unflappable when things went haywire. Our friend Casey gave us some dry clothes for him, as she had brought some spares for her son Cedar; I carried no spares.

Camping there with Casey and Mark and their kids Anna and Cedar was being up there with family. They were our most constant companions on these trips, and at home too. My older boy David had been friends with Anna since they met at age two in the Rivendell Nursery School in our neighborhood, and Cedar and Tim had been friends from birth. Casey and Mark were skeptical of my lightweight ethos, and over distances as short as ours it was true that weight didn't matter, but I couldn't change my ways. They brought up complicated meals to cook on their stove, and laughed at my freeze-dried backpacking food. I learned from them how to eat better in the mountains, and how to identify flowers, and how to relax. We had a lot of fun. Sunsets and storms, card games and skipping stones. Watching the marmots and waterfalls. Neil and Cindy and their boys, also family, were often up there as well, and Neil and Mark played music on guitar and mandolin while I whistled along. One night the three of us watched the wind break up the moon on the lake below us, very late into the night. Nothing then was lacking.

Those days were sweet. There was never any sense of hurry, except on the drive to the ranger station. My boys enjoyed exploring, or playing by the lake with their friends. Some parents would watch the kids while other adults and kids took off on short jaunts. There was a lot of swimming in the lakes, and group hikes. The ascent of Peak 9441 was a big deal, also going up Snaggletooth. Ridge runs took off in all directions, and the descent to Smith Lake involved crawling under a giant boulder. Ridge running northward got us all

Tim and Cedar in Desolation

the way to Rockbound Pass and Lake Doris, where there were other campsites we liked as well. This led to loop trips, in which we got back to the cars by way of Rockbound Pass and the trail going down the Silver Fork.

That the Rockbound Pass extensions revisited my youthful haunts was a satisfying thought, when it occurred to me, but it very seldom did. That was a previous incarnation. Who was that young man, so faintly recalled? The lakes and peaks were the same, but not me.

Family life. A few families together, and therefore a band. A tribe on the move, in the wilderness: this seemed to evoke something primal. The postmodern Paleolithic, glimpsed as a program and then relaxed into, for a week or ten days of chat and play, cooking and singing. Simple pleasures. Then the kids grew up, and we stopped going to Desolation. I refocused on the southern Sierra, which had been happening for me concurrently all along, on separate trips with my old gang. Desolation drifted away — again.

What a beautiful Sierra life we had.

MOMENTS OF BEING (6)

A Sierra Day: Under the Tarp

In the Sierras the ground is never dirty. Granite breaks down into sand, and indeed there's a landscaper's ground cover they call d.g., "dee gee," short for decomposed granite; that's just what the high Sierra is often floored with, and it makes a great camping surface. Meadows are usually too wet and lumpy and delicate to camp on, and bedrock too hard and unflat (although it can work fine sometimes); better are areas that have caught spills of decomposed granite behind a rib of hard rock, after which some grasses and flowers have started to grow. Fellfields, in fact, or young meadows that are not yet fully grassed over. These will take a tent stake well, they will drain well (up to a point) if it rains, they will conform to your body when you lie on them, and they won't poke your ground pad and cause a leak—not usually. Often little bunches of grass are growing out of this ground at regular intervals, which stabilizes a surface that otherwise might shift too much like sand. These grasses never seem much harmed the next day when you take your ground pad off them. If there is dead plant matter mixed with the d.g., it's usually from tree bark and small branches falling apart. The ground in these areas often looks like beach sand and landscaper's bark mulch, incompletely shuffled together. If there are enough trees around, if you're camped in a little glade or an isolated copse, then the ground can be layered by old duff and branches and pine needles and pine cones. But best of all, to my mind, is fellfield.

Tarp set on this, you are still sitting on the ground. You can lie on your ground pad and luxuriate at being at rest, face inches from the ground. Microtextures spring into you: grass clumps, miniature pebbles, pea gravel, maybe a little scatter of old deer droppings. Tiny flowers. Ambient light through the translucent tarp makes the ground glow. Patterns are so intricate that the ground looks groomed, a Zen sand garden.

If it rains by day and you shelter under a translucent tarp, the ground is your delight. Sound of rainfall on the tent, view of the ground beside your head. All your various pieces of gear lie around you, stuffed with their own vitality and usefulness, their intense colors. Like a quilt made of the fabrics of your life, certain favorite offcuts. As you're sitting there sheltered from rain, this kind of contemplation can last for hours. Staying dry despite the persistent percussion of rain on the tarp begins to seem kind of miraculous. I once had a frog join me, very tiny but fully formed; not a tadpole or pollywog, a true frog; it sat next to the round end of my spoon and didn't even extend across a fifth of its width. I had had no idea there were frogs that small.

Once, to get shelter from a quick afternoon thunderstorm, we had to set our tents fast, right next to Palisade Creek. The steep rocky stream crashed

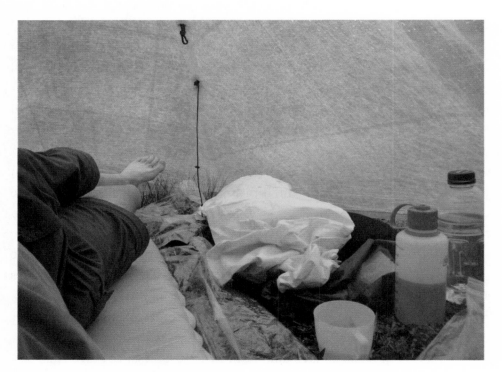

Waiting out a storm

wetly down its channel, the rain on my tent pattered insistently, snare drum rather than tympani; thunder boomed overhead, then echoed off the canyon walls. It was a John Luther Adams symphony!

Little deltas of rainwater meandered under the edge of the tarp; I made microdams to direct them elsewhere, listening to the music of the storm, its slosh and patter. The thunderclaps grew in volume until they reminded me of the time I saw Tchaikovsky's *1812 Overture* played at Wolf Trap, when the cannon fire was provided by a detachment of the US Navy, who completely overwhelmed the orchestra's sound with a stupendous barrage. Here in this deep canyon the thunder now did the same thing, drowning out the other instruments in a crescendo and climax that then rumbled away. After it stopped raining, and we went back outside, the canyon filled with a double rainbow.

Tarp life can be hard to remember. What I don't forget is the joy of lying there on the ground, awake or asleep, in rainy afternoon or early morning sun. Something peaceful and beautiful about it. Harmonious: yes, the world seems to hum a little, in a very tall chord. There's a rightness to the quilting of the world.

Out from under the tarp, after the storm, Palisade Creek

MY SIERRA LIFE (11)
Heart Trouble

By 1994 it had been clear for several years that Terry had a heart problem. His mitral valve was not closing all the way when his heart pumped, and that was causing his heart to enlarge as it attempted to compensate for the insufficiency. When the problem was discovered, Terry was naturally dismayed. At the same time, the diagnosis was of some comfort to him, because it gave him an explanation for why he hadn't performed better in the competitive triathlons he had been entering. No one could have trained harder, as he put it to me, and yet he would always come in tenth or twentieth in his age group. Now that was explained.

Triathlons had become a thing in Davis Aquatic Masters. Terry enjoyed all three activities, and so had done a fair number of them. Once he entered an Ironman, the longest triathlon, consisting of a 2-mile swim, a 120-mile bike ride, and a marathon run; as he had never run a marathon, he wanted to see how it felt before the big day. No sponsored marathons were coming up in our region, so he went over to the university's track in Davis and ran 106 laps on it. He said it felt fine.

But now he knew he had a heart condition, and by 1994 it was getting bad. His heart had grown to two and a half times the size of an ordinary heart, they told him, and they predicted he would die without an operation to replace the malfunctioning valve. He agreed to the idea of an operation.

The valve could be replaced by a mechanical valve, a pig valve, or a cadaver valve. If a mechanical valve, he would have to take blood thinners for the rest of his life. If a pig valve, he would have to have the operation repeated in 10 or

15 years. A cadaver valve would therefore be best, but these were rarely available, and the one they used would have to be the right size to fit his heart. So he got on a waiting list for a cadaver valve, and continued to work out for two or three hours every day, either running, biking, or swimming. When he stood at rest, you could see the carotid artery jump in his neck. It was a scary time.

That summer, Lisa and I took David and made a car trip north to visit Lisa's stepmother Stephanie and husband John, in the San Juan Islands north of Seattle. Before I left, Terry and I had talked of making a last Sierra trip before his operation, so as Lisa and I were preparing to drive home from Washington, I called his house, and found out from his wife Melody that a cadaver valve had been found for him, and the operation scheduled for two weeks later; since I was gone, he had immediately left for the Sierras by himself, just in case it turned out to be his last trip.

Our drive home took two days. When we got home I called Terry's mom, as Melody had mentioned he had given her an itinerary for his trip. I wrote this down as his mom read it to me over the phone, and took it to dinner at a restaurant with Lisa and David. As we ate I went over it with Lisa. Look, I said to her, he's underestimated how far he's going to go, almost every day. Why would he do that?

Maybe he doesn't know how fast he goes, Lisa said.

Maybe he doesn't want people to know how fast he goes, I replied. Or maybe he thinks he'll be slower now. Anyway, I don't know why he did it, but I know him, and he'll be hiking all day every day, and there's no way he's only going from Duck Lake to Silver Pass on day 3, he'll go to Mono Creek for sure, heart trouble or not. Then on day 4 he'll go to Wanda, way beyond where he told them, and the day after that to Upper Basin, even farther off the mark. So, I concluded, if I was going to try to join him by going in over Kearsarge Pass…

You'd have to be there tomorrow, Lisa said.

I nodded. I had been talking to her the whole drive home about joining him on the trail to keep him company on this momentous hike. To hike alone day after day, for 11 days, before open-heart surgery; it seemed to me it would be better to have a friend along. And that had been the plan. If I had been in town when he took off, I would have gone with him for sure.

You'll have to leave tonight, Lisa said. If you get down there late tonight, you can take off in the morning from down there and make it to the Muir Trail by...?

By noon, I hazarded.

It would be a close thing. I had to get to a place on the Muir Trail ahead of him, then wait; there was no way I would be able to chase him down from behind. I knew very well the feel of hiking as fast as I could and yet seeing him disappear ahead of me.

You could call a motel in Bishop, Lisa said. Make a reservation and tell them you'll get in late. You'll have to get a wilderness permit in Bishop tomorrow morning anyway, right?

Right, I said. Good idea.

We usually camped at trailheads, and once Lisa and I had slept in the back of her station wagon, right there in the Bishop ranger station parking lot. But after the long drive down there, a motel would be nice. I wouldn't be getting much sleep as it was; it was already 7:00 p.m.

Call me when you get in, Lisa said, no matter when it is.

Okay I will.

So we went to the grocery store, then home, where I packed up my gear and food and took off. I had already driven from Ashland to Davis that day, but I like driving at night, and the roads were empty. It was the usual timing from Davis: four hours to Lee Vining, another hour to Bishop. It was about 2:00 a.m. when I checked in to a little motel in Bishop and crashed.

In the morning I went to the ranger station and was there when it opened. A woman ranger I had seen before was the only person there. I explained I wanted a wilderness permit to go in from Onion Valley over Kearsarge Pass, and she told me that permits for that trailhead now had to be obtained in Lone Pine, an hour south of Bishop, also south of Independence, where the road up to Onion Valley leaves 395. I groaned and told her about my attempt to reach a friend, and why.

She nodded as I spoke. Well, I have a lot of compassion for you, she said.

My husband died of a heart attack. So I'm going to issue you the permit, but don't tell anybody I did it.

I thanked her fervently as she wrote out the permit, tears in her eyes.

Off I drove, south to Independence, west up the road to Onion Valley. I found a parking spot in the big lot up there and was on the trail by 9:00 a.m., kind of amazed that it had all worked as planned 12 hours before.

I hiked hard that morning, crossed Kearsarge Pass in a hurry, and reached the Muir Trail by noon. Then I rested by the trail and thought it over. By my reckoning, if Terry had stuck to his itinerary, which I didn't think he had, he would still be well to the north of me. I was hoping that he was now in the Rae Lakes area, and would camp tonight somewhere around where I was now, or even farther south. In any case, it came down to this: if I had missed him and he was already south of me, there was nothing I could do. If he was north of me, as I suspected, then I could hike north now, and that would speed up the time when we would meet. And there was a chance he would camp tonight at some ponds just north of Glen Pass that I knew he liked; or just south of Glen Pass, where we had been caught in the Pineapple Express. That meant I could now hike in a more leisurely fashion north to Glen Pass, and wait there, at that great high lookout point on the Muir Trail. If he didn't show, I could pick one of those two high campsites for the night, on either side of the pass. If I was right, I would run into him somewhere that afternoon, coming toward me as I hiked north.

So after my rest and lunch, I headed that way. I was tired. It took me a couple of hours to get up to Glen Pass, and on the way I couldn't locate for sure the place where we had camped during the Pineapple Express; not only did nothing look right, no place even looked campable. But whatever.

I got into the pass. There were a couple of groups there, maybe five or seven people, resting and enjoying the view. I greeted them, and asked them which way they had come; they told me their stories, and I was telling them mine, when a voice called up from the switchbacks on the north side below us:

Robinson, is that you?

Baier!

I had cut him off at the pass.

*　　*　　*

After we celebrated our meeting, and he marveled that I had found him, we headed south. I reminded him of our deluge campsite south of the pass, but even together we couldn't identify where it had been. We dropped to Vidette Meadows, a big drop, 4,000 feet; then headed up the long handsome canyon of upper Bubbs Creek, toward Forester Pass. This is one of the most beautiful sections of the Muir Trail, and one we had traveled together before, but always going the opposite direction. It was good to see it, but I was getting tired; it had been a long day. I requested a stop for the day about halfway up the canyon, and Terry was surprised, as typically we would go for the highest campsite possible, under Forester Pass. But he was agreeable too. It was August 10, and there were already many meteors after midnight. Weather was good, moon wasn't up; we slept out.

The next day we went over Forester Pass, one of the spaciest stretches of the Muir Trail. If Terry hadn't met me, his plan would have been his usual, to hike the full length of the Muir Trail, hitch a ride from Whitney Portal to Lone Pine, take a bus up to June Lake, and lastly hitch a ride to his car, on the June Lake loop near the Agnew Pass trailhead. But with me along, and my car parked at Onion Valley, we made an alternative plan; we would cross Forester Pass, hang a right and go over a short easy ridge into the upper Kern basin, then cross Harrison Pass, and by one way or another get back to Vidette Meadows and up over Kearsarge. That loop would take us to my car, then we'd drive to Terry's car, and caravan home. A good plan.

In Forester Pass Terry only wanted to pause for a couple of minutes; typically in this airy pass we would spend half an hour looking around. But he was trying to reduce his time at the highest altitudes. He pointed to his throat, and I could see his carotid artery bulge like a frog getting ready to croak, over and over. So we hurried down the other side.

The crossing from the Tyndall Creek drainage to Lake South America was easy, and we took a rest at that big lake, which I want to mention would only look like South America if you were lying on the bottom of the lake looking up—really it should be called Lake South America as Seen in a Mirror. In any case, after our rest we headed up the easy broad basin toward Harrison Pass.

We stopped to camp and eat dinner, but then Terry got anxious. He had intended never to sleep above 11,000 feet on this trip, to save his heart that extra work, and here we were in a basin that was everywhere above 11,000. And it wasn't even a very pretty spot. So I suggested we move downhill a few hundred vertical feet and look for a better spot, and he was agreeable. We repacked and wandered in the sunset shadows down to a pond, and found a patch of flat ground where the view to the peaks of the Great Western Divide was vast.

Again that night we lay out under the stars. The Perseids were firing, and for a time after it got full dark we watched meteors shoot off to the southwest in their typical Perseid way. It was August 11, Terry's forty-second birthday.

Then out of the blue, after a long silence, he said, Robbie they're going to cut my heart open.

I had to agree; that was the plan. Then I had an unfortunate question occur to me, which I voiced aloud before thinking it through; I wondered how they were going to stop his heart in order to do the cutting.

Alas, neither of us could remember how surgeons stopped hearts from beating in order to have a steady target to cut. This became strangely upsetting to both of us. Electric shock? Drugs? Nothing sounded at all good. It was a bad topic, and I was sorry to have brought it up. I could hear it adding to his distress. The idea they would simply chill his heart down never occurred to either of us.

Well, it's a common operation, I finally said, lamely. You're strong, you'll be fine. You'll end up better than ever with this new valve. We'll come up here next summer to celebrate.

He didn't reply.

The next morning we headed back up to Harrison Pass. It was an easy walk up a gentle slope. But as so often in the Sierra, and I would suppose any mountain range in the Northern Hemisphere, the north side of the pass was steeper than the south side, because a glacier had lingered longer in the shade there, and thus had had more time to eat back into the rock. Here, the difference was radical; the north side of Harrison Pass was a single steep slope of shaley scree and sand, wet from recently melted snow, almost smooth, and so steep that if you slipped you might slide down hundreds of feet, possibly all the way to the foot of the pass, a wasteland of boulders 1,000 feet below.

Shit, Terry said. I can't go down that. I don't want to get my heart beating too hard on this trip! And it's already beating hard just looking down this fucker.

It's bad, I agreed. Damn, didn't this pass have a trail in the old days?

He shrugged. If it had, and some maps do show a trail (like the old one I used to mark King and Cotter's route, on page 108), it was long gone, eroded by snow and rain back to the original clean sweep. We didn't know the history of this pass, hadn't read the astonishing account by one Force Parker, in volume 5 of the 1890s *Sierra Club Bulletin*, of cutting switchbacks in hard snow with shovels, to make a temporary trail for mules and horses; the ascent of this slope had started for those guys at 10:00 a.m. and ended at 4:00 a.m. the next morning, with along the way some somersaulting horses, and mules that quickly learned to sit on their butts midslide to arrest themselves, and so on. It was not a good pass.

What about Lucys Footpass, or Millys Footpass? I wondered. These were other routes over this section of the Kings-Kern Divide, a bit to the west of us.

Terry shook his head. He had done Lucys, and it was worse than this one; and Millys was said to be worse than Lucys, class 3 as he recalled.

Okay, I said. There's no way over. We'll have to go back. We'll go back the way we came, and get back to my car on trail.

I guess so, Terry said gloomily.

That's what we did. By that night we had retraced our route back over Forester, starting the biggest U-turn of our lives, a kind of fishhook shape of a route, to a camp a bit higher than the one from two nights before, in the great canyon north of Forester, close to where we had always camped in the '70s. Extremely beautiful; and we would go out the next day.

And that night the Perseids ran riot. One of the meteorites, out of scores of them, plowed south the full length of the canyon, just higher than the ridges it seemed, or even down below ridge height, shedding side blazes of green and blue and red as it broke up—it was so low it seemed like it might crash right into Forester Pass! When it missed that ridge, it looked like it was going to go down in the upper Kern. It was the greatest meteor of all time.

That was a sign, Terry said.

Next day we got out by midafternoon. My feet were shot. It had been a tough four days, a typical Terry four days. But we got in my car and drove up to Terry's car, and from there we drove straight home in a single push. I tried to caravan with him, but coming down Highway 50 from Echo Summit he began to go so fast I couldn't keep up. He was always a fast driver, but this was beyond the usual. I eased off and let him forge ahead, lost him in the taillights. Goodbye to that incarnation.

Two days later his parents had a late birthday party for him at their house, including his wife Melody and son Cory, his sister, his younger brother and wife, and Lisa and me. He lay in a lawn recliner by their pool, relaxed and at peace. Whatever happened, he was ready.

The operation a few days later was a success. It's painful having your sternum cut in half and your ribs pried open, and in the days immediately afterward he was in great pain. By day 3 he was walking up and down the halls of the hospital pulling an IV stand on wheels. On day 4 he staged a breakout and left the hospital in his gown without telling them he was going; this freaked them out, and he was told in no uncertain terms that he was not to do it again. A day later they discharged him, no doubt glad to get rid of him. They called him the fastest healer ever.

NAMES (3)
The Ugly

S o, are there ugly names in the Sierra? Unfortunately, yes.

Surrounding the Evolution Basin, and named for the most part by Theodore Solomons back in the 1890s, are several peaks that honor famous evolutionary theorists: Darwin, Lamarck, Wallace, Spencer, Fiske, Mendel, and Haeckel. A bit to the south of these, at the west end of the Palisades, stands Mount Agassiz. And more than one feature up there is named for Joseph LeConte Sr., the Berkeley science professor who helped found the Sierra Club.

So, first it should be said that not all evolutionary scientists of the nineteenth century held racist opinions; but some of them did. "Scientific racism" was in part the invention of Herbert Spencer, Ernst Haeckel, and Louis Agassiz. Add Joseph LeConte Sr., and what do you get? Four prominent public intellectuals who promulgated racist ideas, and are now honored in memory by their names designating peaks in the high Sierra.

It makes sense to judge people in their historical context, as having done well or ill in their time. Judgment is part of the necessary work of thinking historically; we judge the past as part of judging ourselves, creating in that dual process projects by which we hope to do better. This is always complicated work. There's a tendency to feel superior to the people of the past when we see their errors, without making the elementary move of understanding that future generations are going to see our errors and judge us in the same way. People in the future will be amazed that we could be behaving as stupidly and irresponsibly as we are now. Given the facts of climate change, we are going to appear as monsters of self-absorption, like the French aristocracy before the revolution. This no doubt generates some of the current harshness in our critique of past crimes—it's a transference of guilt to anyone but ourselves. But that's hard to see and admit. Every generation thinks of itself as enlightened to the maximum extent possible. To counteract that we really need to make the usual science fiction move of looking at our own time as future generations will see us. This obvious dialectical turn could add some needed humility to our judgments.

After such a meditation on history, I am willing to say this: some of the people honored by our names for Sierra peaks should have their names removed. That doesn't mean these people should be torn out of the history books, in fact they need to be remembered and discussed, so we can learn from what they did. It's the honoring of them by way of peak names that we can justifiably withdraw. We remove their names, not from the history books, but from our mountain range.

It comes to this: we should only honor those whom we still believe deserve to be honored. The names given to features in the Sierra in the years between 1860 and 1920 should not be the end of the story.

Joseph LeConte Sr. is a simple case: slave owner, Confederate munitions developer, lifelong advocate of scientific racism. His name should be taken out of the Sierra. But it gets complicated, because some of the LeConte names in the Sierra honor his son Joe LeConte, who led an unobjectionable Californian life, in terms of his politics and values. Still other LeConte features in the Sierra might refer to both of them. As far as I can determine, the peak called Mount LeConte, just north of Mount Langley, was named for Senior; the canyon under Dusy Basin for Junior; a divide in the west, for both of them; a memorial lodge in Yosemite for Senior (its name already changed); a point overlooking Hetch Hetchy for Junior; a waterfall high on the Tuolumne River for Senior. So the peak and the waterfall names, at a minimum, should be changed out.

This process has already started. The Sierra Club, with the National Park Service's approval and perhaps encouragement, took his name off a lodge built by the club in his memory in Yosemite Valley. The city of Berkeley recently removed Senior's name from an elementary school and a street, and the university took his name off a building on campus. Will this continue in the Sierra? Seems like it should; and this may set a precedent for other cases.

Back to the evolutionary theorists. Each case here is complicated by different vocabularies and frames of reference, and peculiar opinions from these people about other matters. Still, Darwin, Wallace, Mendel, and Lamarck look relatively innocent now, and often admirable. John Fiske advocated for abolition, and yet he was a student of Spencer and disseminated many of Spencer's racist and eugenicist ideas, making for a confused case. Spencer, with his social Darwinism, and some sentences he wrote that supported eugenic ideas, including even the annihilation of weaker humans, was quite bad. Louis Agassiz, teacher of LeConte Sr., Thoreau, and many others at Harvard, was a prominent promoter of scientific racism.

Worst of all in terms of his racist opinions was Ernst Haeckel. His views made him a valued precursor for Nazi eugenicists, despite their rejection of certain of his ideas, as for instance his belief that the human species first evolved on the lost continent of Lemuria. That wasn't Aryan enough for them; they had their own crackpot theories. Of course finding scientists with lunatic opinions is easy to do at any time, including the present. But Haeckel made many blatantly racist statements throughout his career. We should remove his name from the Sierra, and also the names of Spencer, Agassiz, Fiske, and LeConte Sr.

That would give us the opportunity to add new names. Some of these new names should have been there all along, others would be innovations from our time and for our time. Either way, the need is there, and the opportunity.

Having said we should reconsider all the names in the Sierra, an awkward question now arises: What about John Muir? Was he too a racist?

This question has to be addressed because of an assertion that has spread over the last couple of decades, that John Muir disliked Native Americans and harmed their interests. The main accusation made against him is that he

preferred wilderness areas to be empty of people, and that he therefore advocated for the removal of Native Americans from their ancestral lands, in order
to make the newly created national parks more pure. The notion has gotten
around and is now often taken to be the historical truth. I find it frightening
to see how quickly a characterization like this becomes received wisdom.
Because it's not true.

To be more confident of this assertion, I read all Muir's published work,
and a great deal of his unpublished writing in his archive at the University of
the Pacific, in Stockton, California (much of this is now online). At no point in
any of this writing did he advocate for the removal of Native Americans from
their land.

It is true that he wrote some dismissive or scornful things about individual
Native Americans he encountered—nothing as bad as what he wrote about
white miners, sheepherders, and loggers, but still, these sentences were mean,
given the facts of white-settler colonialism and its genocidal destruction of
Indigenous peoples. Like many white Americans in his time, Muir did not
properly register that history, and he cut no slack for anyone he ever encountered, including Native Americans. Recall that he was an abused child (the
beatings he received were "outrageously severe"), which left him with signs of
what people would now call post-traumatic triggers. If he saw people sitting
around in the middle of the day, he got angry. If he saw dirty clothes, he was
disgusted. These overreactions account for almost all his negative statements
concerning the people of color he ran into in his travels.

One of his most negative reactions was recorded in his journal soon after
his arrival in California, when he was accosted by a group of Native American
men in Bloody Canyon, near Mono Pass, and had some trouble convincing
them that he had no alcohol or tobacco to give them. His description of them
is ironic, resentful, and disparaging, but a few pages later he writes, "Perhaps
if I knew them better I should like them better."

Eventually he did get to know them better. And he knew all along that war
was being waged against them by European Americans. In April of 1880 he
was dining at some friends' when they were joined by a cavalry officer involved
in an active "Indian removal" campaign. A daughter of the host family wrote

to Muir's fiancée, "He told Colonel Boyce the other night that Boyce's position was that of a champion for a mean, brutal policy. It was with regard to Indian extermination, and that Boyce would be ashamed to carry it with one Indian in personal conflict." This is just the kind of standing up to racism in social situations that we hope to see from ourselves.

Later, during his two trips to Alaska, he spent around three months living with the Tlingit people. This extended period of contact, during which he traveled with them, spoke with them through translators, and transcribed their statements into his journals at many pages' length, changed him in profound ways. He wrote at length about the Tlingit people, with close observation and sympathy. He was thrilled by their competence in the natural world, which for him was always a sign of moral worth. In one journal entry he wrote, "They should send missionaries to the Christians." In the years following, back in California, he began to contribute money to an "Indian charity" in Los Angeles.

So, contrary to the uninformed accusations being made against Muir in our time, he was not a racist, despite his sharp tongue, and the negative impressions he wrote down concerning some people he met in his journeys. His judgments were of individuals, and did not describe or compare ethnic groups as such. And over the course of his lifetime, his ongoing interest in Native Americans, sparked in his childhood in Wisconsin, strengthened into a sympathetic admiration.

Crucially, since this is the main accusation made against him concerning consequential actions in the world, he never advocated for the removal of Native Americans from their ancestral lands.

For me, the most telling passage in all that Muir wrote about Native Americans is this, written about the Tlingit: "I have never yet seen a child ill-used even to the extent of an angry word. Scolding, so common a curse of the degraded of Christian countries, is not known here at all. But on the contrary the young are fondled and indulged without being spoiled."

Given his own childhood, you can see how that would have caught his attention.

SIERRA PEOPLE (10)
Tree Line Artists

Tree line in the Sierra is a fluctuating thing, because of the recent glaciation. So much of the high Sierra is bare granite, it can be hard to tell if the trees aren't there because you're too high, or because there simply isn't any soil. Trees generally can't grow if there are frosts in the warmest months of the summer, and that happens a lot in the high Sierra. So vast stretches of the land above 10,000 feet are treeless; then you'll come on a stand of foxtail or lodgepole pine, tucked into a south-facing slope that might get more sun and less snow, but it's hard to be sure what it is that allows for these stands to live there.

Above tree line there are still low flowering plants, grass, moss, and lichens. Compared to the Alps the Sierra is not very flowery, because the Alps get as much rain in a month as the Sierra gets all year. But in the summer, in the meadows and on the fellfields, wildflowers do spark the ground with color. Penstemons display a characteristic magenta. Buttercup is a very pure yellow. Indian paintbrush is red-orange, and lasts late into the fall. Columbines are delicate shades of yellow or ivory, usually tucked against rocks. Buckwheats star the sand of the fellfields, always neatly elaborate, no matter which species of their wildly various genus they happen to be. Sky pilots grow right up onto the highest peaks, emerging from bare rocks. They are a specific blue, and have a musky scent. Like lichens, they seem to be able to live on nothing more than rock, sunlight, and water; soil is not required.

Lichens live right on rock surfaces, and are the great citizens of the rocky highland, cheerfully colorful (although the colors include black and gray).

They're like living paint. An alga collaborates with a fungus, and each kind of lichen combines different pairs of symbionts. Some are named for their colors, others for their miniaturized architectures. Battleship-gray lichen. Red jewel lichen, happy to bathe in marmot pee. Button lichen, dog lichen, flake lichen, Iceland lichen, map lichen, pixie-button lichen, crustose lichen—there are scores of different kinds. Frequently they coat rocks in alternating green and yellow and red, like Caribbean flags. Rastafarian rock. One black lichen forms flat plasticky blobs, and makes rocks slick and slippery when wet.

The feeling lichen conveys, that life is everywhere, and can grow right on rock, is encouraging. Life as courage. Lichens make rocks more handsome. It seems like they could survive anything; I'm thinking here of climate change. Lichens will endure those changes, or so I hope. Some scientists recently revived microbes that had been frozen for a hundred million years, they said. So it's not a forlorn hope. Life is tough, life has courage.

At tree line the trees often become singletons, isolatoes all gnarled and stunted. Krummholz, German for "crooked wood" or "elfin wood." Each tree a heroic survivor or pioneer, a work of performance art.

I love the lodgepoles for their stubbornness, as they shrink and gnarl at their uppermost limits, becoming each a little bonsai. Same for the junipers, which fatten to squat gods, or spread out into a dense low shrub, precisely as high as the winter snowpack, which when it blankets the layer of trees, protects them from the coldest winter winds. Those cold winds prune away the branches that stick up out of the snow.

Then also, often bunched in groups that help protect and warm each other, stand western white pines, so tall and stately. Or Jeffrey pines, with their great plates of red bark. These trees are old growth; they live above the loggers' reach. You can tell they're ancient by the way they look. Here the world appears whole, feels right. It's a region of the world that never had any part amputated, and so remains intact.

Of course the giant sequoia is the great god, but it lives lower than tree line. Each encounter with one is stunning, off the scale as trees go. Because they were discovered by Europeans in the time before skyscrapers, the people

An old juniper

of that time were astonished by the sight of these enormous beings. These trees broke everyone's sense of what a tree could be, so people took their seeds all over the world and planted them. I've seen giant sequoias, each about a century and a half old, in Christchurch, New Zealand, at Loch Ness in Scotland, and by Lake Zurich in Switzerland. Seeing them in these distant places made me happy, as does visiting the groves still standing on the western flank of the Sierra. One night on the way to Roads End, we stopped by a fallen one and walked in moonlight through the long high tunnel of its hollowed-out core, a magical walk. Climate change might kill a lot of them, and I recently read that as many as 10 percent of them were killed by the Castle fire of 2020. As I completed this book a fire threatened the Giant Forest in Sequoia National

Park: later it was determined that around 3,600 giant sequoias had died. Twenty percent of all the giant sequoias on Earth have died by fire in the last two years.

Up at tree line itself, there is another giant god of a tree: foxtail pines. They are a close cousin to bristlecone pines, the oldest trees on Earth. The foxtails live almost as long, and are much taller. Their trunks have a spiral grain, obvious in the dead ones; this spiral apparently makes them stronger when a wind strikes. Many of them have been hit by lightning and have blackened tops. The dead ones are tall memorials to a life well lived, sculptures that last for—who knows?—for centuries, it may be. Decades for sure. The highest foxtails on Earth are located in the Miter Basin at around 10,000 feet, just below Sky Blue Lake—that scattered grove where I once stopped for coffee, and the trees suddenly seemed like immense people, ancient and wise. It was that very grove that taught me to pay attention to trees.

The artists of tree line share qualities with the other creatures of that zone: they are gnarly and serene, tough and iconic. Two of California's greatest poets are Sierra people: Kenneth Rexroth and Gary Snyder. A third, Robinson Jeffers, is a mountain man of the coastal range.

The visual artists of the Sierra began with the Native Americans and their pictographs and petroglyphs. When Europeans arrived, Albert Bierstadt brought the eye of the Hudson River school to Yosemite. Muir's Scottish-Californian friend William Keith was very good in the same style. Snyder's teacher Chiura Obata worked in a different style, using watercolors. Then came Ansel Adams and all the great Sierra photographers, including Cedric Wright and Galen Rowell.

In the plastic arts, where it would be a superb achievement to think like a juniper, the great Andy Goldsworthy has taught everyone how to make art above tree line, out of local materials. He comes from a country where tree line and sea level are about the same. His genius is generous and suggestive; anyone can try his kind of art, once you get the idea. We've learned from his inspiration, and have tried little goldsworthies at the end of some days, wandering around our camps assembling little stone things and knocking them down before we leave, to keep from impinging on other people's sense of wilderness. Fun in the late afternoon; artists in the back country. Builders of stone henges! The Neolithics made those at least in part for the fun of it.

A goldsworthy in Dumbbell Basin

John Muir Laws is a wonderful and indeed crucial Sierra artist, having painted every living thing in the range, as illustrations for his naturalist's guide. Each painting is a little masterpiece, and as a practical guide they're better than photographs would be, as he subtly brings out the species' identifying features. Sierra people are lucky to have his great book.

Then there's Tom Killion. He does woodblock prints, like Hokusai. He brought that Japanese art form to California, and over a long career has changed how we see our state.

Killion's woodblock prints look at first like realist works, but on second glance one sees they are not realist, or not just realist; the level of abstraction is high. Very complex landscapes are transformed by his art into discrete blocks of color; chaos becomes geometry. This visionary quality in his work gives the landscapes he depicts a heraldic power; they deploy a kind of surrealism that captures the world in some higher or deeper way. That's what art is always supposed to do, of course, but seldom does it happen so decisively as in Killion's prints. They clarify; they make the shapes of the Sierra's ridges and canyons manifest to the eye. And they convey weather and mood—the feeling of an incoming storm, or the late light of day. In print after print, he manages to suggest the emotions that fill one in the high country. This aspect—the feel of a landscape—is no easy thing to convey, and Killion does it time after time.

As part of his larger project, he often portrays the great trees at tree line, in many prints that feature giant sequoias, lodgepoles, junipers, or foxtail pines. All these appear as the great living beings they are. Has any other artist captured the majesty of trees as well as Killion, with such immediacy, accuracy, and affection? If so I'm not aware of them.

I love in particular his print of Isosceles Peak at twilight, which appears on page 86 of this book, and has the little yellow tent glowing in the dusk like a lamp—an image of a human soul in the wilderness, it seems to me, and by a lucky chance located very near the spot where I spent my first night in the high Sierra. I also love his print of Mount Thoreau, naturally, as it makes our naming of that peak iconic, in the literal sense of creating an icon to represent the deed. He made that name real, and, as in all his art, more real than real.

Big Arroyo Foxtail Pines *by Tom Killion, 2005*

GEOLOGY (6)
Roof Pendants

Roof-pendant rock is an aspect of geology with huge psychogeological effects.

Not all the rock in the Sierra is made of the granite plutons that together form the great batholith. Stuck on top of that granite mass are some remnants

This miniature "roof pendant" serves to show how the larger ones rest on the white granite batholith of the Sierra. Some roof pendants cover many square miles.

of the older rock that the molten granite pressed up against, 80 million years ago and ten miles underground. Some remaining scraps of that older meta-morphosed rock never got worn away, and now perch up there on the granite, areas of rock often dramatically red or black or green, and always weird. Geol-ogists call these remnants roof pendants.

It's not the greatest name. The word *pendant* refers to the notion that some of this older rock melted and sank down into the still hot and liquid magma that would later cool to granite. Thus a pendant hanging from a ceiling. But in fact a lot of the roof pendants lying on top of the Sierra granite were simply roofing the granite as it cooled.

What would be a better name?...Older stuff? Metamorphic remnant? Horrid old black shingles on a beautiful white house? I'll have to keep think-ing about that.

James Moore in his great book includes a map of roof pendants in the part of the southern Sierra he studied, all of them named and identified by age and mineral composition. Some of the most famous divides in the Sierra are roof pendants, most conspicuously the Kaweahs, which are mostly reddish in color, and the Minarets, including the Banner-Ritter double peak at their north end.

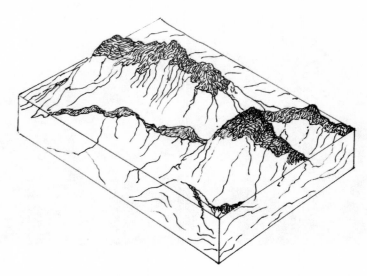

Structure of roof pendants in schematic form. Drawing by Elizabeth Whalley.

This spiky black ridge is dramatic in a Gothic manner quite unusual in the Sierra, and because it is visible from Highway 395, and from much of the Mammoth area, these stark spires are among the most famous in the range. When I hear people say that the Minarets are their favorite part of the Sierra, I think that these are not really Sierra people. Also, that they haven't hiked on roof-pendant rock very much. That said, there's no denying that the Minarets are spectacular in their black verticality and jagged profile. The way I think of them now is this: the Sierras are so great that they even include a dramatic little alien subrange lying on them, to add variety.

The roof pendant that features Red Slate Mountain was well mixed with the granite when it was magma, creating Red and White Mountain, well named, and the colorful swirls near Mount Morrison. A similar mixing of

The Minarets

white and black rock is evident in the Ionian Basin, sometimes in swirls like batter for a marble cake, or, as on the west shore of Chasm Lake, in alternating vertical bands.

The roof pendant that forms big parts of the Ionian Basin is called the Goddard Terrane, and it rises to its high point at Mount Goddard, an immense lump of old metamorphic rock, which a friend of mine calls God's Turd. In sunset alpenglow the west wall of this monstrous lump can turn a deep red, but in the late afternoon it has more variety of color.

Mount Goddard from the west

The Goddard Terrane is one of the largest roof pendants in the Sierra, and it splashes across an area with lots of human activity; the Muir Trail crosses its easternmost corner. The Devils Crags form part of it, as does the Ragged

Spur, and these two ridges bracket the Enchanted Gorge, a black canyon of great notoriety for cross-country hikers. Theodore Solomons named it during one of his typically desperate adventures, when he and a companion, semi-lost and running out of food, dropped down it hoping to reach Kings Canyon before they starved. Whether the name was bestowed ironically or sarcastically, no one can say, but it is definitely a steep deep trench of black rubble, its creek called Disappearing Creek because it keeps running under the boulders.

Hiking around in the Ionian Basin is a great lesson in the differences between granite and roof-pendant rock, because you move between them frequently. White granite is friendly to humans. It breaks down into sand that makes nice campsites, and when it's semibroken into scree and talus and boulders, its rocks tend to lock together in ways that make their surfaces comparatively stable, with lots of flat tops. Very often granite breaks in cubical forms that end up resembling staircases and sidewalks. Really, granite is friendly.

Roof-pendant rock near Lake South America

Roof-pendant rock isn't friendly. It's as hard as granite, but it breaks into clinkers and rhomboids that slip and slide under one's feet, especially when wet. While submerged under ice in the ice ages, this rock resisted ice in ways that left big expanses of it looking like beds of nails.

Elsewhere it got sheared and smoothed by the ice into bossy cliffs, not easy to climb or descend. When broken to rubble, it can hold a higher angle of repose than granite. When you walk on it, it clanks underfoot like ceramic shards. It hosts a different array of ground-cover plants, scrubbier and less flowery. And it's poky and dirty to camp on.

Pete Starr got killed climbing on it, in the Minarets; his friends who found his body thought they saw signs that a rock had come loose on him. The same thing happened to the two climbers who were collecting all the old summit registers on the Devils Crags; a black rock broke, they fell. Ranger Randy Morgenson tried to save the one hurt the worst in that fall, and failed. It's not stable rock.

Alternating bands of pendant rock and granite, at Chasm Lake, Ionian Basin

All that said, you can't get too prejudiced against the stuff, because a fair bit of the Sierra consists of it. It's part of Sierra reality. But I can't say I like it. The fact that some of it jumped up and cut my shin in a way I couldn't stop from bleeding, such that I had to run down from the top of the Black Giant to my pack a thousand feet below, to get some rubber cement from my air-mattress repair kit and pour it into the wound to get my blood to congeal—a descent even faster than my run down from the Muttseehütte to the dread tunnel—of course that has nothing to do with it! It's mostly an aesthetic judgment. Although I have to admit, when I read about Oakland mayor Warren Olney's irrational prejudice against Hetch Hetchy, where, it turns out, he once fell and broke some ribs, I began to wonder if I too had some unconscious—now let's say semiconscious—reasons to dislike roof pendants. I'll confine myself to this: watch out for that stuff.

SIERRA PEOPLE (11)
Fish and Frogs

The early volumes of the *Sierra Club Bulletin* are filled with enthusiastic reports of the efforts made by club members to move the golden trout they had found, an endemic species confined to the upper reaches of a few streams south of Langley, to the rest of the range. Big buckets tied to the sides of mules; forced marches to get the fish to their destinations alive; the pretty trout introduced to streams and ponds all over. These were accomplishments the writers were proud to describe. Later, both the National Park Service and the US Forest Service arranged to introduce golden trout and other kinds of fish to many lakes and ponds in the high Sierra that had never had fish before. Giving fishermen something to catch was a priority. For a while, helicopters and small planes would swoop down over high lakes every spring and drop fingerlings into them as if dousing fires.

It's interesting now to see how complete the lack of concern was for the effects of this move. Aldo Leopold was publishing his books, Muir had made his remark about tugging on one thread and finding it hitched to everything else in the universe, and the nascent science of ecology was studying population dynamics on islands in the Great Lakes. But none of that had penetrated to these people. It wasn't that they didn't care about secondary effects, it was that they had no idea that there would be secondary effects.

That the fish would outcompete the frogs and eat all the bugs, and also eat the frogs themselves, was an easy call. What wasn't as obvious was that the rosy finches relied on those bugs too, so their numbers would fall (no rosy finches seen at Rosy Finch Lake). Then also, it turns out that rosy finches are instrumental in moving certain kinds of seeds around the landscape, by eating them and shitting them out elsewhere, or by tucking them away in hiding places to eat later and then forgetting them. Without the finches doing those things, new trees are not sprouting as they used to. That forest succession would suffer because of the introduction of fish into the ponds was not at all obvious, and took years of putting together observations from different kinds of study. Long-term environmental research—LTER in the scientific bureaucratic language, that technocratic language on which so much now depends—is crucial for discovering secondary and tertiary and cascading effects of this sort. This research is crucial to humanity's adjustment to its home planet.

So, from that time of fish introductions, the frogs in the high Sierra began to suffer. They were outcompeted in their hunt for food, and became themselves food. There are many kinds of frogs and toads up there, but the yellow-legged frog is another endemic Sierra native, and now, like the bighorn sheep, it's in danger of extinction. And again the Endangered Species Act has been brought to bear on the problem.

One part of the effort to secure a future for these frogs is to clear some of the high lakes and ponds of fish. This isn't easy to do. The main methods are gill nets and poison, with occasionally some dynamite. Pretty often now as we hike the high country, we see ponds with gill nets stretched across them, and signs on the shore explaining that the National Park Service is running an experiment, and asking people to please not bother it. I've also spoken with scientists involved in experiments in poisoning lakes to kill all the fish in them; also, in a few small lakes, killing them with shock waves from dynamite explosions. These efforts often kill more than just the target fish; indeed they tend to kill much of the life in the pond; then it becomes a question of who comes back first. Frogs can migrate from nearby ponds, whereas fish typically can't; although sometimes they can, because most of the ponds are connected by streams. So the effort is a work in progress, an experiment in ecological engineering. It's very interesting to watch it unfold, and know that our government (of the people, by the people, and for the people) is in effect working for other species, and against extinction. This is the real work of our time.

Sierra yellow-legged frog, endangered

We now stop and enjoy frogs whenever we see them. They exist in the hundreds when at the pollywog stage. Very few tadpoles are going to survive. Same with fingerlings for fish, of course. It's quite an evolutionary strategy. Even at the young frog stage, there can be a lot of them. They're hopping around trying to find a home. They're croaking.

I was by a Sierra pond one summer night when I was kept awake by an all-night chorus of frogs, and made the discovery that they—this group anyway—were croaking in call-and-response mode. I wrote this into a scene in my novel *2312*, where Swan is on Earth (unusual for her) and listening by a wetland marsh in New Jersey. I myself heard it in the Sierra. First all the frogs were croaking *ribbit ribbit ribbit* in a fluctuating, surging chorus. Then in a gap of silence one seized the initiative and croaked *limit!* And all the frogs croaked *limit limit limit*, until in the flow and surge of voices, another one cried out *robber!* And everyone was off on that line, singing *robber robber robber*. On they went through the night, changing the word they were singing together, and always managing in their group effort to achieve something like the rhythmic flow of Steve Reich's *Music for 18 Musicians*. It was definitely music; it was definitely being produced on purpose by a group, which therefore can be called a choir. There is no one composer, nor is there a conductor, but I had to wonder if the ones changing the word were thinking of that word, holding it in mind, and waiting for a moment of silence to insert it into the flow. Didn't that have to be the case?

Now, through the nights up there, if I hear them I feel happy. People who were camped with us on the night of the great concert complained in the morning— this was one of our big family trips—and I just laughed. Sometimes there are better things than getting a good night's sleep. And sleep itself can be induced by a feeling of calm happiness, and a nice sound. Night sounds are good—as long as it's not the whine of mosquitoes, which is admittedly dreadful.

I recall my mom used to give in, with some pleasure, to my insomniac pleading for a record to be played at bedtime, agreeing that it would help me fall asleep. Listening in the dark, I seldom drifted off until long after the record was over, but I enjoyed the feeling of lying there listening, and so did she. *The Sound of Music* was one of her favorites, and mine. The hills are alive with the sound of music. This is one reason I can sing all the songs of that musical and remember the lyrics, though I'm usually terrible at remembering lyrics. In the Sierras I sometimes pass the hiking time by singing or whistling the entire thing, including the songs left out of the movie, and also the one written for the movie (beautiful). My companions keep a good distance from me.

As for the frogs, what's interesting to contemplate is the idea of habitat restoration being more and more broadly applied, as we realize that these refugia are precious and even sacred areas of the Earth, precisely because of the kind of consideration we give them. It means that the concept of wilderness is thus redeemed and come into its own. With these habitats protected, similar protection might radiate outward, like rings on a pond at sunset when the fish are eating bugs, until the whole world is encompassed. Here the Swiss have already demonstrated a crucial idea: We too live in wilderness. We're part of it.

Once by the shore of one of the Bear Lakes at sunset, we saw the orange water bloom with so many concentric growing circles that the lake suddenly looked like the site of an infestation. It was obvious there were too many fish out there, a die-off was sure to come.

Other evenings, by other lakes, the world goes still, and the water becomes smooth as a mirror. It shifts in color to a sky-colored sheet inserted into black stone—sky-blue right there flooring the ground, even though the sky overhead has turned darker than cobalt. As if the lake were holding on to its memory of the day.

MY SIERRA LIFE (12)

This Is the End

—beautiful friend, the end. Of our elaborate plans, the end—

Jim Morrison. We sang it many times. The Doors were our soundtrack through the early years, the crazy pinball seeker years. *What have they done to the Earth? What have they done to our fair sister?*

Terry loved the Sierras, no doubt about it. He hiked the Muir Trail every year, and he was very often up there. But when he went there alone, he stayed on trail. Was that true? I didn't know for sure, not having been there with him on those solo trips. His accounts made me think that was the case. For sure he never climbed peaks, nor was he enthusiastic when I talked about trying one.

That going off trail made him uneasy was for many years outside my ability to see. There were reasons for that beyond my own obtuseness. We planned our trips through the winters, and then he seemed open to anything, made route suggestions, and so on. And when we were up there, he could put map and landscape together in ways that allowed him to see the best routes. He was ingenious in seeing shortcuts and work-arounds that bypassed difficulties. And hiking cross-country he was unbelievably fast, and always cut the most direct line. All these realities, seen time after time as I followed him, kept me from seeing that he didn't really like hiking off trail. How could he not? I loved it so much, I couldn't imagine that he didn't. It never even occurred to me.

Slowly incidents piled up that should have alerted me to this issue. And I should have pondered a little more the fact that when he was up there by himself, he always stuck to the Muir Trail. I knew the kind of thing I would do, and it sure wasn't the Muir Trail. I thought his repetition of it was just his ritual, a religious act. He was a pilgrim, and that was his pilgrimage. Only later did it occur to me that it made him feel safer. I thought of all the Sierra as safe—gentle wilderness and all that—all except for lightning, which could strike you whether you were on trail or off. But I seldom hiked alone.

And he was so fast. Not that this was exactly relevant, but it was part of what kept me from seeing the whole story. One time we were coming up to Knapsack Pass from the east, cross-country, no trail, and I watched him go right at the head-wall of that perfect glacial U, headed for the steepest part. I veered to the right, knowing there was a use trail up that way because Lisa and I had found it years before. The near-vertical slope under the low point was going to give Terry fits, so for once I would be getting to a pass before him. I pressed it a little, and when I got to the use trail, which was as high as the pass itself, I traipsed around a knob that obscured my view forward, and suddenly saw the whole scene: and there was Terry, already sitting in the pass. It was like Carlos Castaneda watching Don Juan fly through the air. I got to him about 20 minutes later. We had a fast shaman.

But also, when we were crossing new terrain and coming up to a pass, especially from the south, when the topo maps showed that the north side was going to be steep, he would rush up there to have a look. Impossible to stick with him when he was anxious to get a view of how bad it would be. Once he raced ahead of us like that as he and Joe and I came up the south side of one of the small passes northwest of Table Mountain, which the topo had shown would be really steep on its north side. When I caught up to him in the pass, he was looking down with an intense regard.

Well, he said somberly, we can do it.

It was the worst kind of class 2, a steep slope of stacked broken rocks. We would have to test every step to be sure the bowling ball–size talus would hold us. About a 400-foot drop of such touchy work. But the angle was not so horrid as to make it class 3. So we descended it.

Sitting on our packs at the bottom, looking up at what we had done (and as always, foreshortening made it look even steeper), Terry said, One of these days we're going to make a mistake.

Even then I didn't get it.

*   *   *

Through these years he and I kept going for our Wednesday morning runs. As we ran, he aired a lot of grievances. He didn't like his boss in a lab at UC Davis, and took early retirement to get away from him. He often stayed alone at his Sierra house. And along with the Muir Trail, he began to hike the Pacific Crest Trail, hiking from Mexico to Canada in segments. This meant starting in April and finishing in October. The PCT is 2,650 miles long. Seeing that fact on a sticker on a neighbor's car window caused me to reflect that over his mountain life, Terry must have hiked something like 15,000 miles, most of them on his own. Now I think he was trying to outwalk his thoughts, to bathe his brain in a daily bath of beta endorphins. A form of self-medication. We all have them.

After that expansion of his walking program to the PCT, he mostly skipped our trips. Our regular hiking group shrank to Joe, Darryl, and me. We three were still enjoying it. We had fun up there, in fact it was very nice to find out how enjoyable it became when it was just the three of us. So we kept taking the trouble to make it happen. We always invited the others, including Terry, but careers were getting busy, and time was short. Victor was at the mercy of the LA court system's schedules, and Dick was working intensely as a lab manager, with hardly any vacation time. Terry was off on his own. We missed them all, and losing Vic and Dick meant a huge reduction in humor and good fellowship, but there was nothing we could do about it. Joe and Darryl and I went up there and had a grand time anyway, year after year. In some important respects things got easier, while in other ways we made things harder, just for the fun of it. Our trips became epic and were often hilarious.

But also, it was the first decade of the century, a fraught time. 9/11, the Iraq War, Abu Ghraib: everything seemed to be adding to a growing sense of strain and awfulness. On our runs in Davis, Terry became more and more intense and negative. Sometimes we would stop and walk for a while because he was too upset to run, he had to catch his breath so the words could spill out of him in a torrent. He hated Bush Jr. with a fine passion, referring to him as "the torturer." I could only agree with that, but as we talked on, I began to see that his personal dislikes were even more intense, and that there was no one who met with his approval, no one at all. I didn't pursue the implications of that.

A summer came when my dad died, and then Terry's mom. After she became ill, he took a break from the Pacific Crest Trail to stay home for a while and visit her. In that interval he joined Joe and Darryl and me for that summer's trip, which surprised us. But it wasn't a happy trip. He was stressed, impatient, brooding, curt. On the last full day of it, I was awakened by him nudging me with his boot. He was fully dressed, his backpack on his back. I stared up at him from my sleeping bag, surprised. He said he was taking off; he couldn't stand to sit around all morning waiting for us. It was still predawn, fully dark, so cold he was wearing his windbreaker and wind pants. But 10 by 10, as the thru-hikers say.

Okay, I said. We were headed up Deadman Canyon and then over to the Tablelands, it was a route known to us, and we would be able to find each other somewhere. See you up there, I said, and off he went. I may even have gone back to sleep. We did catch up to him late that afternoon, and we went out together the next day and drove home. But that was the last trip.

After it, he wrote reproachful emails to us that got longer and angrier the more we tried to reply. Eventually I stopped trying; it was like throwing gas on a fire. Something was wrong that had nothing to do with that last trip, or even with our Sierra trips more generally. It was bigger than that, and in the airless world of email, it all came out in a furious rush. He was angry at almost everyone in his life, as I knew very well from our running conversations, but now his old hiking buddies were also on the list. Me included. I found that shocking, but it was undeniable. The friendship was over.

What a painful time. Most of all, I felt sad. Surprised, hurt, angry—even frightened—all those bad feelings, but most of all, sad. We had been friends since childhood, and for many years I had admired him as a modern-day Thoreau, and defended him as such to others and myself. Which I now understood was perhaps not a good way to think of it. But this bad analogy did give me one last insight: if he had been a Thoreau to me, I might have been an Emerson to him—remote, inattentive, uncomprehending, and ultimately useless. In any case, he renounced us all and went away. I never saw him again.

SIERRA PEOPLE (12)
Reclusive Neighbors

Once, in Matterhorn Canyon, down in the forest by the creek, first thing in the morning—

A black flash crossing the creek on a fallen log.

Corner of my left eye, jerk my head to look—nothing there. I had to reconstruct what I had seen—long, skinny, slinky, black and brown, fast. A split second only. But I had something from it, an image. Back home with my John Muir Laws guide, I saw it again:

Pacific fisher. Endangered species.

Once, on the Table Mountain between Lake Sabrina and South Lake, early morning horizontal light, just Carter and me on that vast creased plateau, maybe a few hundred acres, wandering separate ways—I saw a movement and looked east.

There trotted a small animal like a coyote, but different. Different ears and head. Light sandy brown, the color of the ground, black tips, brushy tail, absolutely in command of the situation. Canine—no—vulpine. It saw me but trotted on without changing speed or course. I fixed it in my mind.

Back home, in the Laws guide: Sierra fox.

Five or six times through the years, we've heard coyotes howling in the night. They are a choir too, singing their hearts out.

Down in the Kern-Kaweah canyon, as remote as anywhere in the Sierra, on an old trail: a movement across a meadow, under the north wall of the canyon, and suddenly I saw it—a wolf! Huge! Shaggy-coated, long tail. Oh my God.

It turned its head and saw me, and shot off into the trees. As big as a German shepherd, or even bigger.

I looked into that when I got home. There's a small internet group that thinks wolves have survived in the back country of the Sierra. That would be wonderful. But the scientists are dubious. No Sierra scat ever analyzed for DNA has been wolf scat. And coyotes grow really big sometimes, when well fed; and their winter coats can be long. Probably it was a coyote.

Just last week, on the surprisingly extensive sand beach at the east end of Desolation Lake, I saw another coyote, much smaller. It stared at me fearlessly, then trotted away.

Once my son David and I, and our friends Paul and Luc Park, were resting at the confluence of Evolution Creek and Goddard Canyon Creek, near the bridge there. In the shade, having a snack.

A movement caught our eye and we all looked. A small mammal, like a—hard to say—not a weasel, not a raccoon or badger—we weren't really sure, but there it was, intent on some business that made it dash about in tight little triangles—dashing, stopping—dashing in a different direction. Not food; no one else down there; it was hard to figure what it was doing. Dashing around! I wanted to pull my camera from my pocket, but I didn't want to disturb it and cause it to leave. It dashed about for a minute or two, then was off—into the trees and gone.

At home, again the Laws guide: pine marten.

Then there was that raccoon that jumped on Bonin's back.

These rare sightings tell me those species are up there. They were not Ishi, last of his tribe. Even if few in number, they must be abundant enough to reproduce. They're often small and often nocturnal. They might not like people to see them. I don't know. But I've seen these.

They're living their lives apart from us, without our help. We've left that land to them, and they live their lives on it.

All that that implies crashes in on me. No help from people, except to be left alone. They find each other and reproduce; they are mammals with sex lives. The moms give birth and bring up their young, teach them things, and the young go out there and make their way in the world, competently or not, for better or worse, until some other animal kills and eats them, or they die of injury or disease, or old age. Die alone, or among others of their kind. They have feelings. They have thoughts. They are capable in the world. They are mammals and so they are very like us. But wild.

I feel lucky to have seen these horizontal brothers and sisters, even so briefly. Now when I see any wildlife in the Sierra, mammal, bird, fish, reptile, amphibian (salamanders!), insect, spider, plant—I treasure the sight. The high Sierra is not heavily populated, it's too high, too rocky. I go up there for the rocks and the height, so I can't complain when I don't see many creatures, that's not the point of going. But they are up there; and they are so beautiful. The implications of their presence are so beautiful. The Sierras are alive. The Endangered Species Act is the greatest law we have. All the rest of our laws should be written to conform to it, and to enact it. It should be the magnet in our compass.

Mammals getting by, without any help; are we so different?

I feel lucky to have hiked with one of these reclusive Sierra people for so long.

SIERRA PEOPLE (13)
The Sierra Nevada Bighorn Sheep

Then there are the people up there you will never see. It's best that way. Consider the mountain lion for example. Seeing one might be bad for you.

I had read about the Sierra Nevada bighorn sheep with great interest for many years, but had never seen any, and did not expect to. There were few left. Certain areas on the map were marked as closed to humans nearly the entire year, open to people only from December through April, when it was difficult to get there, and few would try. These were reserves for the endemic bighorn sheep. Hunting and diseases transferred from domestic sheep were responsible for a die-off that was likely leading to extinction. The Sierra Nevada bighorn sheep is a close cousin to the Rocky Mountain bighorn sheep, and to the desert bighorn sheep of the American West; both these other species have much bigger ranges, and are doing pretty well. But the Sierra Nevada species was down to its last hundred individuals.

After that count was made, the Endangered Species Act kicked in. Federal law mandates that any species that gets formally listed as endangered deserves and requires concerted efforts to keep it from going extinct. This means money, and thus human time, and also designated protected habitat, all devoted to the saving and restoration of the species in question, if it can be done.

For the Sierra bighorn sheep, this meant going up there and finding them and observing them. Wherever they were found, including in their winter homes, which were far down the eastern slopes of the Sierra, domestic sheep were ordered to be kept away, and later goats. (Owners of domestic goats in the

Owens Valley are currently ordered to keep them east of Highway 395.) Certain mountain lions, protected by California law from being killed for any reason, were sedated and kidnapped and moved away from the bighorn sheep they were eating.

Some of the bighorn sheep also had to be sedated and kidnapped and moved elsewhere in the range, to start up new herds. These true stories of alien abduction are both funny and awful at once, and one has to imagine what it must be like for the sheep in question: there you are in your meadow, with your family and herd, and you know there are these weird people who sit at the edge of the meadow and watch you, very annoying at first, but ultimately just one of the weirdnesses of these people; people to be avoided, but not an immediate danger like the mountain lion people; and then you get stung, feel sick, pass out. When you wake up, some of your family is there, and a couple of other families from your herd, but not the rest of the herd. And you're in a meadow you've never seen before. Things are somewhat the same, but not. Looking around, confused, sick, a little hungry, a little scared, but mostly confused, you find some food to eat. You set to eating, the main occupation of any given day. Find a place to sleep that night that seems safe. Huddle together, missing the rest of the herd, wondering what the hell happened. Making do. And what's with these collars you are all now wearing, which you can't kick off? And the kids have little strange tags clipped to their ears? And they're scared, they're crying, or some of them are just, Hey mom I want a snack, let me get on the teat again please please please please please, and the moms are like, Come on, eat your grass seed and flowers, I'm not nursing you anymore you know that, get away or you'll get kicked. Lots of bleating and crying, throwing up, confusion, dismay. And then the next day is like most days, and you find a better night shelter, wander around a bit, try to figure out this place that is the same but different. Struggle through the first days; carry on coping. Eventually it becomes a memory, a story that you have no way to tell anyone. Do you remember that time we all fell asleep and woke up here? That's not a question you have any way to ask, except maybe with a nudge of the nose, a look at the horizon. You get on with the business of life.

And now, it's said they are up in number, from about 100 individuals to about 600. A postdoc I know at UC Davis is trying to get a current count of them, to help figure out how they are doing; part of his job is to hike up to high meadows on the east side and replace the batteries and data cards in the motion-activated cameras he's placed up there, and download the cards' images. What a great job! I hope to go with him on a trip, up to a high meadow I wouldn't otherwise go to.

On my first morning in the artists' camp that I described in the chapter "Artists in the Back Country," Bill Tweed took a group of us on a walk to a meadow he knew. I carried the spotting scope on its monopole over my shoulder. We stopped in some boulders about 200 yards from this meadow, and slightly above it. And there across a small lake, on the grass on the other side of that meadow — there they were. A herd of about 30 Sierra Nevada bighorn sheep. I was looking at about 5 percent of the species, right there. I was stunned. It was even more surprising than Carter popping out of a tent when I expected Darryl.

Whether with the naked eye or through the spotting scope, they were mesmerizing to watch. They looked healthy, thick-bodied and capable. I stuck my camera lens to the spotting scope and got a funny steampunk-style photo of them, like the view through a telescope, very nice.

Better still, watching them with the naked eye. The kids gamboled; I saw better than ever that gamboling is a very particular verb that captures a very particular behavior. The kids were goofy, they did goofball things. They ran in circles, they popped up in the air without provocation, they landed in heaps, they chased each other and fell, they harassed their moms for milk. The popping into the air, like springboks in nature films (called pronging or pronking), was particularly beautiful.

On a big flat-topped boulder a few youths were looking down over the edge, as if they could jump down to the ground from where they were. Maybe 15 feet down. Don't do it! I cried in a whisper as I watched. You're gonna die, you're gonna kill yourself for sure, it can't be done! Then one of them just *flowed* down to the ground from there. It was like a human dancer's move down a knee-high step. I cried out in surprise and my companions shushed me. But the grace of it was hard to believe.

Muir, always good on animals, says of these:

"I saw a fine band of mountain sheep, light gray in color, white on the backs of hips, with black tails. All horned, they seemed strong and moved with great deliberation, led by the largest. They crossed the river by making leaps on glacial bosses that made me hold my breath.... Then they leaped up the face of the mountain just where I thought they wouldn't, and perhaps couldn't, go. I could have scaled the same precipice myself, but not where they did.... Looking at them I often cried out, 'That was good!'.... I exulted in the power and sufficiency of Nature, and felt like saying to God as to a man, 'Well done!'"

That was good! He caught it exactly.

In the years following, I've seen members of this herd again three more times. Twice it was by accident, hiking in the area; we came on individuals out grazing for the day, high above that meadow. Once, headed up to the pond we call the Riviera, under Mount Mallory and Arc Pass, Joe and Darryl and I came on three of them standing together in a knot. They were the same color

The prey were not amused.

as the rock, and stared at us suspiciously. They didn't like our seeing them, and moved easily but with startling speed up the rocks, in the direction we were going. There was a grassy ramp behind a wall that we could run up without their seeing us, so we ducked down and ran, walking poles clutched in one hand, cameras in the other, running as hard as we could with backpacks on. It was as close to hunting in a pack, and chasing a herd animal, as I ever expect to come. And when I stuck my head up over that rock wall, there they were again. Success of the hunter!

I snapped more photos and they flowed over the ridge above and dis-appeared. That evening at twilight, sitting by our sleeping bags and cooking our dinners over our little stoves, we looked up; on the western skyline stood the black silhouette of a single sheep, curved horns distinct against the sky. A sigil, a heraldic emblem, right there real in the world.

A few years later, I hiked down onto that same herd with my sons, and Paul Park and his son Lucius, hoping to see the sheep again. And we did. Again, as during my first encounter, it was a big group. We sat and watched them for a half hour or so, till the boys got tired of it and we moved down, through the sheep's meadow, and they flowed as a group to the side to let us pass, watching us in an unfriendly way, but not afraid. We begged their indulgence and passed by.

Four sightings in four years, of the same herd. Courtesy of Bill Tweed and Mando Quintero. It's been a blessing, including that little hunting run, trying to keep up with the trio we came on.

And their story is encouraging too. If our purpose as a civilization were to shift to keeping all the species, our fellow citizens, alive—to making space for them and even helping them if they need help (which means helping them recover from the damage we've done to them)—then maybe we could do it. But it would have to be our purpose. And they will need space of their own to live. So many of these animals can't do well in rural areas, can't do well coex-isting with our domestic beasts. They need wilderness, and habitat corridors connecting bigger wilderness areas. It might not always be enough. Bighorn sheep are lucky in that their habitat can't be farmed: they're up in mountains, out in deserts. Even so we can mess them up, and have. But the space is available for helping them come back, and then letting them be. So maybe it can happen.

For the Sierra, it matters a lot that so much of it is preserved as wilderness, and unbroken by roads. This has been crucial for the bighorn sheep. One can suppose that if John Muir had not existed, to be used by the Sierra Club as its own particular charismatic megafauna, leading the human part of an actor network, the range would have been exploited to the point where all the giant sequoia got cut down, and this kind of sheep would already be extinct. They got lucky; lots of species weren't so lucky, and are headed out, or gone already. The sight of that silhouette on the twilight horizon struck me like the statue of Apollo struck Rilke: *You must change your life.*

SIERRA PEOPLE (14)
What Didn't Get Built; and Trail Phantoms

What happened in Yosemite Valley could have happened all over the range. The Sierra Nevada could have turned into Switzerland, or even Disneyland, with roads everywhere and a nice little stone hotel in every pass. It's a historical anomaly that that didn't happen.

But the campaign to preserve it was not a single moment, or just something that happened in the era of Muir and Teddy Roosevelt. It never ended, and it's still ongoing. Lots of people have contributed to the effort. An actor network for sure.

The preservation of the stretch of unbroken wilderness from Tioga Pass to the far south of the range is one of the campaign's most surprising and important achievements. North of Tioga Pass, there's a road crossing the crest every 20 or 30 miles. South of Tioga, there could have been several more of these. One from Fresno over to Mammoth seemed inevitable; a little anomalous road already crosses the crest from Mammoth to the Devils Postpile, so it would have been relatively easy to cut a connector down the North Fork of the San Joaquin River to Fresno, creating quick access to the ski resort. The congressman representing Fresno fought for this road for many years, and a community in Mammoth fought against it for just as long. The resistance won. There's a good book about this called *Stopping the Road*.

Farther south, a road could have crossed from Onion Valley over Kearsarge Pass and down Bubbs Creek to Kings Canyon. That would have required some dynamite in the pass, and would have been a travesty the entire way, but it could have been done. Caltrans, the state highway construction agency, did a study.

Likewise it could have happened farther south, where the bizarre road to Horseshoe Meadows, with its immense switchbacks up from Lone Pine, looks like the start of something trans-Sierran. Caltrans indeed studied the possibility, and although crossing the crest would have been fairly easy at Cottonwood Pass, getting over the deep gorge of the Kern River would not have been. A giant bridge would have had to be built, or more road would have had to swing south toward the path of the old Hockett Trail, a stage road that ran across the far south of the range to Mineral King. It could have been done. There are no easy mountain roads, they all involve big investments of time, effort, money, and dynamite. And yet many have been built. So in other cases, when they weren't, it was because people resisted them.

In this same way, a determined group of people fought to keep Mono Lake from being drained dry by LA, as LA had already drained Owens Lake and the Owens River half a century before. This Mono group succeeded in that, but the fight never ends, because LA is insatiable. LA has still not fully complied with a legal judgment ordering it to rehydrate the Owens River from Bishop to Owens Lake. *Storm Over Mono* tells the Mono Lake rescue story very well. The fight for it, and for the Owens River, and for keeping Long Valley as a grassland rather than desert, continues.

Turning Mineral King into a Disney ski resort: this seems unlikely, even crazy, but Mammoth got built, so it could have happened, despite the awkwardness of the little road with its 800 curves. But it didn't. That wasn't just a local effort, though it was that, but also a state and national effort, led by the Sierra Club, and joined by many. For years when you bought a Wilderness Press guidebook, a little slip of paper in it asked you to support the opposition to the Mineral King development proposal. Finally the locals won. It was another actor network.

Often a win is followed by a new law at the federal level, which makes it look like the battle has been won for good. But in the titanic struggle we are now fighting against the violent destructiveness of extraction industries and their supporters, it's become clearer than ever that the battle never ends.

Mostly these actions defending wilderness have been group efforts, but Bill Tweed has excavated the vast administrative files of the National Park Service to recover a person in that history who should be remembered: Sequoia National Park's superintendent John R. White. He spent much of his tenure in the mid-twentieth century fighting efforts to automobilize (and thus monetize) Sequoia. He was committed to keeping it wilderness, and managed to quash more than one road proposal. His defense of the parks was also part of what kept dams from flooding the Kings River's South Fork and Middle Fork. He deserves to be remembered with a peak or a basin or a trail name, for sure. Remove the name of some stranger who never gave a thought to the Sierra, and replace it with White's name. He deserves it. There's already a White Divide up there, named for the color of its granite; you could add his first name to that. Or you could rename the LeConte Divide the White Divide, and then alter the name of the already existing White Divide to the Other White Divide. Sweet!

That White had a Sequoia National Park to defend, was itself a group achievement fought for over many years. That group was led by George W. Stewart, in a lifelong campaign that he started at age 20 as a Fresno newspaper reporter, first to defend the southern Sierra from destructive exploitation, then to establish a bigger border for Sequoia National Park. That park started early but small, and in the decades following there were several tacked-on protections for the surrounding area. These expansions culminated in the creation of Kings Canyon National Park, a big northward extension of Sequoia that wasn't finalized until 1940, and was a real donnybrook every step of the way, a tale well told in Dilsaver and Tweed's *Challenge of the Big Trees*. Every square inch of protected land had to be fought for in court, and in the halls of power in Sacramento and Washington, DC. It's remarkable just how stubborn and vigorous the attempt to exploit and destroy these areas was. Luckily, those who fought for protection were even more stubborn and vigorous, and the general public backed them, and the national parks and protected wilderness areas of the national forests that now extend for the entire length of the southern Sierra are the result of that long intense political battle. The Sierra's various actor networks have done a good job, at least so far; but they will always have to keep fighting. The generations to come will be grateful that people have protected this mountain range, a gift to all its living creatures. We're lucky some people saw that early, and fought hard.

TRAIL PHANTOMS

In our wandering in the back country, we have often come on trails that are not marked on the map, and often not fully there in the landscape anymore, despite which they can be extremely helpful, and always fun to see. The natural genius has preceded us, and when we encounter signs of them we are archaeologists on the hunt.

This is a game I learned on Mount Desert Island, that little chunk of Sierra tossed into the Atlantic. Though only 10 miles by 10, that little space of granite-and-glacier interaction created the usual complex rockscape, and some locals went mad for it, falling into a frenzy of trail building between 1890 and 1940, making use of the granite slabs and steep slopes to construct stone staircases that look like they came from Machu Picchu, if not Atlantis. There were 250 miles of trails on the island until after World War II, when many were taken off the maps and allowed to fall under the leaves of the hardwood forest. My friend Tom St. Germain alerted me to the presence of these forgotten trails, and to a game played by people who get called trail phantoms. These people go out into the forest with old maps, or just their eyes, to see if they can find some of these old trails, and maybe mark them with ribbons tied to branches. Trail phantoms, looking for phantom trails. It's a great way to explore that island.

So I started looking in the Sierras, and found phantom trails there too. There were several decades in the past when people went more places in the Sierra than they do now. That might seem backward, but the evidence is there to show it's true. A recent clumping process has tended to draw more and more people to just a few popular trails, which these days means mostly the Muir Trail, the Pacific Crest Trail, the Rae Lakes Loop, and some feeder trails that run from trailheads to these two mountain highways.

The earliest Sierra trails weren't made by the Sierra Club or the National Park Service. Native Americans made them, following their own natural genius to find the best ways across the range. Then early European wanderers of various sorts took over, including sheepherders, prospectors, and fishermen. These last looked for lakes no one else knew about; when they found such lakes, they kept going back.

Maybe. The truth is, many of the Sierra's phantom trails have no history; one can't say for sure who made them. They were not designed and constructed. They're called use trails because it's use that made them. The trails that were designed and constructed, Bill Tweed has documented and written the history of, in his book *Granite Pathways*. All the others are the result of people taking what they felt was the best available way, time after time choosing the same route until it got walked into the ground. This process is what I call the natural genius.

Use trails tend to appear only where the terrain is somewhat difficult. Where any way will go, people go any way; they wander, and no trail forms. In more difficult terrain, a best way will be perceived time after time, then walked on by people until a trail is formed, because more and more people see it and use it. No one ever makes much effort to improve these trails, except perhaps by the placement of a trail duck. If trail ducks are ever really useful, it's in terrain so rocky that passing boots will never leave a trace. That's also somewhat true in wet terrain, where new plant growth will quickly obscure any use trail that might have developed. In these two situations, a trail duck marking the best way can be a great thing.

So the typical use trail develops on land with some soil, where not every way will go. The natural genius sees and walks that trail into existence.

A great example of how this process works runs up the drainage of Cataract Creek from Deer Meadow to Amphitheater Lake. A trail once ran the entire way, or so the old maps indicate; now hardly anyone goes up there, and most of the old trail has disappeared. But there's a section about halfway up the route where the east side of Cataract Creek is an enormous tilted talus field, the boulders in it about the size of armchairs. No one would go there if any alternative existed, so everyone has looked to the west side of the creek. Here there's a narrow strip of land between the creek and a cliff that leaps into the sky. So it's no surprise to find a very distinct trail running along the foot of this cliff, up to where a tributary creek drops into the main creek from the west. Here the terrain opens up, and the trail starts to fade away. It comes and goes for a while, marked by a few trail ducks, until you get up into rocky terrain where no trail can be made, and here you might see a duck, but you can't fully trust it; and it's time for cross-country work again.

It's like that everywhere in the southern Sierra.

Many people used to want to go up George Creek canyon, to take the easiest way up Mount Williamson; we joined that crowd of seekers, 130 years after people began going up that way, and found short stretches of trail scattered up and down this gnarly beast of a canyon.

As you hike up beside Milestone Creek to get to Table Mountain and Midway Mountain from the east, there's a forested slope that rises into the rock zone; to the left there's a steep creek, to the right, steep rocks; so there's an old trail winding up that forested slope.

Same next to Vidette Creek, rising between the ridges of East Vidette and West Vidette. Same with Wallace Creek, on the way from the Muir Trail up to Tulainyo Lake.

The use trail from Darwin Bench down to the Muir Trail is a very welcome beauty, as I described.

On it goes like that, even in remote basins where it's kind of surprising to think that enough people ever visited them to walk such trails into being. It's clear evidence of a curious, lively, multigenerational group of Sierra walkers, exploring the range from around 1860 to 1980. And then there's those special few use trails that have been there for thousands of years, distinguishable from the rest by chips of obsidian scattered over the nearby ground, and sometimes right there in the trail itself.

The remaining vestiges of the original route of the Muir Trail are different from these use trails made by the natural genius. That version of the Muir Trail was planned, engineered, improved, and walked on by people and pack animals, from around 1900 to 1933. Then in 1934 they finished two new alternative sections, one going up the Golden Staircase and over Mather Pass, the other, farther south, crossing Forester Pass rather than making two crest crossings at Junction Pass and Shepherd Pass.

In the north, the old route up Cartridge Creek was abandoned, and its lower section is completely overgrown, I'm told, except for the switchbacks by the Triple Falls. I'd like to go see those switchbacks. The upper section, which we have hiked on quite a few times, is still clearly there, because it's above vegetation, and is often used to get over Cartridge Pass. Despite its long absence on the maps, it's very clear on the land, a beautiful trail over a beautiful pass.

Down south, the old Muir Trail still runs very clearly up Center Basin, from the current Muir Trail all the way up to Junction Pass, where it suddenly goes away. This is probably because the south side is such a sandy slot that the freeze-thaw cycle has been enough to erase the trail. The old wooden sign in the pass is very evocative of the 1920s. If you head south from the sign, keep an eye out to your right for a talus-filled chute, called Leonie La, which will take you over the crest to the top of the Tyndall Creek drainage, avoiding the big drop to the Pothole and the rise back up over Shepherd Pass.

It's fun to look for these trails, and it's also fun to come on them by chance.

I don't know what to think about the trails up there that are still on the maps, but seem to be disappearing from lack of use. Maybe in some ways that's a good thing, but damn, they sure are useful when you're on them, trying to get along in a canyon, or up a steep forested slope. Some of them I think should live.

If they don't, people will still go where they used to be, so maybe it's not a serious loss. If the existence of a trail relies on the natural genius, and the genius goes away — the trail will too. Phantoms will remain.

ROUTES (5)

Basins Have Characters

Each basin has its own character, formed by its elevation, its latitude, the compass orientation of its open end, its rock type (granite or metamorphic or both), its plant community, its lake and pond collection, and so on. For me, and a bit to my surprise, I think the critical factor is compass orientation. But they all combine to form a gestalt that makes each of them singular and idiosyncratic.

Here are a few of my favorites.

Kaweah Basin is hard to get into. It's tough to come up into it from below, because its exit is a hanging valley with a wicked hang. An easier way is from the south, following a little creek up to Kaweah Pass, a class 2 pass cutting across the great wall of the Kaweah divide. One of Pete Starr's favorite passes. Easy on the south side, sharp drop down the north side, into the big remote basin. It's on this descent that Secor notes you have to watch out for the invisible cliffs.

Kaweah Basin's floor is mostly absent of trees, and even of lakes (maybe because it has a roof-pendant floor?), but it has a vein system of streams, gathering at the exit from the basin. It's a big red expanse, opening to the northeast, which is unusual. The Kaweah peaks rear up in a grand jagged semicircle of red and black rock. If they were just a few feet taller they'd hit 14,000 feet above sea level, and be much more famous than they are. As it is, this is one of the emptiest parts of the Sierra. It feels austere, otherworldly. Deep inside.

Below the basin, the Kern-Kaweah canyon still holds an old seldom-used

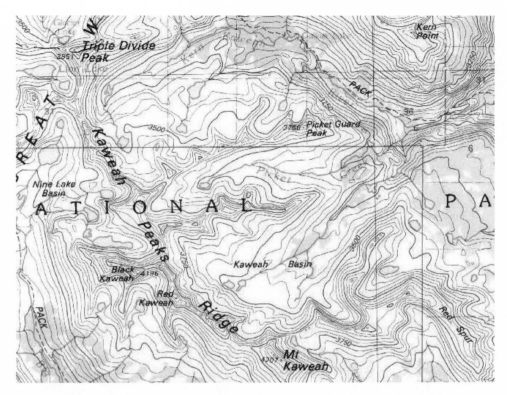

Kaweah Basin, USGS

trail. It runs up to Colby Pass, which William Colby and a few friends discovered in the 1920s, during a ramble launched from one of the Sierra Club high trips.

The glaciers tucked into the bottom of the cliffs that launch up to the ragged peaks of the Kaweah ridge may soon be gone, but for now they provide a nice dash of white to a rusty scene. The Kaweah roof pendant must have a lot of iron oxides in it, although Moore says Black Kaweah is made of "dark metamorphosed crystal-rich dacite." To me even Black Kaweah looked red. Rain or clouds might change that—when we were there, it was dry and sunny. (Now I know that in the rain it can look as black as pitch. Noted with pleasure, August 2021.)

The basin's opening to the northeast gives a long view to the crest, where you can see Mount Williamson poking up over Mount Tyndall. In the summer, sunrise pours over the crest right into the Kaweah Basin, and hits the peaks before it hits the basin floor, creating a dawn alpenglow on the red rock that goes scarlet. Phil Arnot's *High Sierra* mentions this.

On the Mount Clarence King massif, there are three basins. Sixty Lakes Basin is the least of them, constricted, forested, the many lakes (not quite 60) mostly tiny pothole ponds. Crossing over at its top into Gardiner Basin is a shift up to a higher, more majestic world, deep inside the range. The paternoster lakes in the upper part of Gardiner Basin are so long that you can never see more than one at a time. The exit stream plummets down a cliff into Muro Blanco, no one goes that way. The old trail over Gardiner Pass is mostly gone, but the way is still easy. Better, however, to leave Gardiner Basin northward by way of King Col, down into a nameless basin dropping into Woods Creek at

Leaping antelope?

grade. This one is a beauty; there's a sigil on a face of pure white rock that transforms the mural cliff on the northwestern flank of Mount Clarence King into a great cave painting, and the peak itself is seen at one of its best angles. Its granite is very clear and smooth, and breaks off the peak in chunks the size and shape of shipping containers, many carried down the slope by glacial ice and left scattered akimbo. No one goes here: a beyul, a lost jewel, a reward for your efforts to get there.

The little basins and draws under the west side of Table Mountain, on the Great Western Divide, feel remote and lost to the world. It's another space that can be your own, a ruggedly corrugated world, forgotten in that big space between the Great Western Divide and Roaring River, so far below.

I already wrote at length about the Miter Basin, but want to recall it here: a great beauty, Mediterranean and gorgeous.

Under Arrow Peak's southeast flank begins a sweet basin, all the classic features in their Platonic ideal. No one goes there. Arrow Creek leaves this basin in another hanging valley waterfall; better to leave by way of the next stream to the east. Arrow Pass, near Bench Lake, is a good entry at the top.

Dumbbell Basin opens to the southwest, and is framed by the cleanest of granite cliffs, made of the Cartridge pluton's white granite—smooth curving cliffs, better looking than Yosemite's. The basin floor is grassy, and drops hard from lake to lake. Easiest ways in and out are over Observation Pass, and through an easy draw from Lakes Basin. But no one goes there. Although we once ran into a pair of brothers on the Muir Trail who were on their way there, to distribute their father's ashes. He had requested Dumbbell Basin, which amused the sons, it being so hard to get to. They implied it was just like him to want such a difficult thing. But I can see his point. It's the gem of the range, the heart of the Sierra. You can't get more inside than it. No one else will be there if you go. Camp near the outlet of Lower Dumbbell Lake, if your trip allows. You can sleep right on that glossy granite, smooth as a marble floor.

The Lakes Basin, right next door, is almost as fine: longer and skinnier, the original route of the Muir Trail, the summer home of Joe and Helen LeConte, Bolton and Lucy Brown. Filled with—yes, lakes. It's deep inside, but if you're ever there, don't forget to pop over into Dumbbell, the beyul of basins.

Joe and I, traipsing down upper Dumbbell Basin. Note the glacier tucked inside the U of its moraine, to the right of the V of Dumbbell Pass.

However you get yourself into the Ionian Basin, it will be wonderful. It's a mix of white granite and black roof pendant, and as Arnot remarks, you never take a level step in it, it's always up or down. It's not a typical basin in a lot of respects. South-facing—or rather, it has a south exit at Chasm Lake; but really it's ringed on all sides by peaks. There's an easy entry on the east side, right under the Black Giant; and an interesting, tricky entry on the west side, taking advantage of a slot in the black rock that rises from Martha Lake up to the first pond in the west Ionian. This slot is so narrow that it seems certain a cliff or big boulder will cut it off, but it goes all the way. We called it the Mordor Gate, when my son David and I did it with Paul Park and his son Luc; we were hiking in the smoke of forest fires, and that plus the tortured black rock gave the slot a very Mordor feel. The rest of the Ionian Basin is similarly ominous, as

Arnot also noted: remote, lumpy, dark, fierce. The exit from the Ionian to the south is the famous descent down the Enchanted Gorge.

Humphreys Basin, right over Piute Pass, is a giant tilted trapezoid, handsome everywhere, especially next to the astonishing Desolation Lake, under the divide separating Humphreys Basin from French Canyon. The basin is dominated by Mount Humphreys, a beast of a metamorphic peak, set right on the crest.

Desolation Lake astonishes because it is so vast, much bigger than any of the other Sierra lakes, except for Wanda, which, being split almost in two by a long peninsula, doesn't seem as huge. You can see Desolation Lake from airplanes. When you're standing on its shores, the shift in scale looks surreal, it seems like a hallucination. Too big to be real!

It's easy wandering over Humphreys Basin, and there are many ways to get in and out of it. Because it's so smooth and tilted down to the west, the whole world seems to expand up there.

Crucial to mention Palisades Basin, one of the greatest of them all. This one is also south-facing. A very dark hard gorgeous rock forms the serrated cliffs of the Palisades, which rear up so high at the back wall of the basin that while standing under them, you can't perceive how tall they really are. You need to get many miles away to gauge their great height.

There are actually three little basins or drainages that line up together and share the Palisades name with the cliff backing them. Dusy Basin is just to the west of these three, so really it's a tight quartet, and all of them wonderful. Just east of Dusy Basin, over a ridge that features Isosceles Peak and Columbine Peak, is the Barrett Lakes drainage; east again over Potluck Pass's ridge is the Cirque Lake drainage; over the next ridge there's a long skinny canyon running southeast down to Lower Palisade Lake.

The high crossing of Palisades Basin is justly famous as one of the great cross-country routes in the Sierra, and is Roper's High Route alternative to the Muir Trail, which runs in the canyons below. The little internal passes between the drainages are tricky, but the footing is good, and it never stops being spectacular. I'd do it every year if I could. I'd live there.

Sometimes the light at dusk reveals deep clefts like drapery folds in the Palisades.

Best for last, maybe: Dusy Basin, my first and still most beloved. Its open end faces west and gives you a view of the Black Giant and Langille Peak, which we called Yes Mountain because of its resemblance to the cover painting for Yes's album *Relayer*, by Roger Dean. A line of ponds runs down Dusy's lowest crease to an overlook of LeConte Canyon called the Lip. The higher lakes, under Isosceles Peak and the jagged streaked monsters of the west Palisades, are each on a different level, and are ringed by small knots of trees and shapely granite curves. A lovely, lovely basin. The paradigmatic basin, the Platonic ideal.

There are many more basins up there just as fine as these I've mentioned. They are usually off trail, and many can only be reached by way of class 2 passes. Getting into them will be a matter of long rambling, and tough scrambling.

Loop trips will often get you to two or more of them in a week's ramble.

Dusy Basin in the lower center, as seen from space. The Barrett Lakes in the Palisades Basin are to its right. Photograph by Planet Labs PBC.

The circumambulation of a special peak is a Buddhist ritual, a form of devotion: circling Mount Kailash in Tibet, Mount Hiei in Japan (the monks run that one), Mount Tamalpais in California (initiated by Gary Snyder and Allen Ginsberg). Try making a circumambulation! It has a very nice feel; maybe it's a matter of having a goal or a point, something more than sheer wandering around. My favorite circumambulation was of Mount Clarence King. But whatever you do, it's good to have a project.

Visiting remote basins is a very fine project. They will be beautiful. Try one without a name, one never mentioned in any guidebook; there are still many of those up there. The one you pick and visit will be yours forever.

Joe surveying some basin new to us

SNOW CAMPING (4)

Extreme Housekeeping

The Palisades in spring, seen from the southeast. Extreme housekeeping at its finest.
Photograph by Planet Labs PBC.

In the early 2000s, Joe suggested that we try snow trips again, a type of trip he had missed in the early years, having moved to Hawaii. Darryl and I liked the idea. Given Joe's lack of skiing experience, and my badness on skis, Darryl, a good skier, agreed to strap on the plates once again. Back to snowshoes: and as far as I'm concerned, thank God. Much less falling involved, and while moving one can still take the time to look around at the scenery, rather than at the slope you are failing to negotiate. Snowshoeing is just like walking with long serving plates tied to your feet—a little awkward at first, but you soon get used to it, and it's better than plunging hip deep into snow with every step.

We agreed April or May would be best for these trips. The days would be longer, and the snow consolidated and unlikely to avalanche, an important consideration.

On our first trip of this snow renaissance, we went back to Desolation, and ascended Pyramid Peak to spend a night there on its top. This notion came from Phil Arnot's inspiring guidebook *High Sierra*. Spend a night on a mountaintop, he suggests, and time it to the full moon if you can, so you can see the high world at night. Having been on Pyramid Peak in the summer, we knew it had a relatively broad top, with knee-high walls made by visitors over the years, ringing little depressions that we thought would be big enough to sleep in. It worked like a charm: views extended from Nevada to California's coastal range, during an incredible sunset, then a calm night, and an operatic dawn. Dawn of the visible world. Then down the northeast flank of the peak to Lake Aloha, where some rocky knolls were emerging out of the snow. One of them was big enough to camp on the next night.

On our last day we wandered down the Lake Aloha maze, now a rumpled sheet of snow, past a little hollow that concealed the dam that held Lake Aloha in place. None of us had seen it before. Interesting that a little V-shaped brick wall could flood such a big basin, but this is what the undersides of ice caps are like after the ice leaves; not canyons, not cirques, but mazes.

Having thoroughly enjoyed this return to snowshoes, we did it again every spring for the next decade. A different, wilder joy returned to our Sierra repertoire. The trails being under snow, it's as if they don't exist. You're back in

Terry and Joe demonstrate why traversing on snowshoes can be tricky, under Blumlein Pass.

what feels like the original landscape, empty and wild. And stormy: somehow our chosen weeks always seemed to catch a storm. But falling snow is easier to cope with than rain, and we came to consider these storms our fate. *Sturm und Drang:* these trips were Beethovian.

Despite the inherent, adrenalating drama of the stormy days, we came to call our snow trips "extreme housekeeping," because the work of setting camp and breaking it down is so much more time-consuming than it is during summer trips. And as the days are shorter, and traveling over snow is slower, the distances involved could be quite short. A day's hike might start at 10:00 and end by 3:00, and during that time progress might be minimal; many days we only covered three or four miles. That was fine, as long as we didn't plan a loop trip that meant we had to cover a certain number of miles to get back to our car. Quickly we learned not to do that. These snow trips were almost all four days long, so most of them were designed to be out and back, which allowed us to adjust how far out we went according to how much progress we made in the first two days. On the third day, at some point, we'd turn around and go back, and however far we got became that trip's destination.

Once when taking off in a snowstorm we lost our route immediately on departure, and were forced to claw our way back up to our proper elevation, gasping and sweating and using our hands, all less than half an hour into the trip. For sure the physical work of snowshoeing keeps you warm, except for fingers and nose and ears. Lots of people know this just as part of their winter lives at home in city or suburb. For us it was in the nature of a perpetual discovery. When you're living in California and Hawaii, it's always exotic to be hiking and sleeping on snow. We've had to learn the craft of it: the way in the mornings the snow is like concrete, and much more slippery; then the way it progressively softens as it warms, until at the end of the day it loses all structural integrity and turns to a white mush so soft that even wearing snowshoes won't prevent you from sinking waist deep.

Going up to Iceberg Lake we should have had crampons.

The Sierra is particularly good at creating suncups; these egg-carton-shaped hollows can become almost dangerous, especially when the edges are as hard as knives. They look very beautiful, like a blanket with texture, but crossing a field of them is slow work.

If you get on a steep slope of soft afternoon snow, it means a lot of sloppy choppy walking, high-stepping to get the snowshoes out of their holes and into a new one. None of this will be news to people familiar with snow, but for us, and in the continuously tilted slopes of the Sierra, it was fascinating. And also, never a worry about avalanches. *Sierra cement* is a term skiers use for the spring snow up there, and it seems justified. Indeed in the mornings, the snow can be hard enough to cut you if you slip and fall on it.

It's best to stop early enough on the short days to pick a good campsite. Finding some open water is key. This can be difficult, or even impossible if it's cold enough, but typically a lake's outlet to its exit stream will have a little patch of open water, maintained by the flow leaving the lake — either open water, or at least a thin spot in the ice, which you can break with a rock. In the most frozen of afternoons we've had to set our water bottles under trickles of afternoon melt coming down exposed rock faces like tears, with luck falling off an overhang or dripping off an icicle in a way that makes it easier to catch in your bottle. Sometimes it's taken 15 minutes to fill a single bottle. In the worst cases, we've even melted pots of snow on our stoves, which is slow, and wasteful of stove fuel, and results in water with a strange taste. But usually there's open water somewhere.

Then a campsite also needs flat spots big enough for three tents. And some trees around are always nice; they stabilize the snow, and help break any wind that might come up. In fact, now that I think of it, an entirely open stretch of snow really isn't a good candidate for a campsite. (See Kurosawa's *Dersu Uzala* for a vivid demonstration of why this is true.) If we're completely above tree line, big rocks will serve as windbreaks and stove nooks, and provide the sense of hominess that a campsite needs. Some texture in the landscape is definitely helpful.

Occasionally we've been caught by the end of day, and had to settle for what we could find before dark. Then it becomes clear that the only real needs are

A sunny morning in camp

a place to lie down, and water. Aesthetic factors go by the board if necessary, and we've camped in anonymous forests, in the middle of sloping tangles of sage, and between the roots of a giant tree. On those occasions, the comedy becomes what a crappy campsite we've found. But always better than nothing.

Campsite chosen, the task then is to pick your tent site, and manicure it. Sometimes this requires little, and sometimes you don't have much time for it anyway. But it's best not to put a tarp over soft snow. So the prep usually involves keeping your snowshoes on and walking back and forth over your spot, maybe even jumping up and down to smash the snow to a more compact solid surface. That done, or before doing that, you might even do some excavating, using a snowshoe as a shovel, to make an even deeper and harder depression. When you're done, you've made a little graben you can lie in.

Even on snow we use our tarps rather than tents; indeed they work better than ever on snow, because a bit of trenching means the tarp is set higher, giving you more room, surrounded by snow walls that can be pretty high. With some luck you can make a little sunken room, with a kind of sloping entryway down to a floor well below the ambient snow level. Your little room will have a snow floor and snow walls, with your tarp as a roof overhead. This is a substitution for winter camping's famous snow caves, which are said to be well insulated and so on, but look like an enormous amount of work, requiring huge drifts of soft snow, not a common Sierra camping situation; also a shovel, and a willingness to sleep in a cave dug into snow, meaning a thick roof of snow over you. Maybe that might be okay, but we've never tried it. A tarp over a trench is much easier to set up, and once you're inside, very elegant. Packed snow as floor and walls is actually very nice, strange though it may sound. Snow is a great insulator, and even if a tiny sheen on its surface melts from your presence, that watery layer is an even better insulator than snow is. Often the air outside will be a lot colder than the air under your tarp. And the inside is cozy, being lit a little by the snow's whiteness. You can punch holes in your side walls to make open cabinet spaces, or even places to put a candle lantern, although that's only something I did when young, when having a light at night mattered. Anyway, it can look good, and feel great. And if it's windy, being down below ground level will reduce drafts. You can get out and shovel some snow onto the outer edges of your tarp, and create a really windproof seal everywhere but at the entry, which with luck will be on the downwind side.

So a tarp in the snow is often very homey, very comforting, and pretty warm. One thing that helps in terms of temperature is that the Sierra Nevada of California never gets very cold, even in the depths of winter, even at 10,000 feet. This is because the Pacific Ocean is a powerful thermal regulator, creating California's Mediterranean climate. Windchill can make things feel colder, no doubt of that, but the lowest actual temperature I've ever recorded in Sierra snow camping was 10 degrees Fahrenheit, and that was in a storm. On the same trip I saw 12 degrees; once, on another trip, 15. We didn't carry thermometers back in the '70s, and we definitely froze our butts during those winter trips, but that probably had more to do with our gear than the temps. Most of the time, nighttime temperatures bottom out in the '20s; but as this is all happening in snow, you really don't want it to get over 32 degrees anyway, or things will get wet and sloppy, and then feel even colder. So with all factors taken into account, the spring temperatures in the Sierra are as warm as they can be for snow camping, without becoming too warm. People from the Midwest, or New England, or Canada, or all around the top of the world, will know very well that just below freezing is not very cold. In Antarctica I slept in a tent when it was 25 degrees below zero Fahrenheit, and I was fine. Granted my sleeping bag weighed eight or nine pounds, but I was fine with my nose poking out into that air. And at the South Pole I went out when it was 35 below zero — okay, that was cold. And yet in the Midwest or Canada or New England, even temperatures that low happen all the time! And you still have to get your car started and then drive somewhere!

So really, I would say the spring Sierra is relatively comfy. We're geared well, we're exerting ourselves right up to the moment we get in bed; it's just not that cold. A bigger problem is sweating like a pig with the exertion of snowshoeing, then stopping to make camp while dripping inside your stuff. Then you need to change clothes fast and get into your warmies, capture your heat in dry clothes, and go about your business. After that, fingers can and will get cold, and noses and ears. Snow can melt and get your hands wet. But by and large, it's not really a matter of suffering up there. Cold is something to deal with, it's one of the things that make it extreme housekeeping and not normal housekeeping; you have to take care. But done right, it can be very comfy.

Exceptions to this comfort can definitely occur. Lying in your sleeping bag at night, you can wake up with cold feet, or even a chill all through your body; that's a bad moment, especially if you've already got all your clothes on, and are thus maxed out in terms of warmies. This can happen even on summer trips, because temperatures get down into the 20s then also, and often we have much less in the way of warm gear. When you're chilled like that, eating some carbohydrates will help; other times, if it's bad enough, you have to sit up and get the stove going, make some hot chocolate and drink it. That will warm you back up for sure, and then you can go back to sleep. But very often you're cold enough at night, and sleepy too, that there is a real reluctance to do anything except snuggle deeper in your bag, wiggle your toes, tighten the strings of your down hood and sleeping bag, and try to twitch on purpose to generate body heat; then go back to sleep so you don't feel it. Morning and the sun will cure this kind of chill.

Real shivering, the kind your body decides to do on its own out of desperation, is a truly bad sign. I can't recall it ever happening to me while snow camping. Most of the real shivering in my life has happened on the beaches of Orange County after I had bodysurfed too long. Air temperature would be 80 with an onshore breeze, and we'd come out after a two-hour bodysurfing session in 62-degree water and collapse on our towels, and I'd shiver so hard that I'd bounce off the sand. Then the sun would burn me back to warmth and in 20 minutes I'd be getting too hot, making it time to go back in the water. That's my experience of shivering. In the Sierra, no. It would be bad: a sign of hypothermia, and thus a dangerous thing.

So. Night in a tent, meaning under a tarp. Although we also sometimes camp out under the stars, as during the summer. On a still night, clear, no wind, feeling confident in our sleeping bags, etc.: sure. It's beautiful.

But usually we set up the tarps. Flap down when you get sleepy enough; might as well capture a few extra degrees of warmth. The interior surface of the tarp usually sparkles in your headlamp light, because the condensation from your breath has frozen up there, creating a sheen of tiny ice crystals. Best not to smack your tarp wall if you don't want a rain of those ice crystals down the back of your neck. But pretty in the light.

And then, if it isn't windy: the quiet. Nothing like a snowy windless night for quiet. I suppose part of that is the lack of any sound of water falling downhill. In the summer, almost every campsite will include the sound of falling water, either far away or nearby, and often both. A kind of watery chorus, beautiful in its way, but not quiet. Winter, if there isn't a wind, is very quiet.

Then morning. The gray of dawn can be very welcome if the cold is pinching you. And the nights are long, compared to summer, so it's usually welcome to see that gray. Although not so welcome as it was in the old days, because modern ground pads, being air mattresses longer than you are, and filled with down or something else to make sure they capture your heat and insulate you—these are precious things. They're a major factor in making our middle-aged reincarnation as snow campers so much more comfy than the youthful incarnation. It's not just experience over innocence, but better gear.

So, we saw Desolation again. We circled the north side of Hetch Hetchy, and camped on the top of Hetch Hetchy Dome. We wandered the Tablelands and got to the great overlook near Phil Arnot Pond. We went up the Sabrina Basin all the way to the crest between Mounts Wallace and Haeckel. We crossed Piute Pass and wandered Humphreys Basin. We climbed Mount Williamson up George Creek, no doubt our springtime masterpiece; we only spent about an hour on snowshoes that time, and much of the rest of it was bushwhacking, but the airy summit plateau of the peak had a great view and feeling.

Darryl photographing Joe near the peak of Mount Williamson; Owens Valley 10,000 feet below

We tried to climb Mount Agassiz, and were stymied by a giant cornice blocking Bishop Pass. We ascended the north fork of Lone Pine Creek to Iceberg Lake, and watched amazed as extreme-sport athletes from all over the world skied down the cleft on the east side of Whitney that forms the Mountaineer's Route, the route pioneered by Muir in 1873. That entire approach was so steep that it needed crampons and ice axes rather than snowshoes, but we clawed up as far as we could get, and ended up all bloody, cut by hard-frozen snow. On our last trip we floundered around the Little Lakes Basin in snow too soft to hold us.

All these snow trips, stormy or clear, goals reached or not, were spectacular. The hiking by day is almost like ordinary walking, just a little more crunchy, a little more awkward and strenuous. On the plates you are free to look around as you walk, even more perhaps than in summer, as you aren't going to be tripping over any rocks. Crunch crunch crunch on the ups, heart pounding, sweating hard; glissade in big dreamy steps on the downs; traverse with some care, using your poles, as snowshoes aren't so good on traverses. Cross lakes that are suddenly level easy roads through the forest. And all the while a white wonderland around you, punctuated by granite knobs, and walls of colorful roof-pendant rock that are even more striking than in summer, being draped in smooth white blankets as they are, and often wet and glossy. It's very beguiling, even mesmerizing, to snowshoe in the high Sierra. A wildness comes back to the wilderness, and a wild feeling.

Then various things kept us from getting up there in the snow months. We took a pause that we kept expecting would come to an end. Years passed.

Just a few weeks ago I went up snow camping again. It was as beautiful as ever, or maybe more so. As I strapped on my snowshoes, all their straps broke; they're made of rubber, and had gotten slow-cooked by years of standing in my closet, so that they snapped when stretched. Quite a shock, that! I had to tie the plates onto my boots with tent string, a ridiculous fix that worked better than I would have thought possible. We snowshoed around Desolation again, and I felt free of nostalgia, and full of love. I still knew how to snow camp, and that felt like a Bridey Murphy moment, a language I could speak without ever having learned it. The rite of spring: I was back on the plates, back in the snow. What fun! Let's do it again!

Coming to Piute Pass

SIERRA PEOPLE (15)
Gary Snyder

In my life I've been blessed with great teachers, and among those Gary Snyder has been an exemplary figure, my model for how to be a California artist and a human being in this world.

Born in 1930, he was an outdoor kid who grew up in the Depression, and was too young to fight in World War II. He came into his own in postwar America, and veered away from it into a transpacific life of his own making. After Reed College he briefly went to the University of California in Berkeley, and got interested in East Asia. He took various outdoor summer jobs, as logger, trail builder, fire lookout, and in those same years he began writing and

Gary Snyder, early 1950s

publishing poems. He taught the East Coast Beats to pay attention to Buddhism and the physical world. Right in the years when dealing with America's postwar mainstream culture was wrecking Kerouac, and stressing Ginsberg, Snyder took off for Japan for a decade or so, practicing Zen and eventually marrying a Japanese woman and raising two boys with her.

When he came back to California with them, he headed for the Sierras and bought some land there, built a home with his wife and kids, and settled in for the long haul. He's been there ever since.

For a decade he taught at UC Davis, in a deal arranged by our mutual friend David Robertson. I asked to get into two of his classes as an outside member of the community, and he let me join. Watching him teach was a pleasure; he was tactful, scholarly, kind to people in a way both formal and personable, always completely present and engaged.

On the San Juan Ridge he's been an anchor to a community of California hippie Buddhists who are there partly because of his presence. He helps ground them, and it's the same in a less direct way for his readers. His dating system often tacked 40,000 years onto the Common Era date; this is a good thing to be reminded of, a deep-time cognitive map.

Thinking back to my youth, when I first encountered Gary's writing, and saw him give a reading at UCSD in 1972, I recall very strongly how unusual he seemed in the context of American literature at that time. I was a child of the postwar suburbs, and books were my god, and I wanted to be a writer. Who could I look up to?

It seemed to be all men back then, especially if you were a young man. Not the least of the many advantages of getting into science fiction when I did was the powerful presence of Ursula Le Guin and Joanna Russ and many other women, teaching me to pay attention to women writers and making me into a feminist. But I was still looking around for models.

What stuck out about the various men writers, scattered like ninepins over the social landscape, was alcohol. Alcohol, and the bluster of the dominance battle to be alpha male in various forms: the Great American Novelist, the biggest bestseller, the most famous TV celebrity. One could be excused for thinking that being an American male writer was predicated on drinking a lot and treating women badly. How else be a great writer? Even the ones who found jobs in postwar academia tended to be like that.

And then there was Gary. Zen Buddhist, mountaineer, West Coast antiwar culture; marijuana instead of alcohol; family man. Settle into the land and write about that. Hippie intellectual, Asian scholar, Paleolithic utopian visionary. Not about dominance, but resistance; not the *Partisan Review* but the Wobblies; not East Coast confessional poetry, but Chinese landscape poetry; not New York, but California; not the bestseller list, but deep time; not the university, but the wilderness. Or, the university *and* the wilderness; the University *of* the Wilderness, as Muir once named it. What a tremendous corrective to America!

So, thank God for Gary. Because we all need role models.

Of course he wasn't the only one, but especially after the publication of *The Back Country* he stuck out, for me and many others. He was a movement leader. Much later, it became apparent that others were also working the back country of American literature. It's never a single writer who does it all. But when it mattered to me, Gary was the poet, and *The Back Country* was the book. A few years ago, when I gave the commencement address to the English majors graduating from UC Berkeley, I finished by leading them all in three cheers for their moms (it was Mother's Day) and then by asking them to shout out, all at once, the book or writer that had turned them into English majors, which is a perilous path, a fate you shouldn't really choose. Those brave kids gave out a mighty roar, and it was a fun topic in the reception afterward to ask which writer people had chosen to exclaim. Such variety! I myself yelled "Snyder!"

Sierra poems are everywhere in Gary's work, and since he's lived in the Sierra since 1970 or so, the Sierras are the home ground for all his work since then. In that sense all his writing is Sierra writing, it's like a fish in water. As for backpacking in the Sierra, he did that too, and the notes he took while sitting by the fire at night are sharp little accounts of these trips. They're more specific concerning place than Muir's notes, and thus it's possible to map Gary's trips around the southern Sierra, at least the ones he's provided the journals for, from the midfifties through the early years of his marriage to his wife Carole. I reckon he was one of the first people ever to cross Millys

Footpass, because Mildred Jentsch and her companions found it in 1953, and Gary crossed it in 1956. It's not a pass Native Americans would have used very often, if at all, so Gary was probably among the first dozen people to do that one, and he might have been the fourth.

And he got around a lot. He climbed Mounts Whitney (west face), Tyndall, and George Stewart. When he climbed Mount Haeckel in 1969, he left his signature in the summit register; I've seen it in the Bancroft Library, with a Buddhist poem accompanying his name. He took the Japanese poet Nanao Sakaki with him on that ascent, and said it was the only time he ever saw his friend Nanao nervous; it's a class 3 climb up the peak's west ridge, and looks awful. Recently he said to me, there was a chute blocked by a rock that we had to climb over—that was what made Nanao serious for once. Gary also went up the inside route of Mount Sill, led by his wife Carole, who was a more technical climber than he was; his son Kai joined them on that one.

The persistence, continuity, and coherence of the ideas in his poems have led to his being called "the poet laureate of deep ecology," and Max Oelschlaeger in *The Idea of Wilderness* reads Snyder as a "thinking poet" in the way Heidegger was a "poetic thinker," meaning a kind of crossing between artist and philosopher that multiplies the power of the thoughts expressed, and gets them out into the intellectual life of a civilization. Because modern American culture has often been so urban, and so distanced from the land that sustains people, Snyder's work joins that of the transcendentalists, and Whitman, and ecologists like Aldo Leopold; it adds a strong link to that crucial line in American thought.

His poetry, steeped in Chinese poetry, also swims in the sea of West Coast poetry, and American outlaw modernism in the tradition of William Carlos Williams, also going back to Whitman. His translations of Han Shan set a style for his own early work, as did *The Cantos* of Ezra Pound. In his early work he often used short lines, something like Chinese lines, or Williams's variable foot, and placed them like riprap, so there was a lapidary effect. Since then he's developed that line into his own style. As with most poetry, it's a pleasure to read his poems aloud. He's great at that himself, an oral performer with charisma and heart. He makes people feel connected to the larger world of nature and deep time; you can see this at his readings, which always draw big crowds.

From "Four Poems for Robin"

I dont mind   living this way
Green hills   the long blue beach
But sometimes   sleeping in the open
I think back   when I had you

From "Piute Creek"

The mind wanders. A million
Summers, night air still and the rocks
Warm. Sky over endless mountains.
All the junk that goes with being human
Drops away, hard rock wavers
Even the heavy present seems to fail
This bubble of a heart.
Words and books
Like a small creek off a high ledge
Gone in the dry air.

As I was looking through Gary's earliest books to find some youthful Sierra lines to quote, I found this one above in *Riprap*, first published in 1959. Two pages later, I came on a poem called "Above Pate Valley." In that one, Gary eats a lunch in "a small / Green meadow watered by the snow," and afterward:

I spied
A glitter, and found a flake
Black volcanic glass—obsidian—
By a flower. Hands and knees
Pushing the Bear grass, thousands
Of arrowhead leavings over a
Hundred yards. Not one good
Head, just razor flakes

On a hill snowed all but summer,
A land of fat summer deer,
They came to camp. On their
Own trails. I followed my own
Trail here. Picked up the cold-drill,
Pick, singlejack, and sack
Of dynamite.
Ten thousand years.

Ten thousand years: no wonder the last line of my chapter on the first people sounded so right to me! I hadn't read this poem of Gary's for almost half a century, and had completely forgotten that he too had once come on a knapping site in the back country, and written about it. Cryptomnesia: I'm sure that phrase stuck somewhere inside me through all the years, like a line from a song that you can never forget.

Thank you Gary.

At David Robertson's Sierra artists' conference, SNARL (Sierra Nevada Aquatic Research Laboratory), 2009

NAMES (4)
Naming Mount Thoreau

In September of 2014, I drove one morning through hard rain over Donner Pass with Paul Park beside me, Gary Snyder in the back seat. Two of my favorite people. In Reno we headed south on Highway 395, and the skies cleared. We were on our way to the North Lake trailhead; the plan was to rendezvous late that afternoon at a high Sierra lake with a bunch of other people, camp there that night, and next day ascend Peak 12691 and name it Mount Thoreau.

Question: Why do you want to climb Mount Thoreau?
Answer: Because it isn't there.

Nothing in the Sierra is named after Henry David Thoreau—I've heard that's true of the entire American West—and snowshoeing down Piute Canyon in the spring of 2008, I looked up and saw two peaks forming a matched pair—an immense gateway, like Scylla and Charybdis in the Ionian Basin. The one on the left was Mount Emerson, a big serrated gray pyramid, 13,210 feet in altitude. Across Piute Canyon from it, the other peak was somewhat lower than Emerson, but much more gnarly and interesting. Yes, the two peaks had much the same relationship as Emerson and Thoreau, not just in size and aspect but in position, being close to each other but separated by a huge gulf of air. It was just like that in Concord. The map showed me that the southern mountain was called Peak 12691. I shouted to my companions Oh my God! It's Mount Thoreau! They nodded, used to my mountain babbling, and we hiked on.

*   *   *

That would have been that, but some of my friends are good at organizing things. And there's a tradition of gathering in the Sierra to celebrate its art and culture, starting with the Native Americans and including the Sierra Club high trips and their campfire parties. The year after Mando Quintero and Bill Tweed held their final ABC camp, David Robertson organized a meeting at the University of California's SNARL, the Sierra Nevada Aquatic Research Laboratory, just off Highway 395. Like the ABC crowd, this was another great group. We saw petroglyphs in Owens Valley, ascended one of the Mono Lake volcanic cones, hiked up Rock Creek, and in the evenings listened to short presentations, then partied. Snyder was there, Tom Killion, Eldridge Moores, William Alsup, and many others, among them writer and UCD instructor Laurie Glover. So later on, over coffee in Davis, when I mentioned my Mount Thoreau vision, Laurie said, That's a good idea. We should do that.

Do what? I said.

Do like David's thing at SNARL, she explained. Climb this peak, name it, host a party to celebrate the naming.

Good idea! I said.

This is how actor networks get started: some of the people in them know how to act. David Robertson liked Laurie's idea. Gary liked the idea. Mando liked it. Killion liked it. My hiking friends liked it. In fact everyone who heard about it liked it. No surprise, really; Sierra people need very little in the way of excuses to go up there. The Sierras? Some kind of a thing? Hell yeah.

So a little crowd gathered, and under Laurie's guidance the idea became a project.

I've been talking a lot about names in this book, and I should probably mention that you can't just go naming things in the wilderness. Not officially, not anymore. The Wilderness Act of 1964 states that namelessness is an aspect of wilderness, and since that bill passed, official new names in wilderness areas have become exceedingly rare. All my talk of naming has to do only with the unofficial, informal level, where names keep getting made up and applied.

Because people do like to name things. For sure I do, and I see I'm not alone in this. So it keeps happening, law or no law. I've mentioned R. J. Secor's scores of new names in his guidebook, but new names don't come just from guidebook writers. A national park ranger named Randy Morgenson, a classic Sierra lover, disappeared one day on the job, and his bones weren't found for several years; now the Sierra's ranger community is calling an unnamed peak just west of Mount Russell Mount Randy Morgenson. Then also, Mount Darwin is the highest peak on a long ridge; the next peak down is named Mount Mendel, and now the next peak down from Mendel is being called Mount Stephen Jay Gould. That's a nice tribute, also a kind of visual joke in terms of intellectual history.

These new names get spread on the internet and in guidebooks (caltopo .com includes many of them on its map, as an aid to search-and-rescue operations). Sometimes quotation marks have been put around these names, to show they're informal and not on USGS maps. Maybe all landscape names should be inside quotation marks; or maybe we can just dispense with them. It does seem to be a practice that is going away.

So in that spirit of informal naming, especially in the spirit of Mount Stephen Jay Gould, which is more of an intellectual tribute than a personal memorial, we proceeded with the plan to name Peak 12691 Mount Thoreau.

As we drove south that day, we passed Matterhorn Peak, where Gary had taken Jack Kerouac in 1955, as described in Kerouac's *The Dharma Bums*.

I told Gary and Paul that the summit register on the peak was stuffed with slips of paper, signed by an international crowd, with messages like *God bless you Jack Kerouac you are the greatest ever*, and *Thank you Gary Snyder we love you!!!* It had become a literary monument in a California style — not a statue in a square, or a trophy bestowed by a carefully selected jury, but a thing high in the wind, created by devoted readers making a pilgrimage.

Nice, Gary said.

He himself had returned to the peak with David Robertson and some others in 1986, and on the peak he wrote a poem, which he later inscribed on a note card for someone who wanted to take it to the peak and put it in the summit register. That note card had still been there in 1999, I told him. It had on it, in Gary's calligraphic hand:

On Climbing the Sierra Matterhorn Again After Thirty-One Years

Range after range of mountains
Year after year after year.
I am still in love.

Gary Snyder *4 X 40086, On the summit*

For Mount Thoreau, we were going to take up an old metal card-filing box, an antique that Laurie had found in a thrift shop, to serve as its new summit register. Perfect for the job.

We got to North Lake around three and found some of our companions. Gary joined David and Jeannette Robertson, and they began to settle into the car campground at the trailhead, where they would spend the night and wait for our return. Others had already started up the trail. There were six different parties headed for a rendezvous high in a basin none of us had been in before, which certainly created the possibility for the kind of screw-up we call *a real Ed Lane*, but in fact it worked like a charm. Paul, Darryl, Charlie Schneider, and I made our way up to Lower Lamarck Lake, and there ran into Laurie, who was with Dick Bryan. We left the trail and headed west up into the Wonder Lakes basin, a typical glacial maze; we couldn't see very far ahead, but made our way up toward the rendezvous, a pond marked in advance on all our maps.

Before we got there, we spotted the other parties in our group. They had found a better campsite, and waved us over to it. This was lucky in a couple of ways; first, that we had seen each other, and second, that there was a good campsite. Quite a few high basins are floored by nothing but boulders. But our companions had found a large dry meadow, flanking a pond just below our rendezvous pond.

The wind was blasting, and it took time to put up our tents and find pro-tected spots for stoves. Earlier in the day it had been so windy that Tom Kil-lion had almost been blown off his feet. He and the others in the early group (Michael Blumlein, Hilary Gordon, and Carter Scholz) said that the down-drafts had been striking the pond so violently that "everything smelled like trout." Our little meadow, however, was somewhat protected by the side of a granite bluff.

Around dinner we got to know each other. Michael and Hilary and Carter had come up from the Bay Area a few days before, and spent some time on the east side. Tom had been out on a solo backpacking trip, and hiked into Won-der Lakes basin from above. Laurie and her friend Dick Bryan, who had come all the way from Australia, had started up around midday. Paul and I had driven down with Gary; Darryl had driven over from Marin County, Charlie from LA. We were missing one group that had left North Lake before us, but we knew they were capable wilderness people with their own gear, and would be all right. So we had a nice evening's dinner, then went to bed.

No one slept much in that wind. All night it rushed wildly around the basin, roaring and whooshing in an airy chorus. Often we could hear a blast coming for many seconds before it hit us, pouring over rock edges and through pine needles. Our tents were struck from every direction. One gust tore Dar-ryl's tent apart, and as he happened to be standing outside it at the time, his air mattress flew off into the night, not to be found until the next morning. He had to take refuge under a nest of low trees, in a little John Muir nook, tough-ing it out on a bed of pine needles. In the morning he emerged grinning: no harm done, and one more story to tell.

So that night, nine of us lay in our high camp, three more were somewhere nearby, three were down at North Lake, and one was hiking through the night by headlamp. Back in the Sierra, awake in the dark and the wind. It was the kind of party even Thoreau might have liked.

Friday morning we ate breakfast and took off. We ascended the north wall of our basin, headed up toward the peak's summit plateau. This was the steepest part of the climb, but it was still a walk-up, with the looseness of the decomposed granite our biggest problem. It was the two-steps-up-one-slide-down routine so common on scree. Walking poles are a big help for this kind of work. We slogged up for about an hour.

When we reached the peak's long summit ridge, we sat for a while and watched Chris Woodcock catch up to us. Chris takes night photos in the Sierra, very long exposures on color film, making for uncanny results. He had hiked all night by the light of his headlamp, and taken photos of our peak at dawn from a vantage point across the basin. Despite his big backpack, he was moving fast.

After he joined us, we headed west on the summit plateau toward the peak. There was a little scrambling to be done near the top; the rocks got bigger, but they were more secure as well, so ultimately it was a bit easier than slogging up the sidewall of the basin. There was less and less rock and more and more air, so a surge of adrenaline helped in scrambling up the last broken tilt of speckled granite.

It was a big view. The Central Valley to the west was filled with thick clouds like smashed thunderheads. To the north across Piute Canyon we had a good view of Mount Emerson's gray south face, and the red Piute Crags that extend eastward from it. Looking east to the Owens Valley, we could see across to the White Mountains. To the south stood Mount Darwin and the Palisades. Directly below us to the south was our camp.

There were ten of us on top. We left our new summit register box on a flat spot near the highest point. The notebook inside it had been signed the previous day by Gary ("Send off from North Lake") and David and Jeannette; those of us on the summit signed it there. When the box was secure under a big rock, Chris arranged a group photo. Then we sat for a while longer, looking around. As Gary writes in *Danger on Peaks*, "Snowpeaks are always far higher than the highest airplanes ever get." When you're up on a mountaintop, you see what he means.

The descent was easy. You reverse what you tried for going up, and aim for the sandiest places in order to glissade. There's time to look around and think, and for a while as we dropped, I considered what Thoreau himself would have thought of our project.

The Naming Party, left to right: Dick Bryan, Laurie Glover, Michael Blumlein, Paul Park (above), Chris Woodcock, Hilary Gordon, Carter Scholz, Stan Robinson, Tom Killion, Darryl DeVinney. Photo by Christopher Woodcock.

I doubt he would have approved. For him California meant the gold rush, which he considered a stampede of desperate and confused people. More generally, he often said that traveling was a mistake, an attempt to escape a self that can never be escaped. "I am much traveled in Concord," he replied waspishly to someone who encouraged him to see the world. So, a plaque at Walden Pond, maybe. A peak on the far side of the continent: no way.

But as I glissaded down the slope, it seemed to me also that part of him might be pleased by our gesture, simply as an indication that his books had gotten read. When he died, it looked like his books were going to disappear like pebbles thrown in a pond. That they became famous, and are often loved, might surprise him, but would surely please him too. Why not?

Also, during his travels, limited though they were, his few mountain encounters excited him. His vivid description of an ascent of Maine's Mount

Ktaadn (as he spelled it) is one of the most famous passages in American literature, a wild attempt to express the inexpressible.

Then also, there is a very unusual entry in Thoreau's journal, recording a dream he had about a mountain. It's part of the entry for October 29, 1857, and begins, "There are some things of which I cannot at once tell whether I have dreamed them or they are real." After a paragraph discussing the phenomenological status of what we might call the hypnagogic state, he writes:

> This morning, for instance, for the twentieth time at least, I thought of that mountain in the easterly part of our town (where no high hill actually is) which once or twice I had ascended, and often allowed my thoughts alone to climb. I now contemplate it in my mind as a familiar thought which I have surely had for many years from time to time, but whether anything could have reminded me of it in the middle of yesterday, whether I ever before remembered it in broad daylight, I doubt.

He goes on to describe his climb of this dream peak:

> I steadily ascended along a rocky ridge half clad with stinted trees, where wild beasts haunted, till I lost myself quite in the upper air and clouds, seeming to pass an imaginary line which separates a hill, mere earth heaped up, from a mountain, into a superterranean grandeur and sublimity. What distinguishes that summit above the earthy line, is that it is unhandselled, awful, grand. It can never become familiar; you are lost the moment you set foot there. You know no path, but wander, thrilled, over the bare and pathless rock, as if it were solidified air and cloud.... It is as if you trod with awe the face of a god turned up, unwittingly but helplessly, yielding to the laws of gravity.

This is a typically great Thoreauvian description of traversing the higher reaches of the Sierra Nevada, and it sure doesn't sound like anywhere in the vicinity of Concord, Massachusetts. I'm going to claim he had a dream in which he was climbing our Mount Thoreau.

He added a poem rehashing the experience and reflecting on what it might mean. As good a prose writer as Thoreau was, he was almost exactly that bad a poet, and for the most part he gave up writing poetry in his youth. But here in the privacy of his journal he tried again, and says of his dream mountain:

It is a spiral path within the pilgrim's soul
Leads to this mountain's brow

It would have been a comfort to him to know he was on that path, but how could he be sure? His books failed to sell, and his journal wasn't published until 44 years after his death. Near the end of his life, knowing he was dying, he built a stout cedar box to hold the journals, as if building his own coffin, and gave the box to his sister for safekeeping. He could never know what he had accomplished. But we know. And we know also that his books had a huge influence on John Muir, who did so much to save the Sierra. Muir bought, read, and annotated all 20 volumes of Thoreau's complete works when they were published in 1906; I suspect he was one of the first people ever to have read Thoreau's journal in full. Saving the Sierra Nevada from ecocide depended on Muir; Muir depended on Thoreau. So naming a Sierra peak for Thoreau was very appropriate and satisfying.

Back in our high camp we packed up, ate lunch, took off, and immediately got lost in the maze. Everyone had a different opinion concerning the best route, but we blundered down to the Lamarck Col trail without much loss of time, and dropped quickly to North Lake, where we rejoined the others and drove to Valentine Camp, one of the University of California's field research stations, near Mammoth.

There we finally gathered as one group. We ate dinner in the biggest cabin and got to know each other. No one there knew all the others, as friends had invited friends who had invited friends. It was a fun evening.

After dinner we interrupted the party to celebrate Thoreau with some show-and-tell. We didn't make a big deal of it, but despite that, or maybe because of it, after a while it began to feel a little bit like it had on the mountaintop. Paul started this, another New England writer and outdoorsman, reading aloud the famous Ktaadn passage with just the mix of precision and emotion that Thoreau himself so often displays. It was electrifying, and the other talks kept that going. Michael spoke of Thoreau's youthful self-righteousness, so much like our own. Dick, an economist, offered a funny analysis of Henry's personal economics at Walden Pond (his laundered costs included his mom doing his laundry). David spoke of him as a religious writer. Laurie sang a ballad she had written that day, and we joined in on the chorus. Mando told us about meeting some of Muir's descendants, and of reading Muir's childhood primer that had scrawled on its last page, *Tomorrow we're gone to America*. Darryl reminded us that Thoreau himself had also "named Thoreau," in that he had been christened David Henry, and reversed his given names. Tom Killion showed us slides of his Sierra woodblock prints, and Gary read some new poems, including his Ötzi the Iceman poem. Chris showed us

Mount Thoreau to the left, Mount Emerson to the right, as seen from the east

a selection of his night photos, and I finished by reading Thoreau's journal entry about the dream mountain, which by that point definitely sounded like a Sierra climb.

After that we went back to partying. We had made our contribution to the long tradition of mountain campfire storytelling. As Gary's poems remind us, the tradition is now thousands of years old.

Sunday we cleaned the place up and drove to Lee Vining, where Gary headlined a benefit reading and book sale for the Mono Lake Committee. The crowd in attendance was larger than the entire population of the town.

Those of us still around that evening sat under the portico of our little motel in a light snow, drinking leftover wine and eating crackers and cheese. Later we ate at the town's roadside diner.

Michael and I returned after dinner to chat in the diner's bar and shoot some pool. Thoreau has a magical personality, Michael observed as we played. He casts a spell. People think they know him because he has his reputation, but unless you read him, or read him again, you really don't. One of the great things about this weekend has been reading him again. That was what made last night so special—Paul brought him back, and after that the thing just took off! We went transcendental!

Michael's grin was a beautiful thing.

On that note we closed the bar: 10:00 p.m.

I hope the name Mount Thoreau will stick to Peak 12691. It will if people like it. And maybe they will. Thoreau was a small-town guy, an odd bachelor who took odd jobs, lived mostly with his parents, and spent much of his time wandering in the woods. But he wrote down what he saw and thought in prose so precise and expressive that it manages to jump the gap from mind to mind, and change people.

Surely this jump has partly to do with names. All our nouns are names, and often we name things that are huge or various or intangible. We try to name everything.

Of course that includes our surroundings. In the Alps every big boulder has a name, and it's the same anywhere people have lived for a long time. It was that way on this continent too, but we forgot the names the first peoples used, or never knew them.

Now we've decided as a society to stop putting names on wilderness places. For the most part I like that idea. When we cross a Sierra pass in the late afternoon and look down on a remote trailless basin, sunlight banging off nameless lakes, surrounded by nameless peaks, it does feel wild, as if we were exploring some new empty planet—or as if we were the first people to walk into the New World, 25,000 years ago. It's a thrill.

But in this case, as with several others, I think the name is worth bestowing. Emerson and Thoreau changed us. Now their two peaks will form a gate like the Pillars of Hercules, marking a way into a certain kind of American reality, as well as a bit of Sierra back country. *In wildness is the preservation of the world.*

Thoreau's journal, which so often names things, has been criticized for becoming too particular, too concerned with birds and bugs and plants. He

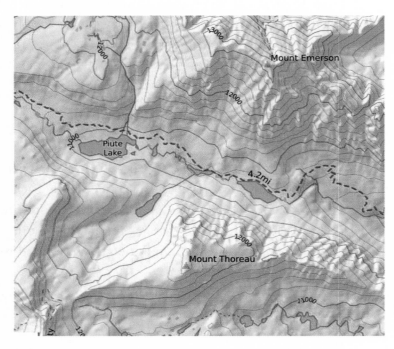

Caltopo.com map showing Mounts Thoreau and Emerson named as such

changed, some say, from a great transcendentalist to just another citizen scientist. It was not a change, but a sharpening of focus. Writing the world became his devotional practice. Now his name stands for that kind of worship. And because of Laurie Glover, and the rest of the Mount Thoreau gang, it now stands in the Sierra too. Seeing the names Emerson and Thoreau on online maps, which now happens, is a sweet thing. Thank you my friends!

And thank you Henry. His famous description of climbing Ktaadn ends like this:

> Here not even the surface had been scarred by man, but it was a specimen of what God saw fit to make this world. What is it to be admitted to a museum, to see a myriad of particular things, compared with being shown some star's surface, some hard matter in its home! I stand in awe of my body, this matter to which I am bound has become so strange to me. I fear not spirits, ghosts, of which I am one, — *that* my body might, — but I fear bodies, I tremble to meet them. What is this Titan that has possession of me? Talk of mysteries! — Think of our life in nature, — daily to be shown matter, to come in contact with it, — rocks, trees, wind on our cheeks! the *solid* earth! the *actual* world! the *common sense! Contact! Contact! Who* are we? *where* are we?

Mount Thoreau by Tom Killion, 2016. This view is from the west, near Piute Pass.

SIERRA PEOPLE (16)

Michael Blumlein

Michael and I knew each other for a long time, maybe 25 years, though neither of us could remember exactly when it was we met. We were both science fiction writers living in the Bay Area, and in the science fiction community everyone tends to meet everyone. We agreed once that it's possible we first met at a party that Ursula Le Guin gathered at her old family place in Napa, which if true would be great.

For years we crossed paths from time to time, and enjoyed talking. One year he brought his family out to Davis for a Fourth of July picnic at our house, and thus we met each other's families, and had a fun time. It was always a pleasure to talk with him.

Then Terry Bisson and his wife Judy Jensen moved from Brooklyn to Oakland, and that made a big difference for a lot of us. Terry likes to gather people, and quickly I was seeing my friends in the Bay Area science fiction community about once a month rather than once a year. We became a little clan. I took Terry and Judy up to Desolation twice, once with Paul Park and Paul's daughter Miranda and my boys, and as I began to socialize with all our Bay Area science fiction friends more, Michael and I often talked about the Sierras. He went to the southern Sierra often with his wife Hilary Gordon, so we shared a love of the range. Once he asked me about Vennacher Col, and I told him we had done it, and had found a sneaky little class 2 route down its west side that could be used instead of the big and obvious class 3 route. He was interested to hear this, and declared that he and Hilary would try it. I was a little worried about that, because only Victor's close examination and

Robin's boldness had found that route for us, but the next time I saw him he said they had loved it, that it went in just the way I had described. That told me they were real Sierra scramblers. Sometime after that, Michael suggested we go up there together, and I said, Good idea! Which it was. This was 2012.

We agreed we should try something new to both of us, and I mentioned I thought there was a class 2 crest crossing between Mounts Haeckel and Wallace, not listed in any of the guidebooks. I had been up the Lake Sabrina side of this pass in snow, with Joe and Terry on a morning jaunt, and that had gone well; up there I had looked down the inside slope, and it had seemed okay. So we agreed to try that way of getting into the Evolution Basin. After that he wanted to go to the Ionian Basin, where he had never been; I was happy to see it again.

Right before we made this trip, the third edition of Secor came out, and in it was listed for the first time "Haeckel-Wallace Col," the very pass I thought I had discovered for myself. I was irritated by this, and thought, not for the first or last time, that the range is a little too well described. Of course here I am contributing to that process.

Anyway off we went, and we had a grand time. Michael took delight in many things, and certainly backpacking in the Sierra was one of them. As he told me, when he and Hilary figured out, on their first trip, that they could leave the trails and wander around up there anywhere, that was it for him; he was hooked for life. I knew that feeling.

On this trip, we snaked our way up toward our own personal crest crossing, and on the second day went over the crest between Wallace and Haeckel, plunging down the immense talus slope on the inside. By the end of that second day we were camped at the outlet of Lake Wanda, high in Evolution Basin. This would have been impossible to do so quickly from any other trailhead—at least for us—I know there are speedsters out there for whom almost anything is possible. But for us, what a great day. Although it's true that the talus slope on the inside of the crest, under Mount Wallace, is so steep and long that I doubted aloud that we could get back up it without a horrid effort. I suggested we should maybe leave by way of Lamarck Col on our way out. No no, said Michael easily. We can get up that no problem! There's harder rock on its west edge, we'll go up that way, it'll be fine.

Okay, if you say so! I said. I was impressed by his confidence.

Over the next three days we crossed Wanda Pass, explored the Ionian Basin, then came back and went over a little draw into the upper reaches of McGee Creek, new to both of us. Every day it rained in a monsoonal way, and we huddled under our tarps, draping them over us like capes and waiting till the rain was done, after which we went on. One day waiting out a storm like this we looked out the air holes of our capes and watched the Muir Trail hikers hike south through the rain like colorful automatons, their giant backpacks encased in rain covers of their own. I laughed at them for carrying such SUVs, and for sticking to their schedules like they were on a time clock, which in a sense they were. Michael was more generous, as so often. They're young and strong, he said. They can handle it. They're enjoying their suffering.

In one of these monsoonal hours, high above Sapphire Lake, we huddled under a boulder that had a two-person-size overhang, and watched the rain turn the glacier-polished rock of upper Evolution Basin into something like glowing white marble, a lovely spectacle seen from such a shelter. We shared our sports autobiographies, and talked about many other things. On our last day, when we were coming back over our pass, it was just as Michael had said; there was harder rock to the left that made it a surprisingly easy ascent. He led the way and we flew over it, and pegged down to the car so fast that we got home that same night, very late, very tired, very happy.

That winter he was diagnosed with stage 4 lung cancer, and from then on he was in the fight of his life. But he didn't just fight; he lived. I've never seen anyone more engaged with life, with people, and with everything one can do in this life to make it good. For six more years he burned like a flare with joy of life, despite the intense suffering he was also going through.

The Sierras stayed part of that life, even though right from the start he agreed to let the surgeons remove much of his right lung. He had never been a smoker, so the cancer seemed capricious at best, but he just shrugged at that, with a little grimace: 10 percent of lung cancers have nothing to do with tobacco, they just happen. So they chopped out two-thirds of his right lung. After that, as he explained (he was a medical doctor), the remaining lobe would expand a little, somewhat filling the emptied space. On he went after these difficult operations. They worked for a while, then they didn't; the cancer returned, and after that all the other therapies came into play, in a rearguard action he never quit fighting.

His first test of his reduced lung capacity came in September of 2014, when we all went up Mount Thoreau. He enjoyed all parts of that project thoroughly, not just getting to the top, but also meeting all the people in that new gang. The affection was mutual. When Laurie later turned the party into a book, Michael's essay "Thoreau's Microscope" was the heart of it. The mountain gave us the book's height; Michael gave us its depth. I was in the audience with Carter when he first read this essay aloud, to Terry Bisson's SF in SF crowd; hearing it for the first time, we leaned into each other weeping. And I was onstage later when he reprised the performance at the Davis Arts Center, so I could see the faces of the audience as he spoke. Never have I seen a crowd so transfixed. Very seldom have life-and-death matters been discussed in public so frankly and with such humor and verve. He did it in Lee Vining too, for the people who came to the 2018 Mono Lake Committee meeting; and at Moe's Books in Berkeley, for the launch party for the book. In all these performances he was our headliner and star. When he was done, nothing more could be said. No one could follow a performance like that. No one, that is, except Gary Snyder, also a member of our group. Gary would follow Michael and finish these group performances by reading, among other things, his Ötzi the Iceman poem, which is also about coming to terms with death. Thus he brought these evenings home in style. The people attending them knew they had been part of something special, something more than just a book event. Laurie Glover, the conductor of our little band, would nod afterward with satisfaction; our dramaturge had created and arranged quite a thing.

In the Sierras, Michael continued to hike. In 2015 he wanted to try the southern Sierras again, but having gone through more therapies, he wasn't sure he could manage it. So first we went to Desolation with Carter and Darryl, and did a sweet little tour of the Crystal Range. He felt fine there, so later that summer he and Carter and I went to the southern Sierras. Alas, it was a big fire year, and the Sierras were smoked out. We drove first to Kings Canyon—closed! It was the Rim fire, and a huge surprise to drive up there at night and have the road to Kings Canyon closed outright. So we slept at Lodgepole in the parking lot, and hoped to go in there, but it was smoky there too. Mineral King the same. Michael needed to avoid smoke for his lungs' sake, so we had to look elsewhere. The young rangers at every station were incredibly helpful—really, young rangers these days are wonderful for their friendliness to hikers—and the one at Mineral King called around and told us the north part of the east side was clear of smoke. We were in the south part of the west side, so he advised us to drive around the south end of the Sierra, rather than wind our way up the western foothills. We did that, a first for all of us—past dry Lake Isabella, then up 395 to just under Tioga Pass, where we slept for a second night on parking-lot asphalt. Next day the ranger station at Tuolumne was jammed with hikers trying to get permits for the Muir Trail, so we left in disgust and drove back to Lee Vining, and found a possible destination on a big 3D map there: Virginia Lakes. Free of smoke. But permits for that area had to be obtained from the Hoover Wilderness station, up in Bridgeport. So we drove up there, our fifth ranger station of the trip, and drove back, and hiked for five days in the Virginia Lakes area, crossing the crest twice and having a wonderful time. We drove home by our usual east-side route, and thus circumnavigated the entire range.

The next year we went up again, Carter and Darryl and Michael and I, to the Tablelands. We camped at Phil Arnot Pond—finally! For Darryl and me it was a case of third time's the charm; and it was charming. A big snowbank overhanging the pond fell in the water the morning we were there and caused a little tsunami that almost washed up into our camp, very exciting. All in all, it was a wonderful tour of that most beautiful plateau. On our way out, Michael led the way up and over Silliman Pass, making a hard push with a big grin on his face. For four years he had thought he might be in his last days, on his last trip; and this one really was his last trip; but he was always delighted to be up there. He knew the flowers and the birds, and loved the hiking, and the life in camp. I'm reminded of one of Thoreau's last letters: "I can report that I am still enjoying myself thoroughly and regret nothing." Michael was like that. If I could learn what he taught by his example, that would be good; but it will be hard.

In 2019, all the therapies stopped working. I saw him often. We took a great day hike in the coastal range in June, up onto the ridge above Cold Canyon, a hike of six miles, including more than a thousand feet up; he led the way, surprising me with his strength. Later in the summer he shifted to hospice assistance, and asked me to come down and see him in San Francisco, and I drove down there in a mournful mood, feeling the end was near. When I got to his house he said let's go for a walk, and told me where to drive us, and after we parked by Golden Gate Park, he led me to the Cliff House and then along the beach trail toward the Golden Gate Bridge, which was invisible in a low cloud, though we could see for miles under the cloud; then up into the city and along its streets for many blocks, to a restaurant he liked. As always when I went for a walk with him in the city, I ended up footsore. We hiked six and a half miles that day, and driving home, amazed and grateful, I thought, Well, he's not finished yet!

But that was our last long walk. I saw him a few more times as he weakened, and he and Carter and I took a walk of about 200 yards in the Berkeley Hills, a couple of weeks before he died. He was the same as ever in conversation, lively and engaged, in the moment. I'm told that on the day before he died, weaker than ever, he insisted on going for a walk, and he and his family took a bus uphill in the city so they could walk downhill to his house, downhill being all he could manage. The next morning he collapsed and died. He had walked right out of this world, dodging by strength of will (and body) the bedridden phase of his ending, which he did not want to go through.

Thus Michael as I knew him. His quicksilver intelligence and warm sympathy, his interest in people and curiosity about them, his friendliness, were shared with many, and they celebrated him in a memorial ceremony in San Francisco, a big affair curated by his daughter into a marvelous retrospective of his life. It was a joy to see how many people regarded him in just the same way I had, as a beloved friend. He gave himself to so many; that was a beautiful thing to see. All those faces.

Shortly after he died, the Mount Thoreau gang had an already scheduled bookstore event in Santa Cruz. We each chose a short passage from his essay in the book, and read it to the crowd without knowing what passages the rest had chosen; it was startling to think all these wildly various sentences came from a single essay, and as we spoke them they became a ramshackle improvised prose poem, impressive and heartfelt. Whether we will ever do more events for that book, I doubt. It may be that with the heart of it gone, it won't be worth it. Carter and I are arranging to get his writing collected properly, and his essay "Thoreau's Microscope" will be in the volume containing his short fiction; and it's there in our Mount Thoreau book too; and also in a small collection of the same name, published by Terry Bisson for PM Press. It's one of his best pieces of writing, a testament to a life well lived.

And I have an idea, inspired by Secor's naming practices. I propose that the

Michael and I, 2012, with Blumlein Pass on the crest above my left ear. Note the talus slope angling down to the right from the pass — 2,000 feet of rock glissade.

pass we crossed together in 2012 be named Blumlein Pass. We're going to have to find a new name for that pass anyway, because as I've explained, Haeckel-Wallace Col is going to have to be replaced, as part of removing Haeckel's name from the range. When that happens, both the pass and the peak are going to need new names. Very few passes are named after the peaks on each side of them anyway, that's the kind of lame idea that gets us the Kern-Kaweah River, and Tulainyo Lake, and other awkward pasted-together misnomers. Passes usually have individual names of their own, and quite a few of them up there now are named for friends of Secor, or for other Sierra people somehow associated with the pass in question. So let it be called Blumlein Pass. No one will ever go over that pass in a happier state of mind.

MOMENTS OF BEING (7)
Late Desolation

A beautiful return to Desolation happened for me in January of 2012, when a dry autumn left the Sierra so free of snow that the road to Wrights Lake was still open, right in midwinter. This was so unusual that I couldn't remember it ever happening, and I was writing *Shaman* at the time, a novel set in the ice age, 30,000 years ago. It struck me that I could do a winter trip starting from Wrights Lake, hope for some insights for my book, and also reach Lake Doris in winter at last! Off I went, driving to the usual parking lot no problem.

I took off toward Rockbound Pass. No snow on the ground, except in a few cracks and shadows here and there, and yet all the water, in streams, ponds, and lakes, was frozen solid. It was weird and gorgeous.

After I crossed the Silver Fork, a white spill of ice in a long granite crack, I took an old phantom trail called the Red Peak Stock Trail up to the crest of the Crystal Range, listening to Brahms's symphonies on my iPod. I don't usually take music to the mountains, I prefer to have just mountain sounds. But being alone, I figured an hour or two of music would be a kind of company. And indeed Brahms was great up there. His Fourth Symphony is the perfect soundtrack for Desolation in winter, as it is for anything sternly majestic.

On the way up to the crest I caught a view of Top Lake, seeing it for the first time since I had passed it with Lisa, 31 years before. It was frozen and white, while the rock all around it was free of snow—startling to see. There were little pockets of snow tucked here and there by the wind, but by and large the Crystal Range was still entirely a rockscape. Low light, sun in the south even at noon. Silence. I was the only person in all of Desolation, it seemed, and even if it wasn't literally true, it was true on the Crystal Range, and that's what mattered. When I got a view down onto Lake Lois, I saw another frozen white plate inlaid into the rock. Down there was the site of my first night in the Sierra, but that barely crossed my mind; the uncanny present filled my thoughts. I hiked south on the ridge and came to the drop to Rockbound Pass. It didn't look too bad. On the left was a patch of manzanita that Bonin and I had gotten caught in long ago; his raucous laughter still rang in my ears. I skirted it grinning at the memory, and dropped right onto the Monolith, as we had named it in 1975. Right in the pass a tall boulder stands on end in a way that reminded us of the mysterious black plinth in *2001: A Space Odyssey*. In the spring of 1990 I had hiked in from Wrights Lake to this monolith with Terry, carrying baby David in his usual backpack. David had been enthralled, head swiveling like an owl's to take it all in, and when we came to the Monolith he regarded it closely, then reached out to touch it when I did. Cosmic!

On this day I stopped to touch it again, and headed on. On the south side of Rockbound Pass I climbed the other side of the pass's deep U, up onto the next section of the Crystal Range, my favorite road in the sky, site of my first ridge run with Terry and Victor. Then past the campsite where Lisa and I had been dive-bombed by owls.

Farther on, in a flat spot on the ridge where we had also often camped, I set up my tarp, expecting January cold. I had with me both of my one-pound Western Mountaineering sleeping bags, so I was pretty confident I would stay warm. Both bags together almost filled the space under my tarp. I kept my head out to see the stars.

I had carried a Duraflame fire log with me the whole day, six pounds of artificial log made of paraffin and sawdust, great at home in the fireplace. I got it set on a big flat rock next to my tent, settled in, and set it on fire. It burned like crap, and there was a wind from the west that gusted and swirled such that the log's poisonous smoke kept washing over me. I couldn't move the burning log, and I was too lazy to move my tent; and if I put out the log's fire somehow, I would have to carry the black remnant away with me. No recourse but to let it burn down to ash, and imagine that my nausea was from some god-awful shaman's brew. I scribbled some notes for *Shaman*, little observations that got into the book later. Finally the shitty fire went out and I slept pretty well, enjoying my moments awake: back in the Sierra again, on my own. I've never done as much solo hiking as I would have liked. This was a shaman night, my novel was coming along, told to me it seemed by the Third Wind and mostly out of my hands; and here I was in one of my favorite places in the world, in midwinter. I had finally gotten to Lake Doris in the winter! Which hadn't even occurred to me as I passed it! But it pleased me that night, as I recalled our old goal from our youth.

Next morning I checked a thermometer I had brought along: 22 degrees. Not so bad. My two sleeping bags had been fine for warmth.

That day I hiked over Peak 9441 and down to Island Lake. As I dropped down the south-facing slope, which my son Tim had named the Wall of Barad-dur, I was stunned at the sight: the lake had frozen, but then a hard wind must have broken that layer of ice into shards, after which the lake had refrozen. So there were two colors, white and gray, in a pattern like a jigsaw puzzle, amazing to see. It was like a rebus of my Desolation life, a pattern made of fragments. I kept stopping to look at it. I didn't want that descent to end.

Island Lake, Desolation, in the snowless January of 2012

It did, of course, and then I walked right out onto the lake, after testing the ice carefully. You could have driven a truck onto it. So I walked out to all the little islands in Island Lake that we had never swum or rafted to before, checked them out for fire rings, found some and was pleased at that (archaeology!), and then left the lake. Down to Twin Lakes, also frozen, and then down the familiar trail to Wrights Lake. Sometimes big lobes of ice slurped over the trail and were so slippery I had to avoid them, but this particular trail was known to me step by step (the little ledge where I had tripped while running and turned to crash into the ground backpack first; the stretch where the older kids always left M&M's for the younger kids to find) and all the plain stone, lined by snow and ice—the frozen waterfalls and creeks—all so beautiful. My place, my home, frozen in time.

It was three years later when I went up there again with Michael and Darryl and Carter, to test out Michael's remaining lung capacity. This time my old backyard felt melancholy. I still knew every inch of it. The big dead tree that has always towered over the intersection of the two Twin Lakes was still standing—surely someday that giant will fall. I wandered through our old campsites, looked into that nest of juniper where we once found a plastic toy lost the year before—seemed like I might find another one. We crossed the little outlet dam at Island Lake, and I recalled chasing Tim across the dam and knocking him into the water. Those had been such lively, lovely years.

But on that trip with Michael, it was just memories. Ghosts filled the campsites, and as we made the usual loop on the Crystal Range, ghost routes. I saw all the places where Tim and I had slept side by side. David and Anna's spots were still the same. It was all the same, of course. Which should have been comforting. But it felt like the touch of a ghost. That there was an even older reincarnation of mine, back there behind the family years, was hard to remember, harder to feel. Clearly I was getting old. My nostalgia was heavier than my backpack. Sharp pangs of love and loss; I had been so happy here for so long, and so crazy here, for long before that. This time—just age. Age and exile. This place was no longer mine. A sudden fear that this feeling would strike me in the southern Sierra pierced me, I exclaimed God forbid! And I suppose it won't happen, the southern Sierra being so much bigger than life. Even when I'm passing through basins I've been in before down there, everything still feels new with discovery, and vividly present. Desolation, no. Somehow, more than ever, it's been well named.

But it's still beautiful. Now, when I go back again, Michael too will be a ghost. His delight in the Sierra will always suffuse the land for me. I will be older still. But—what can you do? That my entire life has included the Crystal Range has been one of my greatest blessings. I'll keep going there; maybe this weekend; and hope never to lose the way.

All this makes me think of Wang Wei's great ode to paradises lost, "Source of the Peach Blossom Stream." There are at least 20 translations of this old poem into English — this is mine:

"Source of the Peach Blossom Stream," by Wang Wei, written 718 CE

Wandering we came on a swift river.
Clear water, granite pebble bottom.
Riffles and rapids and long still pools,
Willows hanging over the banks,
Big fish tucked in the shadows,
And floating down like little boats,
Peach blossoms. Lots of them.

We climbed upstream to find the trees
Dropping these petals of floating pink.
The river narrowed, rose into a defile.
We had to clamber, one side then the other,
Feet wet at one crossing, hands on rock looking down.
Then the gorge opened and we were in a high valley.

Fields of grain, neat houses, and yes: peach trees.
They lined the banks, dropping their blossoms
On the slow meander of a little river.
People came out to greet us:
Where are you from? What's the news?
They fed us and showed us a bower to sleep in.

These people were peaceful, calm, kind.
The valley was fertile and full of animals.
We stayed until we saw what it was: a good place.
To live here would be fulfillment.
So we said to each other, let's get our families
And bring them back. Let's move here.

We left that place and picked a way
Down the narrow gorge, back into the world.
Traveled home and made our accounting,
Convinced who we could to go back with us.
Off we went with packs on our backs,
Back to the place where the peach blossoms fell.

We could not find it. Somehow the hills were
Not the same. No such river where we thought.
Back and forth we made a search, back and forth
But nothing. Different streams, different lands.
That place in space was a moment in time:
You can never find your way back.
Search all your life you will only despair.
Precious beyul, how did we find you?
And where did you go?

THE SWISS ALPS (3)
Seeing Meru

Thinking of time and death reminds me of climbing. My fascinated distaste for it rested like a boulder in my mind, from the time I climbed the Matterhorn until I saw the movie *Meru*, made by the climber Jimmy Chin, who climbed a Himalayan peak of that name with two friends, Conrad Anker and Renan Ozturk, and then made a movie about it.

Chin and his wife Elizabeth Chai Vasarhelyi later made another great movie, *Free Solo*, about Alex Honnold; but it was *Meru* that came first, and was the one that changed me. I went with Lisa to see it at Davis's Varsity Theatre, and as I watched those three friends climb a ridiculously steep spire in the Indian part of the Himalayas, and listened to them talk to the camera in interviews with each other, I began to understand something that all the written accounts of the great British climbers of the '70s had not been able to articulate for me on the page. It wasn't that the three climbers in the film were more eloquent than the Brits; it was more a matter of seeing them talk, and then seeing them climb.

When the movie was over I walked through the dark empty streets of downtown Davis, clutching Lisa's hand and trying to express to her what had hit me so hard. I was quivering, I could barely talk. They can't help themselves, I said. They don't *choose* to do that stuff. It's just in them. You don't get to choose!

Like so often, Lisa suggested. We are who we are.

I could only nod. Those guys were obviously possessed. That activity, climbing, was what they lived for. So, okay, they often had wives and children, and they always had parents. And they were risking their lives in ways that meant a pretty hefty percentage of them were going to get killed by accident and die young. But it wasn't in their power to be different just because of that. They had to do it anyway, because that's the way they were. They were climbers, simple as that. Not many people are, but if you are, you are. And if you're possessed with a project like that, then the difficulties and dangers don't matter.

I had been so judgmental. I had thought climbers were irresponsible fools, getting their jollies in ways that could make their partners widows, or occasionally widowers (Alison Hargreaves left behind a husband and two kids), and would often leave their children without a parent, and always leave their parents without a child. It was a strong opinion, and my own little adventure on the Matterhorn had only reinforced it. When the *Into Thin Air* events happened on Everest in the late '90s, and it became clearer than ever that lots of people were dying for an idea—that "the tallest" as an idea meant more to them than actually being in the mountains—more even than their lives—I was repulsed, and confirmed in my judgments. And indeed I still think that hiring guides to lead you up a mountain, just to say you climbed it, is a stupid thing to do—on Everest, or the Matterhorn, or anywhere on Earth. Even sitting on a raft going down the rapids of the Grand Canyon while an expert rows the boat, which I just finished doing, strikes me as kind of a waste of wilderness time.

But real climbers, like those three in the film? What they said to the camera had me rethinking everything, in a furious whirlwind of thought. What is life for? Why are we the way we are? What possesses some of us to want to do something so badly that we risk our lives to do it?

One thing I was able to say to Lisa, later that night, was that it's a beautiful thing when a work of art can hit you so powerfully that it changes you, right then and there. Rilke again, looking at that statue of Apollo: *You must change your life.* That kind of reorientation. I had an immense feeling of gratitude to Jimmy Chin in particular, for clarifying a thing that had been troubling me for 40 years.

And what about Terry, and his compulsion to hike 20 mountain miles every day? For that matter, what about me? Why did I love the Sierra so much? I felt lucky to feel such a passion, and indeed it seems clear to me that not having such a passion would be a sad thing, might even constitute a kind of existential crisis. Wanting something is a kind of meaning.

So, these climbers; the people who love them have to maybe sigh, like the wife in the movie, Jennifer Lowe-Anker, who had been married to one climber, Alex Lowe, who died in an avalanche, and then later married Conrad Anker, her dead husband's good friend. It would be easier if I were into cowboys, she joked. But she understood about climbers, no doubt better than most. It was fundamental to who they were. So you might lose them. It's as if they were born with a congenital handicap of some odd kind, which meant they only had a 50-50 chance of living to the age of 50—after which, if they survived, they were likely to live a normal span. You had to hold your breath, and love them, and hope they got to 50, after which you could relax a little. And if you lost them, that was what could always have happened, and this time it did, and all you could say then was you loved them while you had them, and were lucky to know them while they lived, but their condition got them. Grieve and celebrate, and live on.

That would be hard. You can wander the cemetery in Zermatt and see that a lot of British parents had to put up gravestones there in the Victorian era, after their sons went from Oxford or Cambridge to the Matterhorn and fell off it and died. *Here lies our beloved foolish son, who loved the mountains more than life itself.* The pain is still etched in those stones a hundred years later, and it will stay there until the stones are washed bare by rain. If you didn't get why they had gone up there, it would feel like such a waste. Even if you understood, it would still be something you would have to struggle to accept. Pete Starr's mom, in Berkeley, was said never to be the same after he fell and died. It must be so hard to lose a child to a game. I still find the idea repellent. Is it the hunger I saw on my friend Steve's face that causes the disgust I feel when anyone risks their life for fun? But if climbing is some kind of condition of consciousness, then when you have it, you can't change it.

I'm very glad I don't have that condition. I don't suffer or glory in that condition. I love the mountains without having the slightest urge to climb. One reason to write this book is to speak for mountain rambling and scrambling as a safe and joyful way of being in the mountains. But if you have that urge, it seems you're stuck with it. Or blessed with it; because having a project is the best thing in the world. And what I think about it doesn't matter. People are who they are.

ROUTES (6)
The High Route

Steve Roper's *Sierra High Route* is a great idea; also a classic of Sierra literature; and most important, a wonderful hike. Recognizing that the Muir Trail, with all its admirable qualities, was designed as a trail for people traveling with pack animals, Roper suggested that a higher cross-country route across roughly the same terrain would provide more adventurous hikers with a better experience than the Muir Trail. And it's true. His route begins in Kings Canyon and runs north to Twin Lakes, just outside the northern border of Yosemite National Park, thus about 175 miles, all of them great.

The first section of his route follows a path reconnoitered and taken by the Sierra Club's high trip of 1934, and this part in itself, after rising quickly from Roads End in Kings Canyon, makes a wonderful traverse of the north side of the Monarch Divide and the Cirque Crest (really two names for the same massif) before dropping onto Marion Lake. The final chute that slices down through the cliff backing Marion Lake still displays the switchbacks cut by the Sierra Club for their nimble mules and horses 85 years ago; kind of shocking to think of cutting a trail for a single trip, but at least the trail is still useful to hikers today. And it was a different time when they did it, with a different wilderness ethos.

Roper's High Route continues north from Marion Lake in an always interesting way, staying above the Muir Trail to the east or west. There are some sections where he uses the Muir Trail itself, which seems too easy, and other sections where he includes class 3 moments, which can feel too hard. Roper apologizes for the class 3 bits, but considers them necessary to keep a clean line. He comes to this project as a Yosemite wall climber, so class 3 to him is really just the way climbers run down from peaks. Those of us for whom class 3 represents trauma may find these points on the way unfortunate. Most of the time Roper provides class 2 detours for these spots, or you can find them yourself; in any case it's a great line, and having hiked most of it, I applaud the conception and the execution. Roper has done many good things as a Sierra person and writer, indeed he is one of the major figures in the history of Sierra Nevada climbing and writing, but this route is definitely his crowning achievement.

It's really the copycats who are beginning to bug me. These are mostly online productions, and of course there's all kinds of things online, but to see the way people construct and talk about these other high routes is to see a good idea get reified and turned into a Thing. Just as doing the Muir Trail, or climbing Whitney, or Everest for that matter, has become a Thing in the culture at large, Roper's High Route is now something you can say you did, as if it were more than any other good backpacking trip. So now online there's a High Route South, starting at Kings Canyon and heading south down the Great Western Divide (an excellent idea), and various Yosemite High Routes, sometimes offered as a set of marked maps and GPS positions and instructions, for a fee. There is even a book called *Sierra Crest Route*, which I feel should have nothing but blank pages, as the title tells the whole story all by itself. Just walk the crest—can't get higher than that!

Reification happens when a thought or action becomes regarded as an object, or a pseudo-object, or a commodity, at which point no more thinking needs to be done. In this case, my advice is that you look at the maps and consult the guidebooks, and make up your own high route. It will be more fun that way when you hike it. Roper would approve.

Can anyone do this? Yes. There are no secrets to the process. Here, I'll do one right now, as an example of how it's done. We'll call it the Robinson High Route, trademark pending. The rest of this book will serve as warning that you might not actually want to try this one, although to tell the truth, I think it would be fabulous.

For sure I'll avoid class 3 entirely. I'll add also that I'm going to try for the least amount of trail possible, except at the very beginning and end of the hike. It will be almost purely cross-country. That means not focusing on staying high so much as on staying trailless. I'll describe it from north to south, starting at South Lake on the east side and ending at Wolverton on the west side. Extensions to both north and south could easily be added, but I'll leave that as an exercise for the reader.

So: Start at South Lake and go up to Bishop Pass on the trail, because there's no good alternative in that stretch. But from Bishop Pass, leave the trail immediately and trend around under Mount Agassiz to the east, to Thunderbolt Pass. This is a common climbers' route and follows a wonderfully clean line, losing very little altitude between the two passes while providing great cross-country hiking and superb views the entire way. Thunderbolt Pass offers a fantastic close-up angle on the Palisades; some of the deep vertical clefts carved into that mighty wall are not visible as such from any other perspective.

The Palisades from Thunderbolt Pass

Alternative route: drop down Dusy Basin to Knapsack Pass, and cross it to the Barrett Lakes.

From Thunderbolt Pass, hang a right and wend your way down the drainage straight to the Barrett Lakes. Again very clean beautiful hiking. From the Barrett Lakes, continue down the exit stream all the way to Palisade Creek, far below, near Deer Meadow. This is a plunge down the side of a big canyon wall, but no problem — except for the alder grove right at Palisade Creek, good luck with that. When stuck, curse loudly. It helps to free you.

Alternative route: go from the Barrett Lakes over Potluck Pass, and drop down Glacier Creek to Deer Meadow. This was the route used by Joe LeConte and his companions in 1904 when they climbed North Palisade.

From Deer Meadow, ascend Cataract Creek to Amphitheater Lake, both named by Joe LeConte and friends, during their first trip to the Palisades.

Above Amphitheater Lake to the south there's an obvious notch usually filled by snow, best called Observation Pass. This is the one that looks so awful from below but isn't as bad as it looks (photo on page 142); maybe call it Foreshorten Pass? Make your way up to it.

From Observation Pass, you traipse down into Dumbbell Basin. Again named by Joe LeConte and friends, for the shape of the lakes there. Wonderful walking gets you all too quickly to Dumbbell Pass, and over into the Lakes Basin. Camp at Lower Dumbbell Lake if you can.

An alternative: Back down at Deer Meadow on Palisade Creek, go west on the Muir Trail for 1.5 miles, then ascend the creek that rises to Mount Shakspere's west shoulder — his left shoulder if he is facing north, as he seems to be. Threading some little slots atop that shoulder will drop you into Dumbbell Basin lower down, and you can continue on as described.

(I thought Mount Shakspere was perhaps named by some Baconian or Oxfordian who believed WS was just the front man for the real writer of the plays — a silly idea, quite popular a century ago. But no, it was just the namer's bad spelling! Though WS himself spelled it that way in a signature or two, so it can serve as a little history lesson.)

Back to the upper part of Lakes Basin. Cross Cartridge Pass, thus making use of one of the best of the phantom trails. Drop into the canyon of the South Fork, still on that phantom trail. Once at the river, struggle up the unnamed creek just to the west of Bench Lake. From there you can get over Arrow Pass, and you're into the unnamed basin that crosses the Arrow Peak massif.

It should be added, before we go on, that from Observation Pass you can run up to Observation Peak, and from Arrow Pass you can run up to Arrow Peak. Also, speaking of peaks, the Secor guidebook currently lists Cataract Peak, which overlooks Amphitheater Lake from the southeast, as being 16,640 feet tall. What a great typo! Imagine if it were true! (It probably should be 11,640.)

Don't leave the Arrow Peak massif by way of Arrow Creek, because it's a class 3 waterfall; instead keep heading south and cross a little ridge, then plunge south on the east bank of the steep little creek that falls to the Woods Creek trail, a mile or two east of the confluence of Woods Creek with the South Fork. Once you're down to the Woods Creek trail, hike east a mile on the trail, then ascend the course of the creek that drains the northwest flank of Mount Clarence King. Going over King Col from the north will mean a slippery climb up a sandy chute. But if free of snow and ice, it will still be class 2. Hold on to the left sidewall of this chute to aid your ascent! You'll be cursing me at this point, I predict.

Atop King Col you can stroll down a gentle ramp into Gardiner Basin. When you reach Gardiner Creek, make your way up to Gardiner Pass. Gardiner Pass used to have a trail over it, so here you'll be hiking on a nearly vanished phantom trail, and can make your way down to Charlotte Lake and then to Vidette Meadows. Cross the Bubbs Creek Trail here and head up Vidette Creek between the great pillars of East Vidette and West Vidette, on another phantom trail, up to Deerhorn Pass. Cross that class 2 pass, unusual in that its south side is harder than its north side. Descend into the glacial moraine boulder hell under the wall of the Great Western Divide, also called the Kings-Kern Divide.

Here you're in trouble. Choices must be made, because there is no good way over this divide. First choice is the very steep and slippery north side of Harrison Pass, the one Terry and I declined to descend. It may be easier going up it, especially if dry. Or you could ascend Lucys Footpass, just to the west of Mount Ericsson, also very steep and rubbly. Or perhaps the next pass around the bend, Millys Footpass, which we did once. It has a brief class 3 section in the cleft at the very top, but the cleft is so narrow it seems like if you fell you would get wedged in it before you died. Does that make it class 2? Maybe not.

A fourth alternative, located between Lucys and Millys, is a pass listed only on the internet, called Little Joe's Pass, very near the place where Clarence King and Richard Cotter recrossed this divide when returning from their climb of Mount Tyndall. Research this pass if you want, because one way or another you need to get over this divide. Given that there are four possibilities within a stretch of three miles, something should work, even though all four are tough. While writing this book, I went to take a look at all these passes from their tops, having come at them from the south, in the hope that one of them would look good for once. No. But it did seem to me that going up Lucys Footpass would work. It did for Lucy and Bolton Brown in 1896, and surely we can be as tough as they were. Maybe. I can add that the topmost section of Little Joe's Pass looked horrible. Be advised.

For now, provisionally, and good luck to you whatever you decide, I'm advising Lucys Footpass, or, if it's completely dry, Harrison Pass.

However you do it (and you could go up Bubbs Creek to Forester Pass on trail, and bypass the problem entirely), you end up in the upper Kern. Wonderful place, expansive and variegated, the Sierra's pocket Mongolia. Head south. Eventually you'll need to cross the Great Western Divide again, but for a while you're in an easy vast basin with use trails all over. Go by W Lake, as we called it, to the use trail rising up into Milestone Basin, and head for Midway Mountain. I think Midway Mountain is the easiest way to get over this part of the Great Western Divide, even though it's the highest point on the whole divide; it's a peak with broad sturdy shoulders. You could also cross at Thunder Pass, or Midway Pass, or Milestone Pass, but these, though lower, are all much steeper than the east and west sides of Midway Mountain.

From the great view on top of Midway Mountain you can see the route to come, far down to the west. Glissade down the west shoulder of Midway all the way to the big lake below, then down again to Colby Lake. There you're on trail again, but only for a couple of miles of descent into Cloud Canyon, where you leave the trail and turn uphill, past some old mining equipment from Judge Wallace's mine. Continue up the canyon on his phantom trail, built for burros carrying loads of copper ore. This abandoned trail, still pretty well incised into the landscape, will lead you up to Coppermine Pass.

Remember that there are two Coppermine Passes. The one I recommend goes right over Peak 12345. That's where the old Judge Wallace trail goes, and the trail is still semilegible, and again, the slopes of the peak are less steep than the nearby passes. From the top of Peak 12345, drop down the west ridge on the ever-more-obvious trail, then you'll see the copper-bearing knob below to the right, high on the headwall of Deadman Canyon.

From the hilarious copper mine you join the "High Ski Route," and hike west over Horn Col, past Lonely Lake, over Pterodactyl Pass, and up to Phil Arnot Pond; then west across the Tablelands, and down to the Pear Lake ranger hut. From the hut, five miles of CCC trail takes you down to the big parking lot at Wolverton.

And there you have it! Oh my God! The Robinson High Route is fantastic! Almost as good as your own will be!

If anyone actually tries mine, I can guarantee you will curse me. The up and down on it is severe. Never a break. But I encourage you to do it anyway. You will also thank me. I've hiked almost every section of it, and I want to do the small bits of it I haven't yet gotten to, in particular Shakspere's Left Shoulder. I know it's continuously beautiful, and never harder than class 2 at any point, although admittedly on the brutality scale it might hit 11 once or twice.

Totals: about 80 miles, with about 57,000 feet of ups and downs.

AN ANNOTATED SIERRA BIBLIOGRAPHY

The Sierra literature is not huge. I've got a stand-alone bookcase dedicated to it, and it's full to overflowing, but that bookcase holds a good percentage of all the books on the topic. From this collection I'll list some books I've enjoyed that have helped me to understand the Sierras better.

I'll start with my favorite eight, then go through the rest by categories: history, guidebooks, art and photography, memoirs, and general aids to understanding. I'll end with a brief description of how the Sierras have gotten into my own books.

MY ESSENTIAL EIGHT

One
Exploring the Highest Sierra, **by James G. Moore, Stanford University Press, 2000**

This is the best geology guide to the southern Sierra, and it also contains an excellent pocket history of the human presence. It's particularly good on early Sierra maps, and Moore is the only writer to have thought to map John Muir's southern Sierra hiking trips. I only wish the book extended its area of focus all the way up to the north end of Yosemite, because I have some questions, and would love to read Moore's answers. But what he's got here is a lifetime's work as it is, and a superb education in the Sierra.

Two

The High Sierra: Peaks — Passes — Trails, **by R. J. Secor, Mountaineers Books, 2009**

This is the Bible for many Sierra people, or perhaps just the dictionary. The history is minimal, and there are things to complain about, but it's indispensable if you're planning to go up there.

Much of it is necessarily based on other people's work, although Secor saw a lot of the range himself. His book is filled with photos, route maps, and information beyond just class ratings. He's not as consistent as Steve Roper is, in the older *The Climber's Guide to the High Sierra,* and he's given some class 3 ratings to class 2 passes, rather inexplicably; possibly he, or whoever reported that pass to him, somehow misplayed the line. It happens.

Now that he has died, I hope Mountaineers Books will keep his book in print, and find someone good to become the next editor. For now, it's a great aid for planning trips. They do need to fix that typo listing a 16,400-foot peak.

Along with Theodore Solomons and Chester Versteeg, Secor may have bestowed more Sierra names than anyone else. For sure he's in the top ten. But since I have quite a few ideas about names myself, I guess I should think of him as more of an inspiration than an irritation.

Three

The Laws Field Guide to the Sierra Nevada, **by John Muir Laws, Heyday Books, 2007**

There are lots of Sierra field guides, some specialized, some general, but this is the best both for beauty and usefulness. Laws as an artist knows how to bring out the features that help people identify a species; his paintings are realistic, abstracted to help understanding, and beautiful. The organization and key systems are very clear. It's wonderful that the Sierras have such a great guide.

Four

***Sierra High Route: Traversing Timberline Country,* by Steve Roper,
Mountaineers Books, 1997**

The most important of Roper's many fine Sierra books, as I've said.

Roper is the best historian of the Sierras. Francis Farquhar, a Sierra Club
leader and longtime editor of the *Bulletin,* and also a good early climber, and
definitely a Sierra lover, strikes me as stodgy and dull in his history of the
range. Roper tells all the stories better. And he himself was a Yosemite wall
climber in his youth, so his memoir, *Camp 4,* is a fine document of that era in
climbing history.

Early on, he accepted the task of updating and enlarging the Sierra Club's
little "totebook," *The Climber's Guide to the Sierra Nevada.* This was a needed
enlargement of the earlier guidebooks that the club put out. Roper's class ratings for passes and peaks are very consistent. You can trust his judgment.

Best of all is this book describing his High Route, a major addition to the
Sierra discussion and an inspiration for many a great trip.

Five

***High Sierra: John Muir's Range of Light,* by Phil Arnot, Wide World
Publishing/Tetra, 1996**

Arnot's is not a comprehensive guidebook, but it is full of great ideas. It's ama-
teurish in its publication, and overlooked compared to Secor and Roper, but I
put it in my top eight because of Arnot's spirit of adventure, his deep experience, and his ideas about how to explore the Sierras — essentially, how to enjoy
them. He's a good photographer and an expressive writer, but the heart of his
achievement comes in his encouragement to hikers to try new things.

His book is organized around the special places he urges you to visit, and
the unusual things you can try that will create intense experiences. Sleep on a
peak's top. Camp out on Christmas Day. Go and see a spring flood. Hike up
the side of some steep endless canyon wall, just to get into a tiny hanging valley with a single pond in it, which afterward will be yours forever. Also, look

for the hardest bushwhacks, the wildest canyons, and go do them! *Go where no one else has gone*—not that this will be literally true, for the most part, but it will certainly feel true in many places.

He flew bombers in World War II, then in the '60s became an antiwar protester. He also protested the American involvement in Nicaragua in the 1980s. He led groups into the Sierra for many years, and made trips of his own as well. He published books of photographs, and guidebooks to the Marin mountains, and to Yosemite, and this one that I like the most, to the southern Sierra.

Well into his nineties he was hiking a lot. I've just learned he died in April of 2021, at age 97. He was an inspiration to many. For sure that pond that he recommends at the northeastern tip of the Tablelands should be named in his honor.

Six

The High Sierra of California, by Gary Snyder and Tom Killion, Heyday Books, 2002

The combination of Killion's Sierra woodblock prints, Snyder's Sierra back-packing journals, Killion's selections from Muir's writing, and Killion's brief history of Snyder's Sierra life, makes this one of the great beauties in Sierra literature, maybe the finest of all in terms of quality of image and text, both individually and in combination.

Seven

Challenge of the Big Trees, by Larry M. Dilsaver and William C. Tweed, Sequoia Natural History Association, 1990

The best history of the southern Sierra. The authors start with a good history of the Native American presence in that part of the range, then move on to a detailed account of the formation of the national parks, and what Sequoia and Kings Canyon have meant for the national park system, and also for our sense of what wilderness is, and how we should treat it.

Eight

Land Above the Trees, **by Ann H. Zwinger and Beatrice E. Willard, Harper and Row, 1972**

This beautiful book is for me *the* great explanation of the living ecologies at tree line and above. Its principal example of this biome is the Colorado Rockies, but it often turns to the high Sierra as well. One of my favorite books, and crucial for my terraformed Mars in my Mars trilogy.

HISTORY

Early Days in the Range of Light, **by Daniel Arnold, Counterpoint Press, 2009**

A great idea for a book, and well executed. Arnold retraced the climbs of the earliest Sierra climbers, while trying to use only their level of equipment. He also provides short biographies of the climbers. His portrait of Bolton Brown is particularly moving, but they are all good. One of the best histories.

Splendid Mountains: Early Exploration in the Sierra Nevada, **edited by Peter Browning, Great West Books, 2007**

To his excellent books on Sierra place names, Peter Browning adds this compilation of early high Sierra explorations, including a rare essay by Frank Dusy and accounts by Theodore Solomons and others that were not published in the *Sierra Club Bulletin.*

Tales Along El Camino Sierra, **volumes 1–3, by David and Gayle Woodruff, El Camino Sierra Publishing, 2017–2019**

The Woodruffs pack a lot of great stories into these three books, rediscovering many interesting people and places from the past of Owens Valley. It seems like the Woodruffs could continue for several more volumes, and I hope they do.

Norman Clyde: Legendary Mountaineer of California's Sierra Nevada, **by Robert C. Pavlik, Heyday Books, 2008**

A short biography that fills in what Clyde never wrote down.

Missing in the Minarets: The Search for Walter A. Starr, Jr., **by William Alsup, Yosemite Association, 2000**

This book functions as a biography of sorts for Pete Starr, and to a certain extent for his father, an early Sierra Club stalwart. It should be read together with *The Last Season,* listed below, to get an impression of what search-and-rescue operations were like in the 1930s and then the early 2000s. And these two lost Sierra people, Pete Starr and Randy Morgenson, were both in that class of persons who fell in love with the range and changed their lives to follow that passion. That they died in the Sierra was a combination of bad luck and the fact that they spent all their time up there, so chances were good that when they died they would be there. Pete Starr's *Starr's Guide to the John Muir Trail and the High Sierra Region* is a memorial volume assembled by his father from his unfinished notes, and Starr senior also gave a bequest to the Sierra Club to keep the book in print in perpetuity. New printings keep appearing, and the map included with the book is useful for seeing the whole range as Pete Starr saw it, because he marked his favorite cross-country routes with faint dotted lines.

The Last Season, **by Eric Blehm, Harper Perennial, 2007**

A really excellent account of the search for Randy Morgenson after his disappearance in the Sierra in 1996, while he was working there as a national park ranger. It's a moving biography of Morgenson, and a great description of search-and-rescue procedures as currently practiced. A detective story on a couple of levels at once, both physical and what you might call psychological, or spiritual. So maybe this is another exploration in psychogeology.

I read online that Blehm is working on a book about David Steeves. This would be a great thing to read. Steeves was flying a navy trainer jet over the Sierra when something in it broke and he had to bail out. He parachuted down onto a high bench just east of the Black Giant and on landing broke both ankles. It was May and the range was snowbound; he had to crawl down the Middle Fork of the Kings River to Simpson Meadow (about 20 miles) using his parachute as a sleeping bag at night. This took almost two weeks. At Simpson Meadow he came on a closed back country ranger cabin, broke in, and found some food. A few weeks later some early horse packers found him. He was first hailed as a hero, then accused of giving his jet to the Russians and making up his Sierra story (it was the 1950s). He quit the navy and died in a private plane crash before Boy Scouts found the cockpit canopy of his trainer, with registration number, lying in Dusy Basin in the 1970s. It's an amazing story, and if *The Last Season* is any indication, Blehm will tell it well.

King Sequoia, **by William C. Tweed, Heyday Books, 2016; also** *Granite Pathways: A History of the Wilderness Trail System of Sequoia and Kings Canyon National Parks,* **Sequoia Parks Conservancy, 2021**

Complementing his first book with Dilsaver, Tweed's continuing histories are great on explaining how the SEKI national parks got the way they are. Many important lessons are here in his descriptions of how the actor networks that protected the Sierra came together, and also how that work will never end. And his new book on the history of the trails fills a niche in the record that no one else has explored.

Water and Power, **by William L. Kahrl, University of California Press, 1983**

This is the best account I know of the LA water grab from the Owens Valley, and some of the subsequent fallout from that event.

Passing Strange, **Martha A. Sandweiss, Penguin Press, 2009**

The secret life of Clarence King after his Sierra years. Fascinating on the complications of living a double life.

Pilgrims to the Wild, **by John P. O'Grady, University of Utah Press, 1993**

Wonderfully illuminating portraits of several early Sierra writers, including John Muir, Clarence King, and Mary Austin. The author is the person I know as Sean O'Grady.

Storm Over Mono, **by John Hart, University of California Press, 1996**

A great account of the battle to save Mono Lake, managing to compress a huge amount of legal maneuvering into a compact and compelling narrative.

Stopping the Road, **by Jack Fisher, Sager Group, 2014**

Add this to *Storm Over Mono*, and William Tweed's books, to get a better understanding of how resistance to "economic development" has saved the Sierra on a continuing basis, as people come together to oppose some threat or other to the Sierra's wilderness status. This one is funny for its portrait of Governor Ronald Reagan riding in on a horse, wearing a white cowboy hat, to take credit for a good move he had nothing to do with.

Sierra Club Bulletin, **1896–present**

Old issues of the *Bulletin* can be obtained in volumes that collect a year or two's worth of issues under one cover. The articles vary considerably in interest, but the best are fascinating. Among my favorites are these:

> "Mt. Barnard," by C. Mulholland, vol. 1
> "A Search for a High Mountain Route from the Yosemite to the King's River Cañon," by Theodore Solomons, vol. 1
> "Up and Down Bubb's Creek," by Helen M. Gompertz, vol. 2
> "A Woman's Trip Through the Tuolumne Cañon," by Jennie Ellsworth Price, vol. 2
> "The Basin of the South Fork of the San Joaquin River," by J. N. Le Conte, vol. 2

"Over Harrison's Pass from the North with a Pack-Train," by Force Parker, vol. 5

"The High Mountain Route Between Yosemite and the King's River Cañon," by J. N. Le Conte, vol. 7

"With the Sierra Club in the Kern Cañon," by Marion Randall Parsons, vol. 7

"Down Tenaya Canyon," by S. L. Foster, vol. 7

"The Mazama Club Outing to Glacier Peak," by Marion Randall Parsons, vol. 8

"Trail Song," by Cedric Wright, 1928

"How It All Began—or Almost Didn't," by William E. Colby, 1931

"Native Daughter," by Harold E. Perry, 1952

"O Tempora! O Mores! Recollections of a High-Trip Tenderfoot," by Peggy Wayburn, 1975

***Mount Whitney: Mountain Lore from the Whitney Store*, by Doug Thompson and Elisabeth Newbold, Westwind Publishing Company, 2003**

The proprietor of the Whitney Portal store, and of the best Whitney website, tells stories collected through the years. Like *Tales Along El Camino Sierra*, these are fun to read.

***In the Summer of 1903: Colonel Charles Young and the Buffalo Soldiers in Sequoia National Park*, by Ward Eldredge, Sequoia Natural History Association, 2003**

A pocket biography, returning to our attention a remarkable man, important to Sierra history, and also to the history of African American achievements in the first generations following the Civil War. Young's name should definitely be up there in the range.

***Mineral King: The Story of Beulah*, by Louise A. Jackson, Sequoia Natural History Association, 2009**

This should be added to those local histories that among other things include a great story of resistance to stupid development plans, in this case the 1970s plan to turn Mineral King into a Disney ski resort.

Francois Matthes and the Marks of Time, by Francois Matthes, edited by Fritiof Fryxell, Sierra Club Books, 1962

Essays by Matthes on various Sierra geological topics, some very good still, others now shown to be pre-tectonically wrong; all interesting for one reason or another. Matthes was the professional glaciologist who most clarified what ice has done to the range. Fryxell collected the essays for his late friend.

David Brower: The Making of the Environmental Movement, by Tom Turner, University of California Press, 2015

Brower was the crucial figure in the environmental movement between the time of Muir and the current era; he led the fight to establish Kings Canyon National Park, among many other significant achievements. He could easily fill a chapter in this book or any other. This excellent biography does the job in a quick and entertaining way.

A Treasury of the Sierra Nevada, edited by Robert Leonard Reid, Wilderness Press, 1983

A wide-ranging collection of Sierra writing from many writers and eras. The combined effect makes for a good history of the range.

The Illuminated Landscape: A Sierra Nevada Anthology, edited by Gary Noy and Rick Heide, Sierra College Press and Heyday Books, 2010

This is another excellent anthology of Sierra writing, organized chronologically from Native American myths to the latest news, and including items not often collected, to make one of the better histories of the range.

GUIDEBOOKS

Desolation Wilderness and the South Lake Tahoe Basin, Jeffrey P. Schaffer, Wilderness Press, 1980

I won't include many guidebooks here, but this is the great one for Desolation, like Secor for the high Sierra. Comprehensive and inspirational for exploring that wonderful postage stamp of mountain greatness.

Trekking California, by Paul Richins Jr., Mountaineers Books, 2004

This and Richins's book on Mount Whitney both deserve mention, because Richins is so encouraging to his readers to try things that they think might be beyond their abilities. As questionable as that might sound, what Richins reminds readers of, in writing that is precise and cheerful, is their ability to extend beyond what they think they can do. And his ideas for Sierra treks are excellent.

Glaciers of California, by Bill Guyton, University of California Press, 1998

The definitive guide to Sierra glaciers. Hopefully its subject won't go away too soon.

Place Names of the Sierra Nevada, by Peter Browning, Wilderness Press, 1986

Browning builds on earlier work by Francis Farquhar to create a complete book, full of interest for those interested in names. He has another volume about the names in Yosemite National Park alone.

Wilderness Press guidebooks

These little "totebooks" from Wilderness Press, edited by Thomas Winnett, take 20 volumes to cover the whole range, and are still full of good information, and good suggestions for hikes.

ART AND PHOTOGRAPHY

***The Changing Range of Light*, by Elizabeth Carmel, Hawks Peak Publishing, 2009**

Beautiful photos of the high Sierra, by my Artists in the Back Country colleague. The cover of her book is her photo of what I call Elizabeth's Pond, with the Miter in the background.

***Above All*, by David Stark Wilson, Yosemite Association, 2008**

Awesome photos taken from the highest vantage points possible, giving an eagle's-eye view of the range. Very evocative.

***West of Eden*, by David Robertson, Yosemite Natural History Association, 1984**

An illustrated history of the early art depicting Yosemite, wonderful for both Robertson's text and his collection of illustrations.

***The High Sierra: Wilderness of Light*, by Claude Fiddler, Chronicle Books, 1995**

Moody, atmospheric photos, with good quotations from various Sierra people.

***Walk the Sky*, by John Dittli and Mark A. Schlenz, Companion Press, 2009**

Beautiful photos of the Muir Trail route, with a good text.

MEMOIRS

***Such a Landscape!*, by William Henry Brewer, edited by William Alsup, Yosemite Association, 1999**

This gives us the relevant parts of Brewer's journal of his Sierra expedition of 1864, with excellent notes and photos by William Alsup.

Mountaineering in the Sierra Nevada, **by Clarence King, James R. Osgood and Company, 1872**

King's little classic, worth reading for the trip to Mount Tyndall. The more you learn about King, the more surprising he gets.

For John Muir

My favorites are *To Yosemite and Beyond,* edited by Robert Engberg and my faculty advisor Donald Wesling; also *The Wild Muir, South of Yosemite, My First Summer in the Sierra,* and *The Story of My Boyhood and Youth.* Both the recent biographies of him are good, by Frederick Turner and Donald Worster. There are good omnibus editions of his books from the Mountaineers; you can get most of what he wrote in two fat volumes.

The Land of Little Rain, **Houghton Mifflin, 1903, and** *Earth Horizon,* **Riverside Press, 1932, by Mary Austin**

These two angles on her life, from first book to last, show her at her best. A great feminist, supporter of Native Americans, and landscape observer. *A Mary Austin Reader,* edited by Esther F. Lanigan, University of Arizona Press, 1996, is an excellent selection from all over her career. She should be read and remembered in the company of Charlotte Perkins Gilman, Emma Goldman, Kate Chopin, Rosa Luxemburg, Louise Bryant (whom she knew), and the rest of that crowd of first-wave feminists.

The Pass, **by Stewart Edward White, Outing Publishing Company, 1906**

This popular turn-of-the-century nature writer provides here a very entertaining account of a summer spent finding a horse-viable pass over the Kings-Kern Divide—which he named Elizabeth Pass, after his wife Betsy. A window into an earlier time, funny both on purpose and by accident.

High Odyssey, **by Eugene A. Rose, Howell-North Books, 1974**

Tells the story of Orland Bartholomew's 1931 winter ski trip up the Muir Trail from south to north, a tremendous feat, well documented by Bartholomew's own excellent photos, and a quick text. He was accompanied during three days of this trip by a curious wolverine.

Close Ups of the High Sierra, **by Norman Clyde, Spotted Dog Press, 1997**

Clyde's spare descriptions of his climbs and the peaks are funny in their Buster Keaton inexpressiveness, but they do give you a sense of his character, as if hidden behind his hat.

In the Sierra: Mountain Writings, **by Kenneth Rexroth, New Directions, 2012**

I edited this one, and can say that Rexroth was a great American poet, and a devoted Sierra lover. This collection of all his mountain writing, from many different sources, is wry, witty, soulful: Rexroth at his best. The five or six years of his life that he spent in the high Sierra meant the world to him. Up there he was content, and the muse often descended on him.

From "Toward an Organic Philosophy," 1940

Here where the glaciers have been and the snow stays late,
The stone is clean as light, the light as steady as stone.

The world is filled with running water
That pounds in the ear like ether;
The granite needles rise from the snow, pale as steel;
Above the copper mine the cliff is blood red,
The white snow breaks at the edge of it;
The sky comes close to my eyes like the blue eyes
Of someone kissed in sleep.

The Dharma Bums, **by Jack Kerouac, Viking Press, 1958**

The chapter describing the ascent of Matterhorn Peak is a great bit of Sierra writing, and the rest of the book adds to a vivid portrait of Gary Snyder circa 1955. As it did with Clarence King, writing about the Sierras raised Kerouac's game. The next book in Kerouac's sequence of autobiographical novels, *Desolation Angels*, describes what happened when he took Snyder's advice and spent a season as a fire lookout on Desolation Peak in the Cascades: very funny. Kerouac couldn't stand it.

For Gary Snyder

Almost all Snyder's books are somewhat Sierra-focused, but see especially *Myths and Texts, Riprap and Cold Mountain Poems, The Back Country, Axe Handles*, and *The Practice of the Wild. No Nature* is a good omnibus compendium from his whole career, and the Library of America will soon release a two-volume complete works that will be one of the great Sierra volumes, as well as a major entry in American poetry.

Up in Our Country, **by George Palmer Putnam, Duell, Sloan & Pearce, 1950**

A charming account of life at Whitney Portal in the early 1950s, by a retired publishing executive.

The Secret Sierra, **by David Gilligan, Spotted Dog Press, 2000**

This is a smart and lively introduction to all aspects of the Sierra: geology, history both natural and human, and some of the author's high-altitude adventures to spark it all to life. I suspect the title is a publisher's title, because there are no secrets here, just wonderful realities.

***And I Alone Survived,* by Lauren Elder, E. P. Dutton, 1978**

Elder was the sole survivor of a small-plane crash on the crest above Center Basin. It was April and snowed over, and she was dressed for a lunch in Death Valley, in a skirt and blouse. She had no mountain experience, and yet had to use her boot heels as crampons to get down the hard snow high on the east side (this I find terrifying), then made most of her descent of the trailless Symmes Canyon barefoot. She dropped 9,000 vertical feet and covered about 30 miles in a single push, and walked into Independence after midnight on the following day. A clear case of her third wind kicking in to help her. Her memoir tells the story well, ably assisted by coauthor Shirley Streshinsky. I think Symmes Canyon should be renamed Lauren Elder Canyon.

***Records of a Broken-Down Mountaineer: A Sierra Nevada Memoir,* by Norman Schaefer, Alcuin Press, 2019**

This memoir, and Schaefer's books of poems, *The Sunny Top of California* (La Alameda Press, 2010), and *Fool's Gold* (La Alameda Press, 2013), all contain great Sierra writing, very evocative of how it feels up there.

***Naming Mt. Thoreau,* edited by Laurie Glover, Artemisia Press, 2017**

Laurie got our group to contribute essays and photos, and Tom Killion provided us with a woodblock print of the mountain that makes the name more than official—it has the stamp of the great California artist now. The book is a record of a fun group and a good project. Anchored by the Blumlein essay, and the Snyder poem.

***Miracle Country,* by Kendra Atleework, Algonquin Books of Chapel Hill, 2020**

What's it like to grow up in Owens Valley now? This book tells one family's story, in a vivid and heartfelt memoir that includes some of the painful parts of Owens Valley's history since Europeans arrived.

GENERAL AIDS TO UNDERSTANDING THE SIERRA

Drifting Continents and Colliding Paradigms, **by John A. Stewart, Indiana University Press, 1990**

This history and analysis of the tectonic-plate revolution in geology is really illuminating for both the topic itself and for how science works when it comes to a paradigm shift.

The Nature of Light and Colour in the Open Air, **by M. Minnaert, Dover Publications, 1954**

Written by a physicist who explains the optics of almost any visual phenomenon one can imagine seeing, sharpening eye and mind in the process. The height of the sky? The green flash? This book has informed me and my books for 50 years now. The touch of craziness infusing it is very appealing.

Why We Run, **by Bernd Heinrich, Harper Perennial, 2002**

An exploration in evolutionary history that makes it clear how and why we evolved to walk, also to run; certainly to go cross-country. It's combined with a memoir of Heinrich's own running career, and a physiological analysis of endurance in animals of all kinds, including the migrating birds that fly from pole to pole. Very entertaining, informative, and thought-provoking.

The Six Mountain-Travel Books, **by Eric Shipton, Mountaineers, 1985**

There are many great climbing memoirs, but in this book on rambling and scrambling, I think it's worth mentioning the collected works of the greatest rambler and scrambler of them all, a man who spent his life wandering central Asia, then Patagonia late in his career. Delightful.

The Idea of Wilderness, by Max Oelschlaeger, Yale University Press, 1991

In trying to sort out what the Sierra Nevada is now as a human space, it's crucial to understand what we mean when we use the word *wilderness*, and Oelschlaeger's history of the concept is a good start and aid in that process. His chapters on Muir as philosopher, and Robinson Jeffers and Gary Snyder as poetical thinkers, are particularly fine.

The Ascent of Rum Doodle, by W. E. Bowman, Pimlico, 2001

This parody of classic climbing literature, originally published in 1956, is wickedly funny, and says all that needs to be said about that genre, and maybe about climbing itself.

Ursula K. Le Guin does this same thing miniaturized, in her short story "The Ascent of the North Face," in *A Fisherman of the Island Sea*, Harper Prism, 1994.

MY BOOKS

What about my own books? Yes, the Sierras have often shown up in them. More even than I realized, until I made this list.

Directly about the Sierra Nevada

My story "Ridge Running" was important for my own sense of how I could write my Sierra experiences into fiction, being my first attempt at it. I wrote it in 1975 at Clarion, and revised it for Ursula Le Guin's UCSD class in 1977. First published in 1982.

Next came a chapter in *The Gold Coast* (1988), when Tashi takes Jim up to the Sierra (over Dragon Pass!) to help him pull his life together, or at least get some perspective on it. That novel is my take on the '70s, from the perspective of the '80s. Tashi is a pretty good portrait of Terry in those years. Terry himself liked it.

Pacific Edge (1990) also includes a brief foray into the Sierra, again to give a place from which to view and judge Orange County. In this one they go to Dusy Basin.

The most recent directly Sierran writing in my fiction is in *Sixty Days and Counting* (2007), the third volume of my Washington, DC, trilogy. The characters go over Vennacher Col as we once did, but I set them in a context of climate change so severe that the high meadows of the Sierra are completely desiccated. It's the chapter called "Sacred Space," filling pages 859–906 in *Green Earth* (2017), the compressed version of that trilogy, which I prefer to the earlier three-volume version.

My other mountain writing

Escape from Kathmandu (1989) is about the Himalayas, from a Sierran perspective. Much of what Lisa and I saw and experienced in Nepal is in this one.

Antarctica (1997) describes the Transantarctics, also from a Sierra person's perspective.

Shaman (2013) is my attempt to imagine how people lived in the last ice age. The snowshoeing in particular comes from my Sierra experiences, and no doubt much else as well.

A novella called *A Short, Sharp Shock* (1991) is set on an ocean planet's world-wrapping peninsula with a lot of Sierran features.

My short story "Muir on Shasta" (1991) is a retelling of Muir's own account of his night on the summit in a storm, "A Perilous Night on Shasta's Summit" (1884). I tried to pierce the veil of Muir's politeness, which kept him from speaking ill of his companion; also to imagine spending a night in a zone of safety "about a quarter of an acre in extent, but only an eighth of an inch thick." It's in a couple of my story collections.

The novella *Green Mars* (1985) comes out of my reading of the British climbing literature, and some of my own Sierra experiences. "Exploring Fossil Canyon" (1982) and "A Martian Romance" (2000) also include many Sierran aspects, and the book they are collected in, *The Martians* (2000), contains most of my Mount Desert Island writing as well. Now that I think of it, the final poem in that volume, called "I Say Good-bye to Mars," describes a Sierra meteor memory from that night under Forester Pass. A lot of things collide in that one.

"Rainbow Bridge" (1986) is a story in my collection *Remaking History*. It's a lightly fictionalized account of a hike I took with my brother Chris, our cousin Jon Hollingshead, and a Navajo friend of Jon's named Lewis Tate, to Rainbow Bridge in 1966. Somehow this first off-trail fiasco of mine, leaving Lewis (with his bemused permission) to head up a cliff route I had cleverly spotted, did not deter me from going off trail later in life.

Other bits of my Sierra life can be found scattered through the rest of my books—as in Hjalmar Nederland's walkabout in *Icehenge* (1984), or when my starfarers try to settle a moon in *Aurora* (2015), or inside certain terraria in *2312* (2012), or when my characters wander the Earth in *The Years of Rice and Salt* (2002). Long walks seem to show up pretty often in my books, and yes, I like it when they do.

Indirect influences of the Sierra are especially prominent in my Mars trilogy (1992–95). In describing the Martian landscape as if it were the high Sierra, I was really fudging it, because only by terraforming Mars could I make that cold poisonous planet into a place anything like the Sierra. Several landscape passages in *Green Mars* and *Blue Mars*, especially when Sax or Ann take walks, were lifted directly from notes I wrote while in the Sierra, sometimes specifically to put into the books. Reviewers who wrote things like "It almost seems as if Robinson has been to Mars" always made me laugh—they had seen through my method. Since that three-decker novel is still my most famous, I think it's right to say that the Sierras have always played an important role in my fiction. How could they not? They are the spirit of the place.

Lastly, I finally got the Alps into my fiction, just recently, in my novel *The Ministry for the Future* (2020). That was a pleasure.

Writing the day on the back of the map: Dumbbell Basin, 2010

MOMENTS OF BEING (8)
The Monsoon Gets Stronger

What will climate change do to the Sierra Nevada?

Higher temperatures and longer droughts seem almost certain.

Another effect of climate change was not predicted in advance, but is already evident; there has been a northward extension of Arizona's midsummer monsoon, which often now comes up from the Gulf of California all the way to the Sierra. This is a change we've experienced ourselves in the last decade.

A day in the monsoon

*   *   *

In 2013, Carter and Darryl and I were at the elbow of Seven Gables Canyon, setting camp in a cloudy sunset. Earlier in the day we had stood under trees waiting out rain so intense that the ground of the entire canyon suddenly turned to water, as it had poured down the tall gleaming stone walls flanking us on both sides, then pooled in a rush at our feet. We had to clamber awkwardly onto big tree roots to get above this surprising flood, which though only a few inches deep, covered the entire canyon floor. We'd never seen anything like it. After a while the water drained into the white roaring creek, and we continued upcanyon over a soaked and slippery rockscape.

Now we stood in an open sandy meadow, damp but nice. We set up our three tarps and bedded down in the cloudy dusk. That night it began to rain again, then blow hard. The wind was barreling down the canyon and then whipping around the elbow bend, throwing rain against our tents in what sounded like sprays from a hose.

There was no sleep that night. Our tarps were barely holding. Mine had water running up its inside, perhaps under the pressure of the wind. And I was camped on the usual Sierra decomposed granite, which looked to be contained in a shallow bowl of bedrock that was now filling with water above the level of the sand, so I was beginning to flood from below. My air mattress floated me above the shallow pool growing under me, so this was the least of my problems. Rain was bombing down, wind hitting in wicked slaps—something could very possibly give—a tent stake in the ground, a loop holding tent stake to tarp—even the nylon fabric of the tarp. If that happened, my widespread incidental dampness would be transformed instantly into total fundamental wetness. I had to plan for that, and I did; this passed the time, sleep being out of the question. When the tarp gave way, I decided, I would quickly pull my rain jacket and wind pants on over my night warmies, get into my boots, wrap my down bag and failed tarp around me burrito style, and sit with my back against the lee side of a big tree, waiting for dawn and the end of this torrential storm. It could be done, if I had to do it; it would not be the worst thing that had ever happened to me in the mountains; etc. In my mind I was prepared to march through all the necessary steps. Meanwhile the typhoon lashed us.

In the event, all our tarps held. The wind relented, then the rain stopped. When the sleepless gray dawn came, we crawled out completely bedraggled. We consulted with each other. We'd all had the same experience, so we didn't have to describe the particulars, merely marvel at them, pretty pleased we had done as well as we had. We concluded we could maybe use stronger tarps. Carter had heard of a new fabric called Cuben fiber, said to be more waterproof than nylon.

Two years later Carter and I had new tarps made of this fabric, since named Dyneema. On the third day of our trip we climbed to the pass between Sixty Lakes Basin and Gardiner Basin. Midafternoon on a warm muggy day, some clouds overhead. We had been rained on for an hour or so on each of the previous two afternoons, so we suspected the monsoon. Even so we were surprised when in about 15 minutes the sky went from half white to dark gray, and just as quickly it began to rain, then hail, then thunder loudly. We didn't see any lightning bolts, but the clouds over us flashed white right before each big rolling boom. Time to gear up and get out of there.

We put on our rain gear and started down. The descent from that unnamed pass into Gardiner Basin is steep and rocky at first, a wall of big boulders that one has to traverse down toward the highest Gardiner lake, a long skinny thing extending as far as we could see, especially in the rain. The deeper parts of the basin were out of sight below this endless lake. The rain was hard and cold. The clouds lit up over us, then immediately banged. Their bottoms were scraping over the ridge to our right, and the boulder slope we were descending was slippery. It was like an immense long room: two gray rock walls, a long black floor of water, a gray ceiling of sky, pelting rain.

I was using one of my blue backpacks, the ones you could cut with your fingernail. I love them, but they're not waterproof, and my gear inside this one was stuffed into stuff sacks that were likewise not waterproof. We had our new tarps, and it might have been possible to pull them out and figure out a way to use them as capes as we had with our old tarps, or at least as backpack covers, but with the thunder now cracking overhead, and no shelter anywhere, and the rocks so very slippery, and everything so cold and wet in a bucketing downpour, we didn't feel like stopping to make experiments in gear deployment. I was going to have to deal with what I found in my pack when we got to a place to camp. Even my wool mittens were packed too far down in my backpack for me to want to stop and get them out. I pulled my rain jacket down over my hands as far as I could and grasped the sleeves against my walking poles, leaving only my fingers exposed. As always, I wondered if aluminum walking poles were in effect little lightning rods. It seemed like they could be. It even seemed like they were humming, although this sound could have been just in my head, an electric buzz like wet tinnitus. Probably the keening of the wind, or nerve damage caused by the thunderclaps.

The descent needed care, and I gave it. The ridge above us to our right was now lost in the cloud. The thunder was getting less frequent, the rain harder. This highest lake in the Gardiner Basin was turning out to be really long. Before the storm struck, we had been planning on hiking to the next lake below it. Now I was thinking that maybe the flat spot I could see at the far end of the lake, where a little promontory pinched off the endless stretch of water, might do. It would be very exposed out there, as the cat's-paws flying across the lake's beaten surface made clear, but it looked flat, and nothing around us was flat or even close; it was a slope of rocks between the size of refrigerators and bowling balls. Nothing to do but clamber down and across this jumble, getting wetter and colder.

This was one of those hours where you just have to bite it and forge on, coldly determined. Total exposure to the elements. Lear on the heath; Beethoven's mad blind energy, as in the *Grosse Fuge* or the end of the *Hammerklavier.* I think Beethoven must have gotten caught out in storms once or twice. Often I like these hours, even while they're happening. It's like sticking your finger in a wall socket, but at a level of electrocution you can stand. Hammered by the elements—unsheltered—focused—wet—cold—at one with the world. Forge on!

Then, as I was getting closer to the little ridge that pinched off the end of the long lake, there appeared a little triangular patch of grass. Real grass, almost flat—certainly not the biggest tilt we had ever camped on. And it seemed like it might be just big enough to fit our three tents side by side. This was like one of Piaget's tests of cognitive development for toddlers: Was the patch big enough for three tents? Maybe?

When Carter reached me I proposed the plan. He nodded. Good idea, he said. I think we'll fit. And if we don't, we still have to.

Darryl joined us and we sketched the idea to him. He nodded. Let's do it, he said. We were all drenched to one extent or another.

In the relentless rain we set up our tents right next to each other. You could barely walk between them, as our tie lines overlapped. I was in the lowest part of the patch, and set my zipper door (so fancy, a tarp with a zipper!) on the side away from Carter.

I got under my new tarp, sat down cross-legged under my poles, and began digging in my backpack to assess the damage. As I pulled things out I grew more and more appalled: everything was wet. Incidental dampness was long gone, although there was a lot of that too, but mainly it was a serious case of fundamental wetness. All my socks were too wet to wear in my sleeping bag. My blue warmies were wet. Down vest only incidentally damp. The sleeping bag was only wet in places, but where it was wet, it was soaked.

It was only about 3:00 p.m., which gave me time to take full stock of the situation. My new Dyneema tarp was pale green, and translucent; I could see the rain running down the outside of it, but as I touched the inside of it, I could tell how dry it was. And it was big—well, bigger than what I was used to. It's not actually that big. But the light poured through it. And I wasn't in the rain, which continued to pound down. The grass under me was wet, but that was incidental dampness; with my ground pad inflated I was well above that, and my gear was resting on my rain pants or jacket, or something else waterproof or irrelevant to my night life.

So I lay on top of my sleeping bag, which was draped on the ground pad, and figured I would sleep barefoot, since I had to. The tilt was pretty steep for a bed, but it was cleanly tilted head to foot, not side to side—I had set the tarp to get that. And the exertions of the previous hour or two—I found I had no idea how long our descent had taken, but probably it was over an hour, and maybe less than two—that work had warmed me up, all but my fingers. I could eat, drink (we had grabbed water from the long lake), and rest. I could listen to the rain drum on my taut new tarp, and even watch water running down the other side of an impermeable translucent barrier, in the usual infinity of delta patterns. I was sheltered! Over the next couple of hours I began to settle into a deep sense of safety, comfort, and even warmth. Damp warmth, but so what! Warmth is warmth, and I wasn't going to get any wetter than I already was. This new tarp was not just a refuge; it was a miracle. In that hour I fell in love with that tarp. I was home.

Gardiner Basin, 2015: the grass patch that saved us

The following year, we went up Center Basin to see if we could follow the old route of the Muir Trail up to Junction Pass. It was easy; the trail is still very distinct, even though it was abandoned and taken off the maps in 1934.

On our way back we decided to try to go over University Shoulder. This is just what it sounds like, a high traverse over the west shoulder of University Peak. We had seen the north side of this shoulder on our way in, and although it was obvious that it would have been really tough to slog up the slope, getting down it had looked feasible. So I suggested to the others that we try it—yes, it was my idea, and yes, I had failed to take in the sentence in the Secor guide that called this shoulder a ski route. Although parenthetically I am amazed at what back country skiers will think to try.

So we left the froggy pond at the bottom of Center Basin, and took off up the slope to the shoulder. This slope is the side of a very big glacial canyon, the upper Bubbs Creek canyon, with the Muir Trail at its bottom heading up to Forester Pass. Soon we were using our hands to pull ourselves up, grabbing on to the exposed roots of small trees at head height above us. It was a vertical forest in decomposed granite, knobbed by big boulders that blocked our way but also stabilized the sand and gravel and trees between them. Ridiculously steep, and we could see, by looking across the big canyon to its other wall, just how slow our upward progress was. Most of 2,000 vertical feet, at the same steep pitch. Frequent breaks. Already far more effortful than staying on trail would have been.

Finally we got onto the shoulder proper, which gave us an easy sandy traverse across a high space where nothing but the big triangular pyramid of University Peak was higher than we were, blocking our view to our right. In every other direction we could see forever. Joe and Helen LeConte, and many other early Sierra Clubbers, had ascended University Peak from this shoulder around 1896, the women wearing long skirts, etc.; those people were tough. We were happy with our high traverse. Our canyon-wall climb was almost feeling worth it.

At the far side of the shoulder, we came to a drop-off and could see down the north slope we had declined to ascend three days before. A steep descent indeed, sand and scree angled hard down a broad shallow funnel that at its bottom shot a gap between boulders—that part looked a little nasty—but we could do it. So we sat on this fine overlook and ate our lunch and enjoyed the view. Which clouded up as we sat there. It had been muggy before, but the clouds had been mostly in the north. Now suddenly they were everywhere; they darkened fast; thunder rumbled.

Kevin Kline, playing the Pirate King in the film version of *The Pirates of Penzance*, said it best: *Here we go AGAIN!* Yes, I shouted his indignant phrase as we poked into our rain gear. We hurried to get off the ridge and as far down the slope as we could before lightning started. It began to rain, cold and hard. Then lightning, thunder, hail, the usual dreadful combo; although again, the lightning was of the flashbulb-in-the-clouds variety, not visible bolts hitting the ground, which is the real heart-stopper, those crackling lines of fire torching reality itself. This was just the usual awful booming overhead, with the whole world flashing before the gloom returned. Disturbing enough, to be sure.

The steepness of the scree slope wasn't helped by its being soaking wet, except maybe it was, as we could stomp into it with our boots a little. I sat down for a lot of this drop, in my usual style. Carter and Darryl, both good skiers, kept on their feet and stepped down skillfully, with me bumping along behind.

We came to the boulders at the bottom of the funnel. I hurried down to have a look and discovered a drop of about 15 feet, maybe a bit more; not huge, but for me an impossibility. It was pouring now, and the thunder frequently punctuated my cries of dismay. I shouted up to the guys concerning what I had found. Darryl immediately cut across the slope of the funnel to the boulders framing it on the left, to see if there was a way down through those rocks. Carter declared he was not to be stopped by any mere 12-foot cliff, and came down past me to investigate for himself. I wished him luck on my way back up, then crossed the funnel as low as I could without slipping down its spillway. Darryl had meanwhile found a nifty staircase down the boulder wall to the left, and was already on the scree slope below the crux. Gratefully I followed him. Pausing on this boulder stairway, I looked across and was horrified to see Carter wedged in a crack partway down the little cliff on his side. He was in a small nook that looked to be 9 or 10 feet above the steep scree under him — no way down, not at all easy getting back up, rain pounding us. I took a photo of him, hoping it would not be needed as evidence in any subsequent inquiry. He took off his backpack and tossed it down to the slope below. Holy moly! I shouted. Carter! The wind and rain and thunder were too loud for him to hear anything I shouted. Then, even though I was looking right at him, he was standing successfully on the slope below. He had jumped. I shouted again, amazed; somehow I had not seen his leap. Another blank-out! But all was well. Carter put on his pack and proceeded. I did too. Darryl was far below, and the slope between him and us was straightforward scree, not as steep as in the funnel. We were past the crux.

But not. Secor mentions some "giant boulders" in his description, and I think these might be completely covered by thick snow in winter, so that as part of a ski route, they wouldn't be an issue. For us they were. These boulders were indeed giant, the size of garden sheds and school buses, all strewn in a crazy broad band that was the ancient lateral moraine of a glacier. The boulders had rested in place forever, and were covered with that kind of black lichen that gets extremely slippery when wet, like thousands of tiny flat lobes of slick black plastic. From the tops of these boulders, gaps between them dropped into cellar holes sometimes 12 or 20 feet down. But if we tried to stay down at that basement level, the corridors would close off in little dead ends with vertical sides more than head high. Nope; it was a fucking nightmare.

The hail had turned to rain and relented a bit; the thunder had stopped. It was now just a matter of being soaked and cold and hiking over a wet boulder hell. Even though we were moving horizontally, and were no more than half a mile from the uppermost of the Kearsarge Lakes, where we had camped on our first night and knew exactly where we would set our tarps, we were now engaged in the most meticulously slow and dangerous work of the day. Though flat, it could still be rated class 3, in that a mistake could kill you; so we had to be sure not to make a mistake. From time to time this involved crawling, the wet black lichen being so outrageously slippery; it was like walking on buttered glass. Many moves had to be made as slowly as we could make them. I was reminded of the *Batman* TV show of the '60s, in which Batman and Robin pretend to climb buildings even though you can see they are on a flat surface and the camera is tilted sideways. A class 3 horizontal surface! Who knew?

The awful boulder field ran right into the eastern end of our lake, and our campsite, the only campsite on the lake, was at its west end. When we finally got over these last and worst boulders onto ordinary ground, for a last walk around the shore of the lake (the lake pictured on the jacket photo of this book), we were soaked and beaten, but also, relieved. Ordinary walking never felt so good. We were going to make it. When we staggered into our first night's campsite, under the Kearsarge Pinnacles, it felt like our long-lost home. We added up the figures for the day as we made camp; it had taken us eight hours to go two miles.

Recommendation: take the trail.

Not that I mean to generalize this! And it has to be added, Helen Gompertz in her trip report in the *Bulletin* of 1896 makes it clear that her Sierra Club group went up and down that very same slope when they climbed University Peak. So they crossed that boulder field twice in one day, presumably when it was dry. And the route is listed in Secor's guidebook, so it is a real pass. Or at least a listed pass. But still. A nightmare. Well, it was because of the untimely downpour that it went a little haywire. That was what made it a day to remember: the monsoon.

May we have more days like it. And given this new northward tendency of Arizona's summer monsoon, we probably will. Before the 2010s, Arizona's monsoon seldom if ever got as far north as the Sierra, but now we've experienced it four times in eight years, and in the scientific literature there is speculation that this is an early localized effect of climate change.

It could be worse. And in fact, some extra summer moisture might help relieve the droughts that are likely to come.

Another obvious climate change effect: the Sierra's glaciers are melting. They were little already, and now they're going fast.

In August of 2021 we hiked across the top of Deadman Canyon, repeating a route we had taken in the fall of 2007. On that earlier trip, we had enjoyed camping in a high narrow curving meadow under the headwall of the canyon, fed by water seeping from the seven small glaciers tucked under the upper-most cliffs of that magnificent amphitheater.

The top of Deadman Canyon with its seven little glaciers, from the 1993 USGS 7.5 topographic map of the area

This time, summer of 2021, all these glaciers were gone.

Actually there was one bit left, the eastern corner of the biggest one in the middle. Without that remaining chip of ice, we would have had no water that night. Every stream we had passed that day, some of which in normal times would have been dangerous to cross, had been just black streaks of lichen mark-ing channels of granite. We had never seen the range so desiccated. So when we hiked under this high remnant ice, we were relieved. We filled our bottles from the trickle glugging down from it through a cleft in the granite, and through that evening in our high meadow we drank the clear cold water thankfully.

The last bit of glacier left in Deadman Canyon

After dinner I walked up to the remnant to say goodbye, and get some ice for our Scotch. The newly exposed granite I ascended was all covered with grit and sand. When I got to the ice, ringed by a band of wet glacial silt, I sat on a rock and looked around. The remaining mass of the glacier was about the size of two or three Olympic swimming pools, I reckoned, tilted against the low cliff of the back wall.

It was solid ice, though white as snow. I spotted a little blue bergschrund near the top, that horizontal crack which shows where lower ice has broken away from a higher verge still frozen to rock. Seeing that blue line hit me hard; it was a fossil bergschrund. Sort of like sitting in a hospice and seeing a gleam in the blue eye there on the pillow.

I knocked off a small chunk of ice and took it back down to camp, feeling old. I thought I would have died before this kind of thing happened. As the great

stone canyon below us filled with shadows, I sipped my glaciated Scotch and tried to comfort myself with the notion that one day, someday, this entire canyon would fill again with ice. People need glaciers; surely they will draw down enough CO_2 to bring them back—to bring the world back! Thus with my usual science fiction exercise I tried to comfort myself. The next ice age will solve this problem, I thought. But all that night the glacier's blood gurgled by us.

So. Higher temperatures are here already, and the Sierra glaciers will soon be gone. The high country will dry out.

Back home, I found myself stricken by this realization. Of course people die; I myself will die; but not the Sierras! Not the Sierras. It was too much to bear. Anguish filled my mind like smoke.

A talk with my friend Mando Quintero reeled me back in from this bad moment. He reminded me that the Sierra's living community is a sky island that has survived up there since the end of the last ice age, through some very long droughts and a little ice age or two. The plants and animals up there are extremophiles, tough and resilient, long adapted to a wildly variable environment. Anthropogenic climate change will add to that variability, and things up there will change; but some survivors will hang on.

Also, this is a global crisis we're in. It isn't just the Sierras. Every life zone on Earth will be stressed by climate change, and the damage will put human civilization at such risk that we will be forced to claw our way back toward cooler temperatures and healthier biomes, in every way we can, just for our own well-being, our own survival. To the extent we succeed in that effort, the relief will be worldwide, in the same way the damage is now.

Thus Mando's calming perspective. And so I worked my way back toward balance. Another compound Sierra emotion got added to the others I'm more used to, like peaceful excitement, or the sublime (beauty and terror), or the feeling of eon and moment together as one. Now: *A fearful joy*, as one of Joyce Cary's great novels is named. But this is one everyone knows already; that's life, at all altitudes and all times.

So now, in our Sierra years to come, we will be greeting any extra doses of monsoon rain with cheers. May they hit hard every summer! We can deal. We will love it.

MOMENTS OF BEING (9)
Hetch Hetchy Restored

Hiking around the north side of Hetch Hetchy in the wet snow of April, we ascended onto Hetch Hetchy Dome from its backside in the late afternoon. It had been raining and sleeting and snowing all day. We were well under 10,000 feet, and in a forest, so we were happy to get a fire going, so rare

Hetch Hetchy, 2005

for us. The rain turned to a mist and it seemed we were just under the clouds, or in their diffuse bottom. Standing on the dome we could look down onto the reservoir. The bathtub ring around it was tall and white. Kolana Rock to the left, the big waterfall just out of sight to the right. The next day we were going to have to get over the river upstream from that waterfall. For now we stood there looking at the sun spearing under the clouds and turning everything into a spangle of silvers and grays and black. A heraldic sight. Down at the far end of what we could see, the concrete line of the dam.

Reservoirs never look right and never look good. Even when you can barely tell they are reservoirs, something gives them away, at the shoreline or just in your head. They look wrong. They aren't good-looking.

It's possible to joke that Hetch Hetchy was saved by being drowned, that otherwise it would be Yosemite North, completely Disneyfied, etc. Instead, the murdered queen. One dawn I ran the trail from the dam to the big water-fall and looked upstream, and the gorge up that way appeared to me as if out

of a dream, it was so tall and so narrow. No people, no animals, no birds, no wind: a frozen landscape. A bronze man in a bronze land (Wallace Stevens). Later I checked the maps and realized it looked bizarre because it was bizarre; very few canyons on Earth are as deep and narrow as the Tuolumne at that point. It looked like something out of Gustave Doré, a caricature of a gorge, now lost behind a reservoir and removed from the sensible world.

We got our fire going and it burned yellow in the dusk. We stood around it, black silhouettes in the blur of a mist like fog. Figures from Bruegel.

I went back to the overlook to see it one more time. The flooding of Hetch Hetchy was a knife thrust into the heart of the wilderness movement. Men had twirled their mustaches like Snidely Whiplash and chortled to each other in their boardrooms, *We'll kill their precious daughter and send them weeping into the night*—no. It wasn't quite like that. We all have our reasons, lame though they may be. We justify ourselves as a matter of course. So they managed to overlook the foothill valleys that would have done just as well as this one, and went for the heart without acknowledging even to themselves the murderous work they were doing. But they did it, and it worked. The later dams on the Colorado, and all over the American West, could point to this one and say, Look, if we could do it there, we can do it anywhere. We all need water. And no place on Earth is above the law of the highest rate of return!

So, a battle lost. But the war is never over. And as I looked down on the scene that misty evening, I saw the water drain away. It will happen someday. There is no rush about this, and given the emergency century we are entering, it isn't even close to the highest priority. But put it this way: if civilization gets itself in a balance with the planet, a day will come when we will drain that misbegotten death lake and let the valley go back to the way it was. It will be one of the greatest experiments in landscape restoration ever conducted.

Plants will return quickly, animals too. Birds even faster, and insects. The river will carve a new course or reassert the old one, or some of both. Studies will be done. Mount St. Helens shows how all that will go, in terms of both natural succession and of the restoration science studying the process. The bathtub ring on the granite walls around Hetch Hetchy will linger longer than most of the damage; lichens are slow growers. But wherever rocks spall off cliffs, in the process that geologists call exfoliation, you can see the speed at which lichens come back; it's slow, but not geologically slow. A century later and you won't be able to tell the reservoir was ever there. Up on Hetch Hetchy Dome, passing travelers will look down on the restored meadow, and see the murdered sister resurrected and basking in love, like Hermione at the end of Shakespeare's *The Winter's Tale*. Forest and meadow, with the Tuolumne River meandering through it, and granite cliffs flanking it. The ghost of John Muir will enter those people, and the ancient ones from all the ten thousand years will enter those people, and they will laugh out loud.

SIERRA PEOPLE (17)

Young People in Love

Like everything else, the Sierras are now on the internet. It makes for a fun form of armchair backpacking, and what I see in that big virtual space is a lively world of Sierra lovers, who are mostly younger than I am, and who show the usual enthusiasm for the back country. There are lots of websites and participants. My favorite is highsierratopix.com, which has many wiki-style features, including a map of cross-country passes with comments added by users, often useful even if you can't judge the standards of the contributors very well. What comes through on that site and many others is boundless enthusiasm for the Sierra, lots of physical energy, and a desire to share ideas for things to try. A nice crowd.

Not that there isn't some trolling there, of course. That always happens. But as so often, nice people form the vast majority of the crowd. Reading the trip accounts and the route suggestions is to realize that there are a few thousand people in the Sierra every summer, rambling happily. The fact that I don't see most of them up there, and they don't see me, is a testament to how big the range is, and how many corners it still has to get lost in. Given the celebrity action on the Muir Trail, and on Mount Whitney, and in Yosemite Valley, it's reassuring to read these accounts, and get a sense of this community's shared appreciation for the back country. They are true Sierra lovers, and nothing I've said in this book will come as news to them, though I hope they'd enjoy reading it anyway.

One recent online report I admired came from a young woman with a jaunty handle who said you could go from the West Pinnacles basin to the

East Pinnacles basin by traversing the big canyon wall from the one to the other, without bothering to drop to the canyon floor. This was such a startling idea that I got out my maps and traced what she had done, and wow—that's a radical traverse! But what a good idea. And it can be made into a general principle of action. Some of these little hanging valleys are so hard to get into from above or below, that only her kind of audacious plan would allow you to visit more than one per trip. It was brilliant.

When we're up there, we occasionally run into some of these people, and in the past decade I've stopped to talk to them for longer than I used to. I've gotten curious. I've even started asking if I can take a photo of them, just to capture that glow I see on their faces as we talk. It's a kind of glory, framing them like halos in medieval paintings.

Once coming up to Bishop Pass, we ran into a young couple and chatted for a while; they were the ones who started me paying attention in this way. They told us they had been hiking the Pacific Crest Trail, going from Mexico to Canada, and when they came into the Sierras and started hiking north on the Muir Trail, they had become more and more impressed, until they said to each other, What are we doing hauling ass through the most beautiful part of this trek? Why don't we slow down? In fact, why don't we give up on Oregon and Washington, and spend the rest of our summer wandering the high Sierra?

We laughed with them, in complete agreement, and a hundred yards up the trail I said to my friends, Damn! Why didn't I get their picture?

And since then, I have. A couple of years ago we were very near that same spot when we ran into a different couple coming down the pass, and chatted on trail for a while, no more than ten minutes, but what an impression they made. He was Iranian by birth, she a Midwesterner, they lived in Chicago and worked in finance; they were perhaps a couple, I assumed so, but in any case, definitely a Sierra hiking pair. At first they had gone on backpacking trips all over the American West, but had come to the conclusion that the Sierras were best for that activity, and afterward kept coming back, for a month or more every summer. Each trip they tried different routes. In the winters they hiked the shore of Lake Michigan, in Chicago's big lakeside parks, with walking poles and 50 pounds in their backpacks, to stay in shape. They had recently descended Frozen Lake Pass, one of Roper's class 3 moments on his High Route, in a complete whiteout fog bank, such that they had had to sit and lift themselves down the slope one little shift of the butt at a time. I could definitely relate to that. And the gleam in their eyes was that of committed Sierra crazies. Their lives were organized around this project. I asked permission and took their photo, and it's beautiful; I wish it was okay to publish strangers' photos in books, but I don't think it is. You'll have to imagine it: man and woman in their early thirties, wind-flayed and sunblasted, eyes alight, giant goofy grins.

Then recently, a pair came flying by us in the Ionian Basin. We were sitting in camp near sunset, tired after a long day, looking across a gap of air at Scylla and the Three Sisters, and suddenly spotted two hikers traversing a snow slope we had declined to try earlier in the day, as being too steep for us. These two clung to it like flies, then dropped out of our sight to the nameless lake below, and we figured they would be camping down there. Fifteen minutes later they popped into our camp, surprising us greatly, and we had a brief conversation. Young women, one tall, with a cut shin bandaged with duct tape; the other short, with dark bangs. Both had big backpacks. That day they had crossed the same rugged late-snow terrain we had, but they weren't done; they were going to head on up toward the western gate of the Ionian in the late light. They were navigating by iPhone map. From their casual speed and power I guessed they might be on a college swim team or the like; gymnasts, lacrosse players, soccer team members, cross-country runners—who knows, but they were strong, really strong. Midtwenties in age. I asked if I could take a photo and they said yes, then after I did they disappeared over the horizon and we never saw them again. We were reading Homer's *Odyssey* aloud at night, in honor of Scylla and Charybdis, and as they disappeared I said to my companions, Those must have been two sirens!

A couple of days later we were headed north on the Muir Trail near Sapphire Lake when we passed two young women setting camp; one tall and thin, the other short and dark-haired. They said hi, and seemed so familiar that I called out to them, Hey, were you in the Ionian a couple of days ago?

No! they said.

I felt like a foolish old man—can't tell one pair of young women from another—really? What was I coming to!

Then one of them said, Hey, I bet you saw our sisters! My sister is hiking with her sister, they're up here somewhere. They're a lot faster than us.

Wow! I said, feeling much better. That's a nice coincidence! Your sisters were definitely fast! I wanted to say divinely fast, but restrained myself.

I wanted to ask to take these sisters' photo too, but I was too shy. Old men asking to photograph young women; it can be misconstrued. Down the trail, when I caught up to Tobias and told him what had happened, he laughed and said, They had to have been pulling your leg. Luckily Yutan had been with me and heard the whole exchange, and he said, No no, they were telling us the truth, you could tell. And you could.

I hope to meet more such people (and I did, just last week: Norma and Tina, headed for the tops of Royce and Merriam Peaks). It's as I've been saying all along: Sierra people are part of an actor network, a community of actors in which the chief actor is the Sierra itself. People visit it, and change for good. It's something deeper than thought, some feeling in the core, a connection that says *This is my heart's home.* It feels like something out of the Paleolithic. If you look at the rate of diffusion of humans across the world, including the Americas when they got here, it becomes clear that people were always going over the next ridge to see what was there. It's part of our nature, going back to before we were the species we are now—it's an urge that predates *Homo sapiens.* It is still in us, it will always be with us. Why it hits some people more than others, I can't say. But for sure if it hits you, you change. You do what you can to get up there and enjoy the walking. I may be crazy in this, an enthusiast, but I'm not alone, and I'm not even unusual. People are doing it by the thousands every year, and they will keep going up there for as long as civilization lasts. No one lives there year-round, it's a wilderness now, Anthropocene wilderness, more needed than ever, and humans are visitors only. But what passionate visitors, oh my God. Flames might as well be bursting out of the tops of their heads.

MY SIERRA LIFE (13)
Still Getting Lost

We found a new way over the crest, because we couldn't find Lamarck Col from the inside. We hadn't planned to go out that way, and hadn't been over the pass in that direction since 1988. So our memories of the region were poor, and it was off our maps. We went up to the top of Darwin Canyon, to the highest pond except one, where many others had also traveled, judging by the footprints everywhere in the sandy slope rising to the crest. Passes are usually located at the low point in a ridge, so we trudged up the sandy slope to the low point, and looked over the other side: cliff. Which is to say: CLIFF!! Straight down 500 feet, maybe a thousand.

Lamarck Col on its outside slope, facing roughly north, is topped by a little glacieret, which people have worn a diagonal traverse across, a trench about knee deep in the snow and ice that covers the final slope right to the pass itself. So we knew we weren't in Lamarck Col—though I wondered briefly if the glacieret had melted away since we had last seen it in 2004, leaving this cliff behind! But no. We were lost. We ranged along the ridge to the west for as far as we thought the pass could possibly be, stopped at a big peak that I thought began the rise to Mount Lamarck. Then we ranged back east along the crest, looking over every point we could and finding nothing but cliff, cliff, cliff. It was spooky. The pass was gone!

We sat down to confer. When you're lost like this, a map's detail often isn't good enough to allow you to locate yourself precisely, so the fact that we didn't have mappage of this area wasn't really the determining factor. Maybe a map would have helped us figure out where exactly we were, maybe it wouldn't. But we had followed lots of footprints up to where we were, so it seemed like we had to be at least *near* the pass. We got up and kept going back and forth along the crest, looking for the pass. Nothing but cliff cliff cliff. It was enough to spook me.

Finally, as far to the east as we had yet ranged, we looked down and saw a steep slide of scree filling an inward bend in the cliff. Right under us it was still cliff dropping to this slide, impossible to descend; but to our left, we could see a crack that led down to a smaller slide of scree that ran sideways into the big slide, meeting it some 300 feet below us. There didn't look to be any place on these scree slopes that was too awful to get down; it was all angle of repose, or the scree wouldn't be there. The only question was, Would the crack to the left allow us down to the top of the high feeder slope?

We worked our way over to look. It seemed to go. With a couple of nifty steps down, big steps, holding on hard, it would be possible to get to the top of the secondary slide. Problem then solved. The drop-in at the top was even still class 2, in the technical sense of, if you fell you wouldn't necessarily die.

So we talked it over. This is one of the comforts of hiking with Joe and Darryl, very important; we talk things over and decide together what to do, in an easy manner, forthright and agreeable, open to each other's opinions, and patient. If anyone's going to get rattled it's me, and then they reel me back in. It was true then too. I said to them, Look guys, I'm having a bit of a crisis of confidence here! Because whatever this is we're looking at, it's definitely not Lamarck Col. I don't even know what we're going down to! I don't recognize it!

But we can get down, Joe pointed out.

This was true; we could see it would go.

And we need to get down somewhere, Joe added.

Darryl nodded. Let's just go down this and then figure out where we are. We'll be somewhere.

This amused us, being one of our regular lines: no matter how lost, we were always somewhere! And at this point any solution was better than staying stuck on the crest of the Sierra with no way down.

So we did it. Darryl threw his backpack down rather than keep it on his back for the first drop, and it tumbled end over end down the upper slope for a couple hundred yards, a clear sign that it was very steep. But we made the facing-in, big-step, hold-on-hard drop, and after that could grab the side wall as we descended the scree. As usual, I often sat as I descended.

A new way over the crest

At the bottom of that first crack, we found an empty water bottle. So someone else had gone this way, probably after making the same mistake we did. In a way it was too bad; we were not literally the first people to cross the crest here. Still, I took the liberty of naming it Lysenko Pass.

After a couple of hours' careful descent, we had worked our way down to a really nice campsite near some high ponds we found, which we later learned are called the Schober Holes. The Schobers had fished these ponds back in the 1930s, I found out in the Browning guide to Sierra names; the drainage we had dropped into fed down to Lake Sabrina rather than to North Lake, which is where Lamarck Col would have led us. But our car was parked at Lake Sabrina, and we had been planning on walking down to it from North Lake, so that was fine. The high narrow basin holding the Schober Holes and Bottleneck Lake had gotten cut off from below by the filling of Lake Sabrina, a reservoir, in the late 1920s. So no one goes up there anymore (although we did run into a single hiker, so again, not literally the case). And it's true that this little high basin is very near roads and trailheads, and in a popular area too, so maybe it gets visited sometimes; but it had the look of abandonment you often see in the upper corners of the high Sierra. Similar high basins are tucked all over, just enough off trail to be very rarely visited; and the range is big. So for sure if you want to go somewhere no one else ever goes (meaning almost no one) you can do it, especially if you don't mind doing something stupid. The range can be new for you, just as new as it is for all those young people in love.

Lysenko Pass, north side

NAMES (5)

Corrections and Additions

After all this talk of names, a summing-up is in order, where all my suggested corrections and additions are listed in one place, to serve as an action list for all those many readers who are itching to petition Congress, or the California Advisory Committee on Geographic Names (CACGN), which makes recommendations to the US Board on Geographic Names (USBGN), run by the US Geological Survey (USGS); or else to add some informal names by direct action to the various online maps that are working as wikis (please feel free!).

CORRECTIONS

Switch the names of Mount Whitney and Mount Muir, conveniently close to each other.

Change the name Haeckel-Wallace Col to Blumlein Pass.

Change the name Mount LeConte, located between Mounts Mallory and Langley on the crest, to Mount Charles A. Young.

Change all the other features named for Joseph LeConte Sr. to something else.

Change the name Mount Spencer to Mount Florence Nightingale.

Change the name Mount Haeckel to Mount Rosalind Franklin.

Change the name Mount Agassiz to Mount Rachel Carson.

Change the name Matterhorn Peak to Snyder-Kerouac Peak.

Change the name Symmes Canyon to Lauren Elder Canyon.

Change the name Mount Fiske to Sagan-Margulis Peak.

Change the name North Palisade to Brower Palisade, as California senators Boxer and Feinstein once recommended to Congress.

Change the name Mount Sill to Nee-na-mee-shee (consult Paiute tribe officials in Bishop to confirm name and spelling).

Change the name Mount Tom to Winuba.

Change the name Birch Mountain to P'o'daranwa.

Change the name of the town of Bishop to Pitana Patu.

Change the name Owens Valley to Payahuunadü, "the land of flowing water."

In general, find Native American names for Sierra places, and bring them back.

Change the name LeConte Divide to Superintendent John R. White Divide.

Change the name of the White Divide to the Other White Divide.

Change the name Bubbs Creek back to the South Fork of the South Fork.

Keep the name Pioneer Basin (or if retaining its peak names, change it to Robber Baron Basin), and change the names of the four peaks surrounding it—Mounts Crocker, Hopkins, Huntington, and Stanford—to Mount Zora Neale Hurston, Mount Willa Cather, Mount Edna Ferber, and Mount Edith Wharton.

If you want to continue this kind of group substitution, and in particular to honor women writers whose work has been specifically concerned with the lived experience of the American West, consider using the following names:

Mount Carol Emshwiller, Mount Molly Gloss, Mount Karen Joy Fowler, Mount Cecelia Holland, and Mount Ursula K. Le Guin.

They could be emplaced around any of those basins surrounded by peaks with uninspired and uninspiring names—as for instance, flanking the Miter Basin on its west side, Mount Pickering, Joe Devel Peak, Mount Newcomb, Mount Chamberlin, and Mount McAdie. Rename those peaks after the quintet of women writers listed above. I suggest that McAdie be called Mount Le Guin; the rest to taste.

ADDITIONS

Name Peak 12691, across Piute Canyon from Mount Emerson, Mount Thoreau. We've already done this, but reiteration and reaffirmation would be nice. Spread the word.

Name the pond on the rim of the Tablelands, at the point that overlooks Big Bird Lake, elevation 11,200 feet, Phil Arnot Pond.

Name the class 2 chute pass crossing the crest from above the Pothole to the pond at the top of Lyndall Creek, Leonie La.

Name the class 2 pass on the Sierra crest located one half mile southeast of Lamarck Col, Lysenko Pass.

Name the first pond north of Lake South America, August 11 Pond.

MORE NAMES TO CONSIDER

Having gone this far, why stop now?

There are still, after all the recommendations listed above, many weak or bad names in the Sierra. And really, keep in mind that there is no good reason why a single generation should have gotten the opportunity to name the features of the range for good and all, especially since they kind of blew it. To the extent that we can find and return Native American names, we should do that; where we can't, we should get creative, and start a process that hopefully will never end.

As a further aid to this game, I append here a preliminary, provisional, and open-ended list of names that should be in the Sierra Nevada but aren't. It's a miscellaneous list of people whose names would honor the Sierra, and also honor those of us doing the naming. They are people whose names should be up there already. They could be substituted for many of the names I've proposed; some of my suggestions above are specific to their locations, but most could be swapped out for other good ones.

So, when thinking about replacing extraneous or irrelevant names, like Goddard, or Williamson, or Tyndall, and on and on and on it goes, consider these people from history, who did good things in the Sierra, in California, and in the world:

Eleanor Roosevelt
Martin Luther King Jr.
Robert Underwood Johnson
Emily Dickinson
George Eliot
Herman Melville
Julia Morgan
Cesar Chavez
Lise Meitner
Emmy Noether
Mary McLeod Bethune
Frederick Douglass
Walt Whitman
Julia Lermontova
Toni Morrison
Octavia Butler
Ruth Bader Ginsburg
Marguerite Vogt

…on and on it should go.

I know that some readers must still be wondering if I am really serious about this name stuff, or if I am playing a game. Again I say, both. I *am* playing a game, because naming is always a kind of game; and also, I am serious about it. We should make these changes and additions, and think of more to make, as a kind of serious play—play that takes the game seriously, because it's a way of assuming our past, and of inhabiting our patch of Anthropocene wilderness, the Sierra Nevada— the Range of Light (Muir's great name for it), which, along with being a place on the planet, is very much a mental space. We should be playfully serious, and seriously playful—this is another Sierra compound emotion, and one of the best.

SIERRA PEOPLE (18)
We Had a Good Shaman

Late in 2018, after seven years without any contact, I got a call from Terry's younger brother: Terry had been diagnosed with ALS, Jeff told me, and had only a few months to live. Amyotrophic lateral sclerosis, a progressive neurodegenerative disease. Lou Gehrig's disease. I asked Jeff to inquire, and he did, and got back to me: Terry didn't want any visitors outside of family. He was already much weakened.

On February 6, 2019, Jeff called again to tell me Terry had died. He died at home, with only his wife Melody there to help him out. She was there with him from the disease's beginning to end, including a full year of home care—she had been a veterinary nurse before retirement, and knew what to do, and did it. They had been together 29 years. He was lucky to have her, in that last year and in all their time together.

Later that day, Terry's son Cory drove to my house to give me the news in person; he hadn't been aware that Jeff had called. A very generous gesture on such a bad day. I hadn't seen Cory in so long that I thought he was Jeff. We shared our grief. When I saw Melody later, to help her arrange a memorial ceremony, she was as exhausted as anyone I've ever seen.

That afternoon, after Cory left, I walked out onto the UC fields to the south of my house, thinking to get a glimpse of the Sierras. Some days we can see the Crystal Range. Not on that day.

His memorial celebration ended up being held in the community center where his son Cory and both my boys had gone to preschool. Terry's family was there, and his old friends, meaning our hiking group; also some newer friends he had made at a swim club in South Davis. One of those swimmers I happened to know, and he told me that a year or two before, Terry had had a seizure in their pool, and someone on hand had pulled him out and brought him back to life. Later Terry had scolded the guy for not letting nature take its course. This was so Baier that I almost laughed, but I would have cried. Baier Baier Baier. How could it be? He had ended up in a place where nobody could help him. What a place. Why couldn't he see he was loved? Even these new acquaintances were fond of him, and had made their way to his memorial. As for Melody, who stuck with him through thick and thin, a few months later she asked me, Why was he always so mad? I could only shrug. There was no answer. Something had gone wrong. And I wanted to hold to an earlier time, when it hadn't been so. Restless and intense, yes, always—but also boisterous, generous, quick to laugh. Always the swift analysis, the sharp insight. A charismatic figure, a mountain shaman.

On the lawn outside the building where they held the memorial, I set up a campsite in which every item had been sewn by Terry: tents, sleeping bags, backpacks, jackets, pants, gloves, gaiters—a complete array for three or four people, a museum of his work. An empty-boots kind of gesture. Alas, the hospice pastor who conducted the ceremony, who did a wonderful job, wanted to do it indoors. So there weren't many people who toured the campsite on the lawn outside, and even fewer who understood that everything there was Terry's work.

No more Baier. That night his old band of brothers gathered for dinner, with our wives who had also known him forever, who were also his friends. We toasted his memory, and remembered the old stories, and tried to overcome the lingering regrets. His death ended any possibility of reconciliation, which, however unlikely, we all had hoped for. Now that could never happen.

I called Daryl Bonin to give him the news, and learned that one of Bonin's closest friends from high school, someone I had often met, had also just died, of a heart attack while out surfing. A tough week for Bonin. Even though he hadn't seen Terry for 25 years, and had been mostly out of touch for almost 40 years, still, those early days had marked us forever. They were the crucible that formed us. It had all been so intense then, so exciting.

It was good to hear Bonin's voice. We've since stayed a little in touch over the phone, a pleasure and a comfort. His raucous laugh is like time travel for me, an abrupt return to when I was young and on fire. Now, we have to admit it: we're getting old. Survivors have to band together. The old nomads stagger on.

Baier donated his body to the UC Davis medical school, and they don't give anything of the donated bodies back to the family. We're thinking of taking up a small plaque and gluing it to a slab of granite somewhere in the Sierra. These foolish gestures. Since he loved the whole range, it's a question where to put this plaque. Surely somewhere near the Muir Trail, but not too near. Joe and Darryl and I will figure it out, and the three of us will take something up there and glue it to a rock. Stitch together an end to the story, and do our best to remember the good times, which lasted for so long.

MOMENTS OF BEING (10)
How Big the World Becomes in a Wind

Once we were snowshoeing over Piute Pass when some skiers came by and told us that hundred-mile-an-hour winds were predicted for that night. We headed down the canyon toward North Lake. Terry, Darryl, Joe, me.

That canyon is tougher in snow than it is when the trail is exposed and available: sudden drops, narrow ledges. We finessed those while keeping an eye out for a campsite that would give us some shelter. Wind was already hitting us hard enough to convince us there was something to the skiers' warning. But glaciers scour canyons in a way that tends to clear away blockages, making them somewhat resemble wind tunnels. Nowhere looked quite right. One or another of us would object to any suggested refuge, and on we would go, getting a little surly. The sky over the giant canyon walls was steely and low, with cirrus clouds scything east at speed.

Finally we spotted something red—someone must have ridden an ATV— no—it was the side of an old pickup truck. We were all the way down to North Lake. The trailhead campground!

Happily the place was completely empty, the road being closed a few miles down the hill. The campground looked long abandoned, old snow covering the picnic tables, filling the concrete fire rings, blanketing the bear boxes, draped thin on the ground. Not, all things considered, such a bad refuge on a night like this. Crucially, it's located in a forest of tall pines.

We picked one of the car-camping areas and gathered downed wood and cleared a fire ring of snow. Cooked and ate our dinner at a picnic table, made a big fire in our fire ring, drank the last dregs of our liquor. I laid my ground pad and sleeping bag out on a concrete slab downwind of a bear box, figuring my tent would just flap in the night. The wind was there, but not yet anything unusual; possibly it had been a false alarm. But we were having a good night, so, no harm no foul.

Around midnight the wind struck. It came down the canyon like a runaway freight train, we could hear it coming. The airy roar of a high wind whooshing through pine needles is very characteristic; sometimes you can hear it swirling across a basin, tearing through trees a mile away, sound being so much faster than wind. First you hear it coming, then it hits.

On this night it was deeper and more sustained than we had ever heard it. The roar just kept growing. But it was all overhead. The forest around us was protecting us. Lying on the ground behind my bear box, I scarcely felt air move at all. A brush, as of fingers on my cheek, nothing more; and yet overhead it sounded like jets taking off at an airport, a barreling steady roar, with little variation—no gusts to be heard—just one immense roar. All night long it roared over us, deep, loud, cosmic. After a while I got used to it and slept pretty well. In the morning it was gone.

Another time Terry and Joe and I were on the west side of the Great Western Divide, just under one of the ridges coming off the giant plinth of Table Mountain. We had crossed Midway Mountain that day and gotten down and around Midway's west ridge, then hiked back up to Talus Lake, an accurate name as it was ringed by rocks, no camping there. A bit farther was our next pass, an easy little draw, and when we were in it we saw just below us a tiny lozenge-shaped pond, perched on a lip overlooking the drop to the basin where we would go the next day. Again there were no flat spots to speak of, but there in the little gnarl of rocks on the far side of this pond, overlooking the grass-floored canyon below, we found three slots just as big as our sleeping bags, and tucked ourselves into those sandy nooks and had dinner and all was well. Rather wonderful, in fact, with the great west wall of Table Mountain towering over us, so that it caught the sunset light, pale salmon below, tarnished gold above.

In the middle of that night, wind dropped on us so hard it woke us up. I felt my windbreaker take off over the cliff, down into the basin below: damn. Nothing to be done but snuggle into my sleeping bag and pull the drawstring around my head to form the smallest hole I could.

The wind pummeled us. It felt like a downdraft; seemed like it was falling off Table Mountain onto us. A katabatic demon, flailing us. Tucked into my bag as far as I was, it took me a while to realize that the wind was hitting the little pond next to us so hard that it was tearing water off and tossing it onto us. We could potentially become soaked by way of wind dashing water out of a pond onto us—an unprecedented situation! But nothing to be done. Had to hunker down and hope for the best. As there were no trees, the sound of the wind was different from the way it sounds when it pours through pine needles—not an airy choral roar, but rather some kind of keening, a giant's whistling, a ripping, shrieking sound, the air itself getting ripped apart on the rocks, as loud as a roar but crazier. No sleep at all that night. I spent some time wrestling my tarp around my sleeping bag in burrito fashion, twisting and grabbing to make sure it was well under me and wouldn't fly off after my jacket. That made my arrangement noisier, but it would protect me from the spray flying off the pond, which was freakish enough to have me wide-awake.

When dawn came it was not quite as windy, although it still pummeled us in hard erratic gusts. The pond surface, while crazy with backwash and cross chop, like a wave tank run amok, was holding its integrity. Spray was not flying off it. We could sit there in our bags and reassemble our packs. In doing so I found my windbreaker was actually in the bottom of my sleeping bag, a nice surprise. I wondered what had flown off in the night, if anything. When we were packed we hunkered down into the wind and staggered to the other side of the pond, where the back wall gave us some shelter and we could jam down a breakfast, stunned, sleepy, impressed. Then we were off again, down the drop to the valley below. When we got down to the floor of that little high valley, we lay on the grass and ate again, napped in the sun, repacked our stuff. Off again, up to the next pass, the next drop, the next climb. Someday it will all end, but not this day. Nomads, alone on the side of a strange windy planet. Just how we liked it.

MOMENTS OF BEING (11)
Have I Mentioned How Much I Like the Fall Colors Up Here?

This is what Terry used to say two or three times a day, on fall trips. One of his little jokes, Norman Clyde–like in its clumsy effort to hide his soulfulness.

The grass goes yellow and brown, the flowers wither, all but a few Indian paintbrush, which being orange merely add to the autumn palette. The land looks sere and drab. The light is dimmer and slants out of the south, the air is visible to the eye. The harsh, actinic, almost radioactive glare of midsummer day is replaced by a lambent sepia.

In the east-side canyons, the aspen leaves turn a yellow almost like buttercup flowers but lighter, a yellow very pure and striking, the leaves often quivering together in the breeze. Maybe the prettiest yellow.

It's the ground itself that goes red, like maples in New England. It's a ground-cover plant, called by some alpine blueberry, by others ground willow, by others dwarf bilberry. Whatever the name, it grows out of the fellfields in expansive diffuse mats, its tiny leaves almost like rounded blades of grass, or pika ears, gathering sometimes around the base of big rocks, and during most of the year not noticeable to the eye, being a drab olive or even a granite color. But in the fall these little leaves go red, so that when you are standing in certain basins and look in the direction of the sun, all the little leaves go incandescent, as pure a red as the aspens' yellow is yellow. The ground itself glows, the ground incandesces. You walk over ground glowing scarlet in the direction of the sun; look the other way and it's a dusty crimson.

The slant of the light, the cool days, the austere rock, the last late flowers;

the absence of thunderheads and thunderstorms; the ceilings of low cloud, threatening snow; the looming winter, already felt in the air. The very fat marmots trundling about. Orion, climbing over the eastern horizon to announce the dawn. The welcome dawn. Frost on your sleeping bag, ice in your water bottle. The slow roll of the world, that first ray of sun, bringing an instant touch of new warmth. The feeling that even though winter is coming on, you are still up here, still alive. Still in love.

MY SIERRA LIFE (14)
For Wilderness

I hope to keep going up into the Sierras for as long as I live. My life at home is partly organized around trying to extend my Sierra years. But what you plan and what happens aren't the same, as I know very well.

What remains for me up there? I have a list in my head of places I still want to see. I don't write this list down, although I do write down lots of lists. But this one is easy to remember. It's a kind of utopian imaginary which I often visit to fill my insomniac hours, or just in idle daydreams. The list is longer than I will get to complete. Which is fine. Although I do wish I could see all the places on my list. If any readers of this book are young Sierra hikers, recall here the Baier's admonition: Don't waste your precious youth! It only comes once, and it can be a zone of freedom. Be a pinball in your pinball years. It's a big range. Go up often and wander.

As for me, I'll take it one trip at a time, and keep in mind what they used to chant together at my kids' preschool, almost every day:

You get what you get and you don't throw a fit.

As for the why of this lifelong project of mine, well, it's a traditional question, but there's never a satisfying answer. Mallory's *Because it's there* is the standard reply, blowing off the question by suggesting it is unanswerable, or self-evident, or oversimplifying, or irrelevant. Why live? All the variants of that question assume many things, and throw us back to our basic existential situation: we have to make up whatever meaning or project we find.

So, one of my projects was the high Sierra. I like being up there. I felt it on that first trip, and the feeling never went away, so I kept going back.

This might also be expressed as, I did it to be in wilderness. The Sierra Nevada of California is a particular wilderness, and my favorite, but I have loved visiting wild landscapes anywhere I've encountered them. I've sought them out. So I feel an urge to defend wilderness, both the places the word designates, and the ideas orchestrated by the word and concept. I've already been doing that throughout this book, so I won't go on again about it too long.

But I say *defend* wilderness, because the concept has recently come in for a lot of criticism. And it's true that all our ideas prescribing how we live in the world always need close examination, especially in this time of crisis and extremity, sliding as we are into a mass extinction event and general catastrophe.

Wilderness, its recent critics claim, is just an idealized Western construct that erases Indigenous peoples, who always lived everywhere on Earth. There was never any such thing as wilderness, these critics say, until it was created by philosophers in the nineteenth century, and then turned into land policy in the twentieth century. It was an invention of settler colonials, who removed Indigenous people from their homelands in order to create utopian spaces that had been emptied to suggest an antihuman purity which had never before existed.

This is a description with some truth in it, but not the whole story. It emphasizes the land designated wilderness by legal decree, which shifts a big burden of guilt away from the people telling the story this way. Because it wasn't actually the idea of wilderness that erased Indigenous peoples; it was invading Europeans building cities and farms, all based on the idea of property. Later, when Muir advocated for the protection of some regions containing forests and mountains, he did it to keep white people from cutting down the forests and devastating the meadows of a mountain range he loved. He thought the high Sierra had been mostly empty before the arrival of the miners, loggers, and sheepherders who immediately set about destroying it for profit. He was wrong about that preexisting emptiness, although not entirely, because no one ever lived in the high Sierra year-round; it was too high, too harsh. Indigenous people, when they had the continent to themselves, tended to live mostly where they could obtain the food they needed to live; which turns out to be right where the critics of wilderness now live and write and teach.

So yes, Native Americans did get evicted from their land. That land we now call Los Angeles, San Diego, San Francisco, Berkeley, and so on. Some of them lived in Yosemite Valley, yes. In the high Sierra, not so much. So when a fuss is made about their eviction from the areas that became national parks, but not from Fresno, Bishop, Los Angeles—that's indeed a displacement, of settler colonial guilt. Davis, my town, was a Patwin village called Putah-toi. More Indigenous people lived here than ever lived in the high Sierra.

So these new objections to Muir and his supposed advocacy for removal of Native Americans from their land—something he never did—and also these new objections to the creation of spaces called wilderness, because they displaced Indigenous occupants—these are convenient distractions from the real dispossession, which was of the rich fertile lowlands that we have now urbanized. It's a classic case of transference; it's not our crime, oh no—it was John Muir's crime! Which also means that now, very conveniently, people who persist in advocating for wilderness can be portrayed as anti-Indigenous, imperialist, and so on.

With that transference accomplished, suddenly, and also very conveniently, we're back to anthropocentrism. Nothing matters but people; so if you advocate for animals, or for areas of land that are or could be free of human occupancy, you are therefore being anti-Indigenous, and also antihuman. And all this in a historical moment when biocentrism and wilderness are more important than ever, both for themselves and for the way they support and enable the survival of human beings.

The bad timing of this attack on wilderness is not a coincidence: it both displaces our historical guilt, and it shrinks our present responsibility. Our land use is leading us into a mass extinction event that will kill thousands of species of living creatures, expressions of life that will never come back, that can't be restored. Ecocide: the killing off of our horizontal brothers and sisters, as Muir liked to call them.

So now wilderness needs defending as part of a larger project of biosphere survival, and avoiding a mass extinction event. And in fact there is a new and powerful movement coming to the fore, calling for us to leave a big portion of the Earth's surface free of human impacts, for the sake of the wild animals, as part of forestalling and avoiding the coming mass extinction event. In other words: *more* wilderness!

E. O. Wilson named this project Half-Earth, and in the book of that title he advocates for leaving half the Earth's land and ocean empty of humans, and thus free for the wild creatures, as part of humans living up to our moral responsibilities to our cousins on this planet, and also passing along a viable home to our descendants, who otherwise might be given a world wrecked by our ecocide. Tony Hiss has just published a book called *Rescuing the Planet* that recovers the pre-Wilsonian history of this idea of leaving big fractions of the land free of human alterations, and he marshals the scientific justification for this policy, and describes its many manifestations in the world today.

In this Half-Earth framing, the academic exercise of critiquing the idea of wilderness begins to look a little retro, indulging in a 1990s historical revisionism that was no doubt useful in its time, but has now been superseded by the onrush of events, in particular climate change and the human-caused mass extinction event now destroying the fabric of the biosphere. These catastrophes were already known to be happening in the 1990s, so this recent anthropocentric antiwilderness moment was at best poorly timed, at worst an attempted transference of guilt and dodging of present responsibility.

In any case, now we are here. The 2020s are going to be a time of radical change. Currently we're killing off thousands of species, all of whom have as much right to this planet as we do. We're changing the climate in catastrophic ways. The two are parts of a single problem. From today's news headlines: UN: CLIMATE AND EXTINCTION CRISES MUST BE TACKLED TOGETHER.

So: it's time for wilderness. We need it; the biosphere needs it. Maybe it began as a nineteenth-century American project, transcendentalist in origin, full of category errors, and dodging or even adding to the guilt of crimes committed against Native Americans. There's no doubt some of its assumptions were wrong. Be that as it may, now its time has come. Now it's a crucial component in any realistic plan to avoid the mass extinction event we've started.

If you want to see what the next step in this intellectual and moral reexamination of wilderness looks like, the website of the International Union for Conservation of Nature will show you. Here wilderness has been refined as a concept, and redistributed in a taxonomy of land use practices as precise and variegated as geologists' subdivisions of granite. From the biocentric point of view, a view that is now crucial for human survival, this evolving scientific-philosophical-ethical set of land practices joins all the other work of decolonialization. All people are equal, yes; and it will take equity work to make that proposition real, for sure. But also this needs extending, because *all living creatures are equal*. And the work on that front is just as important. Luckily the two projects, human and animal/plant/biome, are parts of the same larger project: sustainable justice for all living beings.

That the Sierra Nevada's protected wilderness status now makes it a big early link in the habitat corridors that eventually will stretch from the Yukon to Tierra del Fuego, as part of a worldwide network of protected land that will help to keep innumerable species from extinction—this I find beautiful. If this new use also creates a bit of redemption for bad aspects of wilderness's historical foundation as an idea, that's fine too. Redemption is real, and now we need wild land more than ever before. In this perilous moment of world history everyone should approve of wilderness, including all remaining Indigenous peoples, who will indeed have lessons to teach the rest of us about how to care properly for the land that nourishes us. Their lessons will sometimes be practical and ecological, but more important, they will be ethical and spiritual—a matter of seeing the Earth as our sacred home and parent. It's quite true that everyone used to see it that way, right back to the beginning of our species; and now we need to see it that way again.

All these thoughts are part of the peripatetic musings of someone with lots of trail time to ponder such questions. I'm sure that thoughts about wilderness are clarified by actually spending some time in wilderness, and maybe the more time the better. Practice helps.

For me, backpacking in the Sierra Nevada has been an immersion in a particular wilderness. It's been a deep joy, impossible to express in full, but nevertheless real. I can bear witness to the experience of wilderness as a space of human joy. We were gamboling up there like kids in a meadow. Yes—seeing those young bighorn sheep fooling around that day in 2008 gave me the clearest image I've ever had of the feeling of being up there. I recognized what they were doing, and that made me laugh. Run in circles, pop suddenly into the air, collapse in a tangle—get up and do it again! It's not virtuous; it's not useful. But I've enjoyed it. And it taught me things. I'm grateful it struck me so young and so hard.

MOMENTS OF BEING (12)
The Thicket

I love to go through a patch of shrub oak in a bee-line,
where you tear your clothes and put your eye out.
—Thoreau in his journal, December 1, 1856

This is one of the classic bushwhacks of the High Sierra," Secor says of the Muro Blanco, echoing a common sentiment. Phil Arnot says the same, with his usual enthusiasm for any wild challenge. Most of those who have ventured down this deep trailless canyon, which holds in its bottom a stretch of the South Fork of the Kings River, recall it with a kind of shudder. I don't think many people have done it twice.

A trail would make it relatively easy, as the drop down the canyon is never very steep. Why such a direct route from the Muir Trail to Kings Canyon doesn't have a trail running down it is something I used to wonder about, and believed the explanation to be perhaps because the easy Woods Creek trail is located just one canyon to the south. Now I know that it would be very hard to keep a trail clear through the broad spills of brush dropping from the cliffs on each side right down into the river; also hard to make a trail in the first place through the big steep boulder fields that likewise drop from cliff to water. In the canyon's ten miles, there are only two or three miles where normal trail making would be possible. So it remains one of the great trailless canyons in the range.

I had wanted to go down the Muro Blanco for a long time. In 2015 we were on our way there when the Rim fire closed Kings Canyon. A couple of years later, we decided at the last minute to go elsewhere, because if we got delayed in our descent, we might have missed a Mount Thoreau party in Lee Vining. Both times, it was lucky we didn't try. Finally in 2019 we went for it.

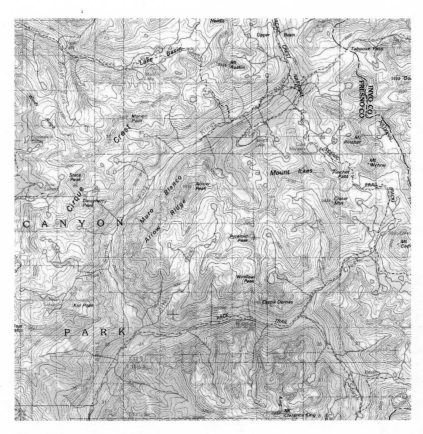

Muro Blanco canyon, USGS

We got to the top of the Muro Blanco by way of the Roper High Route. Up the Copper Creek Trail from Roads End, then off trail in the way recommended by Roper, following the Sierra Club high trip route from 1934.

It has to be said, if you want to save your energy for the Muro Blanco itself, you should go from Roads End up Woods Creek, then over Pinchot Pass on the Muir Trail. That would be a much easier approach, as you would always be on good trails, right to the moment of departure down the Muro Blanco. But we couldn't get a permit to go that way, and the High Route turned out to be a great alternative start, adding to the trip's beauty and its epic quality.

The High Route begins at Roads End and runs north over to the Monarch Divide's north flank, then east over the little ridges that drop northward off that great divide. Each of these little ridges has a sweet crossing, and between them are high traverses with huge views, good footing, and remote high campsites in classic Sierra style.

So, Gray Pass, White Pass, and Red Pass, as Roper prescribes. Such fun. From Red Pass we dropped hard to Marion Lake, using the chute on the left that the Sierra Club cut its switchbacks into. Marion Lake was as gorgeous as ever. The glacier feeding silt into the lake creates an opaque blue water unlike that of other lakes — certainly nothing like the famous glacial lakes of Canada and Switzerland, which often look like radiator fluid. Marion has the finest blue of any lake, I think, and it's a slightly different blue from year to year, depending on how much silt is suspended, I presume.

Marion Lake's blue, 2005

On a tall triangular stone with a clean face fronting the lake, we saw again the memorial bronze plaque to Helen Marion Gompertz LeConte. A lonely monument to a great Sierra life. From there we headed up the Lakes Basin toward Cartridge Pass, enjoying occasional traces we saw of the old Muir Trail. As we ascended the broad rubble chute on the north side of the pass, these traces cohered into full trail again; the phantom recorporealizes there because every person that goes that way finds it useful. As it is also for going down the south side of the pass, all the way to the floor of the South Fork's canyon. We never lost it, and on the fourth morning of our trip we finished this long descent and finally came to the top of the Muro Blanco.

Okay. Three and a half hard days, and we were ready to start. It was lightly snowing on us, but whatever. Time for our descent.

Ready for the descent: me, Carter, Joe; photo by Darryl

Soon we found it lived up to its reputation for difficulty. Not immediately, because at first it was ordinary grassy cross-country, rather easy. Then tilted boulder fields became unavoidable, and we crossed them carefully. Lanes of brush also dropped across our way, blocking it almost entirely. This "brush" is made of some species of massed small trees, perhaps more than one species, but all much alike, and thickly packed together. Alder, willow, chinquapin — I don't know. In any case, walls of chest-high or head-high brushy trees, such that if you were to try to push through them, it would be a matter of bashing through networks of upright branches, often flexible, but stubbornly reinforcing each other. It was a real job to muscle through even a ten-yard stretch of such brush. Wider spills of it were not to be contemplated.

We began to look for any way we could find to avoid these confrontations. Even boulders were better. Maybe the river was better, but as it had been snowing for much of the morning, and was still gloomy and cold, getting in the river seemed a bit much. And it wasn't completely low water; it was still a real river, crashing whitely downstream. All our Sierra experience had taught us that rivers flowing like this are deadly dangerous, to be forded with the utmost caution, and only if a fallen tree doesn't provide a bridge. And there were still some grassy areas high on the slopes to our right, just under the cliffs — lanes above the brush — so on that first day we kept going high to get above and around the brush and boulders. That meant some hard little uphills, even though we were descending the canyon. We had already spent the morning descending the great wall from Cartridge Pass, not a trivial thing, so in the late afternoon, when we came on a big open grassy flat, tucked into a looping bend in the river, we stopped and settled there happily. We had only gotten down the canyon a couple of miles.

We were low enough to have a legal fire that night, and the surrounding dense forest made it feel okay, and we loved it. Next morning we got off as early as we could, given that it was freezing cold. This was to be the big day; we hoped to get to Paradise Valley, on the Woods Creek trail, by the end of it. All day to descend six miles; it seemed possible.

Quickly we were back in the thick of it. Brush or boulders. Finally these both got so difficult that we went down to the riverbank and had a look. We had brought shoes specifically dedicated to getting wet in the river, so we put them on, and slowly, carefully, stepped down into the cold water of the South Fork of the Kings River, and began to slosh downstream in the shallows by the bank. For the most part we were about calf or knee deep in rushing water.

It worked pretty well! This I found amazing. It went against all the Sierra wisdom and logic I had acquired over the previous 46 years, again revealed to be rather meager, all things considered. But really: Sierra streams are where you break legs and drown. Aside from lightning, and maybe slides down hard steep snowbanks, they are the most dangerous thing that walkers face up there. When we had to cross them we were always in emergency mode. And yet now here I found myself sloshing downstream right in the river, feeling with my front foot to make sure I was stepping onto a rock that wouldn't slide under me or otherwise deposit me in the stream. My booted feet were cold but not disastrously so. I had my walking poles, and employed them constantly to support me through the little slips and slides of my footwork. I followed the advice of my brother when he taught me to climb: only move one of your four points of contact at a time. Go completely quadruped, and make sure three of your four points of contact are always secure. This worked well, and I never fell. Progress was slow but steady, and much, much easier than getting through the brush, or over the boulders.

Sometimes the riverbed spread out enough to reveal white boulder roads to each side of the low water, rock fields unstable but not very steep, and we could hike down those. It became clear that the lower the water level, the easier this descent would be. And knowing what this day taught us, we would certainly have gotten in the water on the previous day. In any case, now we were there.

Sometimes the stone banks would choke together and make a short falls, the river dropping into pools so deep that we had to get out and find a way around the blockage. Each time we did that, the superiority of the stream as a road, compared to anything else available, was made clearer to us.

As we hiked, I paused often to look around. The Muro Blanco is called that because the southern wall of the canyon, under Arrow Peak, is an immense curving white wall, about 4,000 feet tall at its highest, and never less than 3,000 feet. A glacial canyon wall of the finest quality, beveled and burnished by the passing ice. Because of the overall leftward curve of the canyon, and its tightness at the bottom, and the steepness of the walls, and the fine granite — not exactly mural precipices, as Muir called them, but more like shallow rib-and-gully patterns, making parallel avalanche chutes — this was surely one of the great Sierra views, constricted and yet still immense. Down below us, where the canyon seemed to make a hard left, almost an elbow turn, it also appeared to get very narrow, and drop harder, as if into a gorge. If it became a true gorge, we were screwed. This happened in some Sierra canyons, making them impassable. But we knew this one wasn't one of them, despite the fearsome pinch we saw ahead of us; we knew it because of all the accounts of previous descents. In the event, as we proceeded downcanyon we found there was always a narrow verge on each side of the stream—the canyon floor was never just the riverbed, cliffed off on both sides. But even with this verge, the river itself continued to be the easiest way.

Looking down the Muro Blanco canyon to the start of its big left turn

So: in and out of the water, in and out, down and down. Left bank sometimes, right bank other times; never very far from the water. The water was cold, the many riffles and rapids loud in that riverine way, liquid crashing of water over rock; we had to be right next to each other if we wanted to talk.

We stopped for lunch. Then we had to get around a deep pool, and the rocks we clambered over were particularly bad; Carter slipped and fell, breaking the little finger on his right hand. We stopped, talked it over; we had a Garmin GPS device with us, and could have signaled for help. Carter shook his head, taped his little finger to his ring finger, and on we went. Our feet got colder and colder, but this also reduced the sensation in them, so we felt less the impact of walking on slippery rounded rocks all day, which included all kinds of twisting and dropping into holes and sudden toe-jamming stops.

When we had completed the leftward turn and drop, and were headed straight south, the river got harder to stay in, and the banks harder to negotiate. We had to slow down. Finally a moment came where the river was unwalkably deep and fast. We were on the right bank, now the west bank, having been back and forth all day. There were patches of meadow here, separated by thickets of brush and trees—alders, chinquapin, willows—they all looked alike, whatever they were. We came down to one band of these brushy trees, which we could see did not go on forever; it was maybe 30 or 40 yards wide, extending from cliffs on our right to the unwalkable river on our left. No way forward. River definitely not walkable. This band of brush blocking us had a steep tilt toward the river, and it appeared also that it had grown over a boulder field; what we were facing now was both brushy and bouldery at the same time! But it also looked like, if we could get through this thicket, we'd then be on a more open floor of the canyon below. So we plunged in.

Quickly we were all separated from each other, at least by sight. The thicket was thick. Shouts could be heard and answered, but questions like "Where are you?" were pointless. "I'm in the fucking thicket!" It was every man for himself, although afterward Joe said that by chance he came on Darryl hung upside down in the branches like an insect in a spider's web. Darryl is six foot three, and thus was at a comparative disadvantage in terms of getting through the branches. Joe helped him get back upright, and then they were a bit of a team. Carter had found that the mesh of branches tended to point down toward the river, such that by going that way he got less resistance, so soon he was well off to the east of us, just barely within earshot. I was somewhere.

The branches grew out of the ground in clumps. Many-trunked trees, or immense shrubs, whatever. Each clump held maybe a dozen branches that grew upward like spray from a fountain, each branch the thickness of a finger or maybe three fingers together. Heavy crushes of snow had smashed the branches down into each other, where they interlocked; then in the following spring, after the snow had melted, they had all sprung up a bit, and grown new branches reaching up toward the light overhead. It was a complete and total 3D maze.

While we were struggling through, it was always possible to put a boot on three or four or five branches together and put your weight down, and be supported by the resistance of all of them together. By pushing the ones in front of your face to the sides, it was possible to dive forward and keep finding footholds. Really the footholds were everywhere, and it was always possible to stick yourself face-first into a gap and squirm forward. I could see that I was about 10 or 12 feet above the bouldery ground, seldom glimpsed below, and also that I was 10 or 12 feet below the top of the canopy. It was arboreal; it was jungle. Even a bad mistake could only have caused you to drop a foot or two before you'd be stopped by the interlocked mass of branches. Maybe.

Twice my glasses were snatched off my face, as if by a mischievous spirit. Like most nearsighted people, I can't see well enough to find my glasses when they're lost. I figured I was doomed to lose them, but both times by squinting around I found them within a minute, hanging from branches below me. It was easy to search under me, because I was no longer upright; more and more I was swimming forward, first horizontally, then sometimes even trending downward, lying in the direction I was trying for. My walking poles were inconvenient most of the time, but I was too preoccupied to collapse them and get them into my backpack, and besides they might have been worse poking up out of it; then also, when I held them in one hand together, I could thrust them forward as part of my body, and use them as a kind of sled, or an extra branch set before me to lie on. Not my biggest problem by any means.

I began to work my way down toward the floor of the thicket, where I saw a gap between the boulders flooring the brush. These boulders were big, like maybe room size, and between them were gaps like tunnels where the bushes hadn't been able to grow. I levered my way down, and got between two giant stones and started crawling forward. In this position I was under most of the branches, and there was a way forward, although often my backpack stuck on the lowest branches above me. Nevertheless, it was the best progress I had made in a long while, and when I came to a fork in the tunnels, I picked one and crawled on. I tried to shout to the other guys that I had found a way to make good progress, but when I realized I was crawling on the ground like a snake, face right in the dry leaves and dirt, about to proclaim to the others that this was a really superb form of locomotion, I began to laugh too hard to shout. It wasn't that easy to get down to my level anyway, and when the giant boulders came together and blocked my way, I had to push back up through the thicket to my previous level, where the branches were flexible enough to allow me to shoulder a way through. Whether there had been any overall advantage in taking the low road was impossible to tell.

That's how it went, squirm after shove after squirm, up, down, left, right. I was back midthicket, well above the ground and well below the canopy top, in a world of branches and dusty green leaves, sunlight blinking overhead and lancing down in myriad little fluttering shafts. Where I found myself seemed now to be the optimal level, as the branches were both strong enough to support my weight, and yet flexible enough to allow me to shove them aside to make a passage. There wasn't really any danger, except laughing to death.

Finally I saw some light ahead, and after a while came crashing out of the morass and slithered to the ground headfirst. I pulled myself all the way out of the last grasp of the branches, freeing my boot from one last clutch, after which I crawled a few feet, stood up, staggered away. I was standing on an ordinary Sierra scree slope, sage bushes ankle high at most, no impediments anywhere to be seen. I walked 20 yards or so away from the thicket and yelled back at the guys. Hey! Where are you guys! Come out, come out, wherever you are!

Carter had already freed himself, far down toward the river. Joe and Darryl emerged shortly thereafter, roughly between us. We gathered and stared at each other speechlessly. How much time had passed? We asked this of each other but had no answer. How wide had the thicket been? Again, we couldn't see uphill far enough to be sure. We would never know any of those kinds of particulars. Maybe 40 yards of thicket, maybe an hour? It was impossible to say. It had been a complete existence, a total world. We chattered our amazement. I couldn't stop laughing. Carter was grimly pleased at having found his riverward path of least resistance. He was as amused as a man with a broken finger can be. Joe and Darryl were still getting over Darryl's upside-down moment, which they compared to the spider scenes in *The Hobbit*. I could feel the grin stretching my face.

We all agreed: no more thickets. They were too thick. We would walk in the river neck deep if we had to. As great as the thicket had been — and I would say without hesitation that it was one of the greatest hours of my life — it wasn't something you want to do twice. Not on the same day anyway.

We had lost so much time that as sunset approached we were still well inside the Muro Blanco, with immense cliffs soaring to left and right. A lost world. The only question was, Could we find any place clear enough of brush, and flat enough, for four people to lie down? This wasn't an automatic yes by any means.

Luckily we came on a bear trail. These were real trails, and obvious as to their origin; bear shit was frequent on them (proving that bears eat lots of different things), also broken branches, and claw-scraped ground, even clumps of fur, all adding up to a bear trail, a cleared way that didn't exist anywhere else in this forest. Bears had crashed through the brush in the same places until they had made a road for themselves. The ursine natural genius! Probably their sense of smell made these breaks an obvious highway for them. So late that day, somewhere on the east bank of the river, long since deep in shadow, we came on a stretch of this kind of bear trail where about 20 yards of flattish ground had been knocked clear. We camped in four good depressions along that stretch, all of us nicely laid out. We tied our empty Ursacks to a tree about 10 yards from where we were sleeping. There was even an obtruding mass of flat-topped bedrock overlooking us, where we could make a fire. Wonderful evening. Although it was true that we were still two or three miles from the trail, and the next day was our last; and we no longer thought two or three miles was a short distance.

Still, it was a great night in camp. We lay in our bags, as there was no room to set up tarps, and we were down to about 7,000 feet by then, so it was warm. Wind soughed downcanyon, stars blinked in and out of existence in the network of tree branches overhead. I kept remembering the thicket. I saw a meteorite in a brief interval of wakefulness. At dawn I was so deeply under that the others couldn't rouse me. I came to only when Carter said very loudly and firmly, "Stan Robinson." That hauled me up; that was me.

The next day brought more action. The canyon opened up, after some more sloshing downstream in the river. The west bank here was wide and flat, and forested; but the trees in this forest had fallen in all directions, and no matter where we went, there were chest-high tree trunks sprawled across the land, blocking our way. An unpassable maze of fallen trees! We had never seen anything like it. Finally we clambered back down toward the river and got back in the streambed, and made our way downstream. The river became flatter, wider, easier. I was sloshing along happily, wondering if I would run into anything definitive before we hit the South Fork's confluence with Woods Creek, when I saw some kind of berm or ramp to my right. And there was Carter steaming along on it, looking maniacally satisfied.

Carter, are you on trail? I called to him.

I am!

Okay, well wait a second there. Let's wait for Joe and Darryl to catch up with us.

Oh yeah, he said. It was like he was coming to.

So we regathered, ate lunch. It was two o'clock in the afternoon, and we had started hiking at about seven in the morning. The day had flown. We still had something like 14 miles to go to reach our cars. But it was trail, big trail. People were coming by on it. We hadn't seen people in six days. They were like aliens. Or maybe that was us.

When we started down the trail, it was just as simple as thump thump thump. It was like standing on an escalator.

As we flowed down this trail, we were passed by a young woman, a trail runner in gym shorts and tank top, holding a water bottle. I guessed she might be a trans-Sierra runner, and called out to ask her where she had started.

She said as she passed me, Roads End!

I exclaimed after her, But you're headed to Roads End!

I know! she called back at me. I went up Bubbs Creek and around!

Holy moly! I shouted, amazed. You go girl!

Well I'm dying now, she shouted back.

It's all downhill from here! I shouted in a final encouragement, and she laughed and disappeared down the trail.

After that I had less of a feeling that we were in for a tough evening. Her circuit that day was going to end up being about 30 miles, with 7,000 feet of up and then down. Hiking down the trail after her was turning out to be slightly harder than standing on an escalator, but not by much. We let gravity do the work, and kept not falling down. The trail was a great trail, built by the Sierra Club in 1909.

Near sunset we came on a black bear. Despite all the bear shit in the Muro Blanco, this was our first sighting of the trip. It was as black as a black cat, and most Sierra bears are brown or blond. It stood out in the shadowed forest like a black hole, like an intrusion from another dimension. It was just 20 yards off the trail.

We sidled by it, all of us begging its indulgence in low conversational tones. Nothing to see here, big guy. It was preoccupied in the meticulous devastation of a pine cone, its front claws as dexterous and capable as human fingers; this was wonderful to see. It glanced at us once, aware we were there, uninterested in us. Nearsighted, as if it had lost its glasses long ago in a thicket, and no longer cared to look at things. We blessed it as we hurried by. If we hadn't been losing the light, we would have stood and watched it for an hour. As it was we gave it five minutes, and that was mostly to move by it slowly. Then on down the trail.

Where the Woods Creek trail meets the Bubbs Creek Trail, we collected ourselves in the twilight. Took off our sunglasses and got out our headlamps. Again it seemed to me that it was an unfortunate failure to have put the road's end at Roads End, two miles to the west of us, at the lower end of a long sandy trough in the great canyon. They could have run the road up that trough to where we now were, and they should have. No one would have minded, and two miles of weary flat sandy trail would have been erased for everyone. Instead we hiked by headlamp to get to the parking lot and our cars. It was weird hiking in the dark by failing mini headlamps that scarcely illuminated the trail three steps ahead, but we were going to get home that night.

In the parking lot we threw our packs in our cars, speechless and slack-jawed. We made sure Carter was going to be okay; he said he was fine, and took off for Berkeley. We three took off for Davis. The crazy Kings Canyon entry road almost made Joe sick, it was so twisty. Down in Fresno we started to look for a fast-food place to eat; Darryl was driving and passed some opportunities, because, he said when we grilled him, he needed to stop at a Jack in the Box, because he had worked at one in high school, and so nothing else would do. We cursed him roundly and demanded he stop at the next fast-food place no matter what it was. Reluctantly he agreed, and the next one was a Jack in the Box. We laughed and ate as we drove north to Davis, hour after hour. The technological sublime: covering hundreds of miles while sitting on our asses, after working like fiends to cross just a few miles. We were back in civilization, for what it was worth: Highway 99, trapped forever in the 1950s. Got to my house at about 3:00 a.m., and Joe's flight left for Hawaii at 7:00 a.m., so I got him to the airport at 6:00. Tight timing, but he could sleep on the plane. And we had done the Muro Blanco.

It had taken us three days to go eight miles. About half that distance we were walking in the river itself.

And then there was the thicket.

To me, this is joy: that thicket. This is what the Sierras can give you, hours like that. Hours stolen from the gods. We are primates. We evolved to do that. I laughed so hard.